MANGO RAIN

BERTA ISABEL ARIAS

To my biggest supporters—

my daughters,

Ilianna and Melissa.

CHAPTER 1

Anaís

October 1999

"¡VAMOS, JIM!" STANDING NAKED AT THE FOOT OF THE BED STILL FLUSHED and sweating from lovemaking just a short while before, Anaís tossed a pillow at the body sprawled on her four-poster bed. His silly smile made her blush. "You are quite a lover. I'm going to miss you!"

"What?" Jim teased, stretching his arms over his head, showing off his beautifully tanned body. "We have time to fool around some more." He made some pelvic thrusts in her direction. "Maybe one more time?"

Anaís' smile broadened. "Aren't you tired yet?"

"What do you think. Come over here," he beckoned, thrusting his body as he moved closer to the head of the bed.

"What I think, *mi amor*, is that you want me to miss my plane. I still have so many things to do before I leave."

Just when she was close enough, Jim grabbed her around the waist, pulling her on top of him. "No, what I want is a little more time with you." Taking his time, he lavished soft kisses on her lips, on her forehead, on her cheeks, on her neck. "Just one more time," he said rolling his body onto hers. "I can't bear the thought of you going off to Havana, though I know you feel compelled to go. God, you are an exotic beauty. I hate that you'll be away, but I understand your decision to make this trip."

"But, come on," he breathed into her ear. "One more time."

"Once more," Anaís whispered. Locking into his dark brown eyes, she put her arms around his neck and thrust her tongue into his mouth, giving way to the moment, all thoughts of packing and planes slipped away.

At her window, taking in all that she knew, all that was part of her life, Anaís thought the lake had never looked more beautiful, sparkling in the late evening sun. The lights of Navy Pier and its iconic Ferris wheel twinkled at her in the distance. She thought of how she loved to ride the Chicago landmark at every chance she had, relishing the feeling of exhilaration when the wheel reached the top of the 200-foot structure, suspending her and her fellow riders in midair. Her heart swelled each time she looked down on her beloved Chicago, the place she called home.

Yet, she had another home. Cuba. A place though unknown to her, it cast a soft, stealthy signal that had enticed her most of her adult life. Ever since...

Snapping back into the present, she shook her head, her long ebony locks bouncing down her back. "I need to finish packing, finish all the tasks on my to-do list," she said aloud to the empty apartment.

Gazing around her living room, bathed in the last rays of an unusually warm, Indian Summer October day, she felt the rich warmth and comfort her home, a Michigan Avenue lakefront condo, provided. Chicago had it all.

With Jim's departure a few minutes earlier, she tried to refocus on her packing. But the beauty of the sweeping crystalline view fringed with autumn yellow, reds and orange, impeded her progress. Questions formed in her mind as she wondered if Cuba would be everything she had heard or read about. She pulled herself away from the window and suddenly conscious of the time, she scurried around her apartment, gathering all she needed, making sure she was not leaving anything important behind. As butterflies began to dance in her stomach with anticipation, she doubled checked her purse for her wallet, passport, and plane reservations. Satisfied she was ready, Anaís picked up her phone and called the bellman of her building.

"Alberto, it's Doctor Moran. Yes, I'm ready...yes thank you. I think it will be great, too. Can you please call me a cab for the airport? The cigars? Well, maybe I can sneak one past customs. Uh-huh. Yes, I know you'd love to have one. Uh-huh. Yes, I'll be right down."

Taking one last look around, she sighed at the realization that tomorrow morning she'd be in a very different place. Slipping her arms into the straps of her backpack and lifting each of her two suitcases packed for the month-long trip, she uttered out loud "Bye, bye house. I'll be back soon."

As the taxi driver navigated to Chicago's O'Hare Airport, she was grateful rush hour traffic had died down and she could enjoy the ride without anxiety despite the tight timetable created by her lingering with Jim.

Anaís was grateful to have been selected to make the trip to Havana. When she had found out that the Governor was planning to send a delegation to begin fostering cultural and business ties between Illinois and Cuba, her heart had jumped at the prospect of joining the group. However, there were many others hoping to be chosen to make the trip and she had refused to get her hopes up simply because she was the only Cuban-born supervisor in her department.

Still, it had been serendipitous that the story of the Peter Pan children from Cuba had been headline news a few years before. Anaís suspected that the Governor's Office remembered a follow-up story on her own experience of having been secretly sent to the United States by her parents worried about her future in Castro's Communist Cuba. It was a dubious distinction, but she didn't care if that was the key that opened the door to her being on the Illinois/Cuba team.

Anaís was one of twenty members of the delegation that included Senator Fernández, the only Illinois Hispanic senator and the spokesperson for the Illinois Governor who was not able to participate in the month long trip. Others were journalists, businessmen and women, agriculturalists, educators, photographers and colleagues from the tourism office where Anaís worked.

Everything about the trip had happened so quickly, her head was still spinning. She wondered how she would have time to do her personal family research while in Havana, but she knew she would find a way. Too much of her past had been erased with her emigration.

The taxi driver dodged a car speeding into the merging lane of the expressway. Her head back in the seat and her eyes closed, Anaís let her mind wander. She was filled with a strange sense that although she had just left home, she also was going home. It wasn't the home she had been brought up in, but it was her birthplace, and that of her parents, the parents she had never known.

"Oh, you're late, too," effused Cynthia, one of her co-workers who was standing by the curb as Anaís' taxi pulled up at the airport. "Glad I'm not the only one." Cynthia tugged at the suitcases at her feet and pulled a long, nubby scarf around her neck. "It's hard to believe it's almost November. I mean, it's been such nice weather, but it does turn colder in the evenings. I am really looking forward to those great temperatures they say they have in Havana. The internet said it would be in the eighties all this week. Can you imagine that?"

Anaís paid the cab driver and gathered her bags. It wasn't difficult to talk to Cynthia because Cynthia enjoyed hearing herself so much that her questions hardly ever needed a response. The only time that Cynthia was an attentive listener was when she was trying to get what she thought might be some juicy bit of gossip about someone. Then, it seemed to Anaís, Cynthia developed an almost priest-like attentiveness. But whatever one shared with her, "in total confidence, of course" as Cynthia would always say, somehow mysteriously was known by everyone almost immediately. Anaís had been stung once by the "Cynthia gossip line". She swore, never again. She had dubbed Cynthia, *arrancapellejo*, an old Spanish word for a gossiper. She smiled thinking how much Jim had laughed when she told him the literal translation of *arrancapellejo* was someone who rips the skin off someone else.

"So what made you late" queried *Arrancapellejo,* as she struggled with her bags. Without waiting for Anaís' answer, she offered, "I'm late because I got a call from my mother just as I was going out the door. She's not doing well on that new heart medication. She thinks it's making her worse. I just think she's becoming more of a hypochondriac as she gets older."

The two women were walking down the bright airport halls to the check-in line when she repeated, "So, what made you late? Was it Jim?" She emphasized the name with a sly look and elbow jab to Anaís.

"I fell asleep," Anaís said.

Cynthia scrutinized her, searching Anaís' expression for something that might suggest otherwise.

"Oh, look. There's our group," announced Anaís to distract her.

Milling around the airline ticket counter were the participants in the delegation. Anaís smiled happily, recognizing many old friends. The excitement was palpable as the group seemed to fidget with nervous energy, like schoolchildren off on a field trip.

"Here comes our *Cubana*. It's about time. We thought we would have to leave without our interpreter," said Richard as he came over and took Anaís' bags. Cynthia pursed her lips and threw him an angry look as he ignored her bags.

"Remember, Richard, just say *sí* to everything," Anaís joked.

"That's gotten me into way too much trouble with you over the years."

Placing her bags on the scale next to the check-in counter, he said, "Boy, what do you have in here. Rocks?"

Anaís had bought extra t-shirts, jeans and toiletries to leave behind with any family she might find. She had decided that if she didn't locate them, then she'd give everything to workers at the hotel. Considering what she had heard and read about the many shortages in Castro's Cuba, she was hoping her gifts would help someone even a small way.

"Well, everyone is here now. And it looks as if the flight is leaving on time. That's great because I am exhausted." Richard brushed back his thick curly top. "I still don't understand why we're leaving so late, or that we have to fly to Miami, then Cancún, then Havana. You'd think the

Governor's Office would rate better than that and get us a direct flight, even though the Governor is not on the trip with us."

"Remember, Richard, we're going to Cuba. It's a whole different ball game. Remember the embargo and the restrictions that come with that?" Anaís took her passport and boarding ticket from the airline agent. "I'm tired, too. Let's just hope we don't get delayed at any of the airports so that tomorrow morning when we get there we can hit the ground running. We don't have anything special in the morning, do we?'

As she and Richard walked over to the rest of the group, he replied, "I don't think we have anything until the evening reception."

The trip's coordinator was a thickset Mexican-American with whom Anaís had worked on various Hispanic events for the Governor's Office. He had asked her out a few times, and Anaís was thankful that it appeared as if he was at last picking up that her continual excuses were just a nice of way of saying she was not interested. He was not her type. He was too much of a workaholic and a "yes" man. Also, at almost five feet nine inches in stocking feet she towered over him. No, Pablo was a nice guy, but not her type.

She half listened as he handed out packets with the trip's agenda and other pertinent information. Her colleagues joked and laughed as they did a quick review of the planned itinerary and listened to Pablo's cautionary words about decorum.

"...so whatever happens, we all need to remember that we are guests in Mr. Castro's country. Supposedly, we will have access to anyone and anything on the island."

"I'll believe that when I see it," said Richard.

"Well, I said supposedly." Pablo passed out official tags. "And, if you decide to wander off, which I don't recommend, make sure you take this tag with you. Since the Cuban officials will be holding our passports at their immigration office until we leave, it will be your sole official form of identification."

"What if they lose one of our passports," asked a voice from the back of the group.

"I've made copies of everyone's passports for our office here in Illinois and I am carrying additional copies with me."

"Keep those really well guarded, Pablo, because we don't want to have to sneak anyone out of Cuba."

"Yeah," another voice laughed. "I'm not a good swimmer. And I'm not getting on one of those rafts to Miami."

"I'd bet you'd be good shark food, Mark. Good American meat!"

Some of the women grunted in disgust, but mostly everyone laughed as Mark grabbed his sizeable beer belly. "Yes, one-hundred percent American beef!"

They headed down the well-lit concourse festively decorated with international flags hanging from the vaulted ceiling. Whenever her travels took her down this concourse, Anaís remembered her parents. They would make a game of finding the flag of the country of their destination and talking about it.

Anaís looked at the sea of nation flags floating overhead. She needed not bother looking for the flag this time. The Cuban flag, she knew, would not be there, another consequence of the almost 30-year U.S. embargo of the island.

Once on the plane and settled in, the lights dimmed in the cabin for the flight. Anaís thoughts returned to her childhood. The flags had reminded her that she had been truly blessed to have been brought to America and to have been cared for and raised by her wonderful adoptive parents.

She remembered the day she learned that she had been adopted and of her Cuban heritage. Gail and Peter Moran had packed up their station wagon for a week's vacation at their summer cabin in Saugatuck, Michigan. Thirteen-year-old Anaís had thought her parents had been acting somewhat weird long before their trip. Yes, they always made a fuss around her birthday, but weeks before they had left, her parents had seemed overly preoccupied with the preparations. She was glad that she had not been asked to help pack as in previous years.

The trip from their Evanston home had been unusually quiet. Her normally chatty mother had said little and appeared sad. Her father, on the other hand, commented on everything that caught his attention on the road. As vice president of the Latin American Division of a large pharmaceutical company, he spoke Spanish fluently and loved everything Latin. Between his chatter and the constant Latino music playing on cassettes he had brought from home, Anaís had after a while felt overwhelmed and had switched to her own music on her cassette tape player, ignoring her father's comments that she was missing out on some wonderful Benny Moré classics.

That afternoon when they reached their cabin in Michigan, both her parents seemed exhausted. When dinner at the local fish restaurant didn't seem to get her mother out of her dismal mood, Anaís wondered if her parents might be having marital problems. She had never known them to be anything but loving with each other. Still, a few of her friends' parents were divorcing.

She whisked those negative thoughts aside and made herself indulge in the anticipation of her birthday the next day, a day when her parents unfailingly gifted her something special and unexpected. As long as she could remember, her parents would tiptoe into her room with a little cake with birthday candles and sing her awake. After she blew out the candles and hugged each one tight, she looked forward to opening up her birthday gift, which was something special that had belonged to either her father or mother when they were younger. Among her favorite gifts were her mother's collection of *Nancy Drew* books and an old Canon camera with many lenses from her father. From year to year, she never knew what she would find inside the beautifully wrapped box that her mother painstakingly and lovingly decorated for her special day.

The next morning, when she heard her parents open the door to her room, she pretended to be asleep until she heard them start singing. They kissed and hugged her, then sat in the loveseat across her bed. Her father fidgeted in his seat.

"Anaís, you know your mother and I love you more than anything in the world." She kept looking at the box on her mother's lap, at her mother's serious and weepy eyes. Gail Moran was an over-emotional woman who cried easily, so her mother's tears didn't worry Anaís.

Her father kept repeating himself.

"Anaís, you know how much your mother and I love you. You are the most important and special person in the world to us. You are our daughter." He kept rubbing his hands. Her mother stared at the gift box.

"I love you, too, Dad." She wondered if her parents' strange behavior was because it was her thirteenth birthday, and she was now a teenager.

Her father took a deep breath, then he took her hand. "You are thirteen today," he said.

Oh God! Maybe they wanted to talk about sex, thought Anaís.

"You are thirteen today," he repeated. "You are at the beginning of your adulthood." He squeezed her hand. "And we need to talk to you as an adult."

Oh no! This indeed was going to be the sex talk her friends had said they had gotten from their own parents, Anaís thought in disbelief.

"Anaís..." Something in his voice made her shiver. "Anaís, you are our daughter." There was a very long pause before she heard her father's voice say "But, you weren't born to your mother and me."

The words sounded foreign to her, a little like when she heard her French teacher speaking quickly and she understood the words individually without making sense of the total meaning.

Her mother had put the wrapped box down, and had moved to sit next to her on the bed, hugging her and crying while whispering, "We love you so." Her father kept talking while her mother continued her whispery cries.

At some point, Anaís started to make sense out of the words she was hearing. It was as if she was suspended in air, feeling nothing in particular, hearing words that swirled around like a constant wind.

"We are your adoptive parents. You were born in Cuba, at the time of the Revolution. Your birth parents were afraid of what was happening there, like so many parents there at that time. They asked Father Pat, a priest they knew, and who knew us, too, to help them. They asked him to find a way of getting you out of the country. They wanted you safe, and thought it would be easier for them to get out of the country, legally or illegally, once they knew you were safely here in the U.S..." Her father's voice trailed off, and choked. Anaís had never seen him so distraught. "It never came to be," he said quietly.

Anaís learned that day that her birth parents never came to the United States. The Morans didn't know what had happened to them. All they knew was that the organization that put everything together tried to find them, but they lost contact with them. After a while, it had become impossible to find out anything about what was happening in Cuba.

They shared that they had adopted Anaís when she was three years old, after months of trying everything they could to find her birth parents.

"We think your parents would have wanted us to adopt you. They would not have wanted you to be put in a foster home. And we ourselves couldn't bear that thought. We love you so much," he said as they both enveloped her in their arms.

"You are our daughter in our hearts and minds. We didn't tell you before because we thought you were too young, but now felt you needed to know the truth."

Her father picked up the box wrapped in beautiful pink and white ribbon.

"Here. This is for you. It's everything your parents packed with you when we left Cuba. It contains the clothes you were wearing. And the picture," again her father's voice cracked, "it's of your mother, Ana Isabel Romero Buenaventura."

Shaking, Anaís took the gift box and placed it on her lap. The three of them sat shrouded in a spell of silence for what seemed like an eon.

Breaking the quiet, her mother said, "Is there anything you want to ask us, dear?"

Words would not come. She shook her head.

"Do you want to open your box now?"

She shook her head again.

"Do you want to be alone for a bit or...?"

She nodded and heard an audible, sad sigh from her parents as they awkwardly stood up.

"We love you, sweetheart."

She nodded, not able to respond.

"We'll be in the kitchen if you want us." They each kissed her on the head, turned and exited the room. She heard her mother sob.

After what seemed an eternity, Anaís opened the elaborately wrapped box and looked inside at several other individually wrapped items. She unfolded the colorful tissue paper surrounding the top gift and found a black and white picture of a baby sitting on a beautiful young woman's lap.

The woman had thick, dark hair that framed a pale, round face similar to her own. The dark-haired beauty smiled joyously. Her arm encircled the baby, holding tiny fingers in her own. A large banyan tree behind them threw a shadow on the flowers next to the wooden bench. The right side of the photograph was jagged and torn with age.

Anaís looked inside the box once more. This time, the wrapping disclosed a beautiful porcelain-faced doll, its lumpy, cotton body draping helplessly in Anaís' hands. Around its neck, she stared at a tiny gold baby chain with a Saint Francis medal as well as the traditional ebony *azabache,* a popular amulet in the Caribbean meant to protect a person from evil spirits. Looking back at the photograph, she saw the same chain around the baby's neck.

A white cotton dress, white socks trimmed with pink lace, and pink leather baby shoes were the last items she unwrapped.

Anaís stared at the box and its contents for a long time before the enormity of what she had just learned became real to her. She sobbed into the box, hoping her parents would not hear her pain. Who was she, really? She was no longer sure.

The rest of that October week stay at the summer cabin during her thirteenth birthday had been a difficult one. Her parents seemed to walk on eggshells around her, vacillating between being overly cheerful or cautiously detached. For days, they all went about their usual routine as if the disclosure of her adoption had never happened. Anaís found herself waking up in the mornings thinking it had simply been a bad dream.

However, the white and pink gift box on her dresser reminded her each day that she had not been dreaming. Often, Anaís would take out each item, examining it, trying to divine its hidden history. She decided to wear the baby necklace as a bracelet that she looped a few times around her wrist.

The picture of her mother was the most disturbing and painful item of all. The woman's beautiful face was that of a stranger, yet Anaís couldn't deny the resemblance when she looked in the mirror. Throughout her short life, Anaís had rationalized that she must have looked like a deceased grandparent because she certainly didn't resemble either of her parents and had often queried them about this. Now she understood why they had answered in vague terms whenever she asked those questions.

She found it difficult being around her parents. She couldn't bring herself to even say Mom or Dad to them. So, instead, she spent a lot of time alone, trying to deal with her inner turmoil. She started carrying *Gordita*, the name she had given the porcelain doll, everywhere she went.

One evening toward the end of their stay, Anaís and her parents were finishing their customary picnic, sitting at the top of the dunes admiring a sky filled with pink and purple ribbons across the setting sun.

"I wonder what the sunset is like in Cuba," she heard herself say.

Anaís caught her breath, realizing she had brought up the word that connected all of them to the silent pain that had permeated their recent weeks. She looked at her parents, expecting to find them staring at her. Instead, she saw her father pick up his wine glass and before she had a chance to say another word, she heard her father speak in Spanish.

"*Cuba es bella.*" His eyes looked at the horizon. "It is indeed one of the most beautiful places your mother and I have had the good fortune to live in."

"Remember the little restaurant in Playa Varadero," Gail said as she smiled at her husband. Then, they seemed transported to another time of youth and good memories.

"*Sí.*" He leaned over to kiss her. They both looked at Anaís.

"You were born in a wonderful and proud country." He sipped more of his wine and stretched out on the blanket. He leaned on one elbow, the other hand cradling the wine glass on his hip, and as Anaís watched her father relax and begin to reminisce about his time in Havana, her heart filled with love for him.

She began to realize then that although the beautiful woman in the picture had given birth to her, Gail and Peter Moran were the ones who had nurtured her in a safe and wonderful life.

Peter painted vivid pictures of the heady life of an American business-man in pre-Castro Cuba. Gail described the parties, the nightclubs, and the all-night fun. They also shared that their carefree lifestyle belonged only to the well-to-do in Cuba. Whether one was Cuban-born or foreign, life was good for the upper classes. But for the poor, Castro promised changes in the political and social climate for a better life. The Morans had felt hope for the Revolution, until outspoken citizens and journal-ists began to be arrested and the foreign companies were nationalized. They explained that they had hated to leave Cuba, but life for them there had become dangerous. When *Padre Patrick* had approached them with his plan for taking children out of Cuba to be reunited with their own parents at a later date, Gail and Peter had eagerly agreed to help with the plan. It was the least they could do, they thought, for the Cuban people. Never had they imagined that they would become life-long parents.

That evening, they all remained outside on the dunes talking until the two candles that provided them with a soft light as night fell burned themselves out. They were a family again. The shock and hurt of the recent revelation disappeared, and in its place Anaís felt a new freedom and connection with the Morans—her parents.

Before going back to their cabin to bed that evening, Anaís hugged them tightly, and told them that she loved them for everything that they had done for her. In her heart, she said, they were her real parents.

Over the years, Peter and Gail shared stories of Cuba, both of the good times and the difficult ones. Anaís felt she owed them her gratitude for keeping her open-minded in her opinions and for helping her main-tain her heritage as much as possible within their American society.

She never stopped calling them Mom and Dad, and when they died, along with her husband eight years earlier in a tragic car crash, she had buried the only people she had ever known as her parents. She still thanked them in her daily prayers for their love, for their honesty, for having provided her with a stable and safe environment, for having brought her up in a bilingual and bicultural home even though they themselves were not Latino. She thanked them for everything she was and for all she had accomplished. And she thanked them for encouraging her to find out more about her past.

Anaís sighed, looking around at her friends sleeping soundly in the darkened airplane cabin. She reached into her backpack at her feet and took out the old porcelain doll. *Gordita's* cotton body was oddly chubby in contrast to its delicate, alabaster face. Anaís smoothed the crinoline dress over the long knickers, thinking how many childhood stories she had shared with her *Gordita* over the years.

She pulled out her wallet and glanced one more time at the pictures that were ever with her. One was with the Morans on a sand dune in their Michigan home, and the other was the torn photograph of herself as a baby, cradled in a young woman's embrace. Her gaze lingered on the slender woman in her late-twenties who was her birth mother. A round, high-cheek boned face framed by raven hair, smiled back at her. It appeared that her birth mother's eyes were different, not as large as hers, and in the black and white photograph she couldn't tell if they were green like her own. She brought the picture closer to look again as she had countless times, for signs of a dimpled chin. It wasn't clear if her mother had one. Anaís smiled at her younger self in the picture.

As so many times before, she looked at the jagged edge where the picture was frayed as if having been caught in a drawer or book and torn irreparably. As always, she wondered what image had been on the other side of the photograph. Probably nothing important. Still, she wished that at least this bit of her past had remained intact.

CHAPTER 2

Havana

"ANAÍS, WAKE UP! LOOK! THAT MUST BE CUBA DOWN THERE."

It felt like just a minute ago they had switched planes in Miami to the Mexican airline that would stop in Cancún before continuing to Havana. Anaís realized she had slept throughout the last leg of their trip to the island. She blinked at the soft morning light starting to come in through the airplane's tiny windows. In the seat behind her, *Arrancapellejo* kept pointing to the ground below.

Lush green terrain surrounded by beautiful blue waters peeked intermittently through white, fluffy clouds. So that was Cuba! She was not surprised to feel tingling in her stomach and a deep sense of excitement. The sparkling city in the distance was where she had been born, perhaps where she would find her parents.

"You must be so excited!" For once, she believed *Arrancapellejo* was sincere. "This is wonderful for you. I hope you do find a whole bunch of relatives while we're here."

"Thanks, Cynthia. That's very nice of you. But I'm really just excited to be on this trip with all of you."

Pablo was standing in the aisle ahead of them, pointing to his agenda. His raven black hair disheveled in that special way all airplane travelers have after a long night of sleeping in cramped seats.

"Alright everybody, if I can have your attention...we're landing soon and I want to go over a few things..."

"Shit! It's too early for this!

"Can't you wait until we all really wake up, Pablo!"

"Do we have to do this now?"

Anaís listened to the complaints and groans around her, feeling sorry for Pablo, who was in charge of keeping them on track. He had his hands full with this group.

"I'd like to have all of us meet after we've checked in at the hotel so we can go over the plans for this evening and for tomorrow." He looked at his watch. "Does anyone know what time it is here in Havana?"

"It's the same as Miami time. They're one hour ahead of Chicago!" someone shouted from the back of the plane.

"Alright then. So, what if we meet, say, around ten..."

"How about eleven? Some of us need to get some real sleep!"

"Okay, then. Eleven it is. In the lobby," Pablo conceded. "We'll need only ten to fifteen minutes. Then you're on your own for the rest of the afternoon. Remember to carry your official IDs with you at all times. All our passports will be with the Cuban Immigration Office until we get back on the plane, so this," he waved his laminated tag, "is the only proof of who we are and what we are doing here."

"And what are we doing here?" Laughter from the people already awake made Anaís wonder that same question.

"Well, we can talk about that later." Pablo responded. "For right now, let me just say that we don't want to have to leave anybody behind..."

"I'm not swimming or taking one of those rafts to Miami, that's for sure!"

"We heard that already, Mark."

"Alright..." Pablo kept trying to get the floor back.

"Pablo, you don't know what you've gotten yourself into with this crowd," someone joked.

"Alright then. Eleven. Lobby." He started to sit down.

"Oh, one more thing." Evoking more moans, he said, "Be sure to check that your bags are loaded on the bus that's taking us to the hotel. You don't want to be without your clothes and personal things. I hear that shopping here is not as easy as going to Chicago's Water Tower Place." Pablo and the moaners were cut off by the pilot's voice coming on asking the crew to prepare for landing.

Anaís looked out the window as the first passengers descended the metal staircase and walked down the customary red carpet that awaits important guests. She saw a tall, gaunt Castro, dressed in a dark suit, shake the Senator's hand as the interpreters and aides on both sides took their places by the leaders. Butterflies still danced in her stomach and head as she neared the exit door.

The bright early morning sun shone lazily over the horizon, the air already warm and humid in the tropical October haze. She was one of the last to step off the plane, coinciding with the fact that she was one of the least important in ranking of the many delegates on this trip.

As she neared the receiving line, she heard the Cuban interpreter quietly translate the Illinois aide's introductions, after which each person was handed a small Cuban flag and guided by a young child, dressed in the typical white and red Cuban school uniform, to the line forming behind the Senator and Castro. She also noted the sudden quiet that came over the rowdy delegation as they entered the sphere of Castro's presence. She wondered why. Was it his reported charisma that impressed them? Were they in awe of one of the few world leaders to not have crumbled to U.S. political pressure yet, or were they in awe of shaking the hand of probably the last devout Communist in the Western Hemisphere?

"And this is our very own *Cubana*, Mr. Castro. Dr. Anaís Moran."

They shook hands, and Anaís felt Castro's long bony fingers surround her hand strongly for a few seconds while he looked at her with a deep gaze, bushy gray eyebrow arched in mild surprise.

"*¿Una cubana? ¡Pero no! ¿De Chicago?* I thought all the Cubans who were not here in Cuba were in Miami."

"Not all of us, Presidente Castro." Anaís smiled at his attempt at humor.

"*Bueno, pues bienvenida.* Well, then, welcome. We will have to talk *un poco más,* you and me, *¿bien?*"

"Of course. It would be my pleasure."

He took her hand a second time and spoke the words in a very thick Cuban accent.

"Welcome home. "

It was, to be sure, pure propaganda for the newspaper article that the local paper would print later that day. Still, those words touched her heart, because regardless of Castro's intent, it was the sentiment that she was feeling, that, somehow, she was home again.

Once the bags were all accounted for, the ride to the hotel was an incredible mixture of sounds, smells and color. The airport reminded Anaís of other Latin American airports she had seen, the large Canadian-made bus waiting for them could have been any Greyhound bus in the States, the porters hustling for business like at any other airport. However, after settling into one of the seats toward the back of the air-conditioned bus, she consciously blocked out all the external noise and chatter surrounding her and tried to absorb everything outside her window. She was more than a little surprised to see many signs along the road welcoming tourists. With the embargo, nothing was publicized in the States about travel to Cuba. Yet here, tourism was touted everywhere. Billboards depicting beautiful beaches and lush tropical forests welcomed the international tourists.

Once on the highway, the vibrant green landscape again reminded her of other trips to the tropics of Mexico, the Caribbean, and Central America. But there was something definitely different and unusual here, although at first she could not put her finger on what it was. She looked out both sides of the bus. Then she realized what was different here.

There was hardly any traffic! For miles, the bus was the only vehicle in either direction heading toward Havana. Instead of caravans of cars and trucks on the road, the traffic on both sides of the road consisted of small groups of men, women and children trying to hitchhike. They stood or sat seemingly patiently waiting for the next ride. Sometime later, they passed a broken down bus with perhaps twenty or thirty people watching as the driver worked his magic under the hood. The people waved at their bus as it sped by. Anaís thought back to all she had read about the dismal transportation situation in Cuba.

After about twenty minutes of driving, she started seeing a greater number of taxis heading in the direction of the airport and also continued to see groups of people at the side of the road asking for a ride.

Suddenly the bus took a few turns and the city became visible in the horizon. From this vantage point, Havana was a mosaic of bright rooftops, with a deep blue ocean fringing its border on the far end. Her heart fluttered and her excitement again mounted. She could hardly believe that she was really here.

Haltingly, they wound their way onto the narrow streets of Havana. Many buildings were in disrepair and in much need of paint. She was struck by the rubbish lying at the curbs. The quiet of the expressway gave way to the sounds of the very old colonial city waking up as people were beginning to jam the streets. Her first impression of Havana was that it was not clean and the people looked undernourished.

They passed areas that appeared to be under reconstruction, and then they turned into an area of the city that was amazingly beautiful in its colonial charm. She saw their hotel down the block and was glad to see that they would be staying close to the heart of the city.

Neatly suited porters approached the bus and started to unload the baggage. A young, tall woman boarded the bus and introduced herself as their hotel hospitality agent. She welcomed them to Havana, and assured them they were in one of the best hotels in town, where it was very safe and beautiful. She informed the group that she would be in the lobby the rest of the day to help anyone with any questions about getting around town, and that she knew their visit in Cuba would be a wonderful one. Anaís was surprised that the young woman's English was perfect and that she had practically no accent.

Richard was waiting by the door as Anaís stepped down from the bus. "You disappeared on me." He grabbed her arm. "God, that was a long plane ride for a country that is only ninety miles away from Key West!"

"The embargo, Richard. Remember? U.S. airlines can't fly directly to

Cuba. Anyway, sorry I didn't wait for you. I just wanted to have some quiet time to take all this in."

"It must really be wild for you, to be here? What are you feeling?" She thought a moment.

"Strangely emotional, Richard. It's hard to explain...but even when Castro shook my hand, and I know he could care less, it was very touching to me. I don't know. I almost want to cry."

He hugged her.

"Well, go ahead." He hugged her again. "Certainly wouldn't be the first time you and I....Oh, Anaís, look at that over there." He pointed to a dark and handsome man greeting everyone at the hotel entrance.

"Doesn't he look like he just came out of *Esquire?*"

Richard's open homosexual lifestyle was comfortable for her, but she laughed at his drastic departure in their conversation.

"You're something else, you know. I thought you were trying to comfort me."

"Yes, sweetie, of course." He squeezed her arm. "But, that's too yummy not to catch my attention."

"You are incorrigible. And remember, we're here on government time."

"Yes, I plan to do my job. Still, I don't know about you, but I am going to also find some playtime. And wouldn't it be just great to play with him?" They were still laughing when they shook hands with the object of Richard's attention, who ignored his prolonged handshake as he instead stared at Anaís.

"*Bienvenidos.* Please feel free to call me personally if you need anything," he pointed to his nametag. "Ignacio, at your service."

Richard put out his hand hoping to shake hands again with Ignacio, who ignored him and instead continued to flirt with Anaís.

"And your name?"

"Anaís Moran." She pronounced her name in Spanish.

"You are Latin, no? From where?"

"Actually from here. I was born here."

"Really! But you live in the United States?"

"Yes. All my life."

"Your first time in Cuba, then?"

"Yes."

"Well, this is wonderful. You must let me show you around, help you to see some beautiful sights when you are not working."

Richard stood next to them, arms crossed over his chest, silently grimacing at his companion.

"Well, yes, maybe..." Richard was pulling her away.

"Come on, you. Bye, Ignacio." They walked away as Ignacio nodded farewell. "You always do that to me."

"What are you talking about?"

"The guys I like! They like you!"

"Richard, the man obviously is straight. That's not my fault." She knew he was teasing her.

"Well, I'm just going to have to go out by myself and try my charms on these cute Cubans - without you around."

She feigned heartache, her hand to heart. "I'm crushed."

"Yes, I bet." They stood in line behind others to register at the front desk. "But listen, you want to bum around a bit with me?"

"Not now, Richard. I'm tired and I'll probably just rest up until tonight's shindig." She felt guilty lying to him, but she didn't want any company when she ventured out later in search of her family.

"Alright then." They jingled their keys. "See you tonight."

"Hey, there's Pablo. I need to ask him something. I'll see you later."

"Okay then." Richard joined others at the elevator.

Once he was out of sight, Anaís stepped outside again.

Ignacio was still there, now smoking a cigarette and talking to another man. He quickly put out his cigarette as she walked toward him. His smile said he thought he had made a conquest.

"Ignacio..."

"*Sí señorita.*"

"Can you recommend a taxi service that I can use to get around the city this afternoon?"

He smiled pleasantly. "Yes, of course. But why a taxi service when, if

25

you wait until I get off work at two, I personally can show you Havana."

Suddenly she realized Ignacio thought she was interested in him.

"No, you don't understand...I mean, it's very nice of you. But I really can't wait until you...until two. I need a taxi at 11:30. I'm just asking for a recommendation, because I know all cities have taxis that are good and others that are not."

"Well, yes, if you can't wait...I understand. Well, let's see." He looked down the street. Whistling, he motioned to a short, thin man leaning against a taxi mid-way down the line. The taxi driver quickly straightened up and ran toward them.

"José, Dr. Moran is here with a very important delegation from the state of Illinois in the United States, and needs a dependable taxi driver." José smiled even more. "Dr. Moran, this is José. He is an excellent guide and driver. You will be safe with him, right, José?"

"Of course. I know Havana very well and I can take you wherever you want to go."

"That's perfect, José. I'll meet you here at 11:30."

He shook her hand and waved to them as he headed back to his taxi. "Thanks, boss."

"You will be okay with him, Dr. Moran. But you would be better with me..." Ignacio grinned.

"Thanks for your help, Ignacio."

Her room on the fourth floor was small and somewhat musty smelling, but the colonial style furniture gave it a charming Old World look. The shutters darkened the interior, and she immediately went to open them. A stream of light shot into the room and she glanced out on a lovely interior courtyard with trees and baskets of bright flowers hanging everywhere. The soft gurgling of water from a large stone fountain in the center was enchanting. What a wonderful contrast to the noisy streets in town.

She pushed one of her big bags into the corner, knowing she would have no reason to open it until she could give its contents away. Her stomach suddenly ached. The contents of the bag were meant for her family, the family she was going to try to find. It had not been in her plans to start her search so quickly, but Pablo had given them the afternoon off from meetings and she would take advantage of it. After all, it was probably going to take more than one day to get any inkling of where her family now lived, and she didn't care how long it took. In her mind, she had decided that she would dedicate every free moment in Havana to try to find them. Despite how wonderful it would be to sightsee, that was not on her agenda, or at least not until she had exhausted every avenue that led to her Cuban family.

She yawned looking at the small clock on the side table. How could she be tired when it was only 9:30 in the morning! Still, the excitement of the trip had made for many sleepless nights during the past few weeks, and last night Jim had done his part in exhausting her with his lovemaking.

Jim. She smiled thinking about him. He was a terrific lover and she knew he was deeply committed to her and wanted to have a more serious relationship with her but she just didn't see herself with him long term. They had tried to simply be good friends who shared sex from time to time, but she could feel that he just kept falling deeper in love with her, and it wasn't fair to him to stay in the relationship. She would break it off when she returned to Chicago. It wouldn't be easy, but she needed to do it.

She lay down wondering if she could trust the front desk to wake her up in time, and deciding not take the chance. Instead, she set her alarm clock to wake her up in one hour. With the warm but steady breeze and soft fountain sounds filling her room, in moments Anaís fell into a deep, relaxing sleep.

CHAPTER 3

Miramar

THE MEETING WITH PABLO HAD BEEN BRIEF. MOST OF THE DELEGATION didn't show up on time, so Pablo just passed out the information as people showed up. His main point was that everyone needed to be ready to board the bus that evening at 8 p.m. to go to the reception that had been planned by the Cuban government for them. Dinner most likely would start close to ten o'clock. He reminded everyone they were now on Latin time for meals and encouraged them to remain in close proximity to the hotel. Anaís nodded, knowing full well she already had planned her escape.

Anaís reveled in the interesting mix of people bustling about as she sat in the hotel lobby waiting for the taxi driver to arrive. The Hotel Europa was replete with European businessmen and women dressed in what Anaís called Caribbean Chic. Trying to blend in with the native garb, many of the men wore short sleeve *guayaberas*, the traditional tropical shirt for men. Despite their attempts, their foreign roots were betrayed by wearing sandals with socks. The women in light cotton dresses wore too much jewelry, too much gold marking them as European or Asian travelers. Resentment unexpectedly filled her as she realized that for these business and vacation travelers it was just one more trip to Cuba, while until now, this travel opportunity had been denied her.

The Cubans working at the hotel were smiling, friendly people. Equally smiling but in a disturbing sort of way were the well-dressed men who approached single men with their leather portfolios full of pictures of young Cuban girls and boys for hire. Despite Castro's denials, prostitution was rampant in 1999 Havana, and although these despicable

28

sorts were not allowed inside any of the reputable hotels, pimps pretending to be businessmen sat around in the lobby or bar searching out men and women who might be looking for Cuban companionship. Of course, the hotel management was adept at figuring out the scams, and the pimps would be run off the property, only to haunt another hotel with the same ruse. Castro's revolution said that it had eradicated prostitution, but standing in the Hotel Europa lobby, any casual observer would have agreed that prostitution was alive and thriving in Cuba in the last year of the 20th century.

Her thoughts were interrupted by the taxi driver standing in front of her. "Good evening, miss." Anaís recognized the wide, toothy smile of the taxi driver she had met through Ignacio.

"Good evening, José. You are most punctual," she said.

In his broken English, he replied, "We have a reputation for being... how do you say *tarde*?"

"Late," she replied.

"Yes, late. But we're late only for *fiestas*. For business, we are punctual." His accent was charming. "Is it okay if I practice my English with you?"

"That's fine, José. Whatever is good for you."

"Where do you want go?" He opened the door and she sat in the backseat of the taxi.

"Miramar," she said, the word catching in her throat, as if it had been waiting to be said for many, many years.

"Miramar?" She nodded. "Ah, it is a wonderful place." He kissed his fingers."Yes. Magnificent. Many years ago, before the Revolution, Miramar...she is where all rich *Cubanos* live. Today...mainly foreigners live there. Diplomats from many countries." He turned a corner sharply. "Diplomats. But not from America." José grimaced as he said the last word. His taxi was an immaculate '59 Chevrolet, the leather upholstery like new. It was well known that Cuba was heaven for anyone who loved vintage cars of the fifties and early sixties because the embargo had almost totally shut down the import of U.S. cars into Cuba except for those in use by government dignitaries and foreigners.

"José, this is a beautiful car. How do you get parts for it when it breaks down?" she inquired.

"Thank you, thank you. She is my..." he struggled for the correct word in English.

"Pride," Anaís offered.

"Ah, pride. Yes, thank you." José repeated the new word a few times. "In Cuba, we no have parts. We learn how to fix old parts, from other cars. Sometime I buy an old part that's not for my car, but..." he shrugged. "It is difficult, but it's okay."

Anaís looked out the window, recognizing from pictures she had seen of Cuba the old ocean front boulevard called *El Malecón* which ran for miles to the 17th century Spanish fortress of *El Morro*. A deep blue cloudless sky reflecting on the glistening Caribbean waters.

José met her gaze in the rearview mirror. "And you are Cuban? From Chicago?" Anaís smiled back.

"Yes."

"Ah. You have family here, in Cuba?"

What a simple question, yet Anaís couldn't answer it. That was the question she had asked herself for the last twenty plus years. Should she tell José? Should she share with this nice stranger the deep anxiety of that simple question?

"No. I am here on business."

"How nice! Here, we need business. I will tell you a little about Cuba, then, if you'd like."

José began pointing out buildings of interest, and at first Anaís listened intently. Soon, however, she found herself muttering mindless replies and focused, instead, on the Miramar address she held in her hands.

This was the last known address of her parents. Whom would she find there? What would she say? Would whoever was living there let her walk through and see where she had lived the first months of her life? Would she find clues to her parents? Questions raced through her mind in a dizzying fury.

Anaís searched her purse for the photo of herself with her mother. Her hand caressed the face of the young woman smiling back at her.

What had happened to her? And her father? What did he look like and what had happened to him? Anaís understood the reason why they had snuck her out of Cuba and sent her to the United States. She believed in her heart that her parents imagined their separation would be brief. Still, did not part of her wish her parents had kept her with them until they were ready to leave Cuba?

She tried to shake off her doubts and concerns. She didn't want to think any more. She was almost as afraid of her questions as of any answers she might receive. Instead, he looked out the window at the beautiful boulevard bordered by the sea. "We're near Miramar, miss. What is the address?"

Just as she was going to hand the paper to José, Anaís changed her mind. "You know, I think I want to walk around a little bit. Let me out somewhere near..." she glanced at the address, "*Calle León.*"

"Calle León. Yes, I know it." José turned off the highway into a residential neighborhood of homes and estates. "This is Miramar," José said with an exaggerated hand gesture. "What is *Miramar* in English?"

Taking in the spectacular view of the ocean, she said, "I think it would be ocean view."

"Ocean view," he repeated, enunciating each of the syllables.

"Is Calle León far from here?" asked Anaís.

"No. Five or six blocks." He answered.

"I'll get out here."

José pulled over. Anaís handed him a U.S. twenty-dollar bill. The driver looked at it and gave it back to her. "No, miss. It's too much. It's one month's pay here in Cuba. No, I can't take it."

"This was a long trip. Please, take it."

Looking down at the money and shaking his head, he looked up ready to argue with her, but was stopped mid-sentence as Anaís put a warm hand on his, and said, "You have been a wonderful guide. It's not too much."

Reluctance and gratitude visible in his voice and face, José inquired, "Do you want me to wait for you?"

"No. I don't know how long I am going to be here."

"Alright then. I will return to hotel. I will check with you later to see if you need a taxi again. Okay? And, you will not pay tonight."

Anaís smiled. She wasn't quite sure what he meant, but it didn't matter.

"Wonderful. Either I or my friends probably will need a taxi again. Thank you so much, José." Anaís waved to him as he stood next to his cab watching her walk across the street.

"Good luck," he waved back.

She had not even walked a block when a youngster appeared out of nowhere asking if she needed some help. She told him in Spanish that she was looking for the address she had on the piece of paper she handed him, and he suddenly became her new guide and asked her to follow him. However, as they walked together a few feet, he turned to stare with a curious look.

"Are you from around here?" he asked.

"No. Well, yes, I am from here, but not now..." She didn't want to explain that she was an expatriate. As she walked down the street, people working in the front yards of the large estates waved to her and asked how she was doing. She felt as if everyone were smiling at her as if they knew her.

Perhaps she just stood out as a tourist, and Anaís felt upset that she was not blending in like she had intended. She had been careful in choosing her clothes, and simply wore jeans, a short sleeve blue cotton shirt, and rope sandals. She wore no jewelry, very little make up, and her nails only had clear polish. Her long, dark hair was pulled back in a ponytail and tucked into a bun.

Maybe it was inevitable that she would stand out here in Havana. It would be false modesty for her not to admit to herself that she was a striking woman who usually stood out wherever she went, regardless how simply she dressed. Besides, she told herself, Latin Americans are just extra friendly people, so she shouldn't be surprised that people were greeting her like old friends.

They had crossed four streets when Anaís finally heard her guide speak again.

"We're here," pointing to a sprawling estate set back from the street smartly landscaped with bougainvillea, vibrant colored plants and some flowers that she did not recognize. Anaís bit her lip as she unconsciously always did when she felt nervous or anxious.

A heavy sigh escaped her lips and the young Cuban boy looked at her again.

"This is the address? This house?" she asked.

"No. This is the embassy. Your number...is on that side...over there..." he pointed to the right far side at the back of the estate. "Next to the big tree." Anaís couldn't see what exactly he was pointing to, but she said thank you, handing him a U.S. five dollar bill. "No," he said, pushing her hand away. "It's not necessary."

"Please take it," she insisted as she shoved the bill into the tattered pocket of his faded, yellow shirt, remembering José's hesitance in accepting a big tip.

The boy gave her an embarrassed smile.

"*Bueno*," he said. "Hope it goes well." And after yet another long stare at Anaís, he turned and walked back down the road.

A car's jarring honk made her jump. A middle aged man behind the wheel of a blue fifty-seven Chevy smiled and motioned for her to get up on the curb. She waved, and stepping back on the narrow paved sidewalk, she sighed, her heart beating rapidly.

For a moment, Anaís contemplated turning around and returning to the safe, known haven of her friends back at the Hotel Europa. Perhaps she should return to her room and mull over the pros and cons of searching for her past. Yes, she told herself. She didn't have to do anything right at this moment. She was still going to be in Cuba for more than a month. She could come back tomorrow, she could...

Another part of her mind replied that there was no reason to wait one more day. She was here. She needed to know.

Anaís inched up the curving driveway, admiring the beautiful sprawling ranch-style house that the boy had said was an embassy. Yes, she recognized the Belgian flag waving next to the front double doors, but it was too far for her to read the bronze plaque beside the flagpole.

Exotically lush, the landscaping of bright flowers gracing the edges of the house below expansive walls of glass impressed her. The manicured lawns and freshly painted surfaces were a distinct contrast to the areas of Havana they had passed on the drive into the city from the airport. This was Miramar, famous for its old and new money in the forties and fifties, and today the home of foreigners as José had said, his voice tinged with bitterness.

Anaís was now at the point in the driveway where it suddenly turned away from the estate in a separate direction, toward the big tree that the boy had pointed out. She still couldn't see any other house, but she followed the path as she had been instructed. A heady fragrance scented the air reminding her of her early childhood. As she walked around the large banyan tree, she eventually saw there was indeed another structure, a wing that seemed to be attached to the main estate she had just passed. Small windows with drawn drapes dotted both sides of a large door flanked by a trellis laced with small white flowers which were the source of the sweetness in the breeze. Perhaps jasmine?

The number on her paper matched the small, corroded metal sign reading one-hundred-seventy-five.

This was a moment she had been anticipating and dreading at the same time for most of her adult life. Calle León number 175 was the address the Morans had received from Father Pat as being Anaís' home. Her heart and mind told her she was at the brink of either a wonderful revelation...or the dead end in her search for her Cuban roots. She sensed that once the door opened, one way or another, her life would never be the same again.

Anaís knocked on the door. She heard no movement on the other side, and so she knocked again, this time a little louder. She put her ear close to the door, but still could hear no movement from inside. Maybe no one lived here anymore, although a rusty bicycle with a metal basket holding a pair of old gym shoes suggested someone was around. Just as she was going to knock for a third time, she heard some rattling from behind the door, as if a metal bolt were being drawn across the door. A muffled voice was saying something. Yes, it sounded like a woman's voice saying, "I'm coming. One moment."

Anaís could feel her heart in her ears, the blood rising through her chest up to her neck, making her temples throb. Her stomach felt knotted and heavy. She thought she was going to faint.

The door creaked softly as it partially opened, and Anaís felt as if everything stopped and then slipped into slow motion. She could hear her own breath, inhaling and exhaling in a slow cadence.

First, she saw a delicate hand curving its long female fingers around the door jam, pulling the door back with some difficulty. Beyond the door, everything was dark, and Anaís strained in the bright sunshine of the street to see inside. The body of the person began to emerge from the shadows. At first a long, thin yet muscular arm reached the outside sunshine, then a shoulder with the end of a damp towel drooping down its side, the delicate hollow of a neck, a towel draped like a turban around a head, and finally—

A mirror? A beautiful face with wide-set, green eyes, a small aquiline nose, full lips, high rounded cheekbones and a dimpled chin all looked at her with amazement. What was happening? An exact image of herself stared from the other side of the now open door.

CHAPTER 4

The Face in the Mirror

As Anaís and her identical counterpart gaped at each other in utter surprise, Anaís heard another woman's voice asking who was at the door. While the two young women remained speechless and as if frozen to the spot, the woman who kept asking "Who's there?" entered the room. Anaís realized that the screaming came from a petite black woman whose almost toothless mouth now continued to yell while her thick black hands went from her turbaned head to her chest as if trying to hold inside the life that seemed to be leaving her body.

Anaís saw the old woman stumble forward, and crash against a small table nearby. Instinctively both women rushed to the old woman's aid, trying to catch her before she fell. They were not in time, and at suddenly all three of them were on the floor grabbing at each other, looking at each other, in both amazement and dismay.

"Who...?"

"How..?" English and Spanish filled the air as the young women propped up the old woman. "Chencha! Please." Anaís heard her image call the old woman by name. Chencha was starting to open her eyes again. The whites of her large African eyes were yellowed with age. The old woman looked at the woman speaking Spanish, then at Anaís, and almost jumped out of their hold.

"Saint Barbara! *Yemayá!* No. It's not possible!"

Chencha kept shaking her head, first grabbing one of the women by the arm, then the other. Tears streamed down her face. Her initial screams had given way to little gasps. Anaís looked at the young woman across from her, and realized she was looking at an exact copy of herself,

36

except with short tousled hair now visible since the towel had fallen from her head in the commotion.

"Chencha, what's wrong? And what's going on here?" Her double asked the black woman while stroking her face lovingly.

Chencha looked at Anaís and sat up, still supported by the two young women. Anaís sat motionless as the startled and teary stranger caressed her dimpled chin before announcing, "Isa, this is your sister."

The words seemed to shatter the space around them.

"My sister?"

"Yes, your sister Ana Isabel."

Anaís looked at her twin in disbelief.

It was now the young women's turn to feel faint. As Chencha slowly raised herself from the floor, Anaís and her sister, Isa, glanced at each other in disbelief. Chencha was still sighing, all the while beating her chest with a clenched fist. "Thank you, *Dios*. Thank you, God." Her tear-stained eyes looked up as if able to see heaven beyond the dark ceiling above them.

Both Anaís and Isa slowly rose from the floor, staring intently at each other, the words "your sister" still shaking them. Without saying a word, they sat at opposite ends of the small wooden table where Chencha now sat, a happy, toothless grin slowly spreading across her face in an out-pouring of joy.

Her gnarled black hands reached in opposite directions to take each woman's hand. Anaís felt the leathery and calloused tight grip from the elderly woman and she almost winced. Chencha smiled, then throwing her head back, started laughing uncontrollably, speaking words that Anaís did not recognize as Spanish.

Slowly, she became silent, and looking at each of them in turn, said, "It's a miracle. And like all miracles, you don't understand yet, do you?" She squeezed their hands tighter. "Well, I'm going to tell you."

CHAPTER 5

Chencha's Story

IT SEEMED TO ISA THAT WHAT SHE WAS HEARING FROM CHENCHA, THE woman who had been like a mother to her, was completely unbelievable. Chencha had not stopped talking for the last hour except every so often to again raise her eyes and hands toward the skies and thank her Yoruba gods for bringing about the miracle as she called it. And, if what Chencha was saying were true, it was a miracle. Isa could still hardly believe all that she was hearing.

She knew from Chencha that her parents had died under suspicious circumstances when she was just a little girl, about three years old. She also knew that although her aunts and uncles in Pinar del Río had taken care of her at different periods of time during her youth, her main caretaker had always been Chencha, her nanny, with whom she had lived in the small section of what once had been her parents' home before the Revolution and the appropriation of property by Castro. The estate had been taken over by the government in the sixties, and it had been used as a training school for the Russians. After the fall of the Soviet Union in 1989, it was then used as the home of European ambassadors on the island. Through all the changes, Isa and Chencha had been allowed to continue living in what had served as the servants' quarters over an old storage area.

For Anaís, to learn that her parents were part of the counter Revolution was surprising. More shocking, however, was to hear that a few years after the Bay of Pigs, both of her parents had disappeared in one of the many round-ups that Chencha said the government carried out against anti-Castro citizens in the years after the Revolution. Her parents were never heard from again. Chencha said that they were probably incarcerated or murdered by the regime.

It was overwhelming news, and terror gripped Anaís' heart as she heard for the first time the horrific facts about her mother and father's probable demise, realizing she would never meet them.

"I never knew them, either, Anaís," Isa lamented.

They sat in silence, Chencha's hands still holding theirs tenderly.

"Well, and now that you two are together, that you now know you are twins, there is more that I need so share with you, about how you ended up living a world away from each other all these years" she said.

Isa and Anaís were twin daughters of Isabel and Pedro Buenaventura, originally from Pinar del Río, where the rest of their relatives lived. In the first months of the Revolution, both Isabel and Pedro supported Castro like so many other professionals and political intellectuals weary of the Batista brutalities and the social inequities.

Pedro and Isabel had married in their hometown, but had moved to Havana because they thought their future in practicing law would be better there. Chencha, then in her thirties and a house servant in Isabel's home, went with them. Because of their English skills, both were hired to work for American companies with branches in Cuba, Pedro with Hershey Chocolates and Isabel with Coca-Cola. Their salaries, paid in U.S. dollars, soon made them a small fortune by Cuban standards, and in 1958 they built a beautiful home in Miramar, where the three women now sat in the servants' quarters.

Chencha proudly explained how Doña Isabel and Don Pedro always had treated her more like a family member than hired help, and over time as more persons were added to run the home, Chencha supervised the other staff members. She also spoke proudly of the fact that even though the Buenaventuras acquired wealth and properties, they never forgot their relatives in Pinar del Río or where they had come from. Chencha said she was always proud to say that she worked for don Pedro and Doña Isabel, and that she and the other house help were the best paid and best treated servants on the block.

"Yes" she mused, "those were very sweet days," her gaze seemed to wander into deep corners of the room and of her mind.

"And those sweet days became sweeter when you two were born." She looked at each of them, smiling her toothless smile at Isa and Anaís. "And then you two became my main job, and Zaida watched over the house." She leaned over, whispering a secret. "And, of course, I watched Zaida so she wouldn't take advantage of your parents who were so good to all of us."

Chencha stretched her hands over her head in a grateful gesture. She gulped down some water. "Thank you, God," she repeated. "*Gracias.*"

"Let me continue my story..." she added. "You girls were going to be named after your mother Isabel and her mother, your grandmother Ana, may they rest in peace." She made the sign of the cross over her chest as she whispered the words.

"But when your parents saw that you were identical twins, they made a slight change and gave you both names, your grandmother's and mothers. Isabel Ana, you were the first one born." Chencha grinned and patted her arm. "And you, Ana Isabel, came into the world screaming, a few minutes after your sister." She pinched Anaís' dimpled chin. "Soon, we just called you Isa and Anaís or Ani," She threw back her turbaned head and laughed a big hearty laugh.

"Yes, you are identical, but from the start, you were also very different. Isa, you slept all night and napped all day," she said. "For a couple of weeks, we weren't even sure of the color of your eyes because they were never open." The young women laughed with her.

"And you, Ana Isabel, didn't sleep through the night for two months. You just used to take cat naps all day long." She laughed again. "You tired us out."

She paused for a moment, and the lighthearted tone of her voice disappeared.

"They loved you both so much. Your parents loved you both so, so much." She started to cry.

Isa rose and put her arms around her old friend and caretaker.

"No, Chencha. No. Whatever happened, it's over. But please, please tell us how and why we were separated."

Anaís suddenly realized there had to be a connection with what she was hearing and the story from her adoptive parents. Chencha was sobbing so strongly now, her frail body shaking, that she could not talk. Isa kept comforting her.

"I know part of the story, I think" she said in her perfect Spanish, and both Isa and Chencha looked up startled to hear her.

"My parents, well the couple who adopted me, said that they had been asked by an American priest who was friends with a Cuban couple to take me out of Cuba as their own child and watch over me until my parents could get out of Cuba."

Isa listened in silent surprise while Chencha nodded, agreeing with what she was hearing.

"My American parents took care of me at first just waiting for instructions or communication from my Cuban parents, but they never heard anything again. And the priest who had arranged my safe transport died, and with him, any further news of my parents. I was adopted by my parents...my adoptive parents...when I was three."

Chencha continued crying.

"They killed them. The poor things. Poor don Pedro and Doña Isabel. They were so good, so concerned about everyone around them, so worried about what was happening to their Cuba. The government killed them."

"But, Chencha," Isa was sitting again across from the elderly woman and pointed at Anaís. "What's the rest of the story?" Isa realized she didn't even know where to begin asking the questions that were flooding her mind.

"Child," Chencha began, wiping tears from her face swollen from crying and the emotion of their meeting. "What Ana Isabel is saying is exactly what happened," she whispered now, as if there were people outside listening. "Father Pat was a good friend of your parents. Your parents had helped many of the poor people in the countryside that Father ministered to. He also was one of a handful of priests who worked with American families who travelled back and forth from the United States to Cuba, people he knew he could trust, to take the children of those Cuban families, like your parents, who wanted to leave the country, who didn't want their children living through the Communism they could see was developing here." Her voice was now a whisper.

"So, your parents talked to Father Pat about getting you both out of the country. They had some old friends from Coca-Cola working on getting the necessary papers to leave the country, but things were getting difficult, and they knew that if they couldn't leave legally, they would do it illegally, but it would be a more dangerous trip, maybe through Mexico or Nicaragua." Chencha said with a deep sigh, "They were going to take me with them, you know. I was part of the family, your father said. And I was younger then, so I wouldn't have been a burden to them."

Isa and Anaís were pinned to their seats, hearing for the first time facts surrounding their separation. Chencha sighed again, dabbing at tears that weren't there anymore, as if she had already cried every tear that she could.

"*Bueno*...well, and so, after many weeks of meeting with Father Pat, one day I remember your father called your mother and me into his study, told us to sit down, and explained that Father Pat had arranged for two different families to take each of you to the United States within weeks. I remember Doña Isabel's initial reaction, jumping out of the chair and clapping her hands happily at the good news. Then almost simultaneously, the horror of sending you two away, by yourselves, with strangers, began to sink in. You were only eleven months old then." Chencha looked at them lovingly. "Two chubby, curly haired, beautiful, happy little angels. The life of this house." She paused, her energy to continue waning.

"Go on. Please." Anaís pleaded softly. Chencha took a deep breath.

"It's important for you to know. Yes. It is time." She took a deep breath. Anaís recalled her own adoptive parents' sighs and concern when they shared with her that she was adopted. It made her brace herself for even more surprising news.

"*Bueno*, I remember that don Pedro asked me to leave when your mother started to cry. He told me to look in on you two, and that he'd come in a little bit. I don't know what they said to each other, but when they came back to your nursery, where I watched you play in the playpen, both of them looked like they had cried their hearts and souls out in that study. But they said nothing. Your mother went directly to the bookcase where you had books and dolls. I saw her pick up dolls, looking at them, comparing something about each of them to the others. She finally picked out two identical beautiful porcelain dolls. Later that day, she asked me to take out all the cotton filling and I saw her fill each one with crumpled U.S. $500 bills and some of her special jewelry."

Isa suddenly got up from her chair, and Chencha stopped talking. The young woman went into another room, and when she returned in a few minutes, she was carrying a very old porcelain doll whose limp cotton filled body contrasted with the rigid alabaster face, arms and legs. She sat the doll on the table and looked at Chencha.

Chencha picked it up lovingly.

"It was so difficult for your mother to get everything she wanted inside her" she said referring to the doll, as her black fingers squeezed the chubby, soft body. "We rolled up the dollars and rubber banded them but they didn't make a normal doll body your mother said, afraid that it would attract the attention of officers at the airport." Chencha stroked the doll's hair. "We ended up crumpling each bill and stuffing the body with it, wrapping the jewelry in some of the bills."

They were all looking at the doll, a link to their past, in disbelief.

"I have a doll just like that," Anaís said, bending over to take her purse from the floor. Chencha and Isa gasped and Anaís pulled out *Gordita*.

Chencha smiled. "Your parents always bought two of everything for you. Dressed you the same, although sometimes in a different color."

"And our parents put things inside, in the dolls—for us?" Each woman held her doll at arm's length, feeling the plump bodies with new interest. Chencha placed a gnarled, black hand on Isa's bare arm. "Even though we've gone through hard times, I've never said anything about the money because...well, I know you, and you would want to spend it on us, our needs. And I've wanted to keep that for you...for when I'm not here anymore."

"Chencha!" Isa looked at her with mixed admiration and reproach.

"But now it's time," Chencha continued. "You should look inside.

Your parents expected you to have these things." She got up and walked her slow, hunched-over stroll to a small table against the wall, and taking scissors from a side drawer, handed them to Isa.

With nervous fingers, she carefully cut the threads holding the seam on the back of one of the dolls. The threads came off easily and as the fabric opened under Isa's careful fingers, through the widening gap they saw the crumpled bills that Chencha had described. Crumpled five-hundred dollar bills disguised as stuffing stared up at them. Anaís had never even seen a five-hundred dollar bill before, yet now the table was strewn with them. Wrapped inside some of the bills, they found another cache, this time of jewelry—earrings, lockets, bracelets and rings. The women gasped almost in unison.

Isa handed Anaís the scissors and slowly the same type of contents emerged from the second doll. The women looked at the collection of beautiful, antique pieces and the crumpled bills in amazement.

"But what happened? How did all this take place?" Isa insisted, hugging the doll to her chest. Chencha sighed, and raised her eyes to the heavens as if asking for the strength to continue.

"After weeks and weeks of waiting, the call came. Suddenly your parents only had a few days' notice to get everything ready, and Father Pat told them it would be safer for everyone if he came to pick you both up and that he take you personally to the American couples who would be waiting in his rectory." She leaned back in her chair. "I think he also didn't want your parents to have to go through the pain of putting you in the arms of strangers." She paused and sighed again as if to replenish her strength to continue.

"It was all set. Father Pat would come for you two with one of the nuns from the church around four in the afternoon The plane was scheduled to leave at eight that evening. You were dressed, as usual, in the same outfits, your dolls were sitting on the sofa in the receiving room of the big house... next door. Your mother and father had spent the whole day with you, not even letting you take your naps." Chencha smiled, eyes closed, inwardly seeing the past. "I see it all as if it were today."

The old woman paused, her thick lips quivering with emotion.

"When the doorbell rang, I felt my heart stop like it was never going to start up again. I can only imagine what your parents were feeling. But I remember that they didn't say anything when I brought Father Pat to the study." She paused.

"Uttering a quick hello, Father Pat immediately said that there was a problem." Chencha looked at each of them.

"One of the families had backed out, becoming afraid of the rumors that were swirling about stricter and stricter inspections and questions at the airport. American tourists were being taken into custody and questioned. Father Pat then suggested that your parents send just one of you, saying he was sure that with a little extra time he could convince a second family to take the other." Chencha got up and went to the small sink to fill her water glass, taking some sips as walked back to the table to continue the painful story.

"Your parents didn't say anything for what seemed like a long time. But Father Pat kept talking, stressing that they should not lose this opportunity. Things were getting more and more difficult for getting the children out. At that point, Father Pat and others had been doing this for two years and it had gone well. But with fewer and fewer Americans in Cuba, he saw the window closing and insisted that your parents not pass up the opportunity to send at least one of you to freedom that day." She drank the rest of the water.

"That's when your mother finally spoke, telling him that they could not choose as to which of you two should go. Father Pat said that they should let God decide through him, reassuring them that he would have another dependable family within the week." Chencha again squeezed their hands tightly.

"Your parents were holding you. I remember that they looked at each other in that special way that they had to communicate with each other without words. They sat both of you down on the floor in front of the good Father and stepped back." Chencha paused. The sisters looked at each other and at Chencha mesmerized, anxiously waiting for her to continue.

"Your mother said. 'Alright then, Father. God will choose.'

"Father Pat looked at both of you, one of you waddling toward him, the other following behind. Finally, one of you grabbed on to the skirt on his cassock while the other sat down and just looked around. Father Pat looked at both of you again, bent over and picked up the one that was hanging on to his skirt. It was you, Anaís ... I will never forget. He said, 'My children... you've made a difficult decision...the most difficult one of your lives, I am sure. But don't worry. I will be back for this other angel very soon. Plus, you two will get your papers in order soon as well, and then all of you will be reunited on the other side,' he said looking directly at your parents.

Chencha looked at Anaís.

"Ana Isabel, your father and mother kissed you, gave Father Pat your doll, telling him that there were special things inside. Your mother hugged you, but I remember that she didn't shed a tear. You were reaching for your sister, and both of you started to cry. Your father talked cheerfully to you saying that you would be right back, gave you one last kiss, and turned with Isabel Ana in his arms and headed for the nursery." Chencha let go of their hands.

"I never saw Father Pat again. He took ill, and returned to the United States. He called your father various times, trying to arrange safe passage for Isabel Ana, but without Father Pat's direct negotiation, your parents wouldn't consider letting you go with strangers. And then..." tears welled up in her eyes, "then, there was no one here to help us."

"I don't want to talk about the day that your parents disappeared, my children," she said. "Not now. Maybe another day. I am so tired."

"Are you alright, Chencha?" Isa asked, getting up and putting an arm around her old trusted friend.

"Yes. I'm better than I have been in a long time, seeing that God finally has brought you two together." She smiled at them. "But I am an old woman, and my heart..." she clutched her chest, "it is old too. I am going to rest a little now." She got up and Isa started to follow her.

"No," Chencha said. "You stay here with your sister."

Chencha's small thin body disappeared through one of the small doorways of the room. Both women watched her go, and then turned to each other. Anaís looked at her sister, still wrapped in a towel and standing barefoot before her.

Isa stared at her sister. The only difference she could see between herself and her twin was the long ponytail down her sister's back, and the American look she had—her polished although simple makeup, jeans, shirt and shoes that did not look worn.

"Now I understand why people around here were greeting me like they knew me. Isa, we are identical."

Both women reached for each other and hugged, feeling for the first time in their memory the special link of sisterhood and family history.

"Sister!"

Chapter 6

Introductions

For hours, the two women sat at the table and talked incessantly about their lives. Like a friendly ghost, Chencha appeared then disappeared from the room, sometimes bringing fresh water, other times a fruit or a bowl of rice and beans. From time to time, she stopped for a moment and caressed each woman's head. The tears were gone, and she had only smiles looking at the women as if they were her own flesh and blood.

Isa had not even taken the time to comb her hair, simply throwing on a pair of shorts and an old tee-shirt that Chencha brought her at some point. It was remarkable how identical they were.

Neither Isa nor Anaís wanted to spend more time talking about the past, rather they seemed more interested in learning about who they were at the present time. Isa was amazed that her sister spoke perfect Spanish, and they were surprised to find out how much they shared in terms of interests, including their choice of career. Isa was an interpreter in Russian and French at the Office of Foreign Investors, while Anaís used her Spanish as the Cultural Specialist at the Illinois Office of Tourism and marketed programs for the Hispanic population in that state.

"It's incredible, right? A world apart, and it seems that we prove all the theories about twins who have been separated at birth."

"Do you like sports?" Isa asked. Anaís nodded. "Let me guess. Your American football."

"Actually, no. We used to have an excellent team in Chicago..."

Isa interrupted her. "Yes, the Bears." Isa said. "We know a lot about your country."

"Really?" Anaís replied. "Anyway, they have been horrible for the last years. And you really have to be a fan to sit through their abysmal games in freezing Chicago weather."

"I can't imagine cold weather," Isa said, her gaze drifting off into the distance. "Our weather here is never cold."

"Lucky you" Anaís replied. "When we left Chicago, during the day the temperature was in the sixties, but they were predicting snow for the weekend."

"Sixty degrees! We would be freezing here with that temperature! What is snow like?"

"It's very, very beautiful," Anaís said. "Especially when it first starts falling, and it sparkles and makes everything look clean and almost magical."

"I'd love to see that," Isa said, still gazing off into the distance.

"Isa, how are things for you here? We hear that there are such shortages in Cuba...such poverty..." Anaís thought she would risk asking that question. "Have you ever considered going to the United States?"

Her sister quickly put a finger up to her lips and shushed her. Isa looked around the room at some imaginary eavesdroppers. Anaís looked around also, but saw no one.

"Every day of my life since I was a little girl I have wondered about your country," Isa whispered. "When I was very young and learned that my parents had disappeared because they did not agree with the government, I cannot tell you the anger and hatred I felt. But my family... our family...in Pinar del Río...they've made me understand that it is our destiny here in Cuba...to go through this difficult political period. But now, hearing from Chencha that our parents wanted for all of us to go to the United States...Well, I don't even know what I'm feeling right now."

She leaned over to Anaís in a softer voice, as if voices might be listening to them from behind the walls.

"From as far back as I can remember," she continued whispering, "I learned from Chencha to be careful about what I say. In Cuba, you learn to have a duality of expression from the time you are very young," she said simply. "You learn what it takes to survive and, you can't always say what you believe." She noticed her sister's puzzled look.

"Anaís, it would take me a lifetime to tell you how I have learned to smile and go along with doing things when my heart has not been in it. But it is the Cuban way. We all do it."

Anaís took her sister's hand.

"If you want to be with me, sister, I will find a way of getting you out of here, like Mom and Dad wanted. I feel so guilty, to have been the one chosen... Isa, right now, the delegation I am with, we have a state Senator with us. I can talk to him about you. Would that be alright with you? I don't want to do anything that would make things difficult for you."

Isa was silent for a while.

"Thank you, my sister. You don't know how wonderful that would be, to be able to leave here, to take Chencha with me. To be with you, on the other side of the moon, like Chencha refers to your country. I think it comes from one of her African stories. I love Cuba, my...our family is here—but life is more and more difficult for us."

"I know we can do it, Isa." Anaís continued, trying to give her sister hope. "And back in the United States, you have a house, you have clothes, you have money," she added, "because everything I have also belongs to you." Her voice broke with emotion as she continued.

"I cannot give you back the years that you have missed with me, sharing my privileges and good fortune," she said. "I am so sorry that... that I was the one to get all the comforts..."

Isa put her fingers up to her sister's lips, stopping the apology. "You apologize for nothing, please. Fate, or God, decided how our lives would be. Not even our parents are responsible for any of this, because, in the end, their dream was for both of us, for all of us, to have a good life, a free life. And I believe that they truly thought they would be around to give us that good life." She was quiet for a minute. "It wasn't meant to be for them."

A lump formed in Anaís' throat, her mind imagining the horror that her mother and father must have endured. She closed her eyes, not wanting to contemplate how they might have died, instead focusing on her sister and what she could for her in the present.

"But now is a different time," Anaís said. "And despite whatever we have to face, we have found each other. That was meant to be." She took her sister's hands. "And I am sure that it is meant to be for us to be together."

Isa smiled. "I hope you are right, dear sister. But I don't think it is going to be easy. And if you do talk to your friend, please make sure it is all very private, that not too many people know." Her face was serious. "Things change here for people who even dream about leaving."

"I'll be very careful." Anaís said. "And I won't do anything without asking you first." Isa nodded.

"Now, I think I need to get going back to the hotel. My goodness, it's already six o'clock. We have spent almost the entire day talking."

"And isn't that wonderful! Let me get Chencha so you can say good-bye to her." She stopped for a moment. "She won't want you to go, you know."

Anaís watched her sister exit through the slightly lit doorway. She stood up and walked around the small room, which served as a living room and eating area, curiously examining bits and pieces of her sister's life. Suddenly, she felt her heart skip a beat as she thought she recognized something in the room. She heard her sister and Chencha talking to her as they entered, but their conversation became a low mumbling in her ears as she slowly walked toward a small wooden console against the wall neatly arranged with knickknacks. There, behind a pair of old, red maracas with a drawing of the Cuban flag and other trinkets she saw a picture of herself as a baby in an old, wooden frame.

She picked up the photograph in total wonderment. It was the picture she carried in her wallet. Or at least that was her first thought. Then she realized there was something different about this picture, and that she was not sitting on her mother's lap. In this picture, strong, hairy arms circled her body. A handsome man with a bright and mischievous smile looked straight at the camera, as if caught in the middle of laughing at a wonderful joke. And his dimpled chin was just like hers. God! Was this Isa with their father?

She felt Chencha and Isa standing next to her.

51

"It's the only picture I have of me with our father," Isa said, placing a loving arm around Anaís' waist. "It's the only family picture I have, period. Chencha and I don't know what happened to all the albums our parents had of us since our birth. The family on the farm doesn't have any pictures of the four of us either." She finished with a soft sigh.

Anaís turned to her sister and hugged her. Then, taking her arm, she walked her back to the kitchen table where she had left her purse. Lovingly, she pulled out her wallet and the precious other half of the puzzle. She showed it to Isa.

Isa's surprise was no less than Anaís had been. Instinctively sharing the same thought, they both ran back to the photograph on the dresser. Isa took it out of the frame, and breathlessly they each brought the two pieces together. Like adventurers who suddenly have found the lost half of a map to a long lost treasure, their yells and screams of surprise and happiness filled the tiny servant's quarters with lighthearted and childlike joy. There they were, their parents and they as babies, the four of them together as a family.

"Tomorrow we go to Secundino's house!" Chencha was saying to them, raising her hands again to the heavens. "My dear God, thank you. Thank you."

CHAPTER 7

Finally Cuba

RIDING SILENTLY IN THE BACK SEAT OF THE TAXI THAT ISA HAD HAILED down for her at the corner of the beautifully tree-lined street, la Quinta Avenida, Anaís felt her mind still whirling from the afternoon's events. She hardly could believe what had just happened. Everything still seemed impossible, and now that she was by herself with time to reflect, she felt an almost numbing sensation in her head.

Yesterday about this time, she was in her ultra-modern condominium on Lake Shore Drive, looking out at a crisp October day in Chicago, leaves the color of burnt sugar and spun gold blowing in the city wind. She had been in bed, making love with Jim, enjoying their time together. Afterwards, she had met up with her colleagues at the airport for her trip to Havana. Yesterday, she had many friends but no family. And yesterday her heart was full with the anticipated promise of what her trip to Cuba might bring.

That promise was now fulfilled, ten times over. She had a sister! A twin sister! And she knew what her father looked like! She took out the torn picture she had exchanged with Isa. What a handsome and happy face he had. Everything she had learned from Chencha was overwhelming, making her almost dizzy. She gazed out the window and breathed deeply, enjoying the warm early evening breeze tinged with the scents of exotic flowers.

She felt she was different now. She had a family, a sister, Chencha and many soon to be met relatives in Pinar del Río. It was more than she had ever imagined.

The taxi drove in slowly moving traffic past what had once been magnificent estates and now were embassies displaying their nations' flags. They turned at a traffic light and soon passed a sign announcing the Naútico Ferretero which Anaís thought might be the old Havana Yacht Club her adoptive parents had mentioned many times as one of their favorite places to visit with their Cuban friends. Her thoughts turned to her birth parents, lost in the social conflict of Castro's Revolution, and her heart sank with sadness.

She could hardly bear to consider how they might have died, having read so many horror stories about political prisoners taken to El Príncipe, the feared interrogation jail in Havana or the Isla de Pino compound where prisoners often died from extreme harshness of forced labor and unsanitary living conditions.

My God. Might her parents have endured such a fate?

The brightness of the day darkened as the taxi entered the Túnel de Línea which led back to the center of Havana, and Anaís shuddered in the momentary musty coolness of the tunnel. Perhaps it was better not to try to imagine anything about her parents' death. It was tragic enough to know that they had died young, disillusioned by the government that they initially had supported. She was proud to have learned about the sort of people that they were and was in awe of the sacrifice her parents had made in trying to give their daughters a safer and better life outside of Communist Cuba. The fact that it had been she who was chosen on that fateful day was, however, disturbing.

Poor Isa. Poor, poor Isa. How had she survived with no parents and under such difficult living conditions? Thank goodness for Chencha. Thirty-eight years and two completely different life experiences separated her from her sister. Could they ever bridge those worlds? Isa was certainly entitled to resent her sister's good fortune for a long time to come.

Anaís sighed so heavily that the startled taxi driver jumped in his seat and looked at her in the rear view mirror. She smiled back to reassure him that she was alright.

But she was not alright, really. She was filled with contradictory feelings of happiness and sadness and timidity. She wished she could tell everyone in the delegation that she had found a sister, but that didn't seem like a safe thing to do. After all, she didn't know most of the people in the group well enough to trust that they would be discreet about what she had learned regarding her parents and sister. What if they discussed it over lunch and one of the many Cuban secret police that they had been told would be hanging around the hotels and tourist places heard the story? What if that caused a problem for Isa and Chencha? Certainly, *Arrancapellejo* could never be trusted not to say anything. What about Richard?

She recognized the street of the Hotel Europa and asked the taxi driver what she owed him. When he told her the fare in dollars, she shook her head thinking how duplicitous it was to pay with American currency instead of the Cuban peso. She handed him the fare plus a tip and stepped out of the cab. She looked at her watch, realizing she didn't have much time to get ready for the evening's reception. Rushing up the stone steps to the lobby elevator, she ran into *Arrancapellejo*, dressed in a glittery evening dress that accentuated her heavy figure.

"Anaís! You're just coming in? Where have you been? We're leaving in half an hour, you know." Anaís nodded as she entered the empty elevator. Thankfully they were headed in different directions. The elevator cut off *Arrancapellejo's* shrill cackling laugh as she bumped into one of the guests in the hall.

They were bused to the Capitolio a few miles from the hotel, and in the early evening light, Havana was simply another old Spanish-style colonial city. The streets of Havana were lined with charming iron light posts that were just lighting up. It was good to see that the huge power outages of the early nineties that she had read about seemed to have disappeared. She wondered what Isa, Chencha and their Pinar del Río family had experienced in those days after the Soviets pulled out, when the island went without running water or power for days at a time. Anaís would never again be able to enjoy ordinary luxuries back in the States without thinking about Cuba.

Anaís thought about her sister and Chencha and how they made it day in and day out in the depressed island economy. Her stomach ached at the thought of the struggles she could only imagine they experienced on a daily basis. Just the idea of not having running water or light for hours on end was incomprehensible. In Chicago, people were in an uproar if they lost their electricity even for an hour after an unusually bad storm. In Cuba it seemed people accepted inconveniences and shortages of all types as their way of life. She shuddered at the thought that her sister had lived in trying financial conditions for all these years while she had enjoyed a totally free and pampered life. There was no justice in their situation. She felt again the urgency to correct it as quickly as possible.

They had arrived at the beautiful Capitol building, its dome shining in the setting Havana sun. She stood in awe of the 1929 neoclassical marvel which housed Cuba's Congress until the Revolution of 1959. Castro quickly had declared that its opulent grandeur was a symbol of the wasteful days of previous dictators who thrived under the influence of the corrupt U.S. government. The once grand building was now closed to public viewing, and had been repurposed as the Ministry of Science, Technology and the Environment (CITMA).

She heard Richard's voice behind her.

"And where were you all day, little miss Cuba?" He put his arm around her shoulder. "By the way, you look stunning in your Caribbean chic. How do I look?"

"Stunning as well." Anaís grabbed his arm. "Aren't you excited that we will get to see the interior of this amazing building, Richard? I know it has been neglected for forty years, but I don't care. I want to see everything inside. Wait until you see what's in the main hall."

"Well, first we have to climb up...what...a thousand stairs?"

"Come on, Richard, you'd prefer an elevator? There are maybe fifty or sixty steps, and, they're weathered and dirty, but beautiful. And look at the bronze statues on either side of the entrance."

Richard allowed himself to be dragged up the marble stairs past a full guard of uniformed police, their bayonets and guns reminding Anaís of the unusual security measures that were being taken for their delegation.

The Senator and his aides were at the entrance. Pablo had told them they would be meeting various ministers of government, and perhaps Castro himself would attend the reception.

Men in the Cuban *guayaberas* and women in conservative suits greeted them in both Spanish and English and as Anaís and Richard were introduced, they asked her if she was the Cuban. When she confirmed that she was, they smiled and spoke words welcoming her back home. Genuine or not, the Cuban hospitality was gratifying to her and allayed her initial fears that she might encounter some hostility or resentment because she was a Cuban from the States. Perhaps the name-calling was over, and Cubans who emigrated after the Revolution of 1959 were no longer called *gusanos,* worms, for leaving Cuba and not staying on the island and being loyal to the Castro regime. Or perhaps it was just 1999 diplomacy at work.

Inside the main lobby of the Capitolio, the light streamed down softly through the glass dome in the vaulted ceiling lighting the third largest indoor statue in the world.

"This is the Statue of the Republic, in bronze, weighing 49 tons and covered in twenty-two carat gold leaf." The young woman leading them paused a moment for effect.

"And here..." she turned around and Anaís and Richard turned as well, "here in the floor is something truly remarkable." They all stared at a cordoned off four foot area. "This stone embedded in the floor is a replica of a twenty-five carat diamond that once belonged to Tsar Nicholas of Russia and that has belonged to the Cuban people for many decades. The original was moved to a safer location. This represents point zero, that is, the distance for the entire Cuban national highway system is measured from this point. Interesting, no?"

They began to walk a long hallway with two huge halls on either side. At the end, their guide opened the door into a semicircular library. "Personally, I think that even after all these years, it still smells like a cigar box." The guide smiled.

"Of interest to you might be the four, one-ton Tiffany chandeliers. The walls, however, are carved mahogany from our own Cuban forests.

But, enough of the tour. You must want something to drink."

Their footsteps echoing on the marble floors, Anaís followed their guide wishing they had time to stroll casually around the beautiful building, with its centuries of colonial, imperialist and revolutionary history. Instead, they followed in a respectful, silent procession past more uniformed police. Suddenly, they found themselves in an indoor courtyard that had been turned into a tropical paradise of stunning linen covered tables topped with exotic flowers and open aviaries with large parrots and cockatiels. A four-piece combo played soft music in a corner. Anaís recognized the melody, one of her father's favorite, but could not think of the title of the song. Servers in crisp white aprons approached them with tall glasses filled with a light green drink adorned with long green sprigs.

"¿Un mojito?"

"Yes. Please."

"What is this?" Ricardo asked, casting a suspicious eye at the cloudy tonic.

"A mojito. A deceptively strong drink..."

"It tastes like an ultra-sweet lemonade."

"Well, Richard, this lemonade will knock you out if you have a few of them."

"Wonderful. That's what I want." He raised his glass. "You know, I've said this before, but don't you look gorgeous. I wish I were straight."

"Thank you. You look mahh-velous, as well, Richard." Anaís always mispronounced that word on purpose around Richard. "By the way, do you think Castro will come by tonight?"

"Who knows, Ani. You know politicians. He already met the Senator this morning, so from here on it may be his lackeys and us." Taking a sip, he said, "Hey, you never said where you disappeared to all afternoon? I looked for you and nobody knew where you were. Cynthia said she saw you running out of the lobby around noon."

"God, she is a gossip. I just went out and walked around. I wanted to see a little of the city where I was born, alone," she said.

"Have you thought about how you're gonna make that connection with your family? And, shit, have you thought about what you will do if you do find them?"

Feeling guilty at her lie, Anaís looked at Richard, certainly one of her best friends ever, and felt tempted to tell him the truth about what had happened that afternoon. She smiled to herself thinking how excited he would be to know she had not just found family, but a twin sister, an identical twin. It was almost too hokey to be true, something from a soap opera. Yet, it was true. She was about to tell him everything that had happened when she felt a hand on her bare back.

"Doctor Moran." A middle-aged very pale-skinned man with light blue eyes smiled at her, slightly bowing his head in a greeting. "I am Engineer Martín Jorge Obrero. I am one of the assistants to the Minister of Tourism here in Havana."

"I'm enchanted to meet you, Mr. Obrero. Please call me Anaís."

"The pleasure is all mine, Anaís." He kissed her hand. "And please call me Martín Jorge. Your Director of Tourism," he pointed to Anaís' boss standing a few feet away, "tells me you are the person I need to talk with about our goals and plans for cultural exchange."

Anaís looked at her own director who waved back.

"Well, yes, I'd be honored."

"Magnificent!" He clapped his hands together. "Then, we can discuss much in Spanish. My English is not so good. You will join our table, no?"

"Of course." Anaís looked at Richard with some disappointment.

"And I suppose this is where I should find my counterpart here in Agricultural Equipment?" Richard asked.

"That is Engineer Ortiz...over there," Martin Jorge pointed to a lithe looking gentleman in a cream colored suit talking to the musicians.

"Well, then, Anaís, I'll see you later," Richard said as he kissed her cheek.

"Nice man," Martín Jorge continued. "Is he your boyfriend?"

"No, just a close friend," Anaís replied, somewhat surprised at the personal question.

"All the better for me," he continued. "You are a most beautiful woman. And, you are a *Cubana*."

His teeth were dazzling white, Anaís thought, and how could he stay so pale living under the scorching Caribbean skies?

"Well, thank you. So you are in the Tourist Office here in Havana?"

She tried to put some distance between them as he held on to her arm. "Yes. Well, we do publicity for all of Cuba. We have many tourists here, you know, from all over the world, except, of course, from the United States." His lips pursed in a grimace. "Maybe your trip can help us change that. Perhaps we begin with cultural exchanges."

"It is our hope as well, Mr. Obrero."

"No, please, call me Martín Jorge."

"Yes, of course. Our Governor and others in our state are eager to establish ties with the Cuban people."

"Ah, yes, and because you too are Cuban this is interesting to you, too, no?"

"Yes." Anaís became nervous. Her sister worked in the government. Could they possibly have ever run into each other? She scrutinized his face to see if he recognized her. After a few moments, she was convinced he did not.

"So what is your story, *señorita?* How is it that we lost such a beautiful and talented woman? How did we let you go?" He was trying to ingratiate himself to her. She looked around the table hoping to catch someone else's attention, but everyone was involved in conversation. She was stuck with Martín Jorge.

"Ah, Martín Jorge. That is a lengthy story for another day," she flashed her most charming smile. "I am here, that is, we are here to learn more about you and Cuba, and how we can help our bosses get our countries to work together."

The comment seemed to remind Martín Jorge that his mission was a political one, and agreeing with her that much needed to be done, his demeanor and tone changed in an instant as he began to explain the tourism aspects of the Cuban economy, emphasizing the large investments that European and Japanese companies were making in Cuba in world-class hotels and resorts.

"Of course, with the embargo, we can have no tourism with the United States. But cultural exchange, that is a possibility, is it not?"

"That's what I am hoping for."

The wait staff served the avocado and tomato salads. One of the musicians tapped the microphone a few times to catch their attention.

"*¡Buenas noches, amigos!* Welcome to Cuba the most beautiful island in the Caribbean. It doesn't matter what other advertising says." Everyone laughed. "You will see, you will see. Anyway, please, forgive my English," he continued in a heavy Cuban accent. "But I will do my best to speak your language. Tonight, we are happy to show you a little of Cuba, in music and dance, two important cultural elements to Cuban people. When we have problems, we sing." The group chuckled. "Yes, you may not believe it, but we sing. And when we have more problems, we dance." His hand around an imaginary partner, he twirled and swayed to the beat from the combo, belying his sixty or seventy years of age. "And, of course, everyone has problems, you, us, the whole world. So, in Cuba, we sing and we dance our little problems away." He danced again with his imaginary partner, and everyone clapped.

"No, no, it's not necessary for me. But you can clap for the first group to entertain you tonight, the children from the School of Revolution Plaza in Vedado, who will sing for you." And with an elaborate move of his hands, pointed to a group of about a dozen children ranging from five to thirteen years of age who formed two rows next to the musicians.

The sounds of guitar, bongos, flute and conga drums filled the air with a soft, familiar melody. The children, in their crisp white uniforms and bright red bandanas tied around their necks in the official Communist Cuba style, started swaying to the music. Cleanly scrubbed faces eyed their audience anxiously. They were white, mulatto and black, the three major racial groups Castro said he would blend into one race in Cuba. She wondered if, in fact, the racial equality that the regime had talked so passionately about achieving had been accomplished after Batista's ouster. Looking at the beautiful mixture of races and heritage of the children staring back at her it seemed, at least for this event, it had been achieved.

One of the older children, a handsome, mulatto boy with piercing green eyes, stepped out from the group and began reciting the old José

Martí poem while his classmates hummed in time with the music.

The poem turned song that had become popular in the United States as the *Guantanamera* gave her goose bumps every time she heard it. This time, Anaís felt a heightened sense of emotion as she looked around at the palm trees, the exotic birds lulling on their perches, the fragrant scents of flowers in the early evening air of her first night in Havana. She closed her eyes and thought about her adoptive parents, thankful that they had told her the truth about her heritage.

The children finished their song, angelic voices now giggling at the exuberant applause at their performance. After a few bows, they followed their teacher through one of the arched doorways and out of sight.

"They were wonderful!" someone at their table was saying, echoing everyone else's opinion.

"And there is more," said Martin Jorge, with a flourish of his hand. "Did you like our salad? Well, now you eat our suckling pig—*puerco asado.*"

"Of course," Anaís replied. "I love Cuban food. And I am sure this meal will be even better than anything I've tasted before."

"Ah, you flatter us. But yes, we enjoy foods that blend much from Spain and Africa and our own indigenous people. You heard our band leader talk about music and dance...Do you know Cuban music? Do you dance, perhaps, a little Cuban, what do you it call in the United States... salsa?"

"I love to dance."

"Well, let's dance." Martín Jorge was on his feet, pulling her out of her chair. Everyone at the table looked at them. She tried to refuse. There was no one dancing, and she instantly felt awkward at being made the center of attention.

"Martín Jorge, no, really. I don't mean that I want to dance now. Everyone is about to eat..."

"No! We dance. It is the Cuban way. We don't leave for later what we can now do." She braced herself for a dance where she would need to avoid getting stepped on by an unskilled partner. Martín Jorge didn't move like a dancer, and he walked with no particular grace.

He took her arm and walked with her toward the musicians. He whispered something in the lead musician's ear and they stopped playing their song and soon the sounds of a lively rumba got everyone's attention. Anaís felt herself blush.

Martín Jorge twirled her toward the middle of the dance floor. His eyes looked up at her, a full head taller. She tried to smile, wishing she were somewhere else. She could feel everybody's eyes on them, an unlikely partnering.

But then as Martín Jorge took his first steps, his arm confidently around her waist, Anaís understood she was in the arms of a true dancer. She saw the look of surprise on his face too, as she followed him first through some simple steps and then as he complicated his footwork. They both smiled at each other, enjoying the pleasure of dancing with an equal.

"Doctor Moran, you're an excellent dancer! I'm most surprised. You are very good!"

"And you lead well, Martin Jorge. You are a true dancer."

"All Cubans are" he said matter-of-factly, moving her into a dip then a triple turn.

Anaís was feeling wonderfully exhilarated, her partner having been transformed on the dance floor from a bland bureaucrat into a Cuban Fred Astaire. More couples joined them on the dance floor, and the band picked up its tempo and pitch. Martín Jorge masterfully moved her in and out of twists and turns that were new to her. She had not danced with such a good partner in years, probably since the last Latin dance lessons she had taken many years ago in Chicago.

She was sorry to hear the music come to an end, and Martín Jorge ended by swooping her into a tight embrace. Breathing heavily, they looked at each other briefly with total enchantment. Then politely he bowed, kissed her hand and took her back to the table. The band struck up with the old Cuban favorite *Te Lo Dijo Adela* and both Martín Jorge and Anaís started singing the popular refrain. The people at the table applauded them.

"That was wonderful," she said. "You are a truly wonderful dancer."

"And you too! And you know this song! We are all very much happy that you have not lost your Cuban-ness."

The delicious roasted pork with sweet plantains and yucca were as plentiful as the mojitos. Martín Jorge's dancing ability made him more gregarious with the other members of the delegation and soon they all were joking and laughing like old friends.

Everyone was caught up in the relaxed atmosphere. Toward the end of the evening, Senator Fernández stopped by her table to thank her for all the good will she was spreading. Anaís was sad to see the evening end. As they boarded the bus to return to the hotel, Richard teased her.

"Well, you certainly had a good time. Even the Senator came over to talk to you, huh. Yes, I saw that."

"Stop it. You know how it is when you're native to the place. It's just natural."

"Yeah, right. But it doesn't help that you are beautiful and that you have those swinging Latin hips."

"You know, you've just had one too many mojitos."

"Unlike you? Anyway, you didn't tell me what you did this afternoon, when you escaped us," he commented.

Isa and Chencha! How terrible that she had not thought about them all night! How had they spent their evening? Anaís' mood changed. Her heart felt heavy again.

"Hey it couldn't have been that bad?" Richard said, looking at her forlorn expression.

"I'm tired Richard. We'll talk tomorrow, alright?"

"Sure. *Hasta mañana.* Is that right?"

He held the door of the elevator as it stopped at her floor. "That's perfect. Keep practicing." She blew him a kiss.

Back in her hotel room, Anaís still felt despondent. What kind of a person was she, to have so quickly put thoughts about her sister aside?

The room spun as she pulled her dress over her head. She grabbed the side of the dresser nearby. Definitely, too many mojitos. Without taking off the rest of her clothing or jewelry, she let herself fall on top of the bedspread and immediately fell asleep.

CHAPTER 8

Secundino

ANAÍS WOKE WITH A TREMENDOUS HEADACHE, AND NOT EVEN THE COOL shower she took totally cleared her mind. Thank goodness she had asked the front desk for a wake-up call for seven o'clock because otherwise she would not have been ready to meet the group as they headed for their first official meetings with the various department heads of the Cuban government. Their schedule for the rest of the four weeks would be grueling, with only a few afternoons and evenings open to be on their own. It was abundantly clear that the Cuban government wanted to cast their visit in the best possible light, and as Pablo had told them all, everyone needed to attend all scheduled meetings and events.

However, today they only had scheduled meetings at the Capitolio in the morning, with a late afternoon lunch at Hemingway's favorite Havana restaurant bar, *La Floridita*. The meetings with various government ministers about the possibilities for trade with Cuba were boring, but lunch at the small café lined with memorabilia of one of her favorite authors had been very enjoyable.

Pictures of Hemingway in Cuba hung everywhere and the staff enjoyed telling them where *el viejo*, the old man, as they referred to Hemingway, sat and what he drank and how much he enjoyed living in Cuba. It was all fascinating, but Anaís' thoughts constantly turned to heading back to Miramar to see her sister.

Her friends were having too much of a good time to notice when she silently left the table. Anaís hailed a taxi, not wishing to use José again and arouse the taxi driver's suspicion about returning to the same area in

Miramar two days in a row.

Back in Miramar, Chencha and Isa were waiting eagerly for her at the door. Chencha said that they had to leave for Secundino's place immediately because they were expected. Anaís was so happy to see her sister and Chencha again that she didn't even think to ask why they were in such a hurry to meet this old friend. Anaís insisted that they take a taxi, and as the old woman looked silently out the taxi window, the sisters hugged and began to ask each other questions, still amazed that they were identical. Same face, same eyes, same expressions. But there was Anaís' long pony tail in contrast to Isa's short and curly hairdo accentuating her heavy use of black eyeliner.

They got out of the cab in Old Havana, the narrow cobblestoned streets crowded with people. This was far from the Hotel Europa area, and Anaís tried not to act like the typical tourist staring at her surroundings. Many people seemed startled as the identical twins walked by.

"What a beautiful part of the city," Anaís said, admiring the architecture hidden behind decades of neglect. "Our group hasn't been brought around here."

Chencha looked up at her and laughed.

"No, tourists don't come here. This is not only Old Havana, it is really old Havana, old and decrepit like me. They don't want you to see this."

"You're not decrepit, Chencha," Isa objected. "And you are beautiful, like these old buildings."

"Yes, they were beautiful at one time," her hand like a wand in the air tried to paint images of freshly painted buildings and flower boxes hanging from the wrought iron balconies, blooming with bright colors and fragrances. "But look at them now."

Anaís continued to admire the once handsome colonial buildings, now weathered by time and neglect.

"We probably shouldn't even be walking under these balconies." Chencha pointed to the corroded wrought iron railing hanging limply sideways just ahead of them. "Some of them are held together with chewing gum. Yes, that is what holds them together." Then she added "... if you can find chewing gum."

The three of them laughed. Nonetheless, the poverty and decay around them could not be ignored. The streets were littered with the day's debris, and in some areas the women skirted small mounds of plaster rubble that had fallen off the buildings. No wonder their delegation had not been brought to this area, Anaís thought.

"And Secundino lives around here?" Anaís asked.

"*Ah, sí.* He has lived here all his life. And that's a long time because he's even older than me, and that is very old indeed," Chencha smiled.

They walked past the open wooden doors of a corner tavern where a group of men stood around the bar in loud discussion.

"Don't look," Isa warned her sister a second too late to catch Anaís' curious glance into the darkened room. She saw the men put down their glasses and rush to the door to whistle at them,

"Imagine our luck, beauty times two." The comments and cat calls trailed behind them as Anaís felt Chencha grab each of their arms.

"That is so funny," Anaís whispered to her sister once they were out of earshot of the men at the bar.

"Funny? Why?"

"Men back home don't usually do that anymore—talk like that to women passing by. Well, sometimes. But not that brazenly."

"Ah, but you're in Cuba," Isa tried to explain. "And here, machismo is still alive and very much in vogue. If you don't want them to follow you, to say something to you, you need to pretend you didn't hear or see them."

They moved past a makeshift cardboard table where men sat on crates playing dominoes. Anaís looked past them as she had been instructed. Whistles and comments followed them anyway. Chencha held on to their arms protectively.

"Look, there's Secundino's house," Chencha pointed her bony finger to a door in the middle of the block.

"Does he know we're coming?" Isa asked.

"Yes, child. That's why you'll see many, many people there. Anaís coming back—this is a miracle that Secundino has always told me would happen. And I am ashamed, because many years ago, I stopped believing him."

The sky was bright with the colorful hues of the tropical afternoon Havana skies. Anaís felt exhilarated. Her second day in Cuba and she was meeting a real *santero,* an authentic priest of Santería, the blended practice of Christianity and African religions. In the past, the Caribbean Santería always had seemed so mysterious when she read or heard about it. Now she was going to meet a high priest. It was incredible!

She glanced around at the poor neighborhood crowded with people sitting on the steps of their homes, many smoking cigars. Lively music and voices reached them from balconies and from behind latticed iron windows Even though she was reminded of other Latin American neighborhoods, she felt that this time she was walking into a forbidden world.

"Have you ever been here, Isa?"

"No, never. Chencha comes here often, though. And she has talked about Secundino my whole life. I know she gets advice from him on some special potion for this or that. I guess santería has been in my life in one way or another always. But this is new to me also."

"I can't imagine why we're here."

"Well, Chencha said that Secundino needs to see us. Last night, after you left, she told me that when we were about six months old, we were deathly ill with a virus no one recognized. Mamá lost faith in the doctors and talked to Secundino, Chencha's *santero* at her suggestion. He saw us and gave Mamá some herbal drink to give us to drink various times a days for many days. Whether coincidence or not, we got well. Mamá was always grateful to Secundino and never questioned Chencha's odd potions or ideas again. Now he wants to see us. I've always wanted to meet him. He sounds like an amazing individual."

"It all sounds so unbelievable." Anaís agreed.

"Here we are." Chencha stepped ahead of them into a wide pathway facing a large, festively painted door. Within seconds, it swung open, and behind it they saw a roomful of people standing behind an ebony-skinned, towering man. Anaís thought that she had never seen anyone as black. His gaze was riveting as he looked first at one woman then the other. His white head tilted to one side, and a smile even wider than Chencha's brightened his face. As he threw back his head, words Anaís did not understand flowed out of the gaping red crevice of his huge mouth.

Secundino raised and extended his long, strong arms to the heavens, continuing to speak in a language foreign to Anaís and Isa. The crowd of people who crammed the ample white painted room began to clap softly in unison. Then they began to chant in sounds similar to those that Secundino was making. Anaís looked around the room at the predominately black faces in the crowd, as they swayed in joyous celebration. Did all these people know about her and her sister? She looked at Isa, who appeared to be as surprised as she at the number of people waiting for them. Chencha had moved over to the crowd, and they saw her become one with the crowd in song and movement.

Somehow, the door had closed behind them. Without the women noticing, they seemed now to have moved into a different room, a spacious courtyard with trees and fountains, and glowing candles everywhere. Anaís and Isa looked up as an even larger crowd of celebrants stood on the second floor veranda encircling the patio. They, too, clapped, swayed and sang. The clapping had reached an almost thunderous level, the bodies swaying as if dancing to a rhythm that had been rehearsed many times before. Secundino stood in the same position, arms still outstretched above his head, eyes wide open, speaking his unrecognizable words that pierced through the cacophony around them. It all seemed surreal and intoxicating to the two women now encircled by the crowd.

Suddenly, Secundino stopped his mutterings and the crowd hushed immediately. His arms seemed incredibly long to Anaís, as if the white shirtsleeves could not accommodate their extraordinary length. His trousers, too, were white, and his clothes seemed to glow in the bright candle light against his gleaming black skin.

Secundino's gaze slowly lowered and fixed itself on the faces of Anaís and Isa staring back at him in astonishment. His smile seemed to recognize that they had no fear in his presence, that the bodies surrounding them seemed perfectly natural and welcoming.

His arms extended toward them, and quickly they were encircled in his embrace that didn't touch them, yet was palpable. Despite their own tall stature, he seemed to tower over them like one of the slender graceful palms in the courtyard, his chin barely touching the top of their heads. Anaís could feel his presence like a current of electricity. In the silence surrounding them, the only things she could hear were her sister's breath and her own, and the soft rustling sound that the fronds made as they were played upon by the wind. She felt transported by the bottomless, depth of Secundino's penetrating stare.

A sudden need to close her eyes made her unexpectedly very relaxed and sleepy. She swallowed, her saliva tasting unusually sweet and warm, creeping down her throat. She started to feel light-headed and worked arduously to open her eyes to find her sister, but could not. She wondered if Isa was experiencing the same feelings.

Ebbing thoughts of Isa disappeared and her mind became a blank. She felt that she was being swept into a kind of sleep even though she thought she was still standing. She tried once more to open her eyes but could not. Her whole body became limp, her mind was unable to hold thoughts or form words. A pleasing, tranquil numbness had overtaken her, as she felt herself as if floating, her feet not touching the ground.

Her mind now glowed with the same soft candle light of Secundino's clothes. She felt a serenity she could not remember ever feeling before, an incredible warmth and lightness. Everything was still outside of her and inside of her.

Then in the center of the glow in her mind, something started to take shape. At first, the outline was fuzzy and unrecognizable. But then, even before the figures were clear for her to see, she recognized her birth parents. They were next to her, picking her up. She was suddenly the tousle-haired child of the picture she kept in her wallet. Isa was there, too, in her mother's arms. No one was speaking, yet her heart heard their loving words, cooing and rocking them playfully to and fro. She heard her father's laughter, smelled the jasmine in her mother's hair. She hugged them with grown up arms, wrapping herself tightly around both of their necks. Anaís had never felt more contented and at peace. Her heart was bursting with joy and sense of wholeness.

"We are always with you," she heard parents say. "And we'll be with each of you always."

Secundino was pouring a murky liquid into small glasses in front of her. Anaís blinked a few times, as if waking up from a deep sleep. Isa was sitting next to her.

"Here drink up. There is no other rum like it in the world. Cuban rum is special," he said.

He handed each woman a shot-sized glass and watched each of them tentatively sip their drinks. Sitting back in a massive, intricately carved mahogany chair, its oval back circling his head like a halo, Secundino smiled at them with a look of pure benevolence.

"It is so good to see the two of you together again." He sipped his glass. "It has been too long. Isn't that right, Chencha?"

"*Sí*, Secundino. Much too long."

"Yes. I have known you almost since the day you were born. Beautiful children that you were. Beautiful women that you have become."

"So much like your mother. She was beautiful too. Especially here" he said, tapping his heart. "So many people in Cuba, well, so many white people in Cuba forgot their soul when they made a little money. But not your mother. She believed in things she could not see, in the old mysteries that we brought from our old homeland across the ocean."

"When you got so ill, your mother brought you here. Your father was not happy. I remember. But I forgive him."

"Yemayá made you well. And she has been with you all these years, working to bring you together.

He sighed heavily.

"There is still much to do, to keep you together. Much water that Yemayá has to cross with you. But it will happen. It will not be long."

He looked at them intently.

"You will have to trust each other... to the other side of the moon..." he sipped his rum "...and back. You will have to trust with the eyes and ears and heart of your souls."

71

He leaned back flashing his compassionate smile.

"And then it will happen."

Anaís and Isa were transfixed by his voice and conversation.

"I know you don't want to be running around the streets of Old Havana at late hours. So, I'll say good-bye. For now. But, my children, come back to see me. I am here for you." With those words, Secundino raised his lofty frame and placed a hand on each of their heads. Again, Anaís felt as if electricity were passing straight through her. Secundino turned, and followed by a small group of men and women, disappeared into the courtyard now dark with the dying candles.

"Let's go, girls. It's getting very late. Our friends will stay with us until we get a taxi closer to the main street," said Chencha.

Anaís finally saw her sister's face, and it looked as startled as she herself felt. Where had everyone gone? There had been so many people, so much noise and now they stood alone with Chencha in the room garbed in silence. They both quietly acquiesced to Chencha's prodding and followed her outside into the night where the air was still warm and inviting. A full moon hung indolently in the sky, basking the darkened street with a shower of light. Chencha lead the way. Behind her, Anaís and Isa walked silently for a few blocks. Finally, Isa broke the reverie.

"Anaís, do you feel alright? What happened with Secundino? What happened to all the people who were there when we arrived? And..."

They interrupted each other with words and questions as they picked up their pace to keep up with Chencha, who was walking at an uncharacteristic brisk trek down the narrow cobblestoned street. They talked simultaneously, gasping at the realization that they had dreamt the same dream about their parents. Both women shivered, not sure if from the night air or an experience that neither one could explain. When they finally were in the taxi and asked Chencha to explain what had gone on in Secundino's house, the old woman only shook her head. "All things from our Yoruba roots. Everything now is as it should be. Secundino was right. Everything happens for a reason and with a purpose."

Nothing they said changed her answer. Chencha leaned back in the seat, closed her eyes and fell asleep.

CHAPTER 9

Thanksgiving Day

FOR ANAÍS, THE DAYS IN CUBA HAD EVAPORATED LIKE THE CUMULUS clouds that idled over the shimmering ocean one minute and were gone the next. Mornings and most afternoons she dutifully attended the meetings her Cuban hosts had planned for their delegation. She had learned much about her native country. The delegation was treated with every courtesy, and everyone had paired up effortlessly with their Cuban counterpart in hopes of future alliances. The Illinois agenda was developing better than anyone had projected.

All the excursions that had been planned for them, from the visit to the cigar factory to grammar school classes and free clinics in towns outside of Havana had been engaging, and were designed to show the country at its best. The other face of Cuba, the barrios deteriorated perhaps beyond recovery, were only experienced by Anaís when she spent time with her sister.

Most evenings, the delegation was feted to sumptuous dinners followed by music and dancing. Even the most two-left-footed people among them in the American delegation seemed to be in the spirit of the moment. They all danced and enjoyed the Cuban hospitality offered to them.

The previous evening, they had gone to La Tropicana, the world- renowned nightclub that had been a tourist hot spot before the Revolution. The show still featured the legendary buxom and curvaceous dancers, but gone were the free spending Americans of four decades before.

Every moment not spent with the delegation, Anaís snuck away to visit with Isa and Chencha. Her long walks with her sister around Miramar had caught them both up on their thirty-eight years away from each other. The more they talked, the more Anaís felt she now understood the void she had felt in her heart throughout her adult life. Also, the longer they were together, the more Anaís felt guilty that she had been the one touched by fate to leave Cuba.

Isa, on the other hand, never showed any signs of resentment or anger. Her sweet temperament accepted her situation, and she was excited about her sister's promise to get her and Chencha out of Cuba. If the roles were reversed, Anaís was not sure she would be as accepting and understanding.

Anaís finally had shared her secret with Richard and had also asked Pablo for a meeting with the Senator to discuss a private matter. Senator Fernández had shown sincere interest and amazement at the details that Anaís was able to share regarding her parents and her new found sister and Chencha. It was like a story or novel, he kept repeating, shaking his head in disbelief. But, he assured them, it should be a relatively easy issue to clear up. After all, their goodwill trip was going incredibly well, and Cuba did have an emigration agreement with the United States for twenty thousand exit visas a year. He saw no reason why Anaís' sister and Chencha could not be granted that type of visa.

When Anaís shared that promise with Isa and Chencha, they screamed and cried, not believing their good fortune. If it all came to be, they said, it would be like winning a once in a lifetime lottery.

Now it was Thanksgiving Day, although nothing felt like Thanksgiving Day to Anaís as she looked out her hotel window at the swaying palms in the courtyard. It was too tropical, it was too warm to be Thanksgiving Day.

She was excited, however, that she was finally going to introduce her sister to her friends and Senator Fernández, and couldn't wait to see the look on their faces when they found out that she had a sister and that they were identical twins. It was a truly soap opera ending to their trip.

Senator Fernández had insisted that Isa come to celebrate with them at the hotel at the Thanksgiving dinner the hotel management was putting together for the delegation. It would be a good opportunity, he said, for them to discuss Isa's emigration.

Anaís had had a difficult time convincing Isa that it was time to meet the Illinois delegation and Isa was still somewhat hesitant about the encounter. Over the last weeks of talking with her sister, Anaís had realized that Isa usually spoke looking over her shoulder as if someone might be watching or listening. She now understood a bit better that Isa could not imagine herself free to speak her mind any more than Anaís could imagine standing in food lines for a pound of rice and some bread. They had lived different lives, and wishing that things were different didn't make them so.

Anaís hoped that Isa would not change her mind about joining them for dinner. Chencha had declined, saying that it would not to be proper for an old black servant to attend with such an illustrious group. Anaís told her that it didn't matter what color she was and what she did in life. Chencha had nodded through Anaís' explanations, and then with a smile refused.

The early morning sun was peeking through the carefully painted wooden windows. She looked at the few dresses still hanging in the wardrobe, feeling glad that the majority of her clothes were now with Isa.

It was difficult to believe that she had been in Cuba for almost a month and that so much had happened. Finding her sister—well, every time she thought of Isa her heart spilled over with joy. And despite the fact that she was sad that she was going to be leaving her sister in Cuba, she was confident that Senator Fernández would keep his promise to help them be rejoined. Anaís had no doubt.

Anaís savored the thought of meeting her sister and Chencha in a very near future at the airport and taking them home. They would drop all their bags at her condo, and immediately walk over to Michigan Avenue to see the glittering holiday lights and decorations. No, they shouldn't walk because of Chencha. A taxi would be much better. And, yes, she needed to get a good sense of what size clothes she needed to buy for the old woman. Isa could wear Anaís' clothes until they could go shopping and she could pick out clothes she liked. Anaís' mind raced from one thought to the next. Christmas would be wonderful this year. Finally, she would have a family again.

The phone rang and interrupted her musings.

"Hello?"

"*Hola, Anaís. ¿Como estás?*"

Richard was trying to again practice Spanish with her. She wondered whether to answer him slowly in Spanish words she knew he would recognize or if she should rattle off a conversation and confuse him a little.

Bemused by his errors and mispronunciations, she said, "Remember what I told you about answering *bueno* in Spanish when someone asks you *¿cómo estás?* It means you're good—in the Biblical sense, that is."

Richard emitted one of his big, hearty laughs.

"Well, yes, I'm that too ...not to brag. Just ask any of my *amigos*."

"You know, that's just a little more than I really want to know. Anyway, I'm fine, thanks. And I really can't wait until tonight, for you to meet my sister."

"I can't either, Ani. I mean, this is totally unreal, isn't it? Finding out you have a sister, and a twin at that! It's unbelievable."

"I know. I wake up sometimes thinking I've had this crazy dream. But no, thank God. It's true. I have a sister. And she is wonderful. Wait until you meet her today."

"Does she really look like you?"

"Exactly like me. It's uncanny. I mean, we have different hairstyles, and she does her makeup differently, lots, and I mean, lots of dark eyeliner like most women here. And her clothes! You know how I always am trying to make my butt look smaller? Well, everything she wears is tight. When she gets to Chicago we're going to have to work on that with her."

"What do you mean *we?* I like your butt. Hard as a rock"

"Stop it, Richard," she laughed back at him. "You're starting to sound hornier than usual."

"Well, I have to admit, these *Cubanitos* simply love babes like yours truly, don't you know."

"I know better. You wouldn't fool around on Franco. Remember Franco...back home? I know you."

"Well, there's fooling around and there's fooling around. Franco and I—we have an understanding."

"You know, I don't want to go there." They laughed, sharing the closeness of their long-time friendship.

"Well, so, are you ready to go back?' he asked.

"Not really. The month here has flown for me. Part of me wants to stay and get to know my sister better. The other part can't wait to get back home to start the paperwork to have her with me always."

"That will be truly fabulous! After all she's gone through. There is so much poverty here, Ani. Every day that we're out and about I'm in constant amazement of the wonderful attitude of the people here. They have so little, and, you know, they take it all in stride. It's a wonderful country with amazing, industrious people."

"You're absolutely right, Richard. My parents, well my adoptive parents, used to tell me the same thing about their years spent in Cuba— about the country being like a natural paradise and the people in general having a supreme love of life."

"They really do. Despite everything."

"Yes, that is what is amazing to me. Here we are, forty years after the Revolution, the Russians came, the Russians left—and the economy is deplorable. Yet the Cubans here like my sister just go with it and make the best of it. It's something I had read about, but you know, it's hard to believe. I mean, I don't know if I could live like this and remain upbeat."

"I couldn't."

"But, you're right. When Isa and Chencha come to Chicago, I think our lifestyle... it will be overwhelming for them."

"And you say that the Senator thinks he can pull it off by Christmas?"

"That's what he said. When I bring Isa today, we're going to talk about how best to do this for her sake. After all, we don't have a problem back home, but we have to consider exactly what to do not to make problems for her while we're working on this situation. You know, Richard, I've noticed my sister is paranoid. I mean, I say what's on my mind most of the time. But Isa," she shook her head. "Isa almost whispers when we're talking about certain things. It's as if she's afraid some government informant is hidden somewhere behind a tree, tape recording our conversations."

"Must be horrible living like that your whole life."

"So true," she agreed. "And I can't wait to get her home, with me. You know, my sister is a graduate of the University of Havana, and she has such a natural gift for languages that she was one of a select group that the government sent abroad for a time to perfect her skills. She spent time in intensive language schools...in St. Petersburg for her Russian, in Morocco for her French and English in Botswana. Can you imagine? And she earns $100 a month and has to stand in line for food."

"Don't worry, Ani. Senator Fernández is one of the good guys. If he told you he can help, it's because he knows he can."

"That's what I'm counting on, and it's one of the reasons I am feeling okay with our leaving in a few days."

"So what's your plan for today? We don't have to meet the rest of the group until, what is it, seven o'clock for dinner here at the hotel?"

"Something like that. I have to check with Cynthia. But I thought today I'd pack the rest of the things that I'm leaving behind with my sister. I'll drop everything off when I pick her up later on after she gets off work. Then we'll both be with you at the Thanksgiving dinner. What a surprise that will be for our group."

"I can't wait to see their faces when you two show up. Because they don't know that you are identical twins, do they?"

"No. Only you. And actually only the Senator and his aide know anything at all about my sister. We thought it better to keep it under wraps until now that we're about to leave because, after all, it is a delicate situation. We don't want any embarrassing moments here for the delegation. So the group doesn't know anything."

"Well, good that you didn't tell *Arrancapellejo*. Listen, I'm gonna go. Looks like you're going to be busy, so I'm just going to get a taxi and get myself to the beach for a few more rays before we go back to frigid weather."

"Sounds good. See you tonight."

"*Hasta luego.*" His accent was getting better, Anaís thought.

While she had been on the phone with Richard, Anaís had been going through the drawers and closet separating the last few items that she would need to keep for her trip back home. Everything else she put in a suitcase to leave with Isa.

Her sister got paid $100 a month! Anaís spent that and more on a pair of shoes at any given moment. She wasn't wealthy, but she had a well-paying job, and she had money in the bank to do just about anything she wanted. She owned her condo and she had money that her parents had willed her, as well as her husband's insurance policy after his death. She would divide everything with her sister, get her on her feet, and enjoy watching Isa and Chencha enjoy a better life. Her plans warmed her heart.

The phone ring made her jump. Richard again, she thought. Yes, he was a good friend, but sometimes he could be clingy. He probably wanted to get her to join him at the beach.

"*Hola Ricardito. ¿Qué pasa ahora?* What's up now, Richard?"

The silence on the other side made her realize she had mistaken her caller.

"Hello?"

"Oh, okay. It indeed is you, Anaís." She recognized Senator Fernández' aide on the other side. "It's Pablo. It didn't sound like you for a minute. Well, what am I saying? Anything in Spanish throws me. Now I wish that my parents had insisted that we kids learn it."

"Hi, Pablo. Sorry about that. I thought it was Richard calling."

"Oh, well, yes. Anyway, how are you?"

"Fine, thanks. And you?"

"Oh, great. It's wonderful to be on this mission, don't you think?"

"Absolutely."

"Yes. It's quite beautiful here in Cuba."

"Well, the reason I'm calling...I don't know if you've heard, although you probably wouldn't have heard yet..." Pablo was a competent aide to the Senator, but his conversations certainly rambled.

"Well, the Senator is having me call everyone in our delegation because there's a situation he wants everyone to be aware about."

Anaís' silence prompted him to continue.

"Well, yes. It seems that...the Senator just got a call from the States that early this morning they picked up a couple of survivors near Fort Lauderdale... in a small boat that left Cuba some days ago. Right now, the Coast Guard is looking for other survivors, although it doesn't look good for finding anyone else, what with it being a small boat and the weather they're having."

"That's horrible. I hope they do find more people. How many were there? And what happened?"

"The Senator doesn't know much more than I just said. And of course, he wants everyone in the delegation to make no comment on this regardless of what we are asked or what we hear any Cubans saying about this."

"Of course. That sounds like the politically correct thing to do."

"Yes, well. We don't want any animosity with anyone here just when we're at the end of a very successful first mission from our state."

"You don't have to worry about me. I'll say nothing."

"Great. Well, yes, so just pretend you haven't even heard anything. If we get any more news, I'll be calling everyone back again with an update."

"Thanks, Pablo. And tell the Senator not to worry. We'll all behave these last few days in Cuba."

"Uh, yes, that's what we need to do, Anaís. Are you coming to the Thanksgiving dinner later?"

"I wouldn't miss it. What time again?"

"Uh, well, seven. You'll have to check downstairs for the specific room, though."

"Great. See you later."

Anaís hung up the phone, her happiness dissipating quickly and turning to dread. She felt a strange and disturbing churning in her stomach. It was never a good day for Cuba/U.S. relationships when Cubans risked their lives crossing the sea and landed on United States soil asking for asylum. Yes, the Senator was absolutely right. It was not a good idea at all for anybody in the group to react to anything they may hear from other people outside their delegation. She wondered exactly what was being said in Cuba about the situation. She called Richard's room, but there was no answer. He was surely already at the beach.

Anaís grabbed her purse and headed for the lobby for a late breakfast and to see if any U.S. news was being discussed by the hotel workers or guests.

The elevator seemed to take forever to reach her floor. Inside, a group of tall, lanky Canadians in shorts and sandals carrying beach bags smiled and greeted her. She was starting to wish she had gone with Richard to the beach and spent a relaxing afternoon, oblivious to the political news now emerging, which somehow felt ominous.

The elevator took its long, sweet tropical time descending from floor to floor, picking up guests. Once in the lobby, everything seemed normal. Anaís walked around, trying to pick up any Spanish conversation from the hotel personnel that might suggest they knew about what was happening in Florida. After five minutes of wandering about, she realized everything seemed the same, and the hotel was going about its daily business of pleasing guests.

She went into the small dining room facing the sunny courtyard garden where she usually ate. The thought of the cold Chicago winter made her thankful for the warm breeze and sunshine streaking through the trees. She sat down at one of the small round tables next to a small fish pond. It was so beautiful here. How sad that people back home could not enjoy visits in Cuba like all the other international tourists sitting around her.

She gave her order to the same waiter who now prided himself in knowing her name and what she liked for breakfast. Today, however, it was near lunchtime and she had an incredible taste for a Cuban sandwich with plantains. The waiter smiled, saying that it was an unusual breakfast, but Anaís replied that back in Chicago this was the beginning of the typical lunch hour. The waiter shrugged his shoulders.

Anaís relaxed her back into the comfortable cushions of the oversized patio furniture. She ran her hand over the smooth, polished dark wood, wondering where the furniture had come from. Spain, maybe? It

certainly was nothing that she had seen in any of the small shops that
they had been shown by their Cuban hosts, and certainly nothing like the
old weathered furniture in her sister's apartment.

Isa! The thought of her sister made her heart leap with elation and
she again started to daydream about having her sister with her in Chicago. Anaís' own condo certainly was big enough for the three of them,
and she hoped her sister and Chencha would want to live with her. But
if not, they could buy something else, maybe in the same building. Isa
would have no trouble finding employment with her skills and training.

There was so much to do once Isa got to the States. She would relish
every minute.

Just as she was finishing her lunch and waiting for the waiter to
bring the bill, Anaís looked up and saw Pablo walking around the ter-
raced restaurant, looking around as if searching for someone. They saw
each other, and he walked at a quick pace toward her table.

"Oh, Anaís. I'm glad I found you. Have you seen any of the others?
Can I join you for a minute?"

"Of course, you can. And no, I haven't run into anyone today yet.
They must be enjoying our day off."

"Oh, well, the Senator wants me to update everyone on that refugee
situation."

"What's going on?"

"Well, they found another survivor. A little boy, maybe five or six
years old. Unconscious and pretty badly sunburned, floating in an inner
tube."

"How horrible! And he's alive?"

"Yes, just barely, it seems. What we're starting to hear from the two
adults they found earlier this morning, there were twenty-some of them
that left Cuba, including this boy's mother." He paused. "At this point, we
understand the boat sprung a leak and they all probably have drowned."

"Oh, my God!"

"Yes, it is tragic. And we don't know what the press here and in the
U.S. are going to do with this story, so again, no comment from us on
anything. Except, of course, that we're happy about the survivors."

"Of course. But I don't understand. What is the Senator so concerned about?"

"Well, you know how the Cuban community is in the Miami area. It could be another event that turns ugly in the ideology battle."

For once, Pablo appeared not to ramble.

"Goodness, I hope not. Here we are on a mission of goodwill..."

"Exactly. Well, we're here only for a few more days. But still, the Senator thinks we're going to get caught up in this somehow. See you later, Anaís."

Anaís nodded in agreement.

She sat in stunned silence as she watched Pablo disappear into the darkness of the lobby's interior. She looked at her watch, and was surprised to see it was almost two o'clock in the afternoon. Almost time for her to go to Isa's house. She wondered if any of the news about the survivors was being released in Cuba yet, and decided to go back into the lobby.

There was a change now in the activity inside the hotel. Across from the check-in desks in an area with comfortable and plush sofas, there was a group of both hotel personnel and guests intently listening and watching a program on the small television set sitting in the corner. As Anaís neared, she could see that it was a news report on the Cubans found that morning in Fort Lauderdale. Pablo was standing among them, and Anaís put her hand on his shoulder.

"Oh, Anaís, good, it's you. I don't understand anything they are saying. But you're bilingual. What are they saying?"

The TV host was in the midst of giving details about a little boy who had been rescued at sea.

Anaís listened, and began translating.

"His name is Elián González...a native of Cárdenas." Pablo looked at her. "That's one of the provinces here in Cuba, on the eastern coast."

"She's saying that the reports they are getting from Cárdenas is that the boy's father has been looking for his son since last Sunday." She paused. "She's saying that it looks like the mother kidnapped him" Pablo looked at her in astonishment. "Yes, kidnapped him from his father's house... The parents were divorced... Her boyfriend is also one of the people missing, so maybe they left together. . . Now she's giving the names of others who may also have left in the small boat..." She paused as she heard the names, while Pablo looked at her anxiously waiting for more information.

"She's saying that the reports they are getting from Cárdenas is that the little boy has been taken to a hospital...and that the Cuban government expects the return of Elián to his father and to a hospital here in Cuba as soon as possible." She paused.

"Now she's giving news on a mudslide in Guatemala."

They both turned away from the television set. Pablo was wiping his brow, and Anaís wondered if he was sweating because of the news or from the tropical heat.

"Hmm. I need to see the Senator. Anaís, thank you so much. And do you mind if I call on you if I need more of this translation?"

"Of course not. If I'm around, I'd be glad to help."

"See you later."

Back in her room, Anaís felt the churning she had been feeling since Pablo had called earlier that morning intensify. Something really bad was going to happen. She felt it. Her intuition seldom failed her, and she could feel that a storm was brewing.

And her sister! If this situation in Florida really got ugly like Pablo had said, she knew this would have a negative impact on everything involving Cuba-U.S. relations. She wondered if she should even bring her sister to the dinner. After all, Senator Fernández would have other issues on his mind.

The phone rang. It was Pablo.

"Hola, Pablo. I was just thinking about you. Well, I don't mean about you, but rather...Well, you know, I've been wondering if it wouldn't be a good idea to cancel that meeting with my sister and the Senator today before dinner. What with this thing in Florida..."

"Oh, Anaís. You are really a lifesaver. That's why I was calling you. I was just discussing the whole thing with Senator Fernández. I was telling him how great it was to have you translate some of the news as it was being given on Cuban TV, and I suggested to him that, well, you certainly can meet with him, but..."

"No, I understand, Pablo. He has enough on his mind right now with this."

"Oh, thank you for understanding. The Senator did not want to cancel your meeting, but I was trying to make the point that, well, we've already had two phone calls to the Senator from people here, wanting him to comment, being as he is the only American official in Cuba at this particular time."

"It must be really rough."

"You can't imagine. I wish we were leaving tomorrow, so we could escape all this. But it would not be a good idea to move up our return flight, I mean. So, the best we can hope for is that the little boy is back here in Havana tomorrow."

"Yes, I understand. And as for my sister..."

"Well, by all means, bring her to the Thanksgiving dinner anyway. She is very welcome."

"Thanks, Pablo. That's what I will do. At least you can meet her and she can meet you all."

"Terrific. And thank you, thank you, again for being so understanding."

"No problem."

No, Anaís thought, this was not the time to take up the Senator's valuable time, especially when a political fallout could be forming around his visit. Damn it, she thought. Their trip had been so successful so far. The Americans and Cubans seemed to hit it off and actually liked each other. Somehow, after the first days of some posturing on political ideologies, everyone seemed to put all the differences in politics aside and concentrated on their commonalities. Illinois agricultural technologies would be so useful in Cuba and Cuba represented another economic and cultural opportunity for the state. It seemed like a win-win situation to everyone involved, albeit a situation that they all knew was in its infancy and would need patience and understanding to become a reality. And now this situation in Florida. Her heart broke for all the people lost at sea and the small boy, sunburned and dehydrated who just lost his mother. How tragic.

The storm was definitely brewing, Anaís thought, wishing she didn't have intuition or sixth sense about things.

She wondered how she would tell Isa that the meeting with the Senator had been called off.

CHAPTER 10

Adiós Cuba

"TO US, ANAÍS," ISA SAID, LIFTING HER GLASS IN A TOAST, HANDING A second empty wine bottle to Chencha. "Thank God for sending you here, my dear sister." She clinked her glass with Anaís' and both women emptied their glasses.

"Maybe *He* is a *She*." Anaís tried to give a joking tone to her voice despite her sadness. Nothing had gone right in the last few days, beginning with Isa's refusal to attend the Thanksgiving dinner. And now, Anaís had to say goodbye to her sister. Once more, Isa would stay behind.

Isa shook her head laughing, feeling her head swimming from too much wine. "That's too revolutionary a thought for Cuba. Remember, religion is not something we really can talk about too much here. And when we can or do, we don't have time to quibble about God's gender." Isa put her glass down, and stared deeply into it.

"But when I am in the U.S." she mused, her voice now serious and quiet, "then I can talk about those things. Anywhere and with anybody, out loud. Right?" She looked at Anaís with a deep, sad stare. "Yes, when I am in the U.S. maybe I'll find out that God is a *She*."

Anaís thought her sister looked as sad and somber as she herself felt. She reached across the small table.

"It's going to happen, Isa," she said taking her sister's hand. "As soon as I get back home, I am going to do everything I can to get you to Chicago. I know many people. I know I can do it. I won't rest until I have you with me."

Isa just continued staring at her sister. Her lips opened slightly, and

Anaís thought she was going to say something to her, but instead Isa just shook her head, as if shaking off awful thoughts. Instead of speaking, she took both her sister's hands in hers and she lifted them to her lips. She kissed Anaís' hands, put her cheek to them with such tenderness that for the millionth time since Anaís had found Isa she wished she could be a genie to whisk her sister away from everything in Cuba. Isa belonged in Chicago. After all, it was only a simple choice on the part of Father Pat that had blessed Anaís with a life of freedom and opportunity and had thrust her sister into a totally different experience.

" I promise you. You will be in the U.S. before you know it."

"I know I will," Isa said. "Let's drink to that." She laughed as Anaís stared at another empty glass. Both women were totally intoxicated, their way of hiding the pain they felt at saying goodbye.

Both clinked empty glasses and laughed, then Isa suddenly got up and went to the small cupboard next to the old speckled mirror. She took out two small, round leather-covered bottles and brought them to the table.

"There's more! Let's toast with a special drink, from some very special bottles," she said. "Our parents brought these bottles back from one of their trips to Spain when they visited our grandparents' homeland. Chencha and I always refill them with homemade port that Tío Julio makes in Pinar...too bad you never had time to visit them on the farm... Strong stuff, this wine he makes." She handed a bottle to Anaís. "This one belongs to you."

"Chencha," Isa called out. "Please, come join us."

Chencha wobbled into the room, head downcast. Anaís felt sorry for them, understanding their sadness and disappointment at how events had changed.

"Thank you, Chencha," Anaís said as the old woman set two small glasses on the crisp, white tablecloth. Her expression of gratitude sent Chencha into a loud, sorrowful cry.

"Please, Chencha. Don't get like that. We'll all be together soon. You'll see." Anaís tried to make her voice sound cheerful, but nothing seemed to change Chencha's mood and she left the room still sobbing.

"Maybe I shouldn't have come here tonight," said Anaís. "Maybe we should have met somewhere else."

"Don't be silly," Isa responded. "This is your home too. And Chencha," she sighed. "Chencha is like our mother. And now that she has found you again in her life, she doesn't want either of us to be far away from her. Don't worry. She'll be fine." She took her bottle and poured out some crimson liquor.

"Now to toast. Each from our own bottle, to our own destinies." Anaís poured from her bottle. She lifted her glass.

"Mine looks darker than yours," she remarked. "What are you drinking?"

"We have the same thing," Isa replied. "But we have had this batch for quite a while. It gets better with age, you know. Maybe yours is just a little older than mine." Isa lifted her glass, swallowing its contents.

Anaís stood up, almost losing her balance. She couldn't remember drinking so much since her sorority days. "To being twins!" She swallowed hard. "Identical twins," Anaís corrected herself. The wine was thick and very sweet, with a strange oaky aftertaste. Isa poured herself another glass.

"To us, identical twins. Nobody could tell us apart...if it weren't for your long pony tail." She tugged at her sister's hair.

"So true. People couldn't tell us apart except for..." Anaís stopped, her eyes suddenly wide open. She wobbled to the small sewing machine that sat in the corner of the room and grabbed a pair of scissors.

"That is what we have to do. Send YOU back with the group because we are identical and...they will never know the difference once I give you my..." she reached around and taking her ponytail, clumsily cut it off. "...once you wear my hair." She threw the piece on the table as Isa and Chencha screamed.

"What are you doing—saying?"

"My dear sister, this is your chance. You have to take my place. Once you get to the U.S., Senator Fernández will have to get me back. I'm a U.S. citizen. Ha! To my brilliance!" She drank the last of her drink and then slumped back on the sofa. "And to my Cuban adventure!"

"I can't leave you here..."

"Why not? We left you here all these years." Anaís yawned. "That's it. Just go. I'm going to take a nap." She lay down on the couch and passed out.

Isa and Chencha looked at Anaís then at each other.

CHAPTER 11

Deceit

As THE TAXI NEARED THE HAVANA INTERNATIONAL AIRPORT, ISA CHECKED the baseball cap she had taken off her sister and the long ponytail she now felt hanging unfamiliarly down her back.

Chencha had pinned the ponytail to Isa's own short hair with all the bobby pins they were able to find. Isa didn't know how she would keep the cap and hair in place for the rest of the evening, but there was so much else she was nervous about, the ponytail was a minor issue.

Sitting in the taxi, she scarcely could accept what had happened. The moment her sister said the words that it was Isa's turn to leave, her drunkenness had disappeared as she felt a surge of adrenaline like never before. She and Chencha tried their best to wake up Anaís but she kept blabbering "*adiós Isa*" and "let me sleep." Isa had changed into her sister's clothes and run out to the taxi after its second honk and after kissing Chencha goodbye.

The taxi driver had stopped the car in front of the loading zone and was opening the door for her.

"Thanks a lot," she said, remembering that the Americans used the words "a lot" instead of "very much" in their conversations.

"You are welcome, *señorita*," was the response from the taxi driver, and Isa felt there was a different tone in his voice as he addressed her as an American tourist. Was she just imagining it, or was added respect in his simple thank you?

He was taking out the suitcases and setting them down on the curb, and Isa found herself going over to pick them up to carry them. They were almost empty so it would be easy. She stopped herself. Would her

91

sister carry her own bags or have the taxi driver carry them? She decided to do nothing, and instead followed the taxi driver through the airport doors to the ticket counter.

Isa had been at the airport on various occasions to welcome foreign delegations in her capacity as government interpreter. She had often wondered how wonderful it had to be to be able to travel freely, to have the money and simply decide where in the world you wanted to go. But those thoughts were mere musings, and never had she assigned them any real credence. Yet here she was, being treated like a tourist by the taxi driver. She looked around at the various groups standing around the ticket counters and then recognized Richard from pictures that Anaís had shown her. He looked like the typical tanned tourist leaving the island wearing the distinctive men's Cuban *guayabera*. He saw her and excusing himself from the group jogged over to her.

"Anaís! We were wondering where you could be." He saw the taxi driver standing behind her, and Isa saw Richard take out his wallet. He handed the driver a ten-dollar bill. She was glad that she had run into Richard and that he had paid the tip because she never would have thought of tipping that much. Maybe one or two dollars. She wondered if ten dollars was a common tip in America and she made a mental note to look into what was customary.

"Come on," Richard was saying. "Let's get your bags tagged." He picked up the large, empty suitcase.

"Shit! This is a lot lighter," he said. "Oh, I know," he added. "You probably left a lot for your sister, didn't you? Boy, it's too bad the Senator couldn't do anything for her, but with that Elián thing going on in Miami..."

Isa's stomach knotted up at the mention of her sister. Would Anaís be able to handle life in Cuba? Sure she kept mumbling "*adiós*" and "my adventure" as Chencha and Isa took off her clothes and changed her into Isa's pajamas, but was she ready for the hard life that was Cuba?

Isa saw Richard hand the bags to the group's liaison, who nodded hello and proceeded to tag the bags with the special Illinois Delegation identification cards.

"Your passport, please?"

Oh, my God! Isa thought. The passport! In her nervousness in undressing her sister and putting on her clothes, copying her makeup and finally the entire ordeal with the ponytail, she had never thought about the passport. It must be in the brown leather bag that she took from her sister. Clumsily, fingers and hands shaking she looked in her sister's bag. Nothing! Isa thought she was going to faint. Then she heard Richard behind her.

"Remember Pablo got them to us earlier? Maybe you put it in your backpack?" he questioned.

What's a backpack? Isa wondered. She looked at Richard quizzically. He reached over and took one of the bags that had already been tagged. "Here," Richard said with a small grin. Isa nodded, recognized her sister's bag and inside to her relief was Anaís' passport.

"Come on," Richard was saying. "Let's get our last real Cuban coffee." He took her arm and guided her to a small bar in the corner of the waiting area. "*Dos cafés, por favor,*" Richard said to the waiter behind the bar in a smooth Spanish tinged with American English enunciation. Isa smiled at him.

"Whaaatt?" he said, smiling back. "Did I sound too gringo?"

Isa shook her head. Richard insisted.

"No, really, tell me. What do you think of my Spanish now that I have been practicing non-stop this whole month that we have been here? I think I sound better. Do you?"

Suddenly Isa became terrified at the need to speak English to someone who knew her sister well.

Since she and her sister had met, they had agreed to improve their language skills and tried to copy each other's vocabulary and expressions. At first, it was simply fun, but from the moment Isa learned that the Senator was going to help her emigrate to the United States, she listened for hours late at night at audiotapes she had made of conversations with her sister, trying to work on accent reduction, making note of her sister's favorite expressions, her lilting laugh which caught in a gasp when she laughed heartily. Isa knew she had always had a fine ear for accents and languages. But Richard was her sister's best friend. Was she going to give herself away even before she left the island?

"Come on," Richard insisted. "Be honest. What do you think of your gringo friend?" Suddenly, he tugged playfully at the visor of her baseball cap. Isa put one hand on her hat and the other on her ponytail. Thankfully, nothing had come unpinned. She adjusted her cap and smiled at Richard.

"*Es muy bueno tu español*," she assured him. "Very good."

"That's it! You know, that is what we should do—to speak Spanish as much as possible to each other from now on. Well, as much as I can speak it, anyway. And I can try to figure out what you're saying too." Richard seemed thrilled with the possibility of a Spanish conversation partner.

"If you like," Isa said measuredly. "Yes, I mean, *sí, es muy buena idea*." He picked up the small cup of Cuban coffee. "This is going to be great."

Could she be so lucky, thought Isa.

Richard put down his coffee cup and looked at her.

"How are you doing, really, about your sister and everything? It must be horrible for you, to leave her behind." He paused. "Maybe you don't want to talk about it. It's okay if you don't."

Isa sighed a deep sigh, as her stomach tightened again at the thought of Anaís lying on her bed, drunk, and with a difficult few months ahead. There was no going back now, she knew. She could only hope that Anaís was really ready for what was waiting for her.

She measured her words, focusing all her energies on speaking like her sister.

"It is very painful. I have come to love my sister very, very much."

Richard reached over and put his strong arm around her shoulders. He gave her a light squeeze.

"I know you do. And it's going to be alright. I'm sure the senator will be able to help you once this Elián thing is over. In the meantime, try to be happy that you found each other, that you know she is well."

His kindness was touching, and her pent up emotions suddenly gave way to a flood of tears. She lowered her head, trying to hide her fear and sadness. Richard pulled her toward him, and she sobbed as he held her close to his chest.

"That's okay. Let it all out. It's okay." He kissed the top of her head. Isa felt comforted like when Chencha held her in her strong motherly embrace.

"Hey you two!" They could hear voices calling to them. "We're boarding. Unless you don't want to go back." Isa turned her tear-stained face toward the voice in the distance. She didn't recognize him, but he was wearing the same baseball cap that they all had.

"Are you okay? We can stay here a few more minutes if you want." Isa looked at his caring face. What a nice friend Richard was for her sister. It would be nice to get to know him more.

"Thank you. Yes. I am alright now, Richard," she said looking up at him, noticing something of a surprise in his eyes. Had she said something unusual or wrong in English? Maybe he was just surprised to see her cry.

"Okay," he said, taking her arm and helping her off the barstool.

They were the last ones to join the group and she saw that they were all wearing the delegation's identification tags. She found Anaís' in her backpack and pinned it on, walking with the group. As Pablo presented the passports to the immigration officer at the entrance to the international gate she felt her heart beat as fast as when she ran marathons. People around her were greeting her, and she forced herself to smile back, copying her sister's lilting greeting. She recognized the woman her sister called *Arrancapellejo* from the group picture Anaís had shown her.

"Anaís, honey," the woman said in a brusque tone, putting her arm around Isa's shoulder. "How are you? Is it difficult saying good-bye to Cuba? I bet it is. Well, I know you haven't had too much time for us..." The woman's squeeze was like a vise. Isa remembered her sister had said *Arrancapellejo* was not to be trusted.

"Yes, I want to hear all your experiences," she demanded.

Intervening Richard said, "Cynthia, later, okay" as he pulled her away from *Arrancapellejo.*

Isa smiled at Richard gratefully.

The group had begun passing the checkpoint with the Cuban immigration officers. Isa could feel her heart galloping, her facing flushing.

She heard the persons in her group give their name to the official who in turn looked through the passports and compared the photograph to each person. "I look exactly like my sister," she reminded herself, trying to quiet her nervousness.

Richard was whispering in her ear about *Arrancapellejo.*

"That Cynthia. She's something else." Isa nodded but her mind was elsewhere and her inner turmoil at nearly panic levels. She watched her fellow travelers, admiring their detached and light-hearted banter with each other. If they only knew what she felt inside. She hadn't seen the Cuban officer ask anyone any questions. He simply stamped and handed back each passport. Why should he act any differently with her, Isa thought. It would be fine. She just needed to remain calm, so that the nervous red rash that always crept up her bosom and neck wouldn't give away her anxiety. She knew how the Cuban immigration and police officers were trained to notice every oddity and body language. Oh, dear God. I have to be careful not to give myself away, her inner voice raged.

Richard tugged at her.

"Look over there. Isn't he something else?" Isa looked in the direction of Richard's glance, catching the eye of a deeply tanned, brown haired man in his thirties having a drink at the bar they had just left. The man looked their way with an inviting smile.

"I wonder if he's looking at you or at me?" Isa thought that Richard's comment was unusual.

"You know, here in Cuba, it has been difficult for me to figure who is gay and who isn't," Richard said.

Isa pondered the question for a moment, realizing Richard was waiting for her to say something in return.

"Yes, I think you are right. It is difficult to know if people here are happy." Richard looked at her, squinting as if he hadn't understood her, and then started laughing.

"I mean," she used a phrase she had picked up from her sister, "I think many people here are unhappy but they pretend to be gay, because it's better for tourism." Richard roared with laughter, still looking puzzled.

"You're kidding, right?" he asked.

"It is better to be with gay people than sad people, do you not agree," she said, knowing that she was rambling.

They were the next up to the immigration officer and Isa's anxiety made her look away and not see Richard's confused look. She took a deep breath and started repeating to herself, "I am Anaís Moran. I am an American. I am going home."

"Anaís Moran." The name echoed in her ears as she said it.

"Don't you agree, Richard?" she smiled at her companion, remembering to use the contractions she knew Americans favored.

Richard pursed his lips in an unusual way, looked at her and then smiled.

"Sure. You are spot on, Anaís." Richard took her arm once more. The officer handed them their passports.

"Let's go," he said. Their friends crowded at the exit door to the plane waiting for them a few hundred feet away on the tarmac. Isa took a deep breath and closed her eyes for a second. It was difficult for her to believe that she was walking toward a plane that would take her to the United States. To Chicago. It was she who this time grabbed Richard's arm with a firm grip as they started up the stairs to the plane. She tried to contain the smile she felt creeping up on her face.

She noticed Richard looking at her with the same strange look she had seen before, but she didn't care what he was thinking or why he looked so odd. She had done it. She was getting out of Cuba. All the turmoil and anxiety left her. She was exhilarated. She felt so light, it was as if her feet were flying over the metal steps.

"You must feel very, very gay right now, right?" Richard asked her, looking deeply into her eyes as they stepped into the plane.

"Oh, yes. I feel so gay that I could...I could explode."

Richard roared with laughter and said something under his breath that she did not understand.

"I also bet it is really great to get on this plane, isn't it," Richard said. She nodded.

"Yes, I have to believe that for you, this time it has to be extra special," he said.

"Yes, Richard. You cannot know how special this is," she replied.

"Oh, actually I think I can." Richard patted her hat as they took their seats.

CHAPTER 12

Going Nowhere

As she sat on the edge of the bed, trying to quiet her mind, the sudden wailing sound that came from another part of the house made Anaís jump to her feet. Dear God. Her plane! What was she doing in bed when she had a plane to catch! She looked down at her clothes, and she didn't recognize the pants and shirt she was wearing. "Why am I dressed like this? And, where is Isa," she said aloud.

The plane! All of a sudden that was all she could think about. If she couldn't find her sister, she'd leave her a note. But she had to leave. What time was it anyway? Her watch was gone.

She felt dizzy and had to sit down again, closing her eyes. When she opened them again, her eyes were still unbelievable heavy, and she had difficulty focusing. Her head felt like a bowl of Jell-O. She put both hands to her head to steady the jumble within.

What was going on with her? Why couldn't she even put one thought together? She tried to open her eyes again, to put that thought, whatever thought, together in her head. A muffled, wailing sound crashed through her head. She put her hands around her head tighter, trying to hold it together and to quiet the noise both within and outside her head. She tried to get up from where she sat. Where the hell am I? Her mind raced and the wailing sound nearby pierced her ears.

She decided to lie down again, waiting for her brain to send signals to the rest of her body to move her feet, her torso, her arms. The wailing was actually becoming a comforting sound, something outside herself that she could recognize. She tried to move her legs to the floor. This time they obeyed. Slowly the rest of her body slowly sat up. She looked around.

Out of the darkness, her sister's small room appeared before her, the worn, faded curtain closed over the wooden blinds shutting out all outside light. Was it day or night? Anaís couldn't tell.

Her body still feeling leaden, she moved her legs to the right and stood up slowly. She looked around the room again. Why was she here? *Why do I have a hangover?*

She remembered sitting at her sister's small dining room table, laughing with Isa as they downed glass after glass after glass of wine and then port. Anaís inched to the door. The wailing was now softer, more like a mournful whimper. As she reached the door's opening which lead to the tiny living room area of her sister's place, she saw the huddled, heaving body on the sofa.

It was Chencha.

"Chencha," Anaís hardly recognized the hoarse voice. "Chencha. *¿Qué pasa?* Why are you crying? Where is Isa? Is she alright?"

Her questions made Chencha look up and throw her arms up into the air over her head. Chencha's old lined face looked bloated from the sobbing, and the huge tears running down her face shimmered in the dim light.

"*Chencha, por favor.* I don't know what is going on here, but I have to leave. Remember that I have to catch that plane tonight? Where is Isa? I want to say good-bye to her. Well, if I can. I don't know what time it is, but I'm sure it's time for me to leave." She glanced at her bare wrist. What had she done with her watch? She looked at her clothes. *These aren't mine,* she realized. For a second, Anaís wondered if perhaps nothing was real, and she was having a nightmare. She closed her eyes tight, trying to shut out the room, Chencha, the wailing. She told herself she needed to remember the last things that made sense. She forced herself to stop thinking about the moment and went back in her mind to the moments before waking up with the huge headache.

All she could remember was drinking with her sister...and cutting off her ponytail.

And then...telling her sister to leave Cuba with the group!

Isa was gone!

She sat down next to Chencha. How many times during the last month, Anaís had wished she could change places with her sister, to give her an opportunity to live a different life. And although she had been drunk when she told her sister to take her place, in her heart that is what she had wanted all along.

The thought of her sister getting caught at the airport crossed her mind, but she quickly refused to accept even the remotest possibility of such a horror happening. It was time for Isa to get a break. This is how it was meant to be.

She embraced Chencha.

"Chencha. Please don't cry anymore. Everything will be alright. Isa will be fine. I will be fine. This is how it was supposed to be."

The woman smiled wanly at her, looking at the beautiful pale face now framed by short, uneven patches of hair, green eyes filling with tears. She was a lucky old woman to be living this moment, she thought. Her dear Isa would have a chance at freedom. And for the second time in her life, the gods had blessed her with the joy of taking care of another wonderful soul.

Chapter 13

Chicago

The plane ride was unnerving for Isa at first. Everyone in the delegation seemed to be in exuberant spirits, talking about the positive aspects of their mission as well as looking forward to going back home. Richard said he wanted to sit next to her so that they could talk during the flight.

Isa, however, was both fearful that she would say something to unravel her deceit and also simply exhausted after the long evening of drinking with Anaís. She smiled at Richard and told him that she was too tired to do anything but sleep. Making sure that her ponytail was still firmly pinned to her head, she lowered the baseball cap over her eyes and pretended to be asleep.

However, no pretense was needed. The effects of all the wine she had consumed coupled with the stress and magnitude of what she had done knocked her out. She slept soundly until the plane landed in Cancún where they hurried through Customs to then make the connection on the U.S. airline that would take them directly to Chicago. Once on board the plane, again she surrendered to sleep. She was still groggy when Richard whispered in her ear, "We're here, Anaís."

Richard was shaking her gently. Isa woke up feeling disoriented as she looked at Richard's unfamiliar face and surroundings. A voice over the plane's intercom said, "Welcome to Chicago!"

"Anaís, how about if we share a taxi to your place since we live so close to one another?"

Oh, that's right. She now was her sister and needed to get used to responding to that name. "That would be nice, Richard." His suggestion sounded like a blessing.

Since she had slept through practically the entire trip, they had hardly said a word to each other since they left Cuba. But now that she was lucid, panic was replacing her initial feelings of elation that she had pulled off leaving Cuba as her sister.

What would she do now? How could she pretend to be Anaís sister? She realized that she didn't even know where her sister lived other than that the condo was near the lake. She felt more panicked. What had she done, just leaving Cuba with no plan, simply because Anaís had told her it was her turn at freedom? Their drunken decision would be a nightmare of consequences. Isa felt her entire body tense in fear.

Richard stared at her as he had before, seeming to scan her face intently.

"Hey, there. Why do you look so distressed? Everything will be alright." He touched her shoulder gently.

Isa looked at him, wondering if Richard had guessed that she was not Anaís. No, if Richard had guessed the truth he would have said something. He was simply being the dear person Anaís said he always was. And there was no need to panic. She just needed time alone to think everything through, and she would call Anaís in Cuba. Anaís would tell her what to do.

"What is it, Richard?" she asked, noticing that he was still staring at her.

"Nothing. I was just thinking what an amazing and brave woman you are. Oh, here go. Let's get off this plane...finally," he replied.

The passengers joked with each other as they pulled bags from the overhead bins and worked their way down the airplane aisle. A few people called out her sister's name and she turned and waved. Richard had placed himself between Isa and the rest of the group to help her with her carry on bags, so thankfully she didn't have to be part of the conversations swirling around her.

"We've done it," Richard whispered to Isa as they exited the plane. "You're here. We're here." Isa smiled, realizing this was her first experience of freedom.

The terminal at O'Hare Airport was enormous with hundreds of passengers at the gates and in the corridors. It was so bright, so noisy, and filled with hundreds of passengers laughing or rushing around. She thought of the José Martí Airport in Havana, so empty and subdued in comparison. No armed police here in Chicago, either, making people feel uncomfortable with their bayonets and stares. The feeling at this airport was like being at a party, relaxed and happy. She was really in America.

Families with balloons and flowers, company greeters with signs, and airport personnel crowded around the gates. People who all seemed to be from different nationalities waved or smiled at the arriving passengers. Heavily bundled up in winter clothing, this group looked more like the United Nations than the blonde, tall and blue-eyed people she had expected to see. She heard many languages, and hearing some people speaking Spanish around her suddenly felt like a comfortable blanket.

After a long walk and having to maneuver various escalators they arrived at a baggage claim area. Bags were beginning to spill out of a huge machine in the center of the room. Isa wondered how she would recognize her sister's luggage since they all looked the same to her. Richard was already collecting his bags.

"You did say that it is okay with you if we shared the ride, right?" he asked. "We live so close to each other, that way we can save on the cab fare."

"That's a wonderful idea, Richard," Isa answered. He smiled at her, shaking his head, and suddenly, he hugged her, strong and hard.

"It's wonderful to be here with you...Anaís," he said. "This is going to be wonderful for you."

"Thank you, Richard." Isa wondered if Richard was always this happy when he returned home from a trip. He certainly had been her guardian angel on this trip, she thought.

"Hey you two," they heard *Arrancapellejo's* voice next to them. "Aren't those your bags, Anaís?" She was pointing to three bags sliding past them on the baggage carrier.

Richard checked the tags. "Yep, they're ours. Thanks, Cynthia."

Isa helped him get them off the carrier.

"You certainly came back very light on clothes, didn't you, Ani?" Richard said as he placed her bags on a cart.

"I left a lot of things for...my sister."

Richard smiled at her. "That was a good idea," he said.

They headed toward the exit door. People from the delegation were all saying goodbye to each other, shaking hands, the men slapping each other on the back. No kisses all around like would have been the custom back in Cuba. She followed suit and shook hands with the people who approached her, including with the Senator who said that she should call in a couple of weeks to talk about her situation.

Everything would work itself out. Secundino had predicted it.

CHAPTER 14

Squeaking In

RICHARD PUSHED THROUGH THE CROWD WITH THE ASSURANCE OF THOSE who know where they are going. The coat Richard had helped her put on was heavy on her shoulders. As they approached an exit door, she felt the freezing air creep up to them. Outside, a blast of wind colder than any cold she had ever known made her catch her breath. She felt as if she had swallowed a huge ice cube, one that was now icing her throat. She stopped, shivering uncontrollably.

"Too cold for you, right?" She nodded, not wanting to open her mouth again. "Yeah, I bet you miss Cuba already. Or maybe not..." He looked at her smiling.

Richard was such a wonderful man. She knew he was Anaís' best friend but could he be her friend too? And what would he do if he knew she was Isa and not Anaís?

Richard whistled in the direction of the taxis parked at the curb, and one pulled over to them in an instant. She overheard him give the taxi driver an address with Lake Shore Drive and she remembered it was her sister's street. She was glad Richard lived nearby. Thank goodness she knew at least one person in this strange new place.

They got into the cab where it was unexpectedly warm. Quickly her face stopped tingling and she started to feel flushed. She had never been in a heated car before. She was quickly enveloped in the comfort of the warm interior. Richard was pulling off his gloves and scarf, and she started to do the same. He looked at her, smiling.

"Comfortable in here, isn't it?"

She nodded.

"I am so tired," he said yawning. "But what a wonderful, *mahh-velous* trip." He paused and looked at her.

She smiled at his funny pronunciation, and he looked as if he expected her to say something.

"Mahh-velous," he repeated again, smiling. He stared at her expectantly for a few moments. Suddenly, he threw back his head letting out a hearty laugh.

"Oh, God, this is really good," he said, still laughing and rubbing his hands together, sounding proud that he had come upon the last piece of a puzzle that now had uncovered the truth.

He put his face so very close to hers that she could feel his breath on her lips. He looked intently into her eyes.

"You are not Anaís," he said in an exaggerated whisper.

Isa sat up like a bolt of lightning and looked at Richard staring at her with a satisfied grin.

"You are not Anaís," he said almost tauntingly.

Isa felt faint. He knew! Richard knew! But how did he know! And what was he going to do about it?

"*No problema,*" Richard changed his tone, seeing Isa's shocked and fearful expression. He took her cold hands in his. "It's okay. Really," he said sweetly. "Please don't be scared. It's okay. Trust me."

Her beating heart started to decelerate, and she searched Richard's eyes. Could she really trust him? He obviously knew that Anaís was in Cuba and that she, Isa, was an imposter.

"You know," Richard said, "I don't know how you two pulled this off. It's brilliant. Anaís is ever chasing a new adventure, always pushing the envelope. And this..." He made a grand gesture with his arms. "But this was...is exceptionally dangerous, for both of you. I don't know how you had the nerve...or I should say *cojones*, to do this." He kissed her cold hands. "But you are here, and I will help you. I love your sister. She is my best friend. I want to be a friend to you, too."

Isa started to cry. Richard was indeed the good friend that her sister had described. Perhaps he really could be a friend to her in this unknown land.

"I am so sorry for what we have done," she began, "I am not sure Anaís understands what it is like to live in Cuba...we were drunk, and..." but Richard shushed her.

"Let's leave any confessions for later." He brushed her hair away from her eyes. "Now what we have to do is make sure no one else finds out. Until we figure out what you need to do."

Isa nodded, smiling at Richard through teary eyes.

"How about if I stay with you for the next few days? Neither one of us has to go back to work right away. We can plan what you want to do. How's that?"

"That would be very nice, Richard." The taxi driver was slowing down, winding through streets with exceptionally tall buildings. "But tell me, how did you know? I am so obvious?"

Richard laughed his hearty laugh. "No, you are not so obvious. It's just that...Well, let's say that I've known Anaís for a very long time. And... well, first of all, tomorrow we will work on how you say my name. In American English it's 'Richard' and you say something like 'Ree-chard.' We'll have to work on that."

"Oh, I am sorry. Yes, I will work on that."

"And I am gay," he continued, "and Anaís and all my best friends know that." Isa looked at him blankly. "Here, 'gay' means that I am a homosexual," he said. "Although, yes, I am a happy person too. I guess I am a gay gay." His hand made an effeminate swirl in midair, and Isa understood the play on words and laughed. "See," Richard grabbed her chin. "You're getting it already."

CHAPTER 15

A New Home

THE CAB PULLED UP TO A STRIKING GLASS AND STEEL BUILDING. RICHARD paid the driver and helped Isa out into the cold night air. A stiff, bitter wind buffeted them as they each dragged their bags into the lobby. A dark uniformed man held the door and smiled at them.

"Doctor Moran. You're back! Good to have you back." He took Isa's bags and she simply nodded.

"Hello, Julius. Nice to see you, too. Here, give me that, Ani." Richard took the suitcase and pulled on the lever to extend the retractable handle that Isa hadn't been able to pull out.

"No, let me help you both." Julius grabbed all the bags under both arms and pushed another button, which opened doors into another expansive lobby. Isa looked at the beautiful surroundings, wondering why they were in an office building.

"So how was Cuba, Dr. Moran? We've all been thinking about you, especially since they found that little boy in Miami. Hmm, hmm, hmm" he grunted, pushing the bags into the back of the elevator and holding the door for them. "That sure is turning out to be one big mess alright." They all entered the elevator and Isa was surprised at her reflection in the wall mirror. With the long ponytail and makeup, it was her sister looking back at her. Julius punched the fifteenth floor, and continued to smile at them.

"You know, Dr. Moran, Alberto hasn't stopped talking about the Cuban cigar you said you were going to try to bring back for him." She looked at Richard. "Were you able to do it? I won't say a word, promise." The door opened at the fifteenth floor.

"Yes, Julius, we got him one. But don't say anything." Richard led her by the arm to a glossy red painted door with a decorative wreath framing the number one-five-one-five.

"Your keys, madam?" Richard bowed to her hand outstretched. Isa seemed frozen at the front door.

"Yes, you are tired. No problem. I will find your keys." Richard smiled at the doorman as he rifled through Anaís' purse.

"Here we are. Home at last." He pulled her inside and turned on lights. Isa almost gasped. The beautiful large living area with floor to ceiling glass walls showed off a white full moon hanging low in the night sky and street lights below.

"Thanks, Julius." She saw Richard tip the doorman who waved good-night. Richard took off his coat and gloves and dropped them over a couch. He couldn't take his eyes off Isa, standing in the middle of the living room, her big green eyes suddenly wide-awake and darting around with the look of a child in front of a Christmas tree.

"This is where Anaís lives?"

"This is where you live now. It's your home. And when Ani comes back, she wants it to be where you both live. She told me so."

Isa's face saddened.

"You don't know what I've done, Richard. You don't know..." She hung her head in shame.

"Come on, now," he took off her coat and sat her on one of the cream-colored couches. "You didn't do anything...I'm sure it's what you both wanted to do..." Isa looked at him with tears in her eyes and shook her head.

"Okay, well, maybe you wanted it more. It really doesn't matter now. You are here and your sister wanted it that way. You both decided that. And I'm your friend. I've been Ani's friend since we were in college. That's a long time. We've both seen the good and the bad in each other. And we're still best friends."

He unwrapped the scarf that she had wound tightly around her neck. "Look, I will help you. You're twins, you and Ani. You must be as wonderful a person as she is." His kindness touched her heart and Isa felt a flood of emotion start to overtake her once more.

He reached for the brim of her baseball cap and was startled to see that the long ponytail stayed attached to the cap.

"Shit!" He screamed, jumping away. Startled, she jumped also. The long, black hairpiece lay innocently attached to the baseball cap now lying on the white couch.

Richard and Isa looked at each other and burst into a roar of laughter. Pointing at the hair, Richard picked it up tenderly like a wounded animal and gently placed it on the glass cocktail table. Isa doubled over laughing so hard, tears streamed down her cheeks. Richard's laugh morphed into one loud, hiccuping yell.

Perhaps it was the built up anxiety and excitement of the evening; perhaps it was the absurdity of the ponytail. In any case, Isa felt her first connection of friendship with Richard when he lay on the couch and, pointing to the ponytail, finally said, "Okay, why don't you start by telling me about the hair."

She accepted the invitation to bare her soul, including acknowledging that she had felt cheated when she first met Anaís and found out how she herself had lost out on coming to the United States to live the life that their parents had wanted for both of them. Isa confessed that soon those feelings dissolved into an overwhelming love for her sister and how she came to a genuine happiness for the life Anaís had enjoyed. Finally, she spoke of their drunken evening when Anaís cut off her ponytail and told her to leave Cuba with the delegation so that the Senator would be forced to bring Anaís back once he found out they had switched places.

Richard was mesmerized with Isa's details. He reassured her that, drunk or not, this had been a good decision to make. Even if Anaís was not able to return quickly, since the delegation had firm plans to return to Cuba the following June, even if they had to wait until then, it was not a long time at all. He was positive the Senator would intervene on Isa's behalf to have her legally emigrate from Cuba. Further, he knew Anaís well. She was an adventure-seeker, and being in Cuba, the place she had dreamed about so much would be the ultimate adventure. Richard was so reassuring and comforting that Isa began to think that maybe things would indeed be alright.

They talked for hours. Richard told her about his life, the difficulty of being a homosexual in a traditional family, his various affairs, and his friendship with her sister Anaís. It was hard to believe that as tired as they both were from the long trip they still couldn't stop their chatter. Somewhere in the middle of their heart to heart, they fell asleep on the couch like old college friends.

"Ani...I mean, Isa. Wake up. You have a phone call. Wake up. I think you'll want to take this call."

Isa strained to open her eyes, an unfamiliar voice bringing her out of a deep sleep. When she was finally able to focus, she did not immediately recognize the face staring down at her.

¿Dónde estoy? Where am I? She wasn't in her room.

"Come on, sleepyhead. This was not an easy call to make."

She looked at the man speaking to her as he helped her sit up. Her mind remembered Richard, and her escape from Cuba.

"*¿Qué?*"

Richard covered the mouthpiece with his hand.

"It's Ani" he whispered. "I got the Senator's office to pull a few strings and get a call through to Cuba—a minor miracle, from what I understand. More importantly, remember you have switched places and that you are Anaís, so don't say anything that will give anything away. We don't know if anyone is listening on the other side."

Now she understood. Her heart jumped at the thought of talking to her sister and she grabbed at the phone. He held it away, still covering the mouthpiece and whispering.

"Remember, just talk like Ani would. Don't say anything about yesterday or..." She nodded that she understood and took the phone. Through the static connection, she heard a soft 'hello' on the other side.

"Hello."

"Yes, it's me. Everything is fine here, Ani. Everything is fine. How are you?" her sister asked in Spanish from the other end.

It was very strange to hear her sister call her "Ani." The ruse was on.

"Ani, don't worry about anything. Everything is wonderful. Things here are fine. Chencha says hello...that she misses you...We both are fine and excited that you had a good trip...home." Her sister's voice sounded happy and calm.

"Are you sure? Are you sure that you...that you are alright with... things?" she asked in a tentative voice.

The response was confident. "Yes. Everything is like Secundino said it would be." The static on the phone became stronger. "Listen, we may get disconnected...don't worry about me...I love you... It was good to visit with you. But now, enjoy everything at home...again. And Richard will be there for you...like he always has been. He will tell you...help you with everything you need..." the static almost drowned out her words.

"Thank you for everything, my dear sister," she managed to answer just before the phone went dead. Richard hung it up and put his arm around her shoulder.

"See what I told you? Anaís is fine. You will be fine. Okay?"

She nodded, looking up at him with grateful eyes.

"Now, let me give you a tour of your new home. Then we're going downstairs to the little grocery store, get some food. I'll make you a real American breakfast. Then we'll....well, I don't know, really. We'll just see where and how we start making you into Ani."

She smiled at him.

"Minus the ponytail." They laughed and grabbed their coats and hats and headed for the elevator. "And we need to come up with a story for *Arrancapellejo* for your new short hairdo!"

CHAPTER 16

Anaís-Isa

IT WAS HARD TO BELIEVE THAT ALMOST A MONTH HAD PASSED SINCE SHE had spoken to her sister, Anaís thought, carefully squeezing the last remnants of her fragrant shampoo into the palm of her hand, then rubbing both hands together and lathering up her hair. The smell of flowers was wonderful, and she tried to breathe in deeply knowing that after she finished with the bottle she would no longer have that luxury. Shampoo and other toiletries were a premium in Cuba, and according to Chencha, you bought whatever was available.

Her thoughts drifted back to the specialty stores on North Michigan Avenue where she usually shopped. She thought of Beth, the saleswoman at the bath and body shop who knew exactly what to pack for her when she called and also introduced her to new products as they came into the market. She wondered when she would see that saleswoman again.

Anaís shook her head, trying to dismiss any doubts that she had made the right decision telling her sister to leave Cuba with the Illinois delegation. It was a perfect plan that so far was working out for both of them. However, with the Elián controversy making headlines every day, the two sisters had agreed that it was not wise to tell the Senator the truth, and even more ill-advised to ask that he bring back Anaís, a U.S. citizen, from Cuba. Sharing that story now would only bring dire consequences and embarrassment to everyone.

Anaís thought back to the strangely convoluted manner in which she and Isa had communicated on the phone to get that idea across to each other. Somehow it had worked, but it was one more reminder for Anaís of the differences in the worlds that she and Isa had experienced.

Yes, Anaís was certain that she could enlist Senator Fernández' help to find a way to get her back to Chicago while also having Isa stay in the U.S., but this was not the right time. Besides, Anaís was discovering that her time in Cuba was turning out to be more of an adventure than she imagined, one that might become even a great adventure if she found a way to get to know her sister's supervisor, Diego, better. She had been immediately attracted to this dark, handsome and charismatic man.

Hopefully, Diego did not have have a woman in his life, although it was difficult to believe that such a good looking and intelligent man was single and available. Strange as well that Isa had never mentioned him.

Diego had heard Anaís talking to colleagues about visiting Pinar del Río for Christmas, and had offered to drive her there. She had accepted and hoped it was an indication that he was not only available but also interested in her. The thought of Diego made her smile.

Chencha knocked at the door of the bathroom door, startling her.

"Child," she said. "Your coffee with milk is ready. Do you want some fruit with that?"

"No, thank you, Chencha. Just coffee will be fine." Drying her cropped hair, she grimaced at her new look, missing her long locks. It had taken what seemed eons to grow. She wondered what hair style her sister had chosen. Had she kept the ponytail? Did she pin it on every morning? People at the office, especially *Arrancapellejo*, would be shocked to see her without her long tresses.

Ani continued dressing. The form-fitting, skirt and blouse felt constricting, but that's how Isa and most Cuban women wore clothing. She strained to see her silhouette in the small mirror over the sink. In Chicago, she never would have worn this short, black skirt and peach-colored, clingy blouse to work.

Her biggest difficulty in imitating her sister's look was with the eye makeup. Isa always wore a lot of it, as did most of the Cuban women in Havana. The dark, thick eyeliner made her green eyes appear even larger and more exotic. Perhaps she gradually could move away from that to her simpler make-up and more comfortable clothing. For now, tight clothes, short hair and dark eyeliner would have to do.

She put on the pearl studs and necklace that had belonged to their mother and touched the necklace lovingly.

"Chencha, do I look alright?"

"You look perfect, my dear." Anaís bent over to kiss the old woman's head. What a loving, caring person she was. Anaís felt as if she had known her all her life. They sat down at the small dining room table and drank their coffees.

"Chencha, I'm worried about spending Christmas with the family in Pinar. Isa and I never were able to get out there together...a blessing maybe considering what we have done since nobody but you here know we are twins. But, I am not sure how I can pull off being Isa with them. I don't know anyone...not their names...what they're like. I need for you to tell me as much as possible about them. And is there anything special that Isa does with them that I should do? Anything that is a tradition with them?"

The old woman put down her cup, licking a drop of very dark liquid from the corner of her mouth.

"It is going to be a little difficult for you...with the names. But you will learn them. And something special? Well, Isa always makes the *arroz con pollo*, chicken and rice, for family occasions, including Christmas. It's her specialty."

"But I don't know how to make that dish" Anaís responded. "Do you?"

"Not like Isa." Chencha shook her head.

"But can you make *arroz con pollo*? Or is there a recipe around here that I can follow?"

Chencha lifted the cup to her lips. "No, there is no recipe," she said. "And, yes, I can make the *arroz con pollo*. But not like Isa. No, I can't make it like Isa does it."

"Well, your version will have to do if I'm going to get the Pinar family to believe that I'm Isa. Where do we get the chicken, the rice..."

"Rice we have," Chencha laughed. "That is one thing we usually can get here in Cuba, rice. But the chicken..." She thought for a moment. "Isa always waits until she gets to the farm and she kills the best chickens they have."

"What do you mean, she kills the chickens?"

Chencha did not react to Anaís' altered tone of voice.

"Oh, my child, just as everybody kills a chicken. You catch it, grab the neck, and twist it in the air..." Her hand acting out the scene.

"Oh, my God. No. Oh, no. I couldn't do that."

"If you cannot make yourself do that, I do not know what to say."

"What if I don't make the *arroz con pollo?*"

"Oh, that would not be good. Everyone loves Isa's *arroz con pollo*. It's a well-established tradition. She never fails to make it, as I said, for Christmas and other special occasions. I'm sure people would wonder if there is something wrong with you...with Isa..."

She realized she was upsetting Chencha.

"No, Chencha. Don't worry." She took her hand. "I'll figure something out. I'll find the chicken and you can make it. And I'll watch and learn. And we'll hope that nobody notices that it is not exactly like Isa makes it. How's that?"

Chencha's gray eyebrows shot up in a surprised look "There are no chickens to be bought around here, my child. I don't know what you mean."

Anaís understood the absurdity of her own comment. There were no stocked grocery stores in Havana. The few stores in the neighborhood were full of empty shelves where only coffee and rice were sometimes available.

Maybe Diego could help her. The thought of him again sent a warm glow through her body. Diego, her sister's boss and now her boss. Diego's face and virile body reminded her that she had not had sex in weeks. She could imagine herself in his embrace. Was it acceptable to have sex without commitment in Cuba?

"Oh my." She looked at her watch. "I have to go, Chencha. We'll talk about this later, okay?"

"Don't you want me to come with you, child?"

"No. Thank you. I know where I am going now. It's time I go to work on my own. I know how to get there now—I think." The old woman started to get up. "I'm kidding, Chencha. I will be alright."

She was almost out the door when she suddenly remembered she wanted to give Chencha something.

"What's wrong, child?"

"Nothing, Chencha. But sit right here. I want to leave something with you."

"Remember, child, that this old woman has things to do here before I go for our rations of milk and rice today."

Anaís had disappeared into her room and was back in an instant. She held a small CD player in her hands.

"You still have a little time, Chencha. And I know you will enjoy listening to this first." She inserted a disk into the player, smiling at Chencha's pursed lips. "I forgot I had this...I found it yesterday in one of the bags that Isa didn't take with her to Chicago. Are you ready?"

Chencha crossed her arms in front of her, grimacing. Anaís pushed the start button and in seconds, the sound of a familiar voice filled the small living room.

Chencha lost her annoyed looked, and with a big smile beamed up at Anaís.

"That's Celia! You know her music in the United States? What a surprise!" She listened intently. "I don't recognize that song...but that is our Celia!" Chencha got closer to the CD player as if to hear better.

"We can raise the volume, Chencha."

"No. No. Her music is not permitted here much, you know. Well, not unless artists from other places play her music when they are here for our music festivals. Please do not raise the volume. I don't want the neighbors to hear. This is alright. It is more than alright." She closed her eyes and leaned back in her chair. "My dear Celia. It's been so long since I've heard you."

Anaís bent over and kissed the elderly woman on her turban.

"If you want to hear it again, just press here."

Chencha looked at the red button and smiled. "Yes, I might want to do that."

Anaís kissed her head again, feeling happy at Chencha's excited re-action. Grabbing her purse, she stopped once more at the door as Celia Cruz began her "*Bemba Colorá*" song. Chencha slapped her thigh with glee. "The things that woman says! Go now, you can't miss that bus!" She waved Anaís away, and went back to listening and smiling as she heard Celia Cruz' voice, echoing memories from her past.

Anaís smiled, imagining that Chencha would keep pressing the "On" button all day. She should have thought about bringing batteries to Cuba since she only now understood that one could not buy things like batteries just anywhere, if at all.

The early morning walk down the driveway that separated her sister's small apartment from the rest of the building had become a wonderful ritual for her as she tried to peek through the windows of the residence that had once been her parents' home. She nodded *hola* and *buenos días* to the gardeners working in the yard and the chauffeur waxing the ambassador's limo under the shade of a large fig tree. She felt compelled to finding a way of getting into that house.

Her parents' former home, the sprawling single story house with ground to ceiling glass windows that she had admired the day she first met her sister, called to her sense of curiosity. Today, it seemed that there were many people milling around inside.

The home reminded her of the fifties type residences in Miami Beach and was in meticulous condition, especially considering the decay she had seen in many parts of Havana. But, this was Miramar. Regardless of what the Communist line might say, Anaís was beginning to understand that in Castro's Cuba, class distinctions still existed, especially separating the native Cubans from the immigrant visitors or dignitaries.

The morning air was soft and warm, the sun shining brightly on the slow rolling waves of the Caribbean. In the States, now she would be wearing heavy winter clothing, walking the lakefront only on the sunniest and least windy days. She thought of Isa, and wondered how her sister was handling the extreme, unforgiving Chicago weather. Certainly in this regard, Anaís had the better end of the deal.

"*Buenos días, muñeca.*" The comment interrupted her thoughts of Isa. It was one of the middle-aged men of a landscaping crew she saw most mornings sprucing up the front yard shrubbery of other neighborhood homes which had once housed wealthy Cuban families and now were the occupied by foreign diplomats or businessmen.

Anaís smiled at the diminutive, coffee-skinned man in a torn tee-shirt and grass stained pants who had just called her a 'doll'. Here in Cuba, the cat calls and whistles were not discouraged, and Anaís was getting used to being leered at. She wasn't sure how she felt about it, except that it seemed to fit with everything else around her— the fifties cars, the dilapidated sections of Old Havana, the natural ebullient character of the Cuban people. Here, in the midst of so few creature comforts, the people seemed happy, less stressed than back home, and certainly the concept of sexual harassment had not yet reached the island.

She marveled at the resilience of the people. Everyone she met did so much with so little. It was as if they didn't know that they were missing anything in their lives. And maybe they weren't after all.

The bus stop at La Quinta Avenida was crowded with the usual group of people cueing up to be the first on the bus. She wondered how much time they would wait today since, as Chencha said, the bus comes when it comes. The previous week, she and Chencha had missed the bus and after waiting forty minutes, Chencha's thumb in the air had finally hailed a ride with a stranger. Anaís would not have been so brave.

She nodded her morning greetings to the usual bus stop group, hoping her sister would have done the same thing. Chencha had warned her against smiling at strangers, and Anaís was never supposed to smile at men because it would send the wrong signal. How different from the casual greetings back home.

The bus arrived just as two young women ran up. The crowded group of waiting passengers drew in tighter as the bus screeched to a stop. There was no such thing as forming a line for anything in Cuba, Anaís thought. She realized that, contrary to her normal inclination, she was starting to push back too, afraid of not being able to get on the already packed bus.

Suddenly, she thought of the Christmas crowds in Chicago. This year, Anaís would not be there to see the tacky and overdone outdoor decorations, or the incessant holiday advertising, or experience the bustle of slushing through cold and snowy streets, juggling gifts for her closest friends. With Castro discouraging any religious displays of faith or celebrations, there were no signs that Christmas was in a few days. But Christmas in Pinar with relatives she had never met would be quite different and wonderful, she was sure. She could hardly wait.

"Hey, there's no fire!" Someone was screaming at the bus driver after the third quick turn around a corner that sent those standing in the aisle with Anaís slamming into each other. No, there was no fire, unless you were thinking about the heated cramped quarters of the bus as it sped down the boulevards from Miramar to Havana.

She grew weary of pushing back, not knowing which passengers were innocently bumping into her and which were just trying to get an easy feel of her ass. It didn't matter.

The bus jerked to a bumpy stop at the corner where she needed to get off. It was only a few short blocks to the building tucked away on a side street, the headquarters for Cuban tourism where Isa worked as an interpreter and translator for foreign business entrepreneurs in Cuba.

At her desk, Anaís thought back on her few weeks pretending to be Isa in the small tourist office. In imitating her sister, she was wearing very tight, short skirts and exaggerated eye makeup and she wasn't smiling at strangers. But the one thing she could not bring herself to do was to drink Cuban coffee throughout the day like the other employees.

Everyone enjoyed a cup of coffee as soon as they arrived in the morning. Then again around ten, Mariana walked through the office with thimble sized plastic cups of the scalding, thick liquid. Lunch brought from home was usually a sandwich with a small piece of meat or cheese, and again a thimble sized cup of Cuban coffee. Finally, around mid afternoon, Mariana offered everyone in the office another cup of the same robust liquid, which everyone downed with gusto.

The Cuban coffee seemed to irritate Anaís' stomach. After the first few days of enduring the caffeine overload, she began to nonchalantly make a visit to the bathroom where she flushed it down the age-stained toilet bowl. She felt guilty at discarding the coffee, knowing how seemingly ordinary things were a luxury in Cuba, but her body couldn't tolerate it.

Her sister's duties were relatively easy and she enjoyed the fact that she was using her French skills much more often than she would have back in her Chicago position. In conversations with Isa, she had learned that her sister had not needed to use her Russian in years since business with that country had ceased. Thank goodness, Anaís thought, since she had no knowledge of that language. What if a Russian client appeared? She refused to even consider that calamitous possibility.

Anaís had been pleasantly surprised at how organized Isa had left all her files. Anaís imagined that possibly Isa had been preparing all her office records for whomever was assigned to her duties once she left Cuba with the Senator's help. Whatever the reason, Isa's attention to detail and notes on each current project and client made it easy for Anaís to orient herself without difficultly to Isa's job of communicating information about Cuba to international investors. The work was interesting and not unlike what Anaís did back home for the tourism office for Illinois, although with one especially interesting exception—Diego.

Was it her imagination that he came over to her desk often, leaning over her shoulder to comment about something she was working on? The sisters had cried together about their unlucky marriages that widowed them and about their current loveless social lives. Anaís had talked about Jim and their sexual, though not exclusive, relationship and Isa had said that she was not involved with anyone and had left it at that. Isa never mentioned Diego. In Anaís' mind, that was a green light to whatever might happen between them.

At the beginning of the week, she was thrilled to learn that as part of her work with a Canadian Hotel Management group she would attend a reception with Diego. Last night, the way he had put his arm around her, as he moved her from group to group at the Canadian event, the way he looked at her as she translated the French conversations, the way his breath lingered close to her face when he spoke, all of it was soft and personal.

"This situation with the Canadians" she had queried him during one of those moments when she could sense the sexual tension between them, trying to dispel the awkwardness. "I don't understand why they are so insistent on going to Varadero Beach when it says in the notes... when I understand...that there are no opportunities for them there."

"Well, everyone loves our beaches, and you know how people are, especially in these changing times. I think they dream of the possibilities." His hand made circles in the air.

"I guess that's true." There was another moment of awkward silence.

"By the way, what time will be good for me to pick you up...to go to Pinar tomorrow?" he continued.

"Whatever is comfortable for you. After all, this is a wonderful favor, to drive us there so that we don't have to take the bus."

"Well, you and I have done this before," he said. "It's not any sort of inconvenience, since I still have a few friends there that I'll be visiting."

"Yes, of course," she added quickly. "But still I would never presume..."

"It's no problem," he replied. "On the contrary, it will be a great pleasure to have your company. And I haven't seen Chucha..."

"Chencha" she corrected.

"I'm sorry. Yes. Chencha. I haven't seen her in quite a long time."

Anaís was surprised to hear that Diego and Isa had driven to Pinar together and that he knew Chencha. But he had said it had been a long time ago, so even if Isa and Diego had more than an office relationship, Anaís saw no reason for her not to follow her instinct and heart with this attractive man, especially when Isa had clearly said that there was no man in her life. To some this might seem like a complicated situation, being with a man who thought she was someone else, but to Anaís...Her attraction to him was strong enough to ignore that issue.

"Well, how about around eleven in the morning? We can get some lunch somewhere between Havana and Pinar if you'd like."

"Perfect."

"It's set then. Great. See you then."

Yes, it had been a lovely evening. Anaís sighed.

Suddenly, she felt her co-workers looking at her as she stood at her desk daydreaming. She smiled back, hoping she was not blushing. She looked down at her desk, searching absentmindedly for a pad and pen and pretended to make some notes. She realized that she was writing in English, and quickly scratched out her scribbling.

"So, what are you doing this weekend, Isa?" Mariana had come over with the morning coffee brew.

"I'm going to visit my relatives in Pinar del Río." Her fingers circled the tiny thimble-like cup with the dark liquid. Anaís realized that if Mariana didn't move, she might have to drink the coffee after all.

"Oh, that will be nice." Mariana sipped her own coffee, apparently with no intention of moving away from Anaís' desk. Anaís continued cradling her cup, hoping Mariana would leave. Everyone else in the office had gone back to their tasks on the phone or on files, but Mariana seemed intent on continuing the dialog with the Anaís.

"So, what bus gets you there best?"

Anaís felt as if she were talking to *Arrancapellejo* back home, always curious about everyone else's life, and she quickly felt more confident about how to respond, which meant that she would give as little information as possible.

"Oh, I think the number sixty-seven bus is the best one to take, don't you think?"

"Well, I don't think I know that route" she answered, a little flustered. "But, then again, I don't live in Miramar."

Anaís pretended to sip her coffee but said nothing. A few minutes later, Mariana turned around and went back to her own desk.

Anaís' sense of relief was short lived. Another co-worker approached her asking for the Brunswick file and report. She had difficulty finding it in the drawer and was glad when finally she saw it in the pending file on her desk. After handing it over, she decided to go through her sister's drawers and files once again to become more familiar with everything she was responsible for, including past and pending cases. Luckily, she felt that last night she had made a good impression and good contacts with the new Canadian clients and was beginning to understand her role in the office. It was the office politics that she was still trying to decipher.

She immersed herself in going through the files in the old wooden cabinet next to her desk marked French Queries and Russian Queries. The latter drawer made her heart stop. She calmed herself remembering her sister's conversations about not having spoken Russian since the early nineties when the Soviets pulled out of Cuba. It wasn't that there were no Russians in Cuba, because, in fact, there still were a significant number of them. But, since the nineteen-eighty-nine decision by the Soviets to discontinue economic support to the island, resentment from the Cubans had grown steadily and the Russians were no longer accorded special privileges. Interpreters were one of those special privileges. Still, she would ask Chencha to have Secundino work his magic so that she would never be found out with a Russian client situation.

The lunch hour came and went, and Anaís still was reading through files. It was amazing to see the number of enterprises that had visited Cuba in the last nine years seeking to establish some type of business liaison with the island, not only in the areas of hotels and resorts, but also clothing, perfume, toiletries and even agricultural products.

Food! She was suddenly reminded that she needed to figure out how to deliver on Isa's *arroz con pollo* for her Pinar del Río family. How in heaven's name was she going to be able to pull that off? Where was she going to find chicken? And even if she did, how would she keep it cold until they got to Pinar? What a nightmare.

"Again you have that absorbed look about you, Isa. Still working! What is going on with you these days?"

Diego was standing at her desk, behind her. Anaís turned around and realized that everyone in the office had left. She smiled feebly, putting back some of the files she held in her hand.

"I guess it's just one of those days. I started to look for something, and you know how it goes, I ended up organizing some of these old files. I did hear people say goodnight to me, but I guess, I didn't realize everyone had left."

"Well, it's time to stop." He closed the drawer as she finished putting the folders inside, and crossing his arms on his chest, continued to watch her as she went back to her desk and put her paperwork away. She took her purse from underneath her desk and realized her short skirt was inching up her thighs. Why did her sister wear these hemlines? She felt Diego's eyes on her. She blushed as she caught his smile.

"I'll walk out with you." He took her arm. She felt hot.

"Are you going straight home?"

"Well, actually, maybe you can tell me where I can buy chicken around here?"

"Chicken?" He seemed surprised.

"Yes. I make *arroz con pollo* for Christmas for the family, usually right there, at my uncle's farm. This year I thought I'd take it all ready so that I have more time to visit with everybody. I don't get to see them often enough."

He didn't say anything and she continued speaking nervously.

"Of course, I don't know how I'm going to keep it fresh, once I make it, that is. Because our refrigerator is really small, and then there's the long drive. I'm not complaining. I just don't know how..."

His unexpected squeeze of her hand stopped her in mid-sentence.

"Alright. I get the picture. But have you forgotten that my pass will get us into the *diplotienda?* They have everything there. I'm sure that we can find one of those fancy Styrofoam coolers—and chicken."

Her surprised look must have in turn surprised Diego.

"I can't believe that you've forgotten the things we can get at the diplomate's commissary. How about that? I always think you have the memory of an elephant—and we all know that an elephant never forgets."

They both laughed, and Anaís realized that her sister and Diego must have been friends outside the office setting. There were too many non-office related comments from Diego for her to ignore. Nonetheless, although she couldn't understand why whatever they had had was over for her sister and not for Diego, she was extremely thankful for that fact. She found him intoxicating.

"You make me laugh."

"No, you make me laugh," he said, squeezing her hand again tight, while hailing a taxi that was parked down the street.

"Young man, take us to *CUBALSE*, please." Diego's tone with the taxi driver was firm but kind.

CUBALSE. Anaís had not heard this word before. It didn't matter. She was with Diego, and in a taxi instead of the daily afternoon bus ride.

They didn't say much as the taxi driver dodged pedestrians crossing in front of the cab in the late afternoon city traffic. As she glanced out the window, Anaís smiled, still finding it difficult to believe that she was in Havana. The city was beautiful and neglected, old and lively, mysterious and simple, all at the same time. Anaís glanced at Diego out of the corner of her eye. He excited her, and she could not remember a man causing such feelings in her since Charlie.

Her heart skipped as she thought of Charlie, her college sweetheart, the man with whom she had shared a wonderful five-year marriage. Her husband. Charlie had made her heart race, as all true first loves do. He had been not only a wonderful husband, but also her best friend.

Just as both of their careers had taken off and they had begun plans to start a family, he had died. Along with the two other people she loved, her parents, Charlie had perished in the freak car accident on the way to meet her for a concert on a cold and icy January evening.

She remembered that evening clearly, bundled in her warm fur coat under a light snowfall, feeling cold and annoyed that their tardiness would make them miss the first act.

After an hour, her annoyance turned to anxiety and finally to heart-stopping fear that her parents and husband were still not at the theater and that they had not called her. Her entire world of love and support had collapsed when she arrived home and answered the ringing of her phone. A police woman's voice on the other end told her there had been an accident.

It had taken her a few years to realize that she needed to get on with her life, that it would have been what Charlie and her parents would have wanted for her. Richard had been her shoulder to cry on those many years, and only after countless psychotherapy sessions did she admit that she indeed wanted to live and love again and open herself to other relationships.

There had been more than a handful of lovers and partners in the last eight years since Charlie's death. But no one, not even Jim, had made her feel the tingling in her neck and toes that she had felt for her husband—and that she felt now sitting next to Diego.

Diego paid the taxi driver and held the door open for her.

They stood in front a beautiful two-story building with a large sign welcoming them: "*CUBALSE: Cuba al Servicio del Extranjero,*" So this was CUBALSE: Cuba, a Store for Foreigners! No wonder she and Chencha had not shopped here! She tried to disguise her curiosity.

"So," he said as they headed for the door. "You need chicken...and a cooler. What a combination!"

Within seconds they were inside a huge, ultra-illuminated room, where a couple of Cuban soldiers stood at attention at the door. Past the guards, she noticed a middle-aged man in a dark blue suit smiling a welcome to them.

"What a great pleasure, Don Diego! It's been a while since we've seen you here."

Diego took out an identification card and handed it to the greeter. The man dismissed it with an air of familiarity.

"You know that's not necessary." He smiled at Anaís. "And welcome back, *señorita*. It has been a while."

Anaís smiled back in silence.

"So what can we help you with today?" the man inquired, looking back at Diego.

"Well, Enrique, today I'm looking for chicken and a big cooler that we can fill with ice."

"That's an interesting request, Don Diego. But, as always, I think we can help you out. Of course, the chicken and ice I will have to get from the other store, the market, but it will be here by the time you are ready to leave." He snapped his fingers and a young man in a white apron appeared from nowhere.

"How many chickens will you need?"

"Isa?"

"I don't know. There will be about 40 people..."

"I understand. We need many." Roberto whispered something into the clerk's ear, and the young man was off in a second. "The other, the cooler," he motioned to an area behind him. "I'm sure we have something that will fit your needs. And, of course, you may just want to look around. We have some very nice things that have come in lately." He paused. "Things that maybe the young lady may want to take some time to look at and try on."

He ushered them past the guards as he continued to talk, and neither man heard Anaís' gasp as she found herself in a department store setting that looked like any upscale store back in the United States! Anaís could hardly believe her eyes. After almost a month of being in Cuba, of shopping with Chencha in small, old neighborhood stores where shelves were bare and quantities limited, of standing in long lines for the bi-monthly rationing of food, she now stood in a department store like any back home.

They walked behind Enrique to the area of the coolers, but Anaís couldn't help looking longingly at the shampoo and soap counter, the racks of shirts and blouses and pants, the walls decorated with beautiful straw hats and leather belts. Was she dreaming? Certainly this was not the Havana that she had known since October when she landed with her delegation, and definitely not the Havana that Chencha had introduced her to in the last weeks. This store had everything! Why hadn't she known about it before?

"This might do for you, Don Diego." Roberto was taking down a small Styrofoam cooler. Diego looked at it from all angles and glanced at the interior space and gave it back to Roberto.

"No, I think we need something bigger, if you have it."

"How about this one, then?" Roberto was reaching up to a Styrofoam cooler twice the size of the previous one. He smiled with pride as he looked at Diego's approving glance.

"Yes, this one will do. We'll take two. Don't you think, Isa? Will these two hold your pots with the famous *arroz con pollo?*"

"Yes, I am sure they will." She couldn't believe how easy this was all becoming.

"Well, the chicken and ice will be here very soon. And, *señorita*, won't you need some onions and green peppers? Perhaps some Italian olive oil?"

"Yes," Anaís responded quickly. "Enrique, yes, I forgot. And anything else you know I'll need for the *arroz con pollo*. Thank you."

"Of course. And in the meantime, why don't you look around?" Enrique left them alone with a deep bow from the waist.

Anaís and Diego were left standing in front of a counter glistening with picnic utensils and baskets. They looked at each other for a moment, Anaís hoping desperately that her surprise and awe were not written all over her face. She still wasn't certain how this type of store existed in Cuba. It was like waking up to a Christmas morning of unexpected, extravagant gifts under the tree when you are poor.

"So, what else do you need?"

Anaís was still tongue-tied. Then she thought of her hair. "Shampoo!" she almost shouted.

Diego threw back his head in laughter. "In a store as big as this—you think of shampoo. Well, I think we can find some shampoo for you here. Let's look."

Slowly they worked their way through the aisles lined with a variety of goods, more than Anaís had seen since leaving the States. She started to notice the shoppers, most of them speaking foreign languages and dressed, not in the tattered or worn clothes of the everyday Cuban, but rather in fashionable clothing. CUBALSE was a department store exclusively for foreigners, but why? She also didn't understand why Chencha hadn't mentioned this place even after they found the crumpled bills inside the porcelain doll. Didn't Chencha know they could get anything they wanted here? How could that be?

"So which of these shampoos is your favorite?" Diego was asking as he picked up some bottles from the crowded shelf.

"This one," he showed her a beautiful brown bottle that Anaís recognized "will make your hair shine like the sun and it will smell like wild-flowers from the Swiss Alps." He pretended to smell the fragrance and made a mocking grimace.

"Or this one, more organic, from Australia." Again, he pretended to smell. "Ooohh, I think I like these violets much better."

Anaís started laughing at his teasing and ignoring his selections, started searching for her favorite brands. She selected two, then realized that she could not pay for them since the price marked on them was in U.S. dollars, which she did not have with her.

"My treat," Diego said. "Please."

"No, definitely not," was her response. "I have some American dollars that...that a cousin who came to Cuba recently...left me. I will pay you tomorrow."

"No, they are my gift to you...for the season."

"Then I don't want them. I mean, it's most kind of you. But I can't."

"Always so independent. Why can't you accept my gift?"

"I just can't."

"Well. Let's get them now. So that we don't have to come back. You can pay me whenever. Alright?"

"Yes. That I can do."

Enrique, the store manager, was approaching them.

"I have your other items, Don Diego. Whenever you are ready one of the young ladies at the front can help you check out."

"Thank you, my friend." Diego said as he patted Enrique on the back "As always, you do a wonderful job here for our foreign guests."

"Yes, we try to have a selection of goods so that our diplomats and their families are happy. And we are always glad to see our comrades visit us and try our products."

"Well, you are very good for our business. I'll come back soon. *Gracias, Enrique.*"

They were followed out the door by a few clerks who put the items in the waiting cab. Anaís still couldn't believe her good fortune with the chicken.

"Would you like to get something to eat?"

"No, thank you. I think I better go home and get this chicken ready for tomorrow. And Chencha and I will be ready at eleven, right?"

"If that's a good time for you?"

"Yes. That will work great."

They had placed the packages between them in the taxi yet Anaís could still feel the electricity between them. They chatted about work, the continuing plans for the Canadian delegation, interspersed with moments of exchanged silent glances and smiles, as if their minds were communicating at a different level than the banal details of their daily work together. Anaís felt disconcerted as to how to react to Diego's veiled suggestions, wondering what had taken place between Diego and Isa. How could she find out? She had tried calling her sister every evening for about a week now, and it was always the same answer from the operator: All lines are busy at this time. Try again later. Maybe Chencha knew something. Yes, she would ask the old woman and see how much she had gleaned from anything Isa may have told her about Diego.

The taxi pulled up behind a line of foreign cars parked in front of the sprawling estate next to her apartment. There was some sort of event going on in the ambassador's residence and the mansion was lit up like a Christmas tree. Anaís overheard the conversation of the well-dressed guests getting out of cabs or private cars and noticed that they were speaking not only Spanish but at least half a dozen other languages. She craned her neck to continue looking at everyone as the taxi was finally able to get around the arriving cars and pulled around close to the back of the property where her apartment was located.

"I forgot that the ambassador is hosting a reception here at his home tonight, yes, right next to your place," Diego said to her, noticing her interest in the party. "If I had remembered I would have asked you if you wanted to come...seeing that you are right next door and all...and that they speak French, and you could help me with that."

"Yes! I'd love to," Anaís responded to the vague invitation. She didn't want to think about what she would do about the *arroz con pollo*. She didn't care. The opportunity to go into her parents' former home, her and Isa's childhood home, was not one that she could pass up.

"You mean you would like to go? You'd still like to make the party?"

"Yes! I've wanted...You know, living next door and all. It would be wonderful." She stopped. "I'm sorry." She apologized. "How rude of me to think that you don't have other plans...with someone else."

"I don't. Remember I just asked you out to dinner a little while ago? This would be magnificent." He sounded as excited as she was, a big smile on his face. "This is great. Do you need time to change? Of course you need time to change! How much time to you need? I need to go back and get into more formal attire. This particular ambassador forgets he's in the tropics and always is dressed to the hilt."

"Uh, I don't know...it won't take me long."

"Great! I'll be back for you in say, forty-five minutes?"

"Yes! I'll be waiting."

CHAPTER 17

La Casa

"CHENCHA! IMAGINE! I'M GOING TO GET TO VISIT THE HOUSE!" ANAÍS RAN in almost screaming with excitement. "Can you imagine! Diego has an invitation to the party at the big house! And I'm going!"

Chencha emerged from the kitchen, drying her hands on an old ragged towel discolored by wear and age. She shuffled her way up to Anaís who hugged her tightly.

"Can you believe it? I'm going to get to see the big house, our old house! Tonight!" She headed for the bedroom. "What do you think I can wear! Oh, my goodness! I don't have anything here that's fancy enough." She searched through the old armoire that Chencha said had belonged to her parents, a beautiful piece of carved dark mahogany in exquisite condition that somehow Chencha had managed to get out of the *casa grande* as she called the mansion next door.

"I can't believe it!" She rummaged through clothes hanging on flimsy wire hangers, then through the drawers. Nothing seemed elegant enough.

"I can't go, Chencha. I will look like a fool, and I will embarrass Diego." Chencha had sat on the small twin bed in Anaís' room.

"What about something that you brought with you from your country?"

"That's it! Isa left almost everything that I brought with me the night that I was supposed to leave Cuba. And there is one beautiful dress that I wore for one of the delegation's receptions." She spoke as she dragged out the large black suitcase that she had stored under the twin bed for lack of other space. Chencha watched as Anaís unzipped the bag and pulled out a beautiful black beaded floor length dress that made Chencha smile with approval. She searched further in the bag and took out a pair of black high-heeled pumps.

"You will look beautiful. But did you say that you are going next door...with Don Diego?"

Anaís was already undressing in the small bathroom and hoping this would be one of those nights when the water spigot would offer more than a trickle of water. She had already gotten used to the cool temperature that she needed to bathe in, but it was exasperating when the water almost turned to droplets that were barely enough with which to rinse her body or hair.

"Yes...Don Diego. What do you know about him, Chencha?" Chencha was quiet for a few moments before responding.

"Diego is from Pinar. He was raised by his grandparents, on his mother's side. That's what I heard at your uncle's farm, anyway. They don't seem to know anything about this father's side of the family except that his father died tragically at the beginning of the revolution but I don't remember any details."

Anaís knelt in the tub, filling the bucket under the faucet with the tepid water, listening to Chencha through the half-opened door between the bedroom and the small bath area.

"But it was here in Havana that your sister got to know him, at work. Isa was invited by Don Diego to many events for a while."

"Do you know if they liked each other, in a romantic way, I mean. Or was it just work?"

Chencha didn't answer right away. Anaís held her breath waiting for the answer. The bucket was half full now, just enough to get her hair and body wet and lathered. She waited for Chencha's answer.

"Child, your sister didn't tell me everything. She knows I am very conservative and traditional, so she never told me everything. But the devil knows more because he's old than because he's the devil." Anaís was always surprised at Chencha's Spanish sayings. Chencha nodded.

"I'm too old to be fooled easily. Regardless of what she was telling me, I knew that it was more than work. You could see the interest in Don Diego's eyes."

Anaís felt a shiver down her back, and it wasn't simply from being naked in the tub and feeling the coolness of the water that she poured on her head and that trickled down her body. She sighed out loud, as she put down the bucket and started to lather herself. That was not the information she was hoping to hear from Chencha. There was no way that she would step between her sister and Diego if they had feelings for each other, regardless of the attraction she felt. Tonight would have to be the last time, she thought, with heaviness in her heart that she would see Diego outside of a work situation.

"Your sister, on the other hand, never liked Don Diego." Chencha's words sent an immediate rush to Anaís' spirit. "And I don't know why. He certainly is a handsome man. And very important in the government. And while your sister was seeing him, she was able to bring home many things that she was able to buy from that special store, the CUBALSE, that they have for the international visitors. Fuck! Oh, child, I'm sorry. I shouldn't use profanities in front of you. But it bothers me to no end that we Cubans cannot go to stores like that in our own country. Well, I lie. We can go, but all we can do is look. Shit! Oh, I'm sorry, for swearing again. But we can't buy anything there unless we have dollars and a special identification card as a tourist, visiting diplomat or the like. That just doesn't seem right to an old woman like me."

Anaís was only half listening to Chencha's diatribe because she was still savoring the thought that Isa had never been interested in Diego.

"So what do you think happened between them and how long ago did they stop seeing each other?"

Anaís stepped out of the tub, half shivering in the coolness of the room. She opened the door fully and saw Chencha purse her lips in her usual fashion as she pondered the question.

"You know, here in Cuba many times we have to pretend. It's how we all get by. What we feel in our hearts is not always what we say with our words. How we want to act is often not the way we do act. It's not a happy thing to do. It makes us feel like hypocrites. But we all have to live here, together. And so, yes, we pretend a lot."

She got up and started to help Anaís dry her hair with the towel as she sat at the edge of the bed. Anaís felt like an Amazon woman next Chencha. Ana's sat, shoulders hunched, so she could be eye level with Chencha and they could look at each other as they talked.

"And so Isa went to these events with Don Diego, first because it was part of her job at the office, but then, I think he got more serious..." she stopped and looked Anaís straight in the eyes. "I think she thought she had to...be nice." Anaís understood. They probably were sleeping together.

"But your sister is a good person, and she said that he wanted a more serious relationship with her. One day all she said to me was that Don Diego would not be coming by anymore. And I hadn't heard Don Diego's name in maybe four or five years, until you mentioned him again."

Anaís' heart felt joyous. It was wonderful to know that she was not cheating or interfering in any way in that failed relationship. Obviously Diego was picking up on Anaís' interest in him and was reacting in kind. Maybe she should care that he thought she was Isa, but she didn't care. She was her own person and if anything developed between them it would be their own new experience.

She slipped the dress over her head and walked to the oblong mirror in front of the dressing table, then turned to Chencha, looking for her approval.

Chencha's hands held Anaís at a distance as she admired the slim figure of the woman in front of her. "You look beautiful...and so elegant." The beaded gown draped Anaís' curvaceous body, sensually accentuating her full breasts and curves.

Chencha smiled her almost toothless smile. "You're going to drive him crazy."

She said thank you as she rimmed her eyes with the black eyeliner and dabbed on some apple red lipstick.

Chencha handed her an old glass jar. "Here," she said. "I make this cologne from the jasmine flowers that grow outside our door." She took off the cap and the heady scent filled the air as Anaís dabbed some behind her ears and on the nape of her neck.

"It's wonderful, Chencha. You'll have to show me how to make this."

"Yes. Of course. We need to keep that plant well pruned—it is so old. But not as ancient as me, of course." She chuckled.

"I wish I had some nice earrings to go along with this," she said as she looked again in the mirror, brushing her short hair first behind and then in front of her ears.

"What about some of the jewelry the two of you found inside the doll?"

Anaís had forgotten the beautiful antique treasures in her porcelain doll. She took down the porcelain doll that now was held together at the back with large pins. As she unclasped the back, Anaís thought of her mother, of her ingenuity in preserving for her daughters some of her special possessions, not only valuable but more importantly, sentimental.

Carefully, she reached inside the doll, moving aside the crumpled pieces of paper she knew to be U.S. bills, her fingers feeling for the jewelry that she and Isa had admired many weeks before. Slowly as to not disturb the dollar stuffing that made up the body of the doll, she pulled out each piece, as both she and Chencha once more uttered sounds of disbelief at the beautiful jewel-encrusted gold pieces that spoke of a long-gone elegant past. Chencha took each piece and used the hem of her skirt to bring out its shine.

From among the many exquisite pieces that they put out on the worn cotton bed cover, she chose a pair of ruby pendants with a matching gold necklace graced with a ruby pendant identical in size to the earrings. A thick rope-like bracelet with tiny rubies and pearls was the next thing that caught her eye. Chencha helped clasp the necklace and bracelet, and Anaís could hardly believe how beautiful the pieces were, and her mind wandered to her mother, imagining her as a young bride wearing them on the way to some special occasion with her father. Her fingers almost trembled as she caressed each piece tenderly.

The knock on the door startled her, and she realized Diego was there to take her around the corner to the *casa grande.* She felt like a high school senior off to the prom, and not the thirty-eight-year-old woman that she was.

"You look absolutely beautiful," Chencha repeated.

They both walked to the front door, and Chencha opened it. Now in his tuxedo, Diego looked even more handsome. His eyes lit up as he saw Anaís walk up to him.

"Isa! You look... incredible!" He smiled at her over Chencha's head, then realizing that he had ignored the old woman, he leaned over apologetically.

"Doña Chencha. How rude of me not to say hello." He pointed at Anaís. "But it's Isa's fault, looking so amazing." He turned back to Chencha. "And how are you? You look wonderful. The years don't have any effect on you. And it has been a long time, hasn't it?"

Chencha seemed almost flustered at the compliments. "*Por favor*, Don Diego. I am a balding, old black woman. Nothing attractive about me."

"You are wrong, Doña Chencha. You are a beautiful woman."

"No, the beautiful woman here is An...Isa."

"She certainly is." His gaze lingered on her, moving slowly from her eyes down to her shoes. "Ready to go?"

"Yes! Definitely. Chencha, please don't wait up for me. And don't worry—I'm just next door. Okay"

"Have a good time. Enjoy yourselves."

Outside the air was warm, with a slight breeze that carried the scent of the ocean nearby. Diego took Anaís' arm and whispered again how beautiful she looked.

"What an incredible dress!" Then, noticing her jewelry, touched one of the earring pendants playfully. "And these are beautiful! Where did you ever get these pieces?"

"They're not real, of course," she lied. "A cousin...Last month a long-forgotten cousin from Chicago...came here. She gave them to me as a gift. She said they make wonderful fake jewelry in the United States, that they are very popular because they look so genuine." She touched her necklace. "They do look real, don't you think?"

"I'll say! Those Americans! If we could only have access to the ma-

terials and technology that they have—we could have things like this
here, for our people, too." He stopped. "But, I didn't know you had any
relatives in the United States."

"Neither did I...until she knocked on my door." This was a dangerous
conversation, she thought to herself, then, she lightly touched his arm
and smiled at him. "Thank you for asking me to join you tonight."

They were around the corner to the front of the *casa grande,* the ambassador's home, which once had been her own. Her heart beat furiously
with anticipation.

"I remember that you loved this house, Isa, although I don't understand why. We have been to much nicer places here in Miramar. And in
Varadero. So what is so special to you about this place? The few times
that we've come here you were like a kid in a candy store... And now you
have that same look again."

Anaís smiled at the thought that Isa also felt the magic of going into
their parents' former home, even if only for a short while. It was obvious
from his comments that Diego knew nothing about her parents or that
this house had once been Isa's home.

She squeezed his arm tighter. "This is...this just seems like such a
special house, Diego. Thanks for bringing me here again."

She was going to walk on the same floors that she and Isa had played
on when they were babies, and she would be able to touch the walls that
had kept the secret conversations between her parents when they were
even younger than she was now. She felt vulnerable to her emotions, and
realized that she would need to try hard not to let those emotions give
her away during the course of the evening.

The Belgian ambassador and his wife recognized them immediately
as they shook hands at the front door.

"*Buenas noches, Diego,*" they said in their best Spanish accent, and
then turning to her spoke in French. "*Enchanté de vous voir encore, mademoiselle.*"

She returned the compliment to them and continued speaking in
French until Diego interrupted laughing.

"Hold on a minute. I don't have any idea what you are saying here.

Some Belgian conspiracy against the Cuban government?" he joked.

"Hardly, Diego. Simply speaking our language to one who speaks it so well, like a native, I would say." He nodded smiling at Anaís.

"*Merci, gracias.*" The ambassador's wife a tall, thin, emaciated-looking woman, echoed her husband's comments. She smiled the pasty, toothy smile of a professional politician. Her eyes fixed on Anaís' jewelry.

"Those are quite exquisite pieces," she commented.

"And, can you believe, they're fake!" Diego laughed. "Isa got to meet a cousin who lives in the United States last month who gave them to her as a gift. She said that over there they make fake jewelry that looks so real everyone is buying them. And they must be inexpensive if she just gave them to her, no?"

"Fake? Really?" Both Belgians peered curiously. "Well, we must get Enrique to see if he can bring such things to the CUBALSE. They would be a hit, I am sure."

"Not a bad idea, Ambassador. I will speak to him about it."

"Well, you two young people have a good time. And *mademoiselle*, let me say again that you are stunning."

The four shook hands and the ambassador kissed Anaís' hand.

The moment she stepped through the double glass doors Anaís felt an overwhelming excitement. Her eyes opened wide, trying to record every detail before her.

They entered a spacious foyer with high ceilings and a beautiful chandelier that hung over their head and sparkled on the soft beige granite floors. From the foyer, she could see that the house was a U-shaped design. Wide glass doors led to a huge terrace and patio where palm trees seemed to sprout up from the terrazzo floor of the terrace. Anaís squeezed Diego's arm.

"Do you think they would mind if we looked around?"

"No, of course not. Although we have done that before." He looked at her smiling. "You must really like this house. It's the only place where you and I have been where you always insist on strolling around."

"Yes, I find it is quite a beautiful and interesting place. Do you mind if we look around, again?"

"With you, anywhere," he said softly in her ear.

They stood in the middle of the living room facing the terrace on two sides, beautiful, modern furniture and paintings everywhere.

"Why don't you pretend to give me a tour? It will be like seeing it for the first time."

"Alright. Well, *mademoiselle*," he said in a bad French accent. "Here we are standing in the main *leevin room*, and to *zee right*," he turned her around to face a large rectangular room "*we ave zee* dining room." Glass walls on two sides faced courtyards, and a third mirrored wall highlighted the immense glass table on marble pedestals that was surrounded by 20 or more tanned leather upholstered chairs. A beautiful console on the fourth wall displayed antique silver dining pieces.

"Do you think any of this is the original furniture?"

"I think the table is. In fact, I'm sure I remember hearing that not only were the ambassador and his wife taken with how beautiful it is, but it weighs a ton and they didn't think it would be easy to move. The rest of the decorations and furniture... I'm sure that it's their taste." He leaned over and whispered in her ear. "Over the top European baroque, if you ask me."

Anaís was barely listening to Diego. She gently touched the dining room table, imagining her parents had dined here.

"And here *to zee left* through these swinging doors..." he pushed the door and they stepped into a large kitchen with full modern appliances, including a microwave oven and a refrigerator with freezer."

"My gosh, I can't believe all the things they have!"

Diego looked at her.

"Well, I mean, I've seen them before, but I'm always surprised to see...the big refrigerators and stoves, you know..."

"Yes, well. Our visitors want to feel that they are not missing out on any comforts from home just because they are on our island."

He turned her around and they exited again through the swinging door past the dining room and living room to the other side.

"And here *wee haf* a second small living area...no, it is a small reception area for small meetings with the ambassador's guests."

The room was not small by any means, with comfortable richly up-holstered sofas on three sides accented by beautiful coffee and end tables. The paintings on the walls looked like works by Flemish painters, and the table lamps were exquisite oriental pieces. A magnificent carved mahogany door was at the extreme end, and when Diego opened it she found herself in a larger room that was set up as an office.

"*Mademoiselle...*" Diego was pointing to the far end of the room where they could admire a large painting of the ambassador standing next to his country's queen. "And guess what is past this wall?" Anaís shrugged her shoulders.

"Your apartment! At one time, there was a door right there," he pointed to the painting in the middle of the wall, "which led to where you live now. Probably the servants' quarters," Diego was saying. "But that was in the days of Batista, when the rich employed other Cubans as their slaves."

Anaís felt blood rush to her head. Was Diego so much of a Cuban revolutionary that he could not see the irony of what he was saying? Were not the Cubans serving the fancy hors d'oeuvres not working as servants for the Belgian diplomat? She looked at Diego's handsome face and for an instant felt anger and disappointment. Defiant words started forming in her mind. But then she reminded herself that she was Isa, and Isa would not say anything in this situation.

"Let's continue, shall we?" She took his arm. "So, tell me, *monsieur...* what rooms are on the other side of this house?"

Diego smiled, lifting his eyebrows in a suggestive way. "*Zee bedrooms!* And let me show you."

"Maybe we shouldn't."

"Oh, no, my services include *zee complete tour.*"

They crossed the living room area once more, and again Anaís admired the openness and grace of the home her parents had built, unusually modern in its use of glass and steel. As they stepped away from the living area, she noticed a stairway with a beautiful brass railing descending a circular staircase.

"And down there?"

"Zee garages and zee, how do you say, ah yes, *zee wine cellar and pantries."*

He pulled her arm. "But, over here, down this long hallway, as I said, *zee bedrooms."*

Anaís walked slowly behind Diego, admiring the lovely garden on the other side of the glass walls of the long corridor.

"One bedroom." Diego pointed inside the first room. Anaís peeked in. "Two bedrooms."

"Three bedrooms."

She curiously looked inside each room, wondering which might have been the nursery, but nothing suggested that children had once lived there.

"And last, but not least, *zee master bedroom,* for mama and papa." He pretended to swing the door open. *"Voilá!"*

With her heart beating and feeling heady, Anaís stepped inside the bedroom that she knew must have been that of her parents. It was a large room with sliding doors that faced the yard and patio now crowded with the ambassador's guests enjoying a perfect, warm, tropical evening. Exotic scents wafted into the room through the open windows and doors and overwhelmed her senses. A second door in the corner led to a large bathroom with a his-and-hers dressing area, and large walk-in closets beyond. The absolute wonder of standing in what had been her parents' home suddenly brought tears to her eyes, and she pretended to pick something off the floor so she could blink them back unnoticed.

"And there you have it, *mademoiselle.* Do you like it?"

"Yes. Immensely", Anaís answered quietly, trying her best to compose herself so she would not do or say anything that would seem out of character with how Isa would have behaved.

"Well, that is the end of the tour. How about a drink?"

"Yes, that would be perfect right now."

They walked back down the corridor, Diego chattering happily about his good relationship with the ambassador, who was said to be a difficult man, while Anaís found herself sinking into a melancholy she did not expect to feel. She had been so excited and anxious at the thought of finally seeing the place that her parents had built and called home, that she never considered what she would feel once she had walked the rooms where they had lived, where they had spent their last happy days alive. Dark thoughts overtook her as she stepped outside onto the terrace with Diego. The happy *merengue* music did nothing to lift her spirits, and she was thankful that Diego excused himself to get their drinks at the other end of the patio.

Elegant couples enjoyed the party atmosphere. Had her parents also entertained in this way many years ago? Had they stood around, discussing politics, the weather, their future, on this same spot where she was standing now? Had they held her and Isa in their arms and planned their *fiesta de quinceañera,* their special fifteenth birthday party? She touched her forehead, feeling almost feverish and faint at the rush of those thoughts and emotions. Diego was walking back toward her, a drink in each hand. His smile disappeared as he looked at her forlorn face.

"What's the matter, Isa? You don't look well. Are you alright?"

"No, actually. Suddenly, my stomach feels very upset. And I have developed a tremendous headache. Do you mind if I go home? Please, you stay. We haven't been here any amount of time, and I am sure that you need to put in your appearance."

"I'll walk you back..." he said, giving the champagne glasses to a young man collecting glassware on a large silver plate.

"No, please..."

He took her arm gently. "Come on."

They retraced their steps to the front door. Everyone, including the host and hostess, were out on the patio and Anaís was glad that she would not have to speak to them again. She wanted to be alone with her thoughts and feelings.

They walked in silence the short distance around the house to the apartment. At the door, Diego took her hand and kissed it tenderly. "It has been a brief, but wonderful evening. Thank you for spending it with me, Isa. I...I have missed you..."

"You're welcome, Diego." She knew she sounded abrupt. "Please excuse my absence to the ambassador and his wife."

"It's done. Tomorrow? At eleven in the morning will still be alright with you?"

She nodded.

"Then, please have a good evening. I hope you feel better." He kissed her hand again, turned and disappeared into the darkness.

Anaís barely got in the room when tears overtook her. She leaned against the door, and sobbed. Her heart seemed to break as she gave in to thoughts about her parents' life and death. She had never felt so orphaned, not even when her adoptive parents had spoken to her about her Cuban past. In those long ago conversations, she had their love and support as she dealt with dark feelings. Now, for the first time, she realized she was truly an orphan, a child still lost in the repercussions of a revolution. She dropped to the floor and hid her head in her hands, giving in to an overwhelming sadness.

"My child."

She looked up at Chencha's face looking down at her, the turban around her head looking like a yellow halo in the deep darkness of the bare lit room. Chencha sank down onto the floor with difficulty and enveloped Anaís in her arms.

"Oh, my dear child."

Anaís' quietly sobbed as Chencha rocked her back and forth, caressing her head, kissing her forehead, saying nothing. It was as if the old woman knew the source and depth of Anaís' pain, and they both sat on the floor among the shadows of the night

Anaís could not get her parents' faces out of her mind. First she would see them smiling in the torn picture that both she and Isa had of their parents. Then she would see her parents lying bleeding and mutilated in an open grave. These thoughts raced through her mind, making her shiver. She fell Chencha's arms encircle her even tighter, and the old woman's hugs helped her to see her parents' smiling faces again.

They sat for a long while. Gradually, Anaís' sobs started to subside, and she buried her head in Chencha's soft chest, feeling the same love and safety of being held in her adoptive mother's embrace. Gail Moran always smelled of roses and cookies. Anaís took a deep breath. Chencha smelled of lemons and garlic.

"Let's go, child."

Anaís got up to help the old woman off the floor. They held on to each other as they got up, Anaís' tall figure towering over the thin, fragile body. They made their way from the small living area into Anaís' bedroom. Chencha helped her unzip and take off the lavish evening dress. Anaís slipped on the oversized Chicago Bears shirt that she wore as a nightshirt, and bent down and kissed the woman's head.

"Thank you so much, Chencha. You are truly a mother to me, to Isa and me." Her heart was full of gratitude for the unconditional of this dear person

Chencha looked at Anaís' and patted her cheek

"There's no reason to thank me. And don't forget" Chencha changed the conversation, "that tomorrow, before we go to Pinar, we have to go the Plaza of the Revolution for the monthly Women's Brigade practices. Why they make an old woman like me handle a bayonet I'll never know, but we must go. So try to get some sleep."

Anaís watched as the old woman inched her way out of the room, leaving the door just a little bit ajar behind her. Thank God her sister had had Chencha to watch and take care of her all those years without her parents.

She closed her eyes and began thinking about her sister, and the pain and hardship Isa must have endured all those years in Cuba while she, Anaís, had only known a life of comfort and opportunity. She thought of the home she was brought up in, the quiet elegance and comfort of every room. She thought of their summer home in Michigan and the carefree childhood she had lived, where her biggest problem might have been which dress or outfit to wear; her vacations in Europe and the Caribbean, Latin America and Asia; dressing up for opening night at the Lyric Opera, going to plays and the ballet. These were all experiences she had more or less taken for granted as a child and as a young woman, and all experiences that her sister had missed because on that fateful day many years ago Father Pat had chosen her and not Isa, to go to the United States.

The more she thought about their lives and how incredibly different their they had been up to now, the more Anaís felt that justice finally was being served. Her sister deserved to be in the States, and she Anaís, deserved to be where she was now. Nothing could undo the past for either of them, but the future had to be different for her sister. It just had to be different.

She was glad that tonight she was the one on the lumpy, narrow bed that belonged to her sister, and happy thinking of Isa in Chicago, sleeping in the large, comfortable queen-size bed under the warmth of a soft, down comforter. Yes, this was how things should be right now.

Anaís moved around to find a non-sagging spot on the creaking bed and dozed off thinking about long ago evenings at summer camp.

CHAPTER 18

Christmas Eve ~ Chicago

BACK FROM HER WALK, ISA FELT ONCE MORE ENERGIZED AND EXCITED AS she thought of the evening ahead. She remembered that she needed to ask Richard what the appropriate thing would be for her to contribute to the night's meal.

"Nothing. It will just be us—my mother and father, you and I. They will have everything catered—oh, yes, just remember to tell Mom that you love when she orders from Estefano's because Anaís always says that."

"But I don't feel right not doing anything for tonight, Richard. Are you sure I can't cook something? Tell me something I can bring."

"Well, your sister never cooks, so that would be a shock to my mother. But Ani does bring wine or flowers. You can do that if you want."

"But what wine? I don't know anything about wine. Maybe I should bring flowers.Where does she get them?"

"Downstairs, next to the small grocery store I've shown you, there's a flower shop. And they have your card, well, Anaís' credit card number, so all you have to do is sign for whatever you want."

"*Perfecto.* That's what I'll do right now. What time should I be ready?"

"How about six? My parents don't like to eat too late."

"That's fine. I will see you then, Ani. Boy, how strange it must be for you to answer to a name not your own. Are you used to it yet?"

"Most of the time, yes. Thanks, Richard. I'll be ready at six."

She hung up the phone and headed for the elevator. The family in the condo across from hers was also just leaving their apartment, arms full of brightly covered Christmas gifts.

"Hi."

"Hello." Isa was finally getting used to the casual friendliness of Americans.

Richard had told her that it was acceptable to greet and smile at most people, like those in the building, at work or in her exercise class. Even joggers and bikers greeted each other although they might be strangers. What odd customs!

Also, in Cuba, decent women simply did go to a lounge unless it was on a date. For her, it felt uncomfortable to get in a taxi by herself to meet colleagues after work at a bar but Richard said it was something Anaís did from time to time, and she should as well. And the men! They looked at her with interest, but never whistled or said anything provocative. She wasn't sure yet how she felt about that.

She found the flower shop next to the convenience store just as Richard had said. Wonderful Richard! Her one true friend! He had even helped her pick out things for the gift exchange and for her supervisors at work. Suddenly, she realized she had not gotten him anything for Christmas, and here it was Christmas Eve. She needed to run over to Michigan Avenue, the only area she knew close by, and get him something special.

Stepping into the flower shop was like entering an exotic other world of lush vegetation, flowers and fragrances filling every inch of space, including the ceiling. Isa again marveled at the elegance and beauty of everything she saw in Chicago. She couldn't remember ever seeing more than a couple of flower shops in Havana, certainly none in Pinar. In this particular store, beautiful arrangements were everywhere, with other displays of small statuettes, knick-knacks and greeting cards. It was amazing to her.

She walked around for a while simply enjoying the beautiful arrangements, looking at the prices of things and shaking her head at how expensive everything was. Any one flower arrangement cost more than a full month's salary for her at the *Oficina de Inversiones Extranjeras* in Havana. And here she was, ready to buy and pay for something so expensive that no one was going to wear or eat. It was still shocking to see how Anaís lived. But like Richard kept repeating to her, she needed to act as her sister or people might consider her new behavior suspicious.

A lovely rose arrangement in a porcelain vase caught her eye. It was the sort of thing she would only have caught a glimpse of in Havana when she attended a function at some diplomat's home, wishing she could have taken it home for Chencha. She looked at the price. Two hundred seventy-five dollars! As she gave the clerk her information and signed the receipt, Isa felt both wasteful and decadently rich. They offered to deliver the roses to Richard's parents later on in the afternoon, another wonderful service she had not expected. She smiled and thanked the clerk, marveling at how things were handled in America.

She headed for Michigan Avenue and Water Tower Place where Richard had taken her to do some of her Christmas shopping for the people at the office. It was a cold but beautiful winter afternoon, and even though she was still in her jogging clothes, she fit right in with the diverse shopping crowd jamming the streets. Everywhere there were signs in stores about last minute sales before Christmas. Anything one could possibly think of or want was in one of these stores, an experience was completely alien to her. She had only been in Chicago a few short weeks, but already the poverty in Cuba was beginning to seem like a dream, something that was not possible only a few thousand miles away.

Finally at Water Tower, she decided to go into Marshall Field's because Richard had told her she could always find anything there, and that it was one of his favorite stores. The bright lights and festive holiday decorations made her look around in awe like one of the young children waiting in line to talk to Santa Claus. Clerks dressed like Christmas elves were offering everyone cookies and chocolates — for free! She took one and thought of Chencha, and how much she would love to eat these delicious treats. When she went back, chocolate was one thing she needed to take back for her old friend.

In the Men's Department, there was less confusion than in the first floor cosmetics area that she had just walked through. She had no idea what to get Richard, what was appropriate for a good friend. At the far end of the store, some colorful sweaters caught her eye and she headed that way. The sweaters were eye-catching, with an unusual and bright weave that was very unique. She picked up one with hues of red and magenta and orange that seemed to fit Richard's personality, wondering if Richard would wear a large or medium. She felt a tug at her sleeve, and turned hoping it was a clerk to help her with the size.

"Anaís!"

A tanned handsome man in a long camel overcoat looked at her with a mixture of joy and surprise. Isa had no idea who he was.

"Anaís? Is that you with short hair? I like it. Yeh, I've been calling you and leaving you messages for weeks. What's wrong? Why haven't you returned my calls."

Isa's mind raced trying to combine the words she was hearing with any information she had about her sister's friends. Calling her for weeks? A lot of people had been leaving messages for her sister for weeks. Who could this be?

"What happened in Cuba? I thought we'd see each other when you got back. You've been back for a while, haven't you?"

Isa nodded yes, still searching her mind to see if the handsome face she was looking at was in any of the pictures she had seen in her sister's apartment.

"Well, why haven't you called me? I've been worried. I've thought about just coming by your place, but I didn't want to...in case you didn't want to see me for some reason. A friend of mine whose mother went to Cuba a year ago said that she came back so depressed from her visit, seeing the situation there, that she cried for weeks. I thought maybe you..."

"Yes, that's exactly what happened to me. It was so sad. I'm sorry. But, yes, I've just been staying at home, by myself...thinking."

"Well, but being alone is not good." He came closer to her. "And I miss you." Something in the intimacy of his voice jogged her memory.

Jim! This was the Jim that had left messages on her sister's answering machines since she got back. The Jim Anaís had told her about, the man her sister said she needed to break up with because she didn't love him and he was falling hard for her. The Jim who was a great lover. She blushed remembering her sister's comments and looked away from his stare.

"I …I'm just getting used to being back, Jim. I hope you understand."

"Yes, but when are we going to see each other?"

"I don't know." She saw the pained look in his eyes. "Soon."

She saw him also look at the sweater she was holding.

"Oh, I see. A gift for a new friend? I know you don't have any family. Pretty expensive for just anybody," he remarked, now somewhat sarcastically. "But, hey, that's none of my business. Well, I hope he likes that it. And if you get bored with your friend, give me a call." He turned abruptly and left before Isa could say anything else about Richard or the sweater. She had hurt his feelings. Still, there was nothing else she could really have said or done to make things any better for Jim.

"Can I help you?"

This time it was a clerk standing next to her, wearing a Santa's cap. The clerk assured Isa that she was making a wonderful purchase, and she would have the sweater gift wrapped, and yes, if it didn't fit, her friend could bring it back. As she signed another receipt for an amount that was more than two months' salary in Cuba, Isa suddenly started feeling depressed instead of happy. What was she doing, leading this crazy life? She was uncomfortable in her sister's skin, always doubting the appropriateness of her actions and behavior. And now, she had hurt someone unwittingly. Isa sighed as she took the beautifully wrapped box inside the shopping bag from the smiling clerk. What had she done, becoming this pretender?

Her walk back to the condo was dark and somber. The happy chatter of carefree shoppers around her sounded like the buzzing of bees, the clanging of the Santa's helpers' bells on each corner was annoying. She waddled from side to side in a strange march with the throngs of people on the sidewalk looking at the window decorations or coming in and out of stores. She held her bag close to her body, thinking that getting robbed would be the last thing she needed, although a thief had little chance of escaping through this Christmas crowd.

She thought about Anaís and what a wonderful time she probably was having at Tío Julio's. It was Isa's favorite holiday, one that her family celebrated despite the fact that it had been strictly prohibited in Cuba until the Pope's visit two years before. She wondered what Anaís thought about the special Cuban food that her aunts prepared--such delicious roasted pork and black beans. She wondered what her sister had done about the *arroz con pollo,* a family favorite.

How different the holidays were here. Partying with her Anaís' friends helped her see that Americans celebrated these holidays in a big way. The office Christmas party at the beautiful John Hancock restaurant had been particularly spectacular. She had never been in an elevator where her ears popped like in an airplane. The holiday cheer that seemed to permeate the city and its people was wonderful, and seeing children sitting in awe and anticipation on the many Santas in stores warmed her heart thinking of the innocent wishes of the young, when anything is possible.

But now it was Christmas Eve, and despite all the comfort and luxury around her, she missed Chencha and her family traditions.

At the corner light, she turned east away from Michigan Avenue, into a street where the crowds lessened. The afternoon sun was beginning to settle in the early evening sky. She looked at her watch and realized it was three o'clock, and in a few hours it would already be the dark of the Midwestern winter.

In Cuba, the sun would still be hanging high in a blue, cloudless sky.

And in Pinar, she would be putting the finishing touches on her *arroz con pollo* in the large kitchen of her uncle's farm, amidst family conversation and gossip. One of her young cousins would be helping her cut the red pimentos into thin slices with which she would decorate the rice. An aunt would be boiling a few hen eggs that Isa would slice into perfect circles to add to the rice as garnish. And then, the youngest of the female cousins would help her place green peas carefully and strategically as the final touches on the rice. It would be a work of art, a work of love.

A tear trickled down her cold cheek, and Isa brushed it away with her glove, hoping it wouldn't freeze on her face. She had spent more than six-hundred U.S. dollars as if it were play money, she had walked through beautiful stores bursting with goods from around the world that she, incredibly, could afford to buy with her sister's money, she had passed several smiling Santa and cheerful street carolers full of good wishes for all. Yet, as she walked up to the front door of her sister's condominium, another tear slowly wet her face. Despite everything around her, she was sad and homesick.

"Merry Christmas, Dr. Moran," Julius smiled happily as he opened the door for her.

CHAPTER 19

Traditions

THE MARVELOUS SMELLS OF HERBS AND SPICES AND SOMETHING COOKING in the next room woke her up. Anaís looked at the small clock on the dressing table and jumped out of the bed realizing it was already eight o'clock in the morning. Diego was coming at 11! And the arroz con pollo that had to be prepared!

She ran out of the room into the small kitchen and saw Chencha smiling and stirring something in an enormous pot.

"It is almost ready." Chencha was adding ingredients to the pot. "Don Diego got us some fat chickens. And the vegetables! The things that man can find in Cuba. No scrawny onions for him."

Still, sleepy-eyed, Anaís looked inside the pot and saw the *arroz con pollo* in a soupy mix cooking on top of the stove.

"Maybe it won't taste like Isa's *arroz con pollo,* but I thought there was no point in my waiting for you to get up. Next time you can watch me make it." She covered the large clay pot with a damp cloth, being careful to tuck in the sides so that they wouldn't reach the flames underneath. Anaís realized that only once before had she seen such an enormous cooking pot on anyone's stove, and that was in Seville with her parents' parents at a local festival. She wondered where Chencha could have gotten such a wonderful piece of cookware that covered all burners of the small kitchen stove.

As if reading her mind, Chencha answered.

"This I brought from the *casa grande* when we moved here. It is very old, but," she added, "not as old as this ancient woman of yours."

They both laughed and Anaís put her arm around Chencha. Anaís

156

was getting used to Chencha regularly stating that she was ancient. "Old yes, and wonderful, too. Thank you for this," she pointed to the pot. "Cooking is not something I know how to do. Although I do bake some wonderful cookies." She said the word in English, not knowing what the Spanish equivalent was.

"*Coo-keys?*" Chencha pronounced awkwardly. "What is *coo-keys?*"

"I think you call them *galletas dulces*, Chencha. But they are nothing like those. My favorites, and the ones I like to bake, are made with chocolate dough, and small pieces of chocolates. They're called chocolate chip cookies."

Chencha licked her lips. "The word sounds terrible," she said, pondering the English, "but the taste sounds delicious."

"I'm going to make them for you."

"Child, you must remember, we are in Cuba, not America. We don't find chocolate here."

"I think I can get some," Anaís said, thinking of the glorious CUBALSE store that she had discovered with Diego.

"That's fine, but right now, what you should be doing is getting dressed and be ready to go to Pinar with Don Diego. He is very punctual, and if he told you eleven, he will be here at eleven. I need to pack a few things to eat on the way—it is more than a few hours."

"Can I help you?"

"No, child. You haven't learned to make *tripa de corazón* yet--making something from nothing is a Cuban art that maybe you will learn while you live here. I need to see what we have and what we can take with us." Anaís watched Chencha look through the small sacks that she kept in a box in the corner of the kitchen.

"Maybe a Spanish omelet." Chencha took out a few small onions and started peeling them with her over-sized, gnarled hands. Anaís walked next to her and took some of the onions.

"How many should I peel?"

"No, don't. Your hands will smell like onions."

"Chencha, that doesn't matter. How many should I peel?"

"You are as stubborn as your sister. Alright. Let's peel four."

"How about six or seven?" Anaís asked, looking at the small size of onions on the table.

"Oh, no, that's too much."

"Come on, Chencha. It's okay. I will get us some more. Remember that I have money that I brought with me."

"But where are we going to find them? They're not easy to find all the time, even when I go early to stand in line at the store."

Anaís sighed, looking at Chencha's worried face. If she could only whisk Chencha away to a supermarket in Chicago! What a thrill that probably would be for her.

"Well, don't worry about that now. Let's use seven, okay? I'm sure we are going to get hungry on that long ride you're talking about." Chencha mumbled something under her breath that Anaís couldn't understand. The old woman pulled back the damp cloth covering the *arroz con pollo* and covered it again. She started to move the pot over onto the counter. Anaís helped her lift it.

"Now it can just sit here and finish cooking in its own heat. And we need the stove for the omelets." She pulled an old iron skillet from a deep drawer under the sink and carefully measured out a little olive oil from the small bottle.

"As soon as the oil heats up, you can put the sliced onions in there and we will sauté them. Along with the green pepper that I have left."

Chencha reached inside another bag. "Here, you slice the green pepper. It won't make your hands stink." She took the onion out of Anaís' hands.

"You, too, are a stubborn woman, Chencha."

The old woman laughed, saying nothing. Anaís smiled, remembering times long ago with her mother in the kitchen. About the only thing Anaís really enjoyed doing in the kitchen was baking, especially cookies and pies. Her adopted mother's death made her regret she had not paid more attention to her culinary instructions. Maybe with Chencha she would have another chance at developing that skill.

They were done chopping and slicing and Chencha had already taken out half a dozen small eggs from the refrigerator. Again, Anaís shook her head at the size of the eggs, which looked to her like quail eggs.

"Here," Chencha handed her a bowl. "Break them and beat them while I finish with the sauté."

As she followed Chencha's directions, Anaís saw her break off some garlic cloves, and after peeling and mashing them with the back of a spoon, Chencha added them to the sauté. The room filled with a new, wonderful aroma, making Anaís hungry. She gave the bowl with the well beaten eggs to Chencha and reached for the small tin cup where she was now used to making her morning breakfast of *café con leche.*"

"Aren't you having some, Chencha?"

"I already had some."

Looking inside the small refrigerator at the remaining amount of milk in the pint-sized bottle, Anaís wondered if Chencha had indeed had breakfast or had simply left the last bit of milk for her. Anaís poured what remained in the bottle into the cup and warmed it on the stove next to the skillet with the omelet.

"Be careful with the handle," the old woman warned, handing Anaís a small towel.

Anaís added some of the Cuban coffee that Chencha kept in a glass jar to the boiling milk and added a couple of teaspoons of sugar and poured equal amounts of the coffee into two cups.

"Chencha. Here you go."

"I told you I already had some this morning."

"Well, have another one with me."

They drank their hot, sweet coffee in silence, looking at the omelet slowly cook around the edges. It looked simply delicious, and were it not for their limited resources, Anaís would have eaten it for breakfast. She was getting used to eating following Chencha's example.

"Go get ready. I'm almost done here."

"I want to see how you turn that big omelet."

"It's very simple. You slide it over the edge just a little bit so you can then slide it on a plate...then you put the skillet over the top of the plate... flip it over...and there you are."

Chencha handled the skillet like a television show chef. And the aromas...they were amazing!

"Now, really, go get ready. It's getting late, and I don't want Don Diego getting angry with me. Me, I'm going to the park for my Brigades exercise!" She shuffled toward the door. "As if I could or would use a bayonet. I'll tell them you're sick, and you get ready for Pinar."

Anaís kissed the old woman on the forehead and went to the bedroom to get dressed. She wiggled into the pants because like everything else in her sister's closet, it was half a size too small. It was not her style, but she needed to dress like Isa.

They would be spending a few days at her uncle's farm in Pinar del Río because Christmas Eve was tonight, and they would not come back to Havana until Tuesday. She didn't understand how her sister had managed to arrange that time off, and of course she couldn't ask. She packed a few other articles of clothing, a baseball cap, her toiletries and was ready to go when she heard Chencha back puttering in the kitchen. Soon Chencha was welcoming Diego into the house. He was greeting Chencha as Anaís entered the room with her small suitcase.

"Ready? Good. We have a beautiful day's ride to Pinar today."

"Don Diego, here's the *arroz con pollo* that An...that Isa made. She said something about putting it in a small ice-box?"

"Yes. Let me. I'll get that. I have a big cooler with ice so that the rice will keep." He went into the small kitchen and came out carrying the large clay pot.

"This smells wonderful, Isa."

"Yes, thank you."

"I'll put it in the car and come back for anything else you want to take." He went outside as Anaís helped Chencha pack some bread, fruit and cheese that she had laid out on the kitchen table.

"I think I'll put the omelet in the cooler too, Chencha."

"Alright. And I'll lock the door."

Outside, Diego was still trying to fit the large pot inside the Styrofoam full of ice that they had bought the previous evening.

"I think we're just going to make it...there!" He covered the cooler, and took the lid off the second one.

"I've got beer and some sausages and cheese...Darn, I forgot the bread."

"We've got that," Anaís said handing him the box that Chencha had prepared. "And there's an omelet that Chencha made that we can put in the cooler too."

It was as if she were going on a picnic with one of her friends back home. Except she was not going to the lake, nor was she with long-time friends. She was in Cuba, on Christmas Eve, with the sun shining brightly on a warm tropical day in the beautiful neighborhood of Miramar. She was a world away from her other life in the States, and she was going to a Christmas Eve gathering probably like nothing before, with her extended family. She was going with a man who intrigued and excited her with his charm and charisma as much as he frustrated her with his political views. Anaís looked at Diego's handsome profile as he continued to work on making everything fit in the coolers and in his trunk. It would be an interesting weekend.

Chencha was closing the door behind her. Diego politely took her arm and helped her get in the back seat of his car, then opened the front door for Anaís.

"Here we go." He started the car, and as Anaís turned to look at Chencha she saw the old woman making the sign of the cross first on the two of them and then on herself.

As the taxi sped down Lake Shore Drive to Richard's parents' home in Evanston, Isa had been telling Richard about her afternoon's experience shopping on Christmas Eve.

"Only crazy people shop on Michigan Avenue on Christmas Eve, Ani. Really, what possessed you?"

"You. I realized I had not gotten anything for my one true friend here in the States."

"That was not necessary. I know how much you hate to shop, decadent *Americanos* that we are, you think everything is way too expensive and it always translates to a month's salary in Cuba." He saw her grimace at him.

"I'm sorry. I don't mean to diminish the economic difficulties that all of you have in Cuba. But I think...no, I know that your sister would want you to enjoy the fact that you have money here. Yes, I'm sure it's hard to believe, but you do. And you can't keep comparing everything or feeling guilty every time you buy something. You will drive yourself crazy.

The taxi made a sharp turn off the drive and Richard slid toward Isa on the seat. "Things here are just different," he continued. "So, I hope you relax and start enjoying this new life. I know your sister would want you to."

He took a breath, smiled and said, "You know, having money doesn't mean you don't have a heart or social conscience. Your sister and I do. My parents do. One thing does not negate the other, although that might be party line back in Cuba." He patted her hand. "All that being said, I hope whatever you got me didn't cost a month's salary in Cuba."

"No. It would have been four months' salary," she replied.

"Oh, shit. How will I ever be able to enjoy it?" he teased.

"Never mind, Richard. I bought you something that I really liked, and I didn't look at the price at all, just as you've been telling me to do."

"Yes, but I give that advice for your personal purchases. Not for me."

"I haven't bought myself anything here. I can't bring myself to doing so when I have so much I can use in Anaís' place."

He pulled on her nose.

"Well, you shouldn't have gone shopping for me."

"Not to change the conversation, but guess who I ran into while I was shopping for you?" Her big, green eyes opened wide. "Jim! You know Jim, right?"

Richard fluttered an imaginary fan and with a coquettish grin said, "Who doesn't know Jim, hunk that he is. If only he weren't straight. I'd be right there. Isn't he just beautiful?"

"Yes, he is very handsome."

"And so what happened?"

"Well, he asked me why I hadn't returned his calls, and it took me a few minutes to realize who he was. I mean, Anaís gets a lot of calls, most of which I ignore or ask you about."

"But what happened? Tell me!"

"He started to tell me that he missed me, I mean, Anaís. And then he saw the...anyway, he saw what I was buying for you and said I was buying it for...that I had a new boyfriend."

"Really?"

"I know. I think now he is angry. But probably it is the best thing. I couldn't pretend to be Anaís with someone close to her ...She can straighten it out when she comes back. The hard part for me was that he looked so hurt, and I couldn't tell him the truth."

"No, you certainly cannot. Please. Don't ever believe that you can tell anyone. Your situation is very complicated. And with what is still going on with that little boy Elián...Well, I don't think anyone should know anything until the time is right. I mean, we agreed not to tell even Senator Fernández. We should not make him part of this ruse, right?"

"I agree with you, Richard."

They both kept silent, as if each were thinking about Anaís in Cuba and that they had to do everything to keep her from being discovered and putting her in danger.

"Well, let's change the subject. It's Christmas Eve. We should be happy. After all, Santa comes today, right?"

"I don't believe in Santa."

"How can you say that, *muchacha?* I believe there is a Santa. Look what he has given me already this year...the twin of my best friend."

"You are truly *dulce*, Richard. Sweet." Isa kissed him on the cheek. "But I don't believe in Santa."

"Well, whether you do or don't, remember that my mother does. In fact, remember to compliment her on her Santa collection like Anaís does every year. Mom loves to hear that from people. And just to remind you, my family has known your sister for a very long time, since she and I were both students at Northwestern in the eighties. And when her parents and husband were killed in that horrible accident...Well, my mother became very protective of your sister. Your sister has spent almost every holiday and Christmas Eve at my parents' place ever since then. Anaís is almost like a sister to me, as you are now."

Isa smiled. "Thank you, Richard. I just hope I don't say anything to make them suspicious."

"Well, maybe just don't say my name too much. You're pronouncing it much better, almost perfectly, but not every time. So call me *Ricardito*. I'll tell them it's something we started in Cuba. And anyway, I like it. It brings out the Latin in me. Yes, *Ricardito*."

"*Buena idea, Ricardito.*"

"Here we are."

The taxi had turned off the main boulevard and was driving slowly through a lovely tree-lined residential area of sprawling brick homes. It was Isa's first time seeing a Chicago suburb, and she looked at everything with the same awe and enjoyment that she felt with each new experience. The Christmas ornaments and lights made everything festive, and her earlier gloom lifted.

Richard's parents must have been waiting for them, for the wreath covered door swung open and a trim couple in their sixties ran out to greet them.

"Anaís! How great to see you again." The tall slim blonde-haired woman hugged her tightly.

"Yes, it's been too long." An older version of Richard with very thick gray hair stepped around to hug her.

"Well, never mind me," Richard teased, standing behind Isa. The couple hugged their son in unison.

"Who are you? Are you crashing this party?" They all laughed. Isa felt drawn by their warmth.

"Come on in. It's really getting cold out here."

They stepped into a large marble foyer with a circular oak stairway leading to a second floor. A beautiful Persian rug beneath a round accent table in the middle of the foyer accented the deep wine colors of the walls and the elegant furniture. On the accent table, Isa saw the flower arrangement she had sent them.

"Anaís, the flowers are absolutely beautiful. My favorite, as you know. Thank you so much. They bring such a wonderful promise of spring, when you have roses in the house in the dead of winter, don't you think?"

She helped Anaís with her fur coat while chattering with her husband and Richard about how lovely Anaís looked with short hair.

"And I love your coat. Is it new? I've told Phil that if any of those radical anti-fur people that walk on Michigan Avenue every so often ever dared to spray my coat...well, I don't know what I'd do to them."

"Alright, mother, let's not get into that again."

"But, Phil. They just did something like that last week, right in front of Saks."

"Oh, my God!" Richard pretended to grab his heart in shock. "In front of Saks, no less. What are we coming to?"

"Don't make fun of your mother, Richie."

Isa listened to the conversation and looked around at the beautiful home. Everywhere, there were Christmas decorations and holiday details that Isa had never seen in her entire life. Finally, they went into what the parents called the great room and Isa almost gasped as they entered and saw the twenty-foot Christmas tree lit up with hundreds of Christmas lights and decorations.

"It is so beautiful!"

"It's the same size as we get every year, but, yes, it still makes me gasp too, Anaís," Richard's mother said.

"And the Santa Claus collection," Isa said as she approached a collection of forty or fifty different types of Santas, "they are so special. How long did you say you have been collecting these, Rose?"

"Well, all my life I think. A few of them were given to me by my grandmother before she died, but the rest...well, every year while we're on trips, I look for a special Santa. Which is your favorite, Anaís? I can't remember which one you picked out last year."

"I can't either, Rose. They are all so beautiful, I don't know how I dared to choose just one. Although," she picked up a very vintage looking Santa, "this one is particularly beautiful."

"That's one from my grandmother's collection," Rose said lovingly

165

looking at the velvet robed wooden Santa. "That's one of my favorites, too. How about if we get the hors d'oeuvres, Anaís, and let the men catch up with each other. I don't think we've seen Richard since you both got back from Cuba. And how was that, by the way? It must have been quite an experience going back to the country where you were born."

They walked into a large kitchen with an extensive island surrounded by half a dozen bar stools. Rose took the prepared dishes out of the double-sided refrigerator and handed them to Isa. The younger woman uncovered artfully decorated bite-sized morsels of food. Rose went to another refrigerator and took out more hors d'oeuvres. Isa stared at the large amounts of food.

"We'll start with these. And the dinner, it's from Estefano's, I think one of your favorites."

"Yes, it is Rose. Thanks for being so considerate and remembering."

"You're like one of our family. You know how much Phil and I loved your parents and your husband. And..." she whispered in her ear as they headed for the door out of the kitchen, "you're my last hope in straightening out our Richard."

Richard looked up at the women as they entered the great room laughing.

"Are you still trying to have Anaís turn me into a heterosexual, mother?" he chided.

"You never know." Rose set down a couple of the plates and smiled up at her son. "If anyone could, this beautiful woman would be my bet." She looked at Isa. "I love you, honey. But I would like to be a grandmother before I die. So maybe you can do that for me, whether you're straight or not."

"Mother!"

They all laughed, and Isa understood why Richard was such a loving man. It was her first experience with a family since arriving from Cuba, and though they didn't speak Spanish and she was in plush surroundings, the friendly, familial bantering was a lot like being in Pinar with her own relatives. The cheese puffs tasted like nothing she had ever eaten before. Richard smiled at her. Christmas Eve would be alright after all.

The ride to Pinar del Río had gone very quickly for Anaís as she and Diego talked about sports. Every time Diego would bring up politics, Anaís changed the subject. So far, the only political opinion that they shared was that the little boy Elián González should be returned immediately to his father in Cuba.

"Can you imagine those Americans holding one of our own Cuban citizens hostage for a month now? That would not be tolerated if the tables were turned around. If we had done such a thing here in Cuba to an American child, you can be sure our skies would be full of U.S. bombers threatening to blow us off the face of the earth. And yet, here they are, giving in one more time to the Cubans in the U.S. who want to see us all dead here in Cuba."

"I agree with you one-hundred percent. We...I mean, the American government, has no business letting the uncle keep that boy one more minute. He belongs with his father. And I am sure many Americans feel the same way."

"No, they don't! They hate the Cuban people. Any chance they have to mess with us—they do so."

"How can all Americans hate all Cubans? We don't even know each other?"

Diego looked at her puzzled. "What are you saying? That they understand our position in Cuba?"

Anaís felt maybe she had sounded much too forceful in her opinion, something perhaps her sister didn't do. "I don't think anyone can understand what someone else is going through, unless they find themselves in that exact position." She realized she was also talking about her own situation with her sister. "But most parents in any part of the world, including the United States, must feel that children belong with their parents, regardless of anything else."

Diego was silent, and Anaís hoped that he would not continue the subject. She remembered Chencha's comment about having one opinion but saying what was politically correct and that Cubans learned to live that way. Probably her sister didn't often express any political opinion, and here she was being her frank American self. She worried that she had somehow made Diego uncomfortable or suspicious. "Oh, look," she said trying to distract them from the confrontation. "Up there. What are they selling by the roadside?"

Diego slowed down as they approached a family of farmers selling produce. "Probably some fruit. Would you like some?"

"Only if it's something we didn't bring with us. I am getting hungry, aren't you?"

"Yes, I am, actually. Let's get out here and eat. I'll buy a few things for us."

Diego pulled his car off the road a few yards ahead of the farmers.

Chencha got out with them and asked Diego to open the trunk so that she could take out the food she had brought. Diego carried the cooler to a nearby tree and set it down underneath its sprawling branches. The old woman followed slowly behind. Anaís walked over to the family by the road.

"*Buenos días.*"

"*Buenos días, señorita.*" Anaís looked at the ruggedly lined faces of the man and woman sitting on makeshift crates. They were both extremely thin, small built people who probably were much younger than they appeared. The man wore a white time-worn shirt and dark pants. The woman's long skirt and blouse were frayed at the seams. They both smiled at Anaís as she looked at the few vegetables and fruits that they were selling.

"How much for the tomatoes?"

"Six for a dime. And the bananas...three bunches for a dime."

"I'll take them."

The man counted the tomatoes into her hands, and looking at the small bunches of bananas, she pulled out her tee-shirt to carry her purchases. Chencha and Diego laughed as she approached with her bulging shirt.

"They look wonderful, don't they? Chencha, did we bring any salt?"

"I'm sure I put some in here for the omelet. In my old age, I'm afraid of putting too much salt on things. My taste buds aren't sharp anymore." She reached inside her paper bag and took out a small piece of folded paper, holding a small amount of salt.

"Would you like a beer? Or a soda?"

"A beer would be fine. How about you, Chencha?"

"Child. A beer for me? No, I don't drink. But a little bit of water, yes." She finished cutting up the cold omelet into quarters, and handed a piece to Diego.

"Don Diego, I hope you like it." She gave another piece to Anaís. "Here you are."

They ate their omelets with gusto under the warm winter sun filtering through the swaying branches above them. Diego sat on the ground across from the two women, and watched Anaís as she carefully washed three of the tomatoes in a little bit of the water from the bottle that Diego had brought and then sprinkling one with some of the salt, bit into its juicy pulp, red tomato juice running down her chin.

"Oh, gosh, excuse me." She dabbed at her chin with the small piece of paper from the omelet. "I'm making a mess. But this is so good. Want one?"

"No, thanks. I'm enjoying just watching you enjoy it." Diego answered.

"No, me neither. My stomach doesn't do well with raw tomatoes," Chencha observed.

"What beautiful countryside this is!" Anaís said between bites of food.

"You've seen it many times! It's the only quick way to Pinar." Diego laughed.

"Yes...but it is so beautiful. I love to be in the country. Everything is...green and beautiful. And the smells. And the blue sky. Not a cloud anywhere."

"You know, we're wasting your talents in interpreting," Diego joked. "We should put you in the marketing department to promote travel to Cuba."

"It is a beautiful country," she said softly, remembering her adoptive father's words. "A really beautiful country."

"And it belongs to us," Diego said. "And we don't have to answer to anyone. How many other countries, especially in Latin America, can say that?"

Again with the politics, Anaís thought. But this time she remained quiet and continued to admire the calm beauty of the countryside. Tree covered mountains in the distance contrasted with the golden hues of the flat landscape around her. Another car stopped next to the farmers.

"Do you think they can make a living, selling everything so cheap?" Anaís pointed to the farmers smiling at the new customers.

"I think our peasants do pretty well now that they can sell some of what they grow themselves." Diego leaned back, folding his hands behind his head. "It was a good move to experiment with a little personal enterprise." He smiled at Anaís. "As long as it doesn't overwhelm our greater sense of personal sacrifice."

He closed his eyes, and sighed. "I could just lean back here and take a siesta, but..." he stretched out his muscular, tanned arms toward the blue sky. "We better get going before I do that so that I can get you to your relatives' place in time."

They picked up the few articles that needed to be thrown away, and Diego carried the cooler back to the car. Chencha walked slowly behind them.

"Why don't you close your eyes and take a little nap, Chencha?" Anaís asked as she helped the old woman into the back seat.

"No, I'm not sleepy. I'm fine. Don't worry about me."

Anaís nodded, knowing that Chencha would soon be snoring.

"Let's get this car going so we can get some air in here." Diego said at the same time that he pulled back into the highway. They all welcomed the warm breeze through the windows, and Anaís angled the small side window to get air directly on her face, remembering her own parents' vintage car.

"Pinar is still about an hour away. Isa, how about putting on the cassette player I left in the back seat next to Chencha. I brought some wonderful old tunes. And out here, we don't get much reception of anything on the radio."

"Anything in particular?"

"Whatever you want." He winked at her, and Anaís was glad to not talk about politics or Elián. She found a Beny Moré tape, one of her American father's favorite singers.

"How about Beny?"

"That's a great selection. Alright, Doña Chencha, get those dancing shoes ready."

Anaís looked out on the green Cuban countryside, dotted by homes that were no more than one room shacks made of scraps of tin, wood and thatched roofs. The smell of burning wood and the scent of flowers filled the air. Behind her, Chencha mumbled something under her breath and closed her eyes in sleep.

Everyone eagerly awaited their arrival. As soon as Diego turned into the long driveway leading up to the big farmhouse, the people gathered on the front porch and began yelling and waving at them. Anaís felt excited and overwhelmed. These were her relatives!

She had already talked to Chencha about the Pinar family and she knew the names of almost all the heads of families. But there were so many of them now smiling and rushing up to Diego's car!

At the head of the group waiting to greet them was Tío Julio, her mother's uncle and the patriarch of the Pinar family. Tío Julio was a man in his early eighties, balding and tanned with deep green eyes like hers. His aquiline nose told of his Spanish birth as did the Castilian pronunciation in his speech. Tío Julio's wife had died a few years earlier, and now he lived alone on the old family farm. Family members who needed temporary shelter or help knew they could always stay with Tío Julio.

A group of about fifty or sixty people, all of different ages, surrounded the car.

"Isa! *Qué bueno* that you're here. Did you bring the *arroz con pollo?*"

said a young boy with sandy blonde hair.

"Goodness, boy. Isa is going to think we only want her to come so that she can bring her *arroz*," Tío Julio said, then adding in a soft voice. "And even if that's true, we shouldn't let on, you know."

Everyone laughed as Tío Julio walked up to Anaís and gave her a big bear hug.

"It's so good to see you, Isa. You have stayed away too long, my daughter."

"Hola, Tío Julio. This is Diego..."

"We know Diego around here, Isa. Although it indeed has been a long time. Welcome back, Diego. We are so glad that you will be spending such an important day with us. Because you will stay with us, won't you? We have a terrific suckling on the spit in back." He winked and whispered. "This year it weighed the same as Aunt Petra." Tío Julio patted Diego on the back, while Anaís continued kissing everyone greeting her.

Saying hello to her real family, a family she had not known even existed until a month ago, was exhilarating. She wished she could memorize their faces, their mannerisms. Instead they simply were a blur of handsome faces with different hair color, some with dark eyes and others green eyes just like hers. Anaís found herself hugging everyone tightly, as if trying to keep a little of them inside. After 38 years, to finally meet people who were part of her bloodline, people who shared her own gene pool and heritage was a miracle, a dream come true.

Diego and Chencha were unloading the food in the trunk with help from a lot of family members. Anaís went to help them.

"No," Diego said. "You go and enjoy your family. It's been a long time since you've been with them it seems. And first things, first," he said taking out the large clay pot with the *arroz con pollo*. "To the kitchen."

"Through here" one of the aunts said, leading the way. Anaís followed along, trying not to stare too much in any direction as she curiously looked at everything around her. Her uncle's farm was a large rectangular adobe place, reminding her a little of houses she had seen in the Southwest in the States. A wide wooden porch wrapped itself around the house. The front door was beautifully carved cherry with bird and flower motifs, and inside, the foyer was ample and the terrazzo floors reflected the light pouring in from all sides through open windows. From the foyer, one could see straight through to the back porch, where some people were sitting around on the ground or on chairs, and beyond the porch, a big open space framed a large brown barn in the background.

The furniture in the living room was old, but looked comfortable and inviting with its wooden frames and soft fabric cushions. Dozens of pictures hung on all the walls, some in black and white, sepia and color. Anaís couldn't wait to come back to look at them. They passed hallways that lead to rooms on either side of the living and dining room areas in the center, and children were running in and out of the front and back doors. This low, rambling home with its buff colored stucco exterior and spacious interior of high ceilings, white washed walls, cool stone floors and red tiled roof was nothing like the poor living quarters they had passed on the road.

"Don't run, little ones." Tío Julio admonished them, and Anaís saw that they slowed down their run until they were out of their uncle's sight and then started their run again.

"Through here, Diego."

Finally Tío Julio swung open a door that opened up into a large, old kitchen where at least a dozen women were milling around tables and counters. "Isa!" some of the women who had not been at the greeting line exclaimed, coming up to hug and kiss her. "Finally you are here. We were wondering about..."

"Yes, I know" Anaís said, "the *arroz con pollo.*" She laughed, feeling she could joke with them.

"I've got the eggs ready," someone said.

"And can we cut up the pimentos with you?" two young beautiful teenagers asked, their swinging, long ponytails reminding her of her once long hair.

"Yes," a small little blonde girl said as she pushed her way between the older girls and Isa, "but I get to put on the green peas with Isa at the end, isn't that right? Her round chubby face looked up at Anaís.

Anaís looked for Chencha. The woman was talking to some of the older women in the room.

"Alright," she finally said. "This is what we're going to do this year. I'm just going to stand back and see if you remember what I've shown you in the past. I'm just going to watch, and you yourselves are going to finish up the *arroz con pollo*. What do you think?"

The teenagers and little girl almost jumped for joy. "Can we? You trust us?"

"Of course I do. And it's time that someone else also made this."

"Oh, no. No one makes it like you."

"*Bueno*, we'll see. But let's get going with it."

"Yes, let's hurry, Isa," the little blonde girl, whose name was Blanca, added. "Because then we have to go make the necklaces for dinner, don't we."

What? Another tradition? Chencha hadn't said anything about making necklaces. And how could they make necklaces for dinner? One thing at a time, she told herself, as she placed the large clay pot with the famous *arroz con pollo* on one of the long counters that lined the large room.

"This is why your cousins can't wait to see you, Isa," one of the older women whispered to her as she took down some spices from the upper cabinets. "You spoil them so with all your special ways with them." The woman kissed her on the cheek. A wonderful warmth filled her as she looked around the bustling kitchen, full of chatter and laughter. "We have missed you," her aunt added.

Anaís looked out the kitchen window at the men taking out long rectangular tables from the red barn and placing them one end butted with the other to form a long dinner table. Diego was among them, in a sleeveless t-shirt that showed off his beautiful and tanned muscular torso. She could hear the men's voices rise in laughter, then become quiet and soft again, as if they were sharing raunchy jokes not to be heard by the women.

Anaís thought how much more she would rather be outside, helping with the tables, out in the beautiful mid-afternoon December sun, than inside in the hot kitchen, pretending to know what the younger cousins were doing to the rice dish. Every once in a while, she would look at their progress and encourage them with a compliment, but her interest was more in looking at all the people, the strangers around her who were, in fact, her family. She tried to remember the names she heard, and some stuck easier in her head than others. There were at least four generations of family members on the farm today, all part of her mother's extended family of eight brothers and sisters. Women who looked her age appeared to be the mothers of the teenagers, and younger women ran after young children or cradled babies. For someone like Anaís, who had spent quiet holiday meals with her American parents or with Richard's family, the festive commotion for this Christmas Eve dinner was quite incredible.

"¡*Perfecto*!" she said looking at the rice. "I think you have done a better job than I could have." She looked at the beaming faces. "And what do we do now?"

"How about if I just cover it up again until we need to warm it up tonight?" Chencha asked coming over. "It looks delicious." She winked at Anaís.

"Okay, let's go!" Blanca was saying, pulling on Anaís pants. "Let's go make the necklaces."

"No, I have to help here..."

"Oh, no, you go ahead." One of the aunts pushed her out the door. "And see if maybe you can get your friend Diego to help you." She smiled a suggestive smile.

Blanca was pulling her out the back door, which slammed loudly behind them on its hinges and stopped the men's low conversation with a start.

"¿*Qué pasa?*" Tío Julio asked from the middle of the group.

"*Nada*. We're going to make necklaces," Anaís waved back.

"You mean you don't want to take a ride before dinner? Lucero has been looking forward to it." Her uncle walked toward her.

A ride? Horses! Of course, they would have horses here. How absolutely wonderful. It was indeed one of her passions since childhood. "Oh, Tío, *sí*. I'd love to ride." Anaís looked at Blanca's dejected face. "But I promised Blanca...." She said looking around at half a dozen little ones that had followed Blanca. "We're going to make necklaces."

"Well, we'll wait for you if you want. We still have some other things to do for tonight. We'll wait for you." Tío Julio patted her on the back. "You go make your necklaces with the girls and I'll see you in a while."

"*Gracias.*" She found herself impulsively kissing him on the cheek. Tío Julio's weathered face crinkled as he put an arm around her shoulders.

"You look so much like your mother, Isa. I miss you when you don't come around. When you're here, I feel like I'm visiting with you and with her."

"I'll come more often from now on, Tío. I promise."

"*Bueno,* off with you and all these kids." He patted some of the little heads.

The girls pulled her along, running and pushing each other to be the one nearest Anaís. She remembered that Isa had told her she had miscarried twice during her marriage. Anaís thought of her own hopes for children and how those dreams had been dashed when her husband was killed.

"Look!" One of the little girls was saying to Anaís as they ran along the dirt road. Anaís caught her breath at the sight of an entire grove of bright red poinsettias. She had never seen anything like it, and they seemed so odd amidst brambly bushes and other vegetation.

"We're going to make a whole bunch of necklaces today, don't you think Isa?" Blanca was saying.

"I should imagine so, Blanca. These are beautiful!"

The girls dropped to the ground next to one of the red bushes and started picking flowers with long stems and putting them on their laps. Anaís watched the small troupe of florists. It was enchanting to watch them carefully and intently wrapping the end of one stem with another, allowing the red flowers to dangle beautifully as they finished making the necklaces. She was reminded of making leis in Maui on a trip with her parents when she was young.

"Now, how many do you think we should make?"

"Oh, at least a hundred!"

"We don't need a hundred, Blanca! Boys don't wear these," another cousin argued.

"How about if we just count out loud the names of all of us who are girls?" Anaís suggested, thinking it might help her remember her relatives' names.

The little ones started naming aunts and female cousins until they had reached almost 30.

"And there are the babies too," she added.

"Not for the babies!" her cousin disagreed. "Even if they are girls, they'll still want to eat the flowers!"

"Yes, not for the babies." They all agreed.

The ground next to them was soon lined with a few dozen poinsettia necklaces. One of the cousins put one round Anaís' neck.

"You look beautiful, Isa."

"*Gracias, Marisol.*"

"Hey, you can't put them on until dinner," one of the little girls was telling another.

"Yes, we'll all save them for later," Anaís said, placing hers carefully on the ground. "They are very fragile and it's going to be a long night."

Everyone went back to chattering and making necklaces. By the time they counted 30, the group was getting somewhat rambunctious and she realized it was time to go back to the house. She asked the little ones to stand up and stretch out their arms. Ceremoniously, she hung two or three necklaces carefully on each arm. The little girls marched slowly and carefully many feet apart from each other in a single file of glowing red flowers up to the old farm house. As they approached, they could hear the laughter from both outside and inside the house as the relatives saw the red marching band.

"You come up with such things, Isa," exclaimed her uncle. Everyone helped take the necklaces off the tired young arms and placed the necklaces on the tables now covered with white tablecloths. The young girls shook their arms and moaned exaggeratedly about their hard work.

"Well, good. Because it's time for a nap," Tío Julio was saying. "But first, wash those arms and hands. We don't need anyone getting a rash from those flowers. Now, who's going to ride for a while?"

Anaís was happy to hear that they had not gone to ride without her. Diego was standing at the door of the barn, watching her with a smile. They had hardly had any time together since they got to the farm, since all the women and men had separated into their separate groups and tasks. She hoped he would ride with them. Perhaps he even liked horses like she did.

"You're going to ride Lucero, right?" Tío Julio asked as they walked to the barn. "He misses you. I don't think he likes anyone else riding him as much as he likes you."

"Julio!" a woman's voice from the house made them both look back. One of the aunts was motioning for him to come in.

"What's going on now?" he grumbled, as he started to walk back to the house. "You get the horses saddled up. I'll be back in a minute."

A few of the younger cousins were heading into the barn ahead of her. Diego had not taken his eyes of her. Anaís knew because she, too, tried to catch a glimpse of him through the corner of her eye.

"All finished with the girls?" he teased.

"They are a lot of fun. But they can also really tire me out. Are you riding with us?"

"Of course. Although I don't know if your uncle has enough horses. This family keeps growing and there are a lot of people here that I don't know."

"Yes, I know, there are a lot of us."

"Well, lucky you. For me, after my grandparents and great-aunt died, that was it. Now I only come to Pinar when I really need to relax and if I want to see some faces and places from childhood. And I just stay at one of the small hotels in town. But this, to see your family again, it's great." He paused. "I hope you don't mind...I accepted your uncle's invitation to stay for dinner."

Anaís felt her heart quiver.

"No, that's...that's good." She tried not to sound overly happy. "Yes, that's fine."

"Good," he said, opening the barn door.

Inside the dark barn, the musty smells of hay, feed, old wood and rusting tools was surprisingly familiar. The barn was large, with a tall ladder leaning in a corner leading to the second floor where old trunks and farm equipment were stored. At the far end of the barn, she saw her cousins stepping into the sunlight outdoors again, and she guessed that the stables were around the corner. She hoped Lucero, the horse Isa favored, was true to his name and had a white marking on his forehead so that she would recognize him.

The stables were old but well maintained, like everything on the farm. Anaís quickly counted over a dozen stalls and almost the same number of horses. She looked around as each of the cousins started taking their horses out into the afternoon sunshine. She was happy to see that the horses were in good shape, and wondered how Tío Julio managed to do so considering the lack of food she had seen everywhere in Cuba.

There were three horses left in their stalls, and as she and Diego approached, the face of a beautiful dark brown beauty turned toward them, showing off a diamond shaped marking on his forehead.

"Lucero!" she cried entering the stall. Lucero in turn, nudged her playfully as she dug her face into his strong muscular neck as if they had always known each other. She had loved horses her entire life, and her family had owned a few horses over the years when she was young. Her riding lessons had made her a strong and confident rider, and it had been one of her passions throughout college. Then busy with work and marriage the times for riding had lessened to a few times a year. Patting Lucero, the smells of the stable, seeing her cousins and their friends readying the horses—it all made Anaís feel like she was back in her youth. She felt suddenly even more connected to her Cuban family. She heard Tío Julio behind her and they smiled at each other.

"I'm telling you, he misses you, even though everyone rides him to keep him in shape." He took the saddle from the hook on the wall and handed it to Diego, pointing to a beautiful black gelding in the next stall. "Here, you take mine. Marissa wants me to do I don't know what with the grandchildren before their nap. I'll ride with you tomorrow. Enjoy!"

They followed Tío Julio out of the stables with the horses.

"I can't believe your uncle," Diego commented as they both watched the old man jog his way toward the farmhouse. "He looks great, and he's what, seventy-something?"

"Almost eighty, I think."

She looked at Lucero. No wonder he was Isa's favorite. She saddled him up quickly and jumped on.

"Come on," she chided Diego.

"Hold on, woman. I've become a city boy, and I'm slower at this."

"Well, then I guess you'll just have to catch up." Laughing, she led Lucero at a slow trot following her cousins. Diego hurriedly buckled the last strap and mounting his horse, galloped after them into the Cuban countryside.

"That was an absolutely wonderful dinner, Richard."

Isa laid her head back on the taxi seat and looked at her friend in the seat next to her.

"I had such a good time. Your parents are wonderful, and they made me feel so much at home with them. Thank you, thank you, again."

He took her gloved hand in his.

"You are family to us, Isa. Your sister has always been family to us, and now you as well. Of course, my parents don't know there are two of you. But they will love you for yourself when they know the whole truth about all this. And when you both are here, well, there will be five of us for Christmas dinner...Or maybe, if we all get lucky and have significant others, then it'll be a bigger group. My mother loves to entertain."

Significant others. Isa guessed that meant *novios*. Her relationships in the last few years had been short-lived and physical. She missed the closeness of true love.

And Richard. It was so strange hearing him talk about boyfriends. She had known homosexuals in Cuba, but never as close friends.

"You know, I think it's wonderful the way your parents don't have any problem with the fact that you are, how do you say it here again...

happy...?"

"Gay," he laughed. "Yes, gay does mean happy. But nowadays, in this country it means homosexual." He stopped. "Yes, they are wonderful now with my life. But you remember..." he looked at her. "I'm sorry. You don't remember, it's Anaís who remembers, that it wasn't always good with my parents. Ani and I were in college when I finally realized that I didn't hang out with her only because of her, but because of the gorgeous guys that were always around her." He seemed to be reminiscing. "She was very popular at Northwestern. Always had more men interested in her than anyone has a right to have."

"Anyway," he took off his gloves "I think it was sophomore year when I had my first gay sex. And I knew. And I told you...I told Ani...she was the first person I told. Ani was surprised, but not shocked. She never asked why or are you sure like my parents did." He sighed.

"They had a very hard time with it for a very long time. I mean, they said that they didn't, but then there would be the comments to not bring my 'friend' to some function or other. And my 'friend' was never invited to their house, and when I brought him, whoever he happened to be at the time, Mom and Dad were not the warm people you saw today." He stopped again, reminiscing. "Oh, no. My father at first would physically look repelled, and my mother...God bless her, she tried, but it never seemed genuine to me."

A long pause followed, and Isa looked at her friend's pained face. "So how did it get better?" she finally asked.

"I guess it started to change about ten years ago, when Steve and I met, and he was the first man I really, really wanted to spend the rest of my life with. I told my parents that we were going to live together, and when they reacted in their usual shocked 'you can't do that...think about what our friends will say', I told them I wouldn't be back to see them until they could accept me and Steve and my lifestyle. It shocked them into going for therapy, and things have worked out. It took a while, but it's worked out." He paused. "Steve and I didn't work out, sadly enough. But my parents came through for me." He leaned back and laughed. "Although they're still always, I think, secretly hoping that Ani can change me back to straight so I can give them a grandchild."

"That is strange," Isa agreed.

"Do you want children?" he asked her.

"I was married for ten years in Cuba. We married young, and never really took any precautions not to have them. I come...Anaís and I, that is, come from a big family on my mother's side. My father was an only child of an only child...that kind of thing. But on my mother's side, she was one of eight, and each of those aunts and uncles have four or five kids each. Well, the point is that I never wondered about the possibility of having a problem conceiving. But after we were married for a couple of years and I hadn't gotten pregnant, we started to worry...Anyway, we went to doctors. Cuba does have great medical help if you know the right people. They put me on some medication...I got pregnant twice, but miscarried twice."

"I'm so sorry, Isa. I didn't mean to..."

"No, I don't mind. It's been a long time now. My husband was a pilot. He trained with the Soviets. In fact, I stayed with him one summer in the Soviet Union where I continued my Russian studies while he trained. I had one of my miscarriages there." She stopped and looked at Richard. "If you don't have to, don't go to that country. And certainly, don't get sick there. I thought Cuba had problems, but the Soviet Union...and it is cold, even in the summer. And always gray and gloomy. And the people are gray and gloomy, also. A horrible place."

Isa leaned again Richard's shoulder and yawned. "Anyway, we went back to Havana after that, and we tried again and I got pregnant for the second time. Then he went back to the Soviet Union...it was right before the wall came down. He was killed in a military exercise, or that's what they told me. I lost the baby."

Richard took her still cold hand in his. He rubbed it, and kissed it. "I'm so sorry. That must be a terrible thing to go through."

"Yes, I don't wish it on anyone." She looked at his kind face. "And poor Anaís didn't have any children either. That too is so sad. Twin sisters and no children."

"Yes, it is. In her case, I think they both wanted to establish themselves in their careers so they put off starting a family, and then when they were ready...well, another horrible tragedy. But, hey, you both are young women. And nowadays, here in the States at least, you hear of women having healthy children into their late forties."

"I think first you have to love someone and want to have their child. Even here in the States, right?"

"Well, it sometimes happens in that order."

They laughed as the taxi pulled up to her apartment building. "Don't get out, Richard. It's too cold. Thank you for a wonderful evening, and for the beautiful gift."

"You, too," he kissed her first on one cheek and then the other. "Thank you for spending time with us, and for the beautiful sweater." He hugged her tight. "And thank you for being you--my new best friend that I've known forever."

He waved through the window as Isa dashed out of the taxi in the cold, windy night. The night watchman held the door for her.

"Thank you, Julius. And Merry Christmas."

"Merry Christmas to you, Dr. Moran."

CHAPTER 20

First Snow

EVEN THOUGH SHE WAS VERY TIRED, ISA DECIDED THAT SHE WOULD STAY up and wait for the snowfall that they were predicting that evening. Christmas Eve in Chicago in Anaís' beautiful condo was lonely but spectacular. She put on one of her sister's holiday CDs and sat in front of the fire in the living room, looking out at Lake Michigan traffic and the dark lake beyond the breakers.

Snow. It had always held a strange fascination for her when she had seen it in movies. It always looked so beautiful, so white and clean. She couldn't wait to see the first flakes drop.

The sounds coming from the stereo faded into the background as she sipped her hot chocolate and thought about how pampered she felt in Anaís' apartment. She looked at her cup, filled with small marshmallows and whipped cream, all wonderful novelties for her that didn't exist in Cuba. A warmth filled her heart as she remembered her sister's last word in the short conversation that they had a few weeks before: *Enjoy.* It said volumes to her.

As twins, they seemed to understand each other from the moment they met, and so, even though it was difficult to believe that Anaís did not miss all her creature comforts, something inside Isa made her believe that her sister was being sincere when she said she was enjoying her Cuba experience as her ultimate adventure. Anaís had insisted she would make do with everything. Isa hoped that meant she would use the money their parents had left them hidden in the porcelain dolls. Still, she prayed that her sister would be able to weather the hardships that Isa knew were part of life on the island.

Isa thought back to her own big adventure when as a young teenager, she had been part of Castro's mandatory Youth Brigade that went into one of the more remote areas of the Sierra Maestra to set up a school and medical facility for a small farming community. Her life had never been comfortable in the way now she saw was possible, but even her Havana city life had not prepared her for the struggles that she and her companions endured during their six month stay in the Cuban mountain village.

To reach the small community, the trip in the old school jeep had taken 22 hours from Havana due to the lack of good roads outside the city limits. The young group found themselves traveling in sweltering heat on narrow gravel or dirt roads which sometimes disappeared beneath a thick overgrowth of trees and shrubbery. She smiled remembering the youthful enthusiasm with which she and the rest of the group initially tackled the jungle barriers with their machetes. However, after the 20th day of clearing the brush under the blazing heat of the country sun, they were exhausted and complained about the situation, much to the disdain of the group leader, a stout, staunch revolutionary woman in her late twenties who reprimanded them for being soft and not being true to the Revolution. Isa remembered they had all kept quiet after that, but in her mind she kept grumbling and wishing she were anywhere else but there.

Once at the town, they were shown with much respect and gratitude to their home for the duration of their stay, a six by six-foot dirt floor shack with tin walls and a roof made from the fallen fronds of the palm trees that were everywhere in the dense forest. There, her group of ten companions, half male and half female, plus their two team leaders spent the six months in hammocks that hung at different heights and angles from every corner. It was also there that Isa had lost her virginity one oppressively humid and hot afternoon when the rest of the group, except for herself and Sergio, had gone to the river to wash clothes.

Sergio. She still remembered his thick lips, his ebony body pressing on hers, the smell of wood in his short curly hair, his large caressing hands on her breasts, inside of her. They had been inseparable after that. "Students today, laborers tomorrow, soldiers for the revolution, always."

The Revolutionary chant echoed in her mind as she sipped more hot chocolate, grabbing some marshmallows with her tongue.

She simply loved how marshmallows tasted. And she loved the whipped cream that seemed to be on so many types of desserts here in the United States. They were exotic tastes to her, just as the salty taste of Sergio's body had been on her lips when she was fifteen years old.

The memory of that magnificent afternoon of physical discoveries blended with the warmth of the hot chocolate and darkness around her. Isa's eyes started to feel heavy. She fought the drowsiness wanting to stay awake for the snow, but soon she was asleep on the couch.

She awoke to the ringing of the phone. Startled, she stumbled off the couch in the direction of the phone on the console against the far wall of the living room. Who could be calling? She looked at the clock on the table. Two thirty in the morning! Goodness! What could be wrong?

"Hello?" she pushed short curls of hair out of her eyes.

"Are you looking out the window?" She recognized the voice immediately. It was Richard. For a moment, it made no sense to her that he would ask that question, but her eyes still went to the windows across from where she stood. There, through the darkness, it looked like small floating pieces of cotton brightened the blackness of the night.

"Snow!"

"It just started," Richard was saying. "I thought you might want to know."

"Oh, Richard," she muttered, her eyes glued on the snow falling outside. "Thank you, *sí*, yes! I was waiting for it and fell asleep. But I have to go. I want to go outside."

"It's two thirty, Ani," he reminded her.

"I know," she replied. "I don't care. I want to be outside."

"Well, it definitely is beautiful, but remember that it's also going to be very cold at this time of the morning." Richard had that parental tone he used when warning her about life in the States.

"I know." Isa couldn't wait to get off the phone. "I'll put on everything that I have to. Don't worry. I'll see you tomorrow." She was about to hang up when she remembered one more thing. "*Gracias*, Richard."

"*De nada*," he replied before hanging up. "And, Merry Christmas."

"*Feliz Navidad* to you, too, Richard."

She ran into her bedroom and grabbed the clothes she had left on her bed. Throwing off her bathrobe and pulling on her sweat clothes and socks, she wondered if everyone in Chicago also waited for the first snow with anticipation. She couldn't wait to finish dressing and go out to see it.

Running to the closet and taking her coat, she almost forgot her keys in her rush to get out of the apartment. The elevator came immediately. What would Jake, the late evening doorman, think about her going out at this time of the morning?

As she walked through the glass door out into the foyer, Jake was stuffing a piece of pizza in his mouth. Sheepishly, he hid the plate behind his desk and cleaned his mouth with a napkin.

"Dr. Moran. Is everything alright?" he said as he finished swallowing food.

"Oh, I woke up for some reason and couldn't go back to sleep. I saw that it was snowing. I wanted to come out to see it."

"Really?" Jake replied, watching her go through the revolving doors. "You're going out now? Do you want me to come out and keep an eye on you?"

"No, Jake, thank you. I'm just going to walk to the corner for a few minutes. That's all."

"Well, I'm gonna keep an eye on you anyway. You never know. This is Chicago," he replied.

Yes, this certainly is Chicago, a world and a lifetime away from anything she had ever known. The cold air made her catch her breath as much as the sense of awe at seeing the white, weightless flakes falling heavily from the sky. The sidewalk was already covered with snow, and she looked at her footprints in the snow, remembering walks on the sand of Varadero Beach.

She put her hand out to catch flakes, but they didn't last long on the warmth of her glove. Closing her eyes, she felt them falling on her face, hanging on her eyelashes. They were weightless for a few seconds before turning wet on her eyelids. She stuck out her tongue, trying to catch the thick flakes tumbling recklessly down on her. She could not tell if the slight tingling feeling all over her face and in her body was her own excitement over the magical snow which enveloped her like a whirlwind or merely the cold Chicago wind.

"*Feliz Navidad, Anaís.* Thank you for letting me be here," she whispered to her sister across the miles. "I hope you have the best Christmas ever in Pinar with our family."

CHAPTER 21

More Pinar

THE RIDE WITH HER COUSINS AND DIEGO HAD BEEN EXHILARATING. THE cousins seemed to enjoy ribbing each other about everything and telling racy jokes. Even Diego had shown his raunchy streak. After nearly two hours, they all decided to head back, knowing that they needed to rest if they were to be awake for the long night of celebration ahead.

They came into the quiet, sleeping house almost giddy from the energizing ride, but were immediately shushed by Chencha and a few of the older women keeping vigil over the various meals cooking on the stoves. Anaís followed her female cousins as the women and men headed in opposite directions towards darkened bedrooms. She found herself in a large room where more than a dozen children and women napped on cots covered with worn mosquito netting. One working ceiling fan creaked softly, circulating the warm, humid air.

Her cousins took off their clothes and lay in underwear on the empty cots at one end and Anaís followed their example. After a few minutes of chatter, everyone seemed to fall asleep, but Anaís couldn't close her eyes, interested in looking at everything around her.

The room had many windows on one side, where very old blinds were closed to keep the light from disturbing anyone's sleep. It smelled of old wood and fresh flowers. Two old dressers with mirrors were the only other pieces of furniture in the sparsely furnished room. The only other items in the room were a great number of old posters and banners of different Latino singers and baseball teams that covered the walls almost from floor to ceiling, and a few tourist banners from the U.S. The yellowed banners of Washington, D.C. and the Empire State Building were silent reminders of a pre-Castro time when travel between the U.S. and Cuba was common among middle and upper class Cubans.

Anaís wondered which of her relatives had visited the United States during those years before the embargo. Suddenly, she remembered the walls lined with family pictures in the living area and realized that this would be a perfect time to explore the house. It seemed that everyone had taken Tío Julio's advice to take a siesta.

She slowly moved her netting aside and grabbed her jeans. The terrazzo floor felt cool to her bare feet and she quietly slid past sleeping children and snoring mothers and out the heavy wooden door. She paused a minute outside the room and looked around to see if anyone was about. The house was perfectly quiet. The only sound she could hear in the distance was the soft rattling of shades against the windows.

Anaís slid past closed doors, assuming they were bedrooms. Outside a room with the door half-ajar she listened for voices, and hearing no one, stepped in, closing the door behind her. The smell of tobacco was very strong and still fresh, as if Tío Julio and the uncles had just finished their afternoon cigars.

The room was a mini-casino, complete with a large roulette table and smaller tables for playing cards, dice and even chess. In a corner, the humidors on the tables next to comfortable, old armchairs signaled the spot where uncles probably relaxed with a Cuban after a few unlucky rounds at 21. The walls were bare, save for a few water color and oil paintings of rural country scenes that looked like the Cuban landscapes they had passed on their way to Pinar. She wondered if there would be gambling on Christmas Eve.

A door at one extreme of the large game room was also slightly open, and Anaís again listened for voices. She continued her curious investigation. This room was totally different, much smaller and more feminine, with frilly curtains on the windows and soft hued cushions on the brown textured sofas. A small antique looking sewing machine stood silently on one end, anchored on both ends by baskets full of neatly folded fabrics and spools of thread, testifying that it was still used. This room, too, had comfortable chairs with side tables similar to the ones in the casino room, but these tables held no humidors, but rather newspapers and magazines. The walls had pictures of faces she did not recognize.

This room led out to the main living area, which she assumed was the main room in the house. She was quiet as she entered the living room, full of couches, sofas and armchairs of different styles. But the most interesting aspect were the walls with pictures from floor to ceiling.

Anaís started at one end, glancing at unknown faces as if she were looking at a friend's family album. Mostly the photos were in black and white or sepia, but a few here and there were in color. The walls were a mish-mash of periods in time and events. She saw many weddings and birthday parties. Many photographs were of children and couples. She thought she recognized her Tío Julio and a couple of the aunts in younger years and more recently with their grown children and grandchildren.

And then she saw her parents.

The two faces that had now become part of her psyche, the faces that she saw every night before she closed her eyes, and that she saw even after she closed her eyes, looked back at her from the shore of a beautiful beach. Her mother wore a two-piece flowered bathing suit and a wide brimmed straw hat that cast a long shadow on her full cleavage. Her father held a glass in his hand, his profile smiling at his beautiful young wife.

Anaís couldn't resist touching the photograph with her fingers, wanting to caress them. Her eye caught another picture of them, this time sitting on a bench under a beautiful banyan tree, looking dapper in their fifties clothing. She looked above and found at least half a dozen more pictures of her parents in different settings, with family members or by themselves. None, however, were with her or Isa.

"I don't have any pictures of you with your parents" she heard Tío Julio's deep voice behind her. She turned to see the kind, weathered face of her uncle looking at her with sadness. His green eyes were sunken, and dark circles showed the effects of time and hardship.

"I don't have any pictures of you and...I don't have many of you and your parents."

He put his arm around her, and she instinctively embraced him back. She felt they shared a moment of grief, Tío Julio grieving for the family members now dead, and Anaís for only now getting to know her real family.

"*Gracias a Dios* I do have you in pictures of the times you've come to visit, as well as the ones you've sent me over the years of special things in your life." He kissed her forehead. "Thank you for that. You know, you're the only one in the family that doesn't live here in Pinar, and I, we, always think about you. And wish you were here with us."

Anaís just smiled back at her uncle.

"But we understand...just like your mother...you need the big city. Just as long as you don't forget us, okay?"

"Never, Tío Julio." She squeezed his old hand. "How could anyone ever forget you?"

"That's what you say now, but when you don't come around for so long...Well, it's Christmas Eve and I'm just so happy you're here." He hugged her tightly again. "And it's not just because of your *arroz con pollo*." They both laughed. "Although, I don't know... Aunt Mercedes tells me you brought everything done...got those chicken in Havana... and not our fresh ones that we had picked out for you."

"But, Uncle," she protested, "this way I was able to ride Lucero. It was so wonderful...maybe tomorrow you and I can go out?"

"*Sí*, that's a great idea. We'll do that early, before anyone else is up, like we always do. *Bien*. Now I really need my siesta. And you probably do, too."

They kissed on the cheek and she slowly walked back to the bedroom. All the women were still sleeping. She got under the netting, hoping the soft sounds of those sleeping around her would lull her into a nap. However, she was much too excited, her mind racing from one image to another, reliving the day with her family members, the beautiful country home, the ride with Diego. Before she knew it, women and children around her started to stir.

CHAPTER 22

Diego

THE SOFT MOONLIGHT FILTERED THROUGH THE NARROW CRACKS OF THE wood planks around them like a million fireflies shining on their naked bodies. Diego had pulled her into the barn and Anaís had followed willingly. Her body ached for him.

Christmas Eve had been an amazing experience. Anaís could not imagine the closeness of such a large, extended family. With Tío Julio at the head of the longest dinner table she had ever seen, she had sat among her cousins and reveled in a late supper under a cloudless, starry night. Most of the family had gone in the house at some point for shawls and sweaters and marveled that she said she felt fine in her cotton blouse. Diego teased her about having cold blood in her veins, but she knew he thought otherwise when they locked gazes.

The sounds of laughter and singing grew fainter as she and Diego moved deeper into the barn's cavernous belly, and the musty, damp smells of the old barn made her feel lightheaded. Or perhaps it was the many glasses of red wine she had shared while playing dominos after dinner. After winning a few rounds of five-hundred points and being called sharks by the others, at last both she and Diego lost their seats at the domino table. They ignored the comments of 'don't get lost' from the younger cousins and strolled down the moonlit dirt path.

Perhaps it was the wine, or the desire to feel the passion she saw in his eyes every time he looked at her. Anaís did not know. She allowed herself to be pinned against a wall in an empty stable and didn't move as Diego lifted her flowing skirt and caressed her body with his strong, confident hands. In silent complicity, they disrobed each other and fell on the cool hay. His kisses were penetrating, and she could hardly breathe. She felt his fingers slowly descend her body, pausing and stroking gently as he descended to her thighs. Her body seemed weightless on the spindly bed beneath her, the wetness between her legs waiting anxiously for him to penetrate her. Diego was in no hurry to go inside her.

Anaís' arousal was intense, and she saw the surprise in his eyes as she moved herself on top of him. She felt herself grinding her body against his uncontrollably and felt further aroused by his intense stare of her breasts, her body. The rhythm of their bodies in unison, like riding Lucero in the deep, tropical forest, made her close her eyes and she grabbed his chest grabbing to steady herself. Their soft grunts and gasps came faster and faster as their bodies stretched towards the sky, finally convulsing in whispered groans as she fell forward on his chest, heaving with pleasure. Diego felt her body become limp in his embrace, and they both slipped into a quiet sleep.

He awakened to the tickling of her hair on his face, and gently moved her body next to him. Her short, dark hair curled around her pale, slumbering face made her look like a child. He got half way up on his arm and let his eyes roam her beautiful, strong, naked body with total abandonment. He had not been able to get her out of his mind since their brief affair some years ago. But Isa's lovemaking now was aggressive and passionate in a way he did not remember. Tonight was like nothing he had experienced with her before.

Anaís stirred and stretched her long, athletic body. He dared not to breathe so as not to awaken her and end the pleasure of watching her in sleep. She was an exquisite woman. She has become even more beautiful, he thought. He moved closer and felt the hot surface of her skin. His eyes followed the curve of her dimpled chin down her graceful neck. Her full breasts like alabaster mounds seemed to catch the gentle evening light and made his still erect body quiver. He remembered loving to kiss the large, dark beauty mark he remembered beneath her right breast. He leaned over trying to see it, thinking he would kiss it and reawaken those memories in her.

This is strange. He leaned forward, looking at her body intently. The beauty mark wasn't there! Maybe it was the other breast. He saw no beauty mark there either.

Diego's bafflement turned to doubt, thinking perhaps he had seen the beauty mark on another woman. No, it wasn't possible. Isa had never been just another woman to Diego. He had felt something special for her. They had stopped dating because she had said that she did not love him and did not want to waste his time. He remembered everything about their time together, and the pain of their separation. And he remembered that large beauty mark on her right breast.

Anaís opened her eyes and smiled up at him.

"I think I drank just a little too much." She reached up and put her arm around his neck. "You, Diego, are wonderful!"

CHAPTER 23

Anaís' newfound family

HER COUSIN NELSON NEEDED A RIDE BACK TO HAVANA, AND DIEGO graciously offered to take him. Anaís was glad to be able to help out a family member, but was disappointed when Nelson took the front seat next to Diego. Anaís had indeed noticed that the women rode in the back here in Cuba. Soon, she was got bored of the baseball talk and leaning her head against the seat rest, mused on the last two days in Pinar.

Anaís loved being with her new extended family, a sense of personal community that she had never known before. Her adoptive parents had no family to speak of, since her grandparents on both sides had died at an early age and her few uncles and aunts were spread out around the U.S. Anaís remembered looking forward excitedly to weddings and even funerals when she would get to see the handful of cousins who were around her own age.

In stark contrast to those occasional family gatherings, her Cuban family seemed to get together often, and already she had made plans with her cousins for the next few weekends, one to picnic on the beaches at Varadero and another for nightclubbing in Havana. Anaís enjoyed the fun loving way they teased each other, the caring way in which children were watched over by the older members of the family. Still, Tío Julio was her favorite. During the two days that they had stayed at the farm, he searched her out, kissing her on the cheek and reminding her how much they liked her visits to the farm. She reiterated her promises to come to Pinar more often.

After the hectic set up for Christmas Eve, Christmas Day had been a day for relaxation. Everyone seemed to get involved in his or her own interests, and the only serious work was done by the older aunts and Chencha who never left the kitchen and the constant preparation of food. Anaís and Diego had gone horseback riding again with the cousins, but they did not get a second opportunity to be alone. It had been difficult to look at him without thinking of their lovemaking, and she felt the blood rush to her face each time he was near.

Anaís looked at the back of Diego's head, his strong jaw line outlined in the darkness. It was a three-hour ride back to Havana, and they probably wouldn't be there before midnight, but she didn't care. Not only was she beginning to attune herself to the late hours that Cubans kept, but she didn't want the weekend to end.

And what would happen now that they had had sex? What would it be like in the office tomorrow? Would he pretend nothing had happened?

Diego turned his head as if reading her thoughts. Anaís felt herself blush and was thankful for the darkness. His easy smile made her heart jump. She smiled back, wishing they were alone, that she could feel his embrace once more.

Chapter 24

The New Millennium

If Christmas had been an elaborate city event, the preparations for the Millennium New Year's Eve celebrations were even more impressive. Isa still couldn't believe the amount of effort and expense that the city spent on getting everyone in a celebratory mood. The Santas were gone from the street corners and the holiday music and decorations in the stores had all but disappeared. In their place, an ongoing barrage of announcements promoting celebrations for the end of the millennium celebrations astounded her.

At the Tourism Office, thousands of flyers, brochures and posters were thrown in bins to be recycled and even though this effort was well intended, all the wasted paper amazed her. She was not only trying very hard to pretend to know what she was doing promoting events in a town that she did not know, but at the same time forced to keep herself from commenting on the waste of resources that was part of the office routine.

Thank goodness that the events for the holidays were so complex that everything was done in teams. In the few weeks that she had been pretending to be her sister, she had already helped to host almost a dozen parties for out of town visitors in the different venues around the city, each a unique opportunity to learn her job.

And thank goodness for Ricardito, who almost every night after work either walked with her around town or brought videos that described the city and its special buildings, architecture and neighborhoods. Her bedroom walls were now plastered with maps and city information that she tested herself on nightly.

What she did not like about her work day was Cynthia. Isa now understood firsthand what a gossip Cynthia was. No wonder her sister called her *Arrancapellejo*. Every day, Cynthia would make it a point to stop by her desk to inquire about what Isa had planned for the day or to gossip about the other women in the office. Most of the time Isa, smiled without making any remarks. This tactic seemed to work after five or ten minutes and Cynthia would eventually head for another worker's desk.

Thankfully, Isa would have a few days of not having to deal with Cynthia because of the holiday and thankfully as well there were no scheduled meetings with any new clients until after the New Year. The most challenging aspect of her sister's job so far had been calling on contacts and not knowing if Anaís had met them previously or what relationship she had with them. So far, she had not made any huge mistake thanks to Anaís' professionalism in dealing with her office co- workers and her contact list which gave details of each client's personality and his or her unique needs. Still, there wasn't one evening after going over her self-imposed homework that she didn't fall asleep half wishing that things would slow down and be simpler.

Even for the celebrations for New Year's Eve.

Back home in Cuba, New Year's Eve was a simple affair. Chencha would ready the buckets of water to do the yearly cleaning of their house to rid it of any old bad luck and make it fresh for New Year blessings. Sometime around noon, she would hand Isa one of the worn, straw brooms, and together they would commence the cleaning--from the farthest wall in the house. Chencha would pour a little water on the cracked tile floor and swish it around as if trying to collect every visible and invisible particle while at the same time praying softly to her Yoruba gods. Isa would join in the ritual, following Chencha from room to room until finally they were at the front door.

She could see the old woman in her mind's eye, her hands grabbing the doorknob with a strong twist to swing open the door through which she and Isa would then sweep out any remaining water. The smile on Chencha's face told of her conviction and belief that all evil had been discarded and the New Year could enter as untouched as a newborn child.

Isa looked around her sister's apartment. With the exception of the foyer and adjoining kitchen, everything was carpeted. Would the cleaning work if only a few rooms were cleaned according to the ritual? And how could she do a proper cleaning without sweeping the water out the front door?

And, what about the coconut? Chencha would always interpret for Isa what kind of year Isa could expect by the way the coconut pieces fell on the ground after she smashed it against the cement sidewalk outside of their apartment. Chencha herself would have her future read by Secundino that evening. New Year's Eve was one of the rare days when Chencha left Isa alone and spent it in Secundino's home with the other believers, to hear Secundino and the other seers make their New Year's prognostications.

Isa suddenly realized that for the first time in her life, Chencha was not with her to guide her in their tradition, but she could not imagine beginning a New Year without it. She would just have to do it on her own.

She dialed the small store that serviced the condominiums and asked for a coconut. The young grocery store clerk said he didn't think they had any coconuts and he would call her back. A few minutes later, he informed her that in fact, they never carried coconuts, although they did have coconut juice.

Isa knew there were some other grocery stores in the area, but had no idea of their name or how to get to them since she always tagged along with Richard when he shopped. He wasn't home and she left a message on his machine about needing a coconut, hoping he would get back to her quickly. They were both invited to a New Year's Eve party at a friend's nearby condo overlooking Grant Park, where they could easily walk to Navy Pier to see the fireworks at midnight. Richard had been complaining about the party, saying that the millennium didn't start until the year two-thousand-one, and said he was only going so that Isa could celebrate the American way.

The millennium and its promises and dangers were on the news constantly. Isa hungrily read every magazine that her sister subscribed to, relishing the controversial nature of most articles. Everything from Nostradamus and believers saying that the end of the world was at hand, to the extraordinary measures being taken to ensure against disruption of festivities by computer hackers was covered in the news. Isa had never known such diverse journalism. The printed word was controlled in Cuba and she loved this new freedom.

Hoping Richard would return her call quickly and help her find the much needed coconut, she decided to do the cleaning the best way possible given her circumstances. At noon, she was ready with her bucket and broom, and although she didn't know any of the African chants that Chencha invoked, as Isa swished the small amounts of water around the marble floor of the kitchen and out toward the foyer she prayed for a good year, a year in which Elián would be returned to his father and political tensions between Cuba and the U.S. were relaxed. She prayed for a year that would bring her a call from Senator Fernández' office that everything was arranged so that she could go back to Cuba with his delegation, the trip that would give her the opportunity to change places again with her sister while the Senator made the proper arrangements for Isa to legally join Anaís in Chicago. For a brief second, she even prayed that Castro were no longer leader of the government so that things in Cuba would change for everybody, but then she realized that it was too much to ask of Chencha's saints.

At the door of her apartment, she grabbed the two large copper doorknobs of the double doors and turned them forcibly, allowing both doors to swing. She peered down the carpeted hallway and was glad no one was about. Mopping up the water, which as Chencha would say, held any negative energy from the current year, she prayed to the unknown gods to rid the house of any and all evil spirits. She acted quickly, not wanting to be caught by one of the neighbors in her ancient although modified ritual. When she could no longer squeeze any water out of the mop, she placed the broom and mop back in the foyer, and closing the door behind her, carried her bucket into the elevator amidst curious looks from the others descending with her. Head held high, she greeted the doorman as she carried the bucket carefully so as not to spill any of its content.

In her intense focus on accomplishing her cleaning quickly yet effectively, she had forgotten about the cold weather, and she shivered in her jeans and t-shirt as she headed out the door. No matter. It's too late to turn back now, she told herself. I cannot break the pattern of the ritual.

She walked the short block to the inner Lake Shore Drive road and at the corner as taxicabs and cars rushed past her, she emptied her bucket with the old year's tainted water onto the street.

It is done.

She ignored the looks of the people around her and swung her empty bucket as she walked past the doorman's curious gaze.

"Happy New Year, Julius."

"Happy New Year, Dr. Moran."

Anaís waved at Chencha as she lumbered down the street toward the bus stop a few blocks away. Anaís had just experienced santería first hand, helping the old woman sweep evil spirits out of their apartment by mopping the floors and throwing the bucket of water out their front door. The end of the year ritual as Chencha explained, was followed by the smashing of a coconut on the ground so that Chencha could read Anaís' fortune for the next twelve months. Although she didn't believe much of it, Anaís was glad to hear that only good things awaited her in the first year of the millennium. She didn't tell Chencha that the first good thing about the New Year was that she was spending the evening with Diego at his place.

They had not been able to spend any time together since returning from Pinar del Río. The day they returned to work, Diego was called to Varadero to deal with old clients from the former Soviet Union wanting to deal on behalf of a newly constituted Russian hotel chain.

He had stopped by her desk in the middle of the day to tell her he'd be out for a few days. Anaís blushed looking up at him, remembering their deep goodnight kiss the evening before. Pretending to be reviewing one of her files to avoid the stares from the office personnel, he leaned forward and whispered that he'd pick her on New Year's Eve. She had not seen him since that conversation.

Now, she was hours from seeing him again. Chencha said she would be spending the night at Secundino's house and would return after Secundino and the other santeros had met and proclaimed their predictions for the New Year for Cuba and the world. Anaís was glad that with the old nanny's absence, she wouldn't have to explain that she was spending the night with Diego, since she was sure Chencha would not approve.

The house was warm, and she realized that the cold shower would feel good today. She inserted one of Celia's CDs into the player and sang along happily as she stood under the corroded showerhead in the tiny bathroom, trying to take advantage of every drop of water that dripped through. She thought of her sister, probably getting ready to attend an elegant New Year's Eve party. Anaís imagined her under a luxurious stream of hot water, surrounded by the fragrance of scented soaps, shampoos and conditioners. Isa would not be concerned with having enough water to rinse her hair. But was she having as much fun as Anaís in her adventure? She hoped so.

She heard the loud knock on the door and turning off the water, wrapped herself in a towel. The knock got louder, and she cracked the door open just enough to see if indeed it was Diego.

He stood in the late afternoon sun, tanned and handsome, smiling back at her.

"Diego, come in. I'll be right back."

She let him in and ran into the bedroom. Funny that she felt embarrassed to greet him in a towel when only a few days ago they had explored each other's bodies.

"So, what should I wear, Diego. Where are we going?"

She had put on a pair of shorts and t-shirt to keep cool in the increasing heat. When she entered the living area, she saw Diego curiously standing in front of the CD player.

"Where did you get this?"

Anaís started to give the name of the record store back home, and caught herself. She straightened up, taking a minute to think about her answer in light of what Chencha had said about Celia and her music.

"Ah...my cousin from America that I told you about...the one who gave me the fake jewelry...she asked me why she didn't hear Celia's music here. She left me the player and a few of the CDs." Her answer was the best she could offer.

"You have a very generous cousin, Isa," Diego replied, staring at her perplexed.

"Yes. *Bueno.* You know, when someone offers you something you don't turn it down, now, do you?"

She approached him coquettishly. "So, what should I wear?"

"Isa, you've never worried about what to wear."

"Well, yes, but it is New Year's Eve. It needs to be special...we haven't been together on New Year's Eve... in so long, I mean."

"Yes, not since...la Sierra Maestra."

La Sierra Maestra? What did that mean? All Anaís knew about the Sierra Maestra was that it was the mountain range in eastern Cuba where Castro had planned his revolution.

"*Bueno, sí...*it's been a long time. I would like our being together again to be...special." She took another step toward him, and then stopped. He seemed unusually quiet, still staring at the CDs. Anaís wondered if she had said something wrong. But then Diego smiled, and stepping forward, took her into his arms.

Anaís felt herself relax into his embrace.

"Well, tonight, my place and just us." He kissed her gently. "And tomorrow, for the day of the Liberation, we are going to hear your favorite *punto guajiro* poet...he'll be at the Plaza of the Revolution at the rally. I'm sure Fidel will ask him to lead the people's call to get Elián back. Then, we're meeting with the Russians I saw in Varadero...the ones who want to invest in a new hotel there."

Suddenly, Anaís' head was reeling. Her favorite poet? Russian hotel owners? She didn't know what to say, but her puzzled look caught his attention.

"I know it sounds like a lot to do...especially when what I really want to do is be alone with you." He pulled her close to him. "And I don't usually mix business with pleasure, but these Russians are leaving in a few days, and they really want to talk with you. But we'll keep the meeting short and we'll get them out of our hair as quickly as we can...so I can have you all to myself." He kissed her deeply, and she momentarily relaxed.

"But that is tomorrow. We still have all of tonight. Now, go on. I'm going to sit here and enjoy Celia...Shit. I don't understand how we let a woman with all that talent get away."

Anaís left his arms. She grabbed clothing from her sister's wardrobe and applied a lighter touch to the eye makeup routine, all the while feeling panic settling in her veins. In the euphoria of the last weeks, with everything going smoothly in her pretense of being Isa, she had not considered the possibility of Russian clients. And tomorrow she was going to hear Isa's favorite poet in *punto guajiro*. What was *punto guajiro* anyway?

"Come on, gorgeous."

She finished combing her hair and sprayed on some perfume from the States, deciding that she would not ruin their evening worrying. "Alright, I'm ready." She hugged him sensually.

He kissed her deeply. She playfully bit his lower lip.

"Alright. Let's go. If I kiss you again, we will not get out of here." He nuzzled against her neck. "Let's finish this" he grabbed her buttocks, "at my place."

Anaís followed him out to the car. The late afternoon sky was its customary bright Caribbean blue. Chencha had said that the coconuts augured very special things for the coming year. Maybe the good luck would begin tonight.

Isa watched the fireworks break the darkness of the sky into hundreds of colored specks forming beautiful shapes over Lake Michigan. One sparkling eruption reminded her that she had never found a coconut to smash on the ground. That was fine, since she would not have known how to read the pieces anyway.

She continued admiring the glowing sky reflected on the water. Despite the bitter cold, she felt toasty wrapped up in her sister's long, fur coat and understood why polar bears frolicked in the cold, they were warm under all that fur. Richard laughed at the comparison. He looked dapper in his own fur coat, although Isa had not seen too many men wearing furs around Chicago. Perhaps it was a gay man's style. Isa mused that even if she were a straight man, she would still wear fur to minimize the brutal Midwestern weather. She wondered if she could wear the coat to work and to the stores. She would need to remember to ask Richard if it was acceptable behavior.

The party was as elegant as any Hollywood movie she had seen late at night in Anaís apartment in between studying maps of Chicago and its neighborhoods and history. The women all wore floor length, beautiful dresses and most of the men, including Richard were in tuxedos.

Isa had refused to go shopping for a new dress as Richard insisted, and she had instead enjoyed trying on all of her sister's evening wear. Her final selection, a cream-colored silk sheath with thin, beaded straps looked stunning on her and she felt like a princess. Richard laughed as she paraded back and forth in the apartment, watching the long train swish behind and around her.

As she looked through her sister's jewelry box, she remembered their mother's precious pieces inside their porcelain dolls. Anaís had followed in their mother's taste for jewelry, and it was difficult for Isa to choose what to put on because there was so much. The turquoise and pearls earrings, necklace and bracelet that she had decided upon with Richard's help looked stunning. Anaís' lifestyle was seductive.

Seductive! That was the word some of the men at the party had used to describe her, as they flirted with her. Still, Isa didn't find any of them attractive, and preferred staying close to Richard. He was a better dancer anyway, and she didn't have to keep up pretense with him, her new, good friend.

Then Jim appeared at the party.

He had looked intensely at her as he introduced his date, a tall, skinny blonde woman who clung to Jim like chewing gum, as they would say in Cuba.

"He's just pissed, Isa. His loss."

Pissed? Urinating? What a terrible expression, Isa thought, to probably explain that Jim was bothered.

"But, I offended him, Richard. I mean, he thinks Anaís offended him."

"She was going to break if off anyway...isn't that what she told you?
Well, leave it alone. You did her a favor."

It was difficult for Isa to believe she had done anyone a favor. Especially when she obviously had hurt this man, someone she didn't even
know.

Now, standing by the railing at Navy Pier, watching the magnificent
fireworks in the distance as a voice over the loud speaker kept them ap-
prised of the ticking clock, ever closer to midnight, Isa thought about her
sister and wondered if their lives would ever be at peace.

"Five more minutes to the millennium!" People cheered to the voice
booming overhead.

"Millennium, my ass. That's not until next year!"

She smiled at Richard, now wearing a pair of florescent glasses in the
shape of 1999.

"...yes, let's party, like it's 1999..." he sang, keeping up with a song
blaring through the speakers. "Because it is 1999, not the eve of the millennium, but still a fun evening."

Isa smiled, thinking how Richard just was not giving up on his litany
about the millennium. Suddenly, she felt eyes burning at the back of her
head and turning, saw Jim's flushed face. He was a handsome man, but
he looked almost menacing as he stared at her without blinking.

"I don't like the way he looks at me, Richard." She nodded gently in
the direction of Jim and his date.

"He's harmless, Isa. I told you already; he's just pissed. I'm with the
most beautiful woman here...and a few months ago he probably thought
it would have been him with you...with Anaís...here tonight. Don't pay
attention to him."

She knew he was right.

"Alright...get ready...ten...nine...eight..." The crowd joined in with screams and whistles as the sky over their heads lit up like daylight with a constant burst of fireworks.

"Happy New Year, Isa." Richard kissed her on the cheek as he embraced her.

"*Feliz Año Nuevo, Ricardito.*" The mood around them was one of jubilation, and the fireworks kept pace with the music reaching them across the lake from the Grant Park band shell. What a tremendous celebration, Isa thought. She felt joyful at starting the year two-thousand in this new country, a place she had always dreamed of and never really had expected to see.

But here she was, wrapped up in the warmth of her sister's coat and her sister's friends. It was like a dream.

The large crowd had become a sea of revelers dancing, kissing, pushing. Richard was in the distance, hugging and kissing people and people were hugging and kissing Isa. She didn't know if they were friends of her sister's or strangers. It didn't matter.

Suddenly, she lost her footing as she felt herself being jerked back. A second later, she was being held in Jim's tight embrace, his hot breath, heavy with the smell of liquor.

"Happy New Year!" He kissed her hard on the lips, his tongue forcing her mouth open. Although at first shocked, her next reaction was anger and she struggled in his grip to free herself. Jim was having none of it, and the more she struggled, the more he squeezed her, his lips hurtful on hers. Isa could barely breath.

"Hey, you asshole!" Richard's voice next to her and a loud smack were the two sounds she heard before feeling herself free of Jim's embrace.

The tall, dark haired man had reeled back and would have fallen on the ground save for the crowd around him, pushing him back into a stance. "What's wrong with you, man?" Richard was looking at his hand, bloodied with Jim's cut on his lip.

"Fuck you and your faggot friend, Ani. Fuck you!" Jim turned and disappeared into the crowd.

"What...what..."

"Never mind, Isa. He's just drunk."

"But what did he call you? I don't understand."

"Oh, yes. The words that are meant to cut a gay person to the quick! We'll have to spend some time going over certain expressions so you know what they are, when some asshole" he shouted at Jim "thinks he's being funny."

Richard looked at her bleeding lip and dabbed it with his handkerchief. "Did he kiss you...or bite you? No, I know, it's not funny. But you know, I bet Ani didn't know mild-mannered Jim had that side to him... so," Richard lifted his almost empty beer bottle and clinked her glass "good riddance...and let's drink to next year...the real millennium...when you and Ani will both be here to celebrate."

"From your lips to God's, Richard."

CHAPTER 25

Elián Rally

"IT'S ALL GOOD. NOTHING IMPORTANT. YES. NEXT MONTH WILL BE FINE. Enjoy yourselves. *Sí...adiós.*"

Anaís watched Diego smile as he thanked the barman for the use of the phone on the counter of the small tavern.

"Those Russians won't be joining us after all! They said they have a lot of packing to do before they leave tomorrow, but I know better." He hugged Anaís tightly and whispered in her ear. "They probably met up with a couple of our hot Cuban ladies and want to party before they head for Siberia." He laughed, not hearing Anaís whispered 'thank you, God.'

The fun and passion of being with Diego had made Anaís put the Russians out of her mind, and she had refused to spoil her first evening with Diego since Christmas. The Russians spoke Spanish and she decided to say that her Russian was lackluster from years of not speaking it and let it go at that. All she had wanted to do last night was savor every minute with Diego.

And good that she had not fretted. The Russians had just cancelled the meeting.

"Isa, let's go. We don't want to miss Juan Antonio."

La Plaza of the Revolution was packed with people from one end of the square to another, and a party mood vibrated through the crowd celebrating New Year's Day, the day that Batista had left Cuba in 1959 and that Castro had taken over the country as its liberator. As they made their way through the throngs, people patted Diego on the shoulder or greeted him. She wondered where exactly Diego was leading her and was happy but also surprised to see that he was escorting her to the secondary stage at the front of the plaza. Under a row of Cuban flags and signs in Spanish saying "Long live the Revolution, Send Elián Home, and Miami Mafia—Stay Out of Our Affairs" they took their seats among other government officials a few feet from the podium. It seemed that his position in the Ministry of Tourism afforded Diego incredible privileges.

"Do you remember the last time we heard them together?" he smiled at her. "Back in Pinar? But that was before the rest of Cuba discovered him."

Anaís faintly smiled back, deciding that not responding was better than saying the wrong thing. Diego was too excited to notice anything but the event unfolding around them.

"I love these times when we come together as a country...it makes everything...it makes me think that everything will be alright."

What an odd thing for Diego to say. Could it be possible that he had his doubts about the Revolution? Should I dare venture say anything political?

"You know, of course I agree that Elián should be sent back home here, but you know, I bet there are many Cubans in the States who have that same opinion."

Diego looked at her as if she were a stranger.

"What are you saying? That's not how they think over there. If a blonde, blue-eyed little boy had been washed up on our shores and we didn't put him on the first plane back to Miami, the American CIA, FBI, U.S. Army would be invading us to get him back. And the Cubans in Miami would be cheering it all on!"

She realized he was shocked at her comment, but she couldn't help herself from continuing.

"You didn't hear what I said at all, Diego. Yes, I agree with you that the American government wouldn't stand for our keeping one of its citizens. But that's not what I said to you. I was commenting on the fact that Elián's uncle and cousins...they can't really represent the opinions of all Cubans in the U.S. Lots of parents must think that little boy should be sent back to his father...don't you think?"

He stared at her as if not believing his ears.

211

"But why would you say that? Look, it's been over a month, and nothing has changed." He looked at her curiously. "Why would you say these things, Isa?"

She softened her comments.

"Well, I've had the occasion to talk to some Americans, and Cuban Americans. I told you my cousin was here from Chicago, didn't I?" She waited for his nod. "Well, she's very different from the Cubans that you... that we hear about. Not as radical." His face didn't show that he was convinced. "I just think people are different than we think sometimes."

The roar of the crowd clearly signaled that Juan Antonio had arrived, and she was grateful for the interruption to their conversation. She wasn't making any headway to Diego and his hardened position about Americans.

A slight, balding thirty-something man in the traditional *guayabera* mounted the makeshift stairs to the stage followed by an older, shorter man. They both waved at the exhilarated fans, their presence causing the same wild reaction as any rock stars back in the States. The trio of musicians began softly playing in the background, and to the sound of the *laúd*, an indigenous type of lute, Juan Antonio and his partner started to belt out their song. Diego squeezed her hand in anticipation.

"I still can't understand how they can improvise those verses right on the spot...on any subject. And wait until the crowd calls out el *pié forzado*, the requests from the crowd. That's when it gets really good."

From the recesses of her memory, Anaís remembered her father and a conversation about the *punto guajiro*, verses composed on the spot by poets of Cuba's small towns and villages. As a child, she and her parents would play rhyme games, trying to outdo each other, and she remembered her father saying that some countries had special schools for children with talent for poetic improvisation. She wondered if Juan Antonio had gone to such a school.

His strong voice had a country quality that matched his poignant verses referring to the Cuban landscape. It was easy to paint pictures in her mind of places she now had seen firsthand and the verses evoked beautiful images of places in Cuba that she still wanted to see.

After the applause had died down after one of their songs, Juan Antonio spoke of Elián and the injustice of keeping him from his father. The crowd applauded and yelled excitedly, then the two poets began another set of verses on the topic.

"It's hard to believe they compose all this without preparation."

"But of course, that's what they do. You know that, Isa." He looked at her strangely.

"But it all rhymes...well, it reminds me of rap..." The moment she said the word, she wished she could take it back.

"What?"

"Uh, it reminds me of....rap...Rapinche...an old friend of Chencha... He did the same thing."

"I've never heard you mention him before."

"I can't imagine why not. He is very, very good."

"Really?"

The crowd's cheering gave her an opportunity to get out of the difficult conversation with Diego. They were calling out *¡Controversia! ¡Controversia!* in almost a frenzy.

"Now it really gets good!" Diego seemed to have dismissed her comment on rap. "It's like a contest on who can outdo who."

Juan Antonio raised his hand and asked the crowd to give him a topic. The words yelled out were difficult to understand, but soon the poets took up their positions and began rhyming again.

This time their verses spoke of the struggle that they faced, a struggle to be free of American imperialism. The crowd cheered madly as he referenced Cuban heroes such as Martí and el Ché. Diego tapped his foot to the beat of the verses.

"Incredible. I just love them." He looked at her. "But you don't seem as interested as usual, Isa. I thought you really liked him."

"Oh, I do. He is ...my favorite. I'm just...overwhelmed by his talent... like always. And his partner this time is very good too." She squeezed his hand, and gave him a kiss on the cheek.

"You've become much bolder since we last dated, Isa," he commented, taking her hand gently in his own.

"I hope you don't mind."

"But of course not. It's just...different." He looked at her intently. "And you are different, very different." He kissed her tenderly. "I like the new Isa."

She didn't know what to say that would not give her further problems. "Shh. Listen..."

To the sounds of *¡Elián! ¡Elián!* from the crowd, they watched as Juan Antonio and his partner left the stage and mixed with the audience. The hours passed quickly listening to the talented performers. Anaís laughed every time Diego unsuccessfully tried his hand at rhyming. Before long, dusk started settling over the plaza.

"How about if we leave now?" Diego suggested. She grabbed his arm as they made their way past the cheering and chanting fans.

"Where else do you want to be on this first day of the year?"

"It doesn't matter. You pick."

"How about *La Floridita?* Maybe the Old Man's ghost will hang around there."

"*¡Perfecto!*"

Finally, something in Havana that she and Diego both knew and liked—Hemingway! She had gone there with the Illinois Delegation two months earlier as part of the tour of special sights and although it was kitschy and touristy, she had felt honored touching the table and seat that the old master had called his own. She wondered what kind of a crowd would be there on New Year's Day.

"Do you still think that the *Old Man and the Sea* is better than *For Whom The Bells Toll?*" he queried.

"Only because it's set here in Cuba," she smiled. "But all his books are my favorites. What a writer! To have been fortunate enough to meet him."

"He would have loved you, Isa. He loved women in general, and you know how he was here in Cuba...well, legendary with the ladies." Anaís grimaced at Diego's words.

"Yes, I get it. You wouldn't have wanted to be just one of his many conquests. But are you sure that not even for Hemingway, you would have looked the other way with his philandering?"

"I don't think so. But I sure would have loved to have met him."

Old Havana was brimming with people in the streets, dancing to the music from blaring radios. As they walked past old homes with doors swung open, they were invited to join the parties within.

The smells of fried food and coffee filled the air. Anaís felt transported to a different world once more. No champagne or elegant decorations here in Havana, but in its place dancing in the streets under a cloudless, starry night, and pure, unadulterated passion for the man who lovingly held his arm around her shoulder.

Diego stopped in mid step and she looked up at him in surprise. He smiled and she felt the quivering in her loins.

"I am so glad we are together again, Isa. I have missed you. I have missed you very, very much."

"Happy New Year!" people shouted from the deteriorating balconies and cars.

"Yes, it is a New Year!" He grabbed her close. "The Old Man will have to wait." His lips came close to hers.

"What a great way to start the new year, Diego. I, too, am glad I have found you...again."

CHAPTER 26

On the Trail

DIEGO HUNG UP, FEELING BOTH SATISFIED AND UNCOMFORTABLE WITH the conversation he'd just had with his old friend. Arturo was one of the good guys, and they'd met when Arturo recruited Diego into the G2, Cuba's secret police, and to the Revolution. Arturo had also proven to be a true friend when Diego asked him to support his leaving the organization. No one had ever made that request before. Despite Arturo's bewilderment, he had pulled strings to ease young Diego's departure without repercussion. They had stayed friends.

Diego knew he could trust calling on him for a favor and although in truth, Diego didn't know what he was looking for on this search, he knew that something simply didn't feel right about Isa's recent behavior. In every way, she was more exciting and vibrant, and often so different, that he had started to wonder how she had morphed into this more assertive and spirited woman that he couldn't get out of his mind.

Could her American cousin have made such an impact on Isa with her American ideals? And if so, what did this mean to their relationship? Perhaps nothing, but he felt his old suspicious self-rearing inside, wanting to know.

He looked at his watch. A couple of more hours and perhaps he would find out something important about this cousin and her influence on Isa. Perhaps the G2 needed to keep an eye on this stranger if she returned to the island.

He busied himself reviewing the proposals from various hotel chains interested in partnering with Cuba on developing tourism. His background in the G2 had made it possible for the government to use his talents in various departments. Not only was he good at dealing with people, but he also kept tract of certain foreigners while they were in Cuba.

In his latest position with the *Oficina de Inversiones Extranjeras,* his secret police background was peripheral to his main job overseeing foreign investment in Cuban/Foreign Interest hotel development for the almost two million global visitors. Among the major foreign investors involved in these joint-venture agreements were the Russians, not the same Russians of the pre-Soviet exodus, but the capitalist Russians of the new twenty-first century. They were not much different than the Spaniards or Germans that kept the Cuban tourist economy alive. Still, after suffering the superior Soviet attitude for many years, most *Cubanos* were left with a bitter taste in their mouths from the Russian's abrupt departure and total economic abandon in nineteen eighty-nine by the anti-American superpower. Most Cubans still blamed the Russians for the desperate situation that Cuba suffered throughout most of the decade of nineties.

So, it wasn't now going to be easy to let them come in and manage their hotel and casino on some of Varadero's prime beach property. It didn't matter that the Cuban treasury would gain greatly from the foreign investment. The Cuban feelings ran deep. And so Diego understood Isa's lack of enthusiasm every time he brought up the subject of talking to them. Although it was more than resentment for the Russians that he felt from her. It was almost an uneasiness in negotiating with them that seemed contradictory to the assertive and determined woman she had become, the woman who tackled each task with gusto and creativity.

What a woman she was, this new Isa. He leaned back in his chair and closed his eyes, images of her beautiful face, the sparkling deep green eyes and bright smile exciting him instantly. He loved her new aggressiveness in lovemaking, her abandoned enjoyment of his exploration of her sensuous body. Her physical beauty now was even more attractive to him in her uninhibited eroticism.

What had opened the door to her new found sexuality? He doubted meeting her cousin a few months ago could have caused that change. Still, the macho in him preferred contemplating that option in place of conjuring some other lover who may have replaced him in her favors after they broke up.

Yes, aside from maturing with life experiences, he was sure some of the change must have been caused by meeting and associating with her cousin. After all, he had heard that American women were almost like men in their aggressive search for sexual gratification. So, if Isa and her relative had spent a lot of time talking...maybe she had even given Isa literature...after all, the cousin had brought Celia's music...

The ringing of the phone snapped him out of this rumination.

"Hello. Yes, I can come there. I'd prefer to chat in private I'll come immediately."

As he grabbed his car keys from his desk, Diego smiled, not surprised much at Arturo's quick response to his request. Not even an hour, and his old friend's secretary was already calling to say that the information Diego wanted was ready.

The drive to the nondescript old building where some of Havana's most secret planning was carried out was a short drive in the mid-morning traffic. Diego maneuvered around the many bicyclists running their errands or heading towards jobs. The bicycle revolution, as it was called, of the last year had truly changed the face of Havana, and bicycles now outnumbered cars three to one. It was a necessity, but also a big hassle, trying to get around town without running someone down.

"*La necesidad hace parir negros*" Diego's very white, proper, and obviously racist, Spanish grandmother would have said, contemplating the bicyclists. Diego smiled at thoughts of the petite, loving, iron willed woman, full of passion and fire who had raised him in Pinar del Río. It was difficult for him to criticize anything about his grandmother, even now that she was gone. Still the socialist in him said he needed to replace that old racist saying that in times of need, white women would have black babies, with a less offensive one. Interesting, he thought, how words from youth played in your head even in adulthood.

He knocked softly on the heavy weathered door. A tall, muscular man with piercing eyes and shaved head opened it ceremoniously. Diego was ready to hand him the old identification card that he kept hidden in his wallet for special moments like this. Although he didn't smile, the agent's eyes softened and he moved aside courteously as Diego entered the dimly lit hallway.

He knew his way around the building and quickly found Arturo's small office. The young secretary pulled down her short skirt as she stood up to greet him, her tight cotton blouse opened just enough to show cleavage.

"*Buenos días, coronel Mendoza.*"

"Good morning, *señorita*. Is your boss here?"

"No. He told me what I needed to find for you and then left. But he said he can see you Monday...in the usual place."

She handed him a large box.

"I hope what you need is in here. If not, he said you should call him."

"Thanks so much...Matilde. That's your name, isn't it?"

"*Sí,*" she smiled the coquettish smile of an eighteen-year-old trying to make an impression on an older, attractive man.

"Glad I remembered. I'll just go in there..." he pointed to a small empty office with a single chair and table.

"Let me know if you need anything."

Damn that Isa and what she was doing to him! Shaking his head at his genuine disinterest in the suggestive behavior from the nubile young woman in a miniskirt, he closed the office door behind him and shifted his attention to the cardboard box full of manila files and envelopes.

His friend had always had a penchant for orderliness, one of the qualities Diego had regularly teased him about.

"You're like an old woman," he remembered telling Arturo many times, to which his friend would always respond by giving him the finger and mouthing some obscenity at the comparison.

Now he thought, thank goodness for Arturo's meticulous habits which had kept them many a time from acting on misinformation from an overzealous barrio snitch. If there was any real information to be had on Isa's cousin, Diego knew he would find it in Arturo's notes.

Anaís looked at the thick stack of letters on her desk, the Cyrillic writing accusing her ignorance of the language. She sighed heavily, once more feeling grateful for her sister's notes and the Spanish translations of the correspondence she had received from the Russian hotel chain over the last five years.

If she needed to negotiate the Russian contract, given Isa's details and voluminous information, Anaís felt she was up to the task—minus the Russian language. Her business training and experience in the States plus all the background she had been able to glean from doing her home-work on Isa's clients put her in a good frame of reference to deal with the situation in the present. But she couldn't do so in Russian, and it worried her that Diego kept waffling back and forth on whether the Russians should be accorded the courtesy of a translator or should be expected to negotiate in Spanish like all the other business people that came to Cuba seeking investment ventures. She needed him to consider the latter posi-tion or she would be exposed as the fake Isa that she was!

Anaís buried her head in her hands, feeling an ache at the pit of her stomach. The Russians were coming back, and all her fears of being discovered moved front and center. Throughout January she had tried to distract Diego away from conversations about the Russian deal every time he brought it up, hoping deep inside that Diego was wrong and that the Russians would not return until Isa managed to get back to Cuba. In her nightly prayers, Anaís found herself even calling on Secundino, that old master of the Yoruba secrets, to keep her from being discovered. For weeks, no calls had come through from the clients, and Anaís had started to believe she was home free.

Until three days ago, when Diego received a message that the Rus-sians were planning to be in Cuba by the end of the week.

What was she going to do? She was in way over her head.

Last Sunday, she and Chencha had gone to the Parque de la Fraterni-dad for the *Día de la Defensa* drills. The two women had joined a group of about 30 women of varying ages at one end of the park as they performed military exercises, from running an obstacle course to throwing dead grenades at dummies staked to the ground. Chencha hobbled along with the group in her customary housecoat and her rubber slippers, while younger women took off their high heels to climb the wooden walls.

It was difficult to believe that this ragtag army would be considered capable of defending the country, but the banner stating *Guerra de Todo el Pueblo* -- Defense by the Entire Country-- at one end of the makeshift exercise area told the story of the Cuban civilian army. Anaís wondered what Abraham Lincoln's statue thought of them from his vantage point near the Árbol de Fraternidad Americana a short distance away. She shook her head at the incongruent nature of Lincoln next to the Tree of American Brotherhood given current U.S./Cuba relations.

She felt as so often in the last few months that she had fallen into a surreal rabbit hole, where she hardly recognized herself or the events around her. However, pretending to know the women who chatted with her and what exactly they were talking about was the most difficult. She hoped she had not brought attention to herself with her brief replies knowing as she did that Chencha worried constantly that the block committee was watching them and would report them to the MININT, the Ministry of the Interior.

Yes, I am definitely just keeping my head above water, she told herself. But if the Russians did come soon, she might drown.

"A small coffee for you, Isa?" Mariana stood by her desk offering the afternoon drink.

"*Gracias, Mariana, sí.*" The dark, sweet liquid travelled more familiarly down her throat now, but she still didn't like Cuban coffee.

Diego had been pouring over letters and notes on the special Illinois delegation's visit to Cuba, and from what he could see the discussions between the groups seemed to have been successful. He was sorry he had been out of the country during that period of time, since he was among those in government hopeful that the question of the embargo would eventually be resolved. Cubans didn't hate all Americans, just the American colonial and imperialistic attitude that they had always displayed toward Latin American countries. In fact, most Cubans would welcome American businesses and tourists—but on Cuba's terms and not on the demands of the Cuban Mafia speaking through Washington's spokespersons.

According to the file, Arturo's agents had kept their usual close watch on the travelers. Among the first documents he found were the delegation's proposals for agricultural exchanges, followed up by a list of requests for cultural exchanges from the Cuban Department of Education. Diego thumbed through the paperwork, a detailed compilation of letters and forms that helped to set up the visit. Arturo is still as much of a packrat as always, he thought.

He looked for the list of participants. When he finally found it, his eyes quickly went down the list looking for female names. Among the names he found, there was only one belonging to a younger woman according to Arturo's notes—Anaís Moran. Diego found no other information on this Anaís Moran person. The majority of the documentation was background on the governor, although he had participated in the trip, the senator who did visit, and his immediate staff. Diego also found their public declarations and record regarding the Cuban embargo.

He put the file away and read the other file names: Agricultural Equipment, Livestock, Land Rehabilitation...The *Americanos* had certainly come prepared to lay the groundwork for exporting their state's products. But this held no interest to him at the moment. He needed something different, something more personal, on the group's participants. .He was down to the bottom of the cardboard box and had not found the passport copies or background checks he was looking for.

Wait! Photographs! Arturo's men always took pictures of everyone entering Cuba. He stepped out of the office and Matilde immediately stood up and came around the desk, pulling coquettishly at her black mini skirt.

"*¿Coronel?*"

"Yes, Matilde. Is there another box...did your boss leave any other box for me?"

"*No, Coronel.* That was all he gave me." She smiled and leaned against the desk.

"Hmm. That's strange. There are always background notes...photos..." Diego talked to himself as his eyes darted around Matilde's desk and around the room. He noticed a brown envelope next to the telephone. He stepped closer to the secretary and she held her breath.

Diego stepped around her and took the envelope. The label read *Illinois-octubre, 1999.*

"Ahhh! I think I found it. Thank you, Matilde," and without looking in her curious eyes again, he closed the office door behind him.

This is what I need. He poured out the contents, finding among the pictures, a five-page stapled document describing the information gathered by the secret police on the people in the delegation, beginning with the senator and his top aides. *Anaís Moran...Anaís Moran...*He found her name toward the last page.

Graduate from the University of Chicago...Doctorate in Business Administration...Master's in French...Widow...Travelled to China... Perú... Germany...Latin American countries.

He skipped the other travels, his eyes searching for any comments his fellow agents may have made regarding this woman's political activism. Nothing more interesting than working for the Office of Tourism as a Multilingual Specialist. The information didn't seem to suggest that she was overtly the kind of person who could have influence on Isa's behavior.

He sighed, relieved in an odd way, and also feeling somewhat guilty that his old secret police suspicions had made him suspect that Isa's cousin was a CIA agent or even...Miami Cuban Mafia. Thankfully, it appeared she was just a regular American woman.

He began putting away the document and photographs, now so relieved that he didn't even feel interested in looking at any pictures. What did it matter? The facts were the facts. The Cuban secret police was very efficient and knowledgeable on subversives entering the island.

Who knew why Isa was so different. The fact was that he felt more excited than ever before to be around her. And what a beautiful woman she was. He smiled as he looked down at her picture.

Her picture!

Diego stared at the gorgeous, statuesque brunette, long black hair blowing in the wind as she descended the airplane.

He poured all the pictures out of the manila envelope once more, searching past unrecognizable faces for the tall, dark woman in the elegant pale fitted suit. He found another picture of the same figure in profile, waiting in line to greet Fidel. What was Isa doing at the airport with the delegation? Then another picture, this time of Castro himself smiling at a camera with...Dr. Anaís Moran!

Diego steadied his large body against the desk and slowly sat down in front of the shocking collage of photographs of the face he loved.

Isa's cousin was her double!

But...was that biologically possible? It must be! What other explanation could there be?

He quickly shoved the pictures into their manila envelope as if hoping to hide a dangerous secret from invisible eyes. He placed the envelope in the box, and stepping out of the office, handed it to Matilde who had once more jumped out of her chair, tugging at her skirt.

"Thank you, Matilde. Tell him I'll call him later." He hurriedly left the office and the building. Once in his car, he drove quickly away, wanting to put as much distance as possible between himself and the inquisitive minds that worked for Arturo. A few miles down the road, he pulled on a side street and turned off the engine.

Diego nervously ran his fingers through his thick, black hair. What had he just seen? It was impossible, but the woman in the pictures looked like Isa, Isa with a long wig. He felt strange in his muddled thoughts, not accustomed to feeling disconcerted or unsettled. Images of Isa and the photos danced in his head.

Could this Dr. Moran be an identical...cousin? Were those things possible? Of course not. After all, photographs often distorted images. That was it! The cousin's likeness was amazing, and in the pictures, probably the angle from which the photos were taken made her look just like

Isa. Yes, that was it.

Still, now his old suspicious nature had really kicked in, and he needed to know more. He needed to know more about Isa herself, and what other relatives she might have outside the island, and their intentions toward Cuba as well.

Diego realized he was only a few short blocks from the Department of the Interior where he could find documents such as passport applications and birth certificates. He cranked up the car and headed in that direction, still trying to pick apart the remaining memory of the pictures taken by Arturo's men. The woman in the picture certainly was a ringer for his lover.

His lover. It was the first time in years that Diego had thought about Isa in those terms, but here it was. His lover. It felt good to sound out the words in his head, and they conjured up thoughts of her voluptuous body wrapped around his, kissing him, stroking him. He saw himself again running his tongue on her soft skin, wanting to taste every part of her, from her beautiful feet up her well defined calves, legs, lingering on her pubic area and then, eventually, continuing up her hard belly to the mounds of her breasts...

Breasts without ...a mole!

The mystery of the non-existing mole came back to him in a jolt, perhaps triggered by his present agitation from the photographs.

How could Isa have had a mole removed, without leaving any obvious scars! Despite the free, first-rate medical care in Cuba, plastic surgery was not something readily accessible and certainly not to a Cuban government employee like Isa. He had even begun to second-guess himself about whether the mole had existed at all. Perhaps, he began to ask himself, it was another lover...but no. Few women in his life had made a lasting impression on his soul, and he remembered everything about them. And the only one with a mole on the underside of the breast had been Isa.

He was already at the Department del Interior where his old secret police ID again opened doors closed to others. It was easy for him, therefore, to have the clerk in the section that dealt with birth certificates stop her filing to guide him to the damp, subterranean area where the pre-Revolution birth certificates could be found.

Diego could not remember having been in this section of the building since the very earliest days, when he tried to memorize all the nooks and crannies of the old colonial building. There had been clerks and secretaries to do the dirty work then. Now, he was on his own, not only because of a lack of help in all departments but also because his search was definitely a secret one. Although why he thought it was secret he himself still didn't know. I just want to know more about Isa and her family in the States, he told himself. There's nothing secretive here.

The tower of boxes made him grimace. It would be easier to go to Pinar to look for the records, but aside from arousing suspicions, he couldn't get to Pinar for a few days and when Diego got it into his head that he needed some information, he was like a hungry dog with a bone. He would just have to deal with the dust, mold and hassle if he was going to get at the copy of Isa's birth certificate.

Although why? His non-police persona tried to convince his other half that there were better things to do on a lovely and warm February day. Why look for an old certificate whose worth would probably only be information on familial surnames shared by Isa's cousin that could lead him to find information on the U.S. relatives? Why should he care about people who probably had left Cuba a very long time ago? What could be gained?

But I'm here, he spoke the words out loud. He unbuttoned his cuffs and rolled up the sleeves of his cotton shirt. It was going to be a very long afternoon.

CHAPTER 27

Learning the Ropes

ISA SAT IN A CHAIR AT THE SALON AND SPA, IMPRESSED AS SHE ALWAYS WAS by the cleanliness and spacious offices that were the norm in America. Her sister had gotten a reminder phone call on the answering machine that she was due for a bleaching procedure, and after checking with Richard, they both agreed that it would be best if Isa carried out Anaís' schedules as closely as possible until her sister returned.

She had walked eight blocks to her appointment and felt frozen to the bone. The cold, early February wind almost carried her away. Richard had already explained that the city's reputation as the Windy City had more to do with the winded politicians than with the actual weather, but this afternoon it was difficult to believe. She didn't know weather could be this cold. They even gave the temperature with something they called the wind chill factor and today it was below zero!

Isa was getting very used to getting around the city by walking or using public transportation since she still had a difficult time paying for short taxi rides. Richard's insisted Anaís would want Isa to lead life as she herself would, but ten dollars for a five-minute ride! It was ridiculous!

She thought of Anaís in Havana, wearing at most a light sweater and momentarily yearned to be back there in warm, tropical weather. Still, it was certainly heady to lead the type of life her sister had in the States.

Just yesterday a call from one of the doormen announced to her that the cleaning service was ready to come up to her apartment to do the bimonthly chores. She had not been in the apartment the last couple of time that the service had cleaned the apartment, and the visit had been supervised instead by one of the condo staff.

Isa watched intently as the crew of three women speaking Polish among themselves took over the rooms with buckets, dusters, polishing sprays and vacuum cleaners The tall, blonde one who directed the other two in their chores and apparently was the only one who spoke English had asked her about the towels. Since Isa had no idea what she was talking about, she had taken the stocky blonde to the spare room closet where Anaís kept towels and bed linens, but the woman had laughed and said something to the other girls that Isa had not understood. Isa saw later that the cleaning woman had found thick, colored towels in a bin next to the kitchen. Throughout the morning, Isa watched as they used them to dry and clean, towels that back home would have been the envy of everyone she knew, being used here as rags.

And, now she awaited to have her teeth bleached. Back in Cuba, there were no cosmetic procedures for teeth. Actually, people prayed that they would not need a dentist since painkillers were almost nonexistent. A visit to the dentist came after a bad toothache and not for cosmetic purposes. Her sister's life was almost too much to believe.

"Good afternoon, Dr. Moran. I am Amala, your technician for today's procedure. "The stocky, short Indian-looking woman spoke with a heavy accent. She pulled up a rolling chair next to Isa and smiled.

"Hello. Nice to meet you, Amala."

"Well, do you have any questions about the procedure before we begin making your smile even prettier than it already is?" She asked the question even as she began taking out trays and gels and setting them up on the counter.

"No," Isa gulped. "Only, is it going to hurt?" Richard said it would not, but Richard would suffer anything to look good.

"Not at all. Actually, today you are only going to get half the treatment, for 30 minutes. The next appointment will be a bit longer and might leave your gums a little sensitive, but there is no pain." She approached Isa with the gel and tray. "Here, open your mouth...that's it...Good! Now put these goggles on...yes, because of the laser..." Amala positioned the laser appliance next to Isa's teeth. "Ready?"

She handed Isa a small radio and earplugs.

"Just lean back and relax. I will be back before you know it." She smiled at Isa and lowered the lights as she left the room, closing the door behind her. After the first few minutes of discomfort, Isa almost fell asleep with the music playing in her ears. If Chencha could see her now, she thought. Amala's soft hand on hers startled her.

"All done, Dr. Moran." She took out the trays and handed Isa a small mirror. "What do you think?"

Isa wiped the drool from her lips, looked in the mirror and smiled. Her teeth glistened as white as the teeth of a one-year old child. How much did this just cost?

"Well, we're done with you until...about July. Now remember to read this pamphlet with the list of foods and drinks to avoid for the next few days since your teeth are so porous now."

They walked together down the long hallway, and Isa wondered how many other different beauty procedures were being performed behind the closed doors.

At the front desk, her printout on the procedure read six-hundred dollars! Isa stared at the figure and looked at the receptionist.

"Everything alright? Will you be using a credit card?" The young woman took Isa's card. "Well, then, you're done. I'll send you a copy of the transaction when it goes through...our connection is down."

Isa nodded and took the heavy coat that the technician handed her. "Have a good one!"

Six hundred dollars for 30 minutes getting her teeth to look whiter! The last time she had traded dollars for pesos with money Anaís had given her when they first met, the exchange rate in the Cuban black market had been twenty pesos for one dollar! Not even people high up in the government, like Diego, earned anywhere near the equivalent of what she had just paid. No wonder some of Chencha's friends with relatives in the United States always talked about how rich Americans were.

And the longer she lived her sister's life, the sadder she became thinking about how meager the Cuban economy was and the hardships this brought to the people she cared about in Cuba. No wonder people risked their lives, crossing in rafts and inner tubes. She had always thought they were crazy. Now she understood a bit more. They must have heard from their own relatives what was on the other side.

The other side of the moon. Isa smiled, thinking of Chencha's old African story of the children who found their way to the other side of the moon where craters were made of caramel covered flan and the lakes and rivers ran with the sweet taste of mango juice that had fallen from the skies as rain. Like the night of seeing her first snowfall, the thought of the old children's story was her example of pure perfection.

She was tasting the sweetness of freedom and opportunity. Would she ever be able to live without those again?

The cold, gusting winds had picked up, and Isa wrapped herself tighter inside her coat, teeth chattering in the sub-zero weather. When she went back to Havana, this weather was not something she was going to miss.

Five thirty! Shit! He had spent the entire day looking through boxes and still had not found the birth certificates he was looking for.

What had appeared like an orderly file keeping system had become a disorganized mess by the time Diego had gone back to the early years of the Revolution. It was as if the chaotic feeling of those days had infiltrated even the record keeping of births and deaths, compounded by the mixing of information from the different provinces so that the Pinar del Río records mistakenly included documents from Matanzas and Havana as well.

If it weren't that he had already invested the greater part of his day, Diego would have given up hours ago. That, and the fact that it was not his nature to give up until he got the information he wanted or needed. Unfortunately, this time he could not delegate the tedious chore of searching for forty-year-old paperwork to an assistant. He still didn't know what he was searching for. It was his dog with a bone mentality that kept him digging further and further, refusing to quit.

He leaned back and sipped the still hot Cuban coffee that the clerk had brought him for the fifth time. His adrenaline was failing, but the caffeine kept him on task. But what task exactly? To find Isa's birth certificate? And then what? To see if other surnames on the certificate would lead him to find the mysterious look-alike cousin? And then what? To find out, if she had been born in Cuba, when she left the island? To go back to Arturo to see if he had any information on her about possible subversive anti-Cuban activities in the United States?

And then what? He had no idea what he would do with any of the information. He just knew he needed it.

Putting his cup down, he put the lid back on the box and placing it carefully back on the wooden shelf, picked up one of the last boxes, *La Habana-1960 a 1963.*

CHAPTER 28

Feeling Cuban

ANAÍS HAD NEVER HEARD SUCH HIGH NOTES COMING FROM A TRUMPET. She had never seen such lightning fingers playing piano jazz. And all of it was amazing to her, even coming as she did from jazz town itself in Chicago, where her parents had exposed her to the dynamic music that was best played in the narrow bars of that old city of grit and verve.

Thousands of people, including foreigners had again converged on Havana. Anaís was getting used to the partying spirit of the Cubans. She wondered if their readiness to celebrate was in part fueled by a need to forget the daily hardships they all faced. Just a few short weeks ago, Diego had taken her to the José Martí celebrations honoring the great Cuban hero's birthday, and the crowds there, also, were wildly enthusiastic.

"You look tired, Diego."

"*Sí, un poco.*" He thought of his marathon day searching through old records, which yielded nothing.

"But I'm glad we're here. This is definitely one of my favorite events."

He looked at her smiling profile, thinking it was uncanny how much Isa looked like the U.S. cousin in the pictures.

"It's unbelievable! How can these men still have such energy?"

There they were, the old men of the Buena Vista Social Club exciting the crowd to dancing and screaming like teenagers at a rock concert. The world-renowned Havana Jazz Festival had brought together the best of the best, and Anaís could not believe she was listening to the winners of the nineteen-ninety-nine Grammy award.

She had heard of the Buena Vista musicians a few years earlier after Ry Cooder brought back the group's music to the States. She had even seen the video of them playing live at various venues in Cuba. But in real life, these prodigious musicians were beyond anything imaginable, especially given their advanced age. Francisco Repilado in his Panama hat could not possibly be in his nineties, could he? And the voices of Ibrahim Ferrer and Omara Portuondo, with their rich haunting melodies belonged to 30 year olds, not septuagenarians.

Anaís looked at Diego, enjoying the late afternoon of music in his white Cuban *guayabera*. How tanned and handsome he looked. Her gaze caught his eye and they smiled at each other, his hand squeezing her thigh in a tender yet sensual manner.

"They are magnificent, aren't they?"

"Absolutely. And I can't believe Los Van Van and Irakere are also going to show up."

"But why not. We're the best in this music and the world is here to hear us." He pointed at the many nationalities represented in the audience sitting in the bleacher style open courtyard of the Casa de la Cultura.

"They're not here only for our beautiful beaches and beautiful women. We have much to be proud of. And our music...Well..."

His pride was infectious.

"Now, that crap that they call hip-hop...we could do without that influence from America. Reggae is alright. After all, that's the music of our black brothers. Although we will not allow our young men to keep dreadlocks like that..." he pointed to the Trinidad group waiting on the side.

"It's just hair," Anaís heard herself saying, and Diego looked at her perplexed.

"Yes, but that's how it begins. First, hair that doesn't conform to anything anyone approves of..."

"But who is anyone else? I mean, I don't like it...I can't see you like that, but even if you had a strange hair style, it wouldn't change who you are, would it?"

What was Isa saying? Diego asked himself. History proved that youth left unchecked eventually became troublemakers.

"Well..."

"Oh, look, it's the one with the cowboy hat! I can't believe he's... what...eighty, ninety?"

"I lose track. They're all between 70 and 90 something. Isa, my apologies that I was late in picking you up. We missed Los Muñequitos de Matanzas. But I got caught up in...something."

"That's alright, Diego." She smiled at him. "I was watching a Brazilian *telenovela* with Chencha. She loves to watch her sopa operas." She paused.

"By the way, Diego, do you think you could take me to the CUBALSE store? Our refrigerator isn't working too well, and Chencha...she says she's been on the list waiting for a brassiere for about a year and a half. I'd like to go shopping for her."

He looked at her astonished. Anaís noticed the surprise in his eyes.

"Oh, you're wondering about the money. Well, you know, that cousin of mine whom I met a few months ago. She left us dollars. I think she felt guilty..."

"*¡Ahhh! La prima.* Yes, this cousin of yours was certainly very generous with you. I don't remember you ever mentioning her, Isa. Tell me about her." His brown eyes narrowed as he fixed his gaze intently on her flustered face.

"*Mi prima...sí.* Her name is...Ana Isabel." Anaís felt herself stumbling, and swallowed hard. "I didn't know about her either. She looked us up... Chencha and I, that is. *Sí*, it was nice to meet her."

"*Ahhh. Claro que sí.* Of course. But how strange that you didn't know about her. How did she know about you?"

"You know," she swallowed again, "I'm not sure. We didn't see each other that much. Just a few times. And she left us money and a few other things, like the cassette player you saw a while back." Suddenly, she remembered that it was illegal for Cubans to own dollars, although everyone who could did indeed own them. "I know it's not right to use dollars." She looked into his eyes, looking for signs of what Diego might be thinking.

"Oh, no. It's alright. You and I know that many of our citizens get monthly money grams from relatives in Miami. Is she from Miami?"

"No. No. Actually, she is from Chicago. Her family moved there many years ago." Anaís felt her entire body steaming from the anxiety. She heard herself speaking in measured syllables to make sure she said the right words. Applause and screams to the musicians of *otra, otra* for an encore thankfully interrupted her explanation.

"Oh, good. They're going to play again. *¡Qué bueno!*" She grabbed his arm, and hummed along with melody. Diego looked at her, feeling struck as always by her beauty and vivacity, and something else that was new in Isa. Perhaps an air of devil-may-care attitude and confidence she had not had before.

Diego liked this new Isa, despite the fact that some of her ideas and comments seemed somewhat radical to him. Yes, he smiled at her angelic face. He liked this new, even more exciting woman. But he still needed to know more about the look-alike cousin and what business and interest she had in Cuba.

———

Diego had left a note on Isa's desk that he needed to go to Mexico on urgent business and would not be meeting her for Carnaval, or Mardi Gras as it was called in the States. In fact, his trip might take a few weeks. His note was full of allusions to their lovemaking, how much he was already missing her and how much lovemaking they would need to make up when he got back. She smiled, thinking about their intimate moments and Diego's sexual hunger. He was the most passionate and tender lover she had known.

She felt her body tingle just thinking about him. She had not felt so alive and excited in a very, very long time. Perhaps not since her relationship with her husband.

Tears welled up in her eyes as she pictured his youthful, smiling face. They had been so in love.

Was it love she was feeling now for Diego? Perhaps it was simply raw lust?

She looked at his note, scribbled in a large, strong penmanship, and signed with his initials. Her body tingled again.

They had made plans to go to the Malecón for Carnaval, and she certainly wasn't going to miss that. In fact, while Diego was gone, perhaps she would do some exploring of Cuba on her own. But first, Carnaval. She asked Chencha if she wanted to go with her.

"Oh, child, what are you telling me? You want to go to Carnaval? That's only for low people, it's not a decent event. No, no. You can't go there."

Chencha made the statement with a finality that amused Anaís, and she wondered if her sister was often persuaded by the old woman. Certainly, she was not going to be told what to do, yet she did not want to offend Chencha in any way. She took the old woman gently by the shoulders, bending over her gently.

"However, Chencha, dear Chencha, I've never seen *Carnaval* here. This will be probably my only chance." Anaís towered over the woman, and bent further to look pleadingly into her eyes. "*Por favor.* Remember, I'm from Chicago. Like you said, gangsters, Al Capone...I can take care of myself. I really can."

Chencha pursed her big, red lips.

"And why don't you go with Don Diego? It would be alright with me if he accompanied you...although, in truth, if he is a true gentleman he wouldn't let you go either."

Let me go? Anaís grimaced at the thought that she would need anyone's permission. But Chencha was old school and traditional.

"Diego is in Mexico on business. So, why don't you come with me? This way, I will feel protected. And we can come back whenever you want. Please." She smiled, her green eyes sparkling in anticipation.

Chencha's lips were still pursed as she looked up at Anaís. She was starting to understand that Isa's sister had a totally different temperament, very strong willed and fearless, not qualities Chencha liked in a woman. But then, she was from America, where she heard women thought they could act just like men.

"I think it is a bad idea." She looked at the unwavering green gaze.

"But I can see that you might get it into your head to go on your own. And that would not do. No, that would not do." She shook her turbaned head, and hearing the knock on the door, went to answer it.

"Okay, we will go for a bit."

A knock at the door stopped their conversation. Anaís knew who was on the other side and let Chencha open the door wanting to get the full effect of the surprise. When the old woman saw the two scrawny men handing her some papers and showing a brand new small refrigerator, Anaís felt this was the best gift she had ever purchased for anyone. In shock, Chencha was still standing at the door, when the men began to drag out the Russian refrigerator that Anaís nicknamed *el dinosauro*.

"*Gracias, señores.*" Anaís closed the door behind them, handing Chencha a brown paper bag the men had left on top of the new Canadian brand appliance.

"Chencha, this is for you, too."

The small black figure continued staring speechlessly. She absent-mindedly took the bag that Anaís handed her, her gnarled hands slowly taking out three white brassieres.

The large cups stared up at the two of them in silence. When she finally spoke, Chencha's eyes were brimming with tears.

"How in the world did you get these? I have been waiting almost two years for one at the store. It should be in soon. But these beauties..." her rough fingers touched the silky fabric gently. "Nothing like these beauties." She let the bag drop to the floor as she looked up at the refrigerator.

"And this!" Opening the door, she looked in amazement at an interior not dilapidated or corroded. "How did you manage this? This costs a fortune."

Anaís smiled at the joy she saw in the old woman's face. It felt wonderful to be able to do something for the person who had taken such good care of her sister all those years since their parents' death, someone who was now taking such good care of her.

"Chencha, I don't want you to think any more about having to *resolver*, to make do. We have money, dollars, in the dolls, and I have money back home which is for you and Isa too."

"I can't believe we have such a beautiful refrigerator. And these brassieres...Can I put one on?"

"They're yours. Of course. Tell me if they're the right size."

Chencha ambled to the small bathroom and a few minutes later came back into the room smiling happily, still wearing the housecoat, but her ample bosom now a few inches higher than usual.

"It is so comfortable. Many thanks, my child." Coquettishly, she looked at herself in the small mirror over the table against the wall.

"But this is enough. Please no more purchases. Or the neighbors may start to wonder."

"You look wonderful, Chencha. And don't pay any mind to the neighbors. Tell them, tell them you found out you have rich relatives in America and they are sending you money grams, like so many other people here receive. That can't get us in trouble, right?"

Chencha was still admiring her transformation in the small mirror.

"Yes, we could say that. Oh, we need to put our food back in the refrigerator."

Anaís helped her place the few items back into the new appliance. It wasn't much bigger than the old Russian one, but there was no rust on this one.

Diego had given her a card so that she could shop at the store whenever she wanted, telling her to have the items charged to his name. Of course, she wouldn't do that, but she certainly planned to make many trips to CUBALSE and if possible, replace everything in her sister's apartment. However far the money in the doll would take her. Her next trip to CUBALSE she would stock up on food.

"As long as I am here, and even after I leave, Chencha, I don't want you to ever have to worry about *resolver* again." Her arms circled the frail old body. "You deserve this and more."

Chencha was not a sentimental kind of woman, but Anaís saw tears in her eyes. Anaís could only imagine the economic hardships that Chencha and her sister had endured all these years. The old woman patted her hand, and looked up at her.

"*Bueno*, we will see. Now, let's get going to the Carnaval before it gets to be too late and the real craziness begins." She ambled over to her small bedroom, mumbling under her breath how it was not proper for them to mix with the riffraff that would be out in the streets that evening.

Chapter 29

Varadero

Diego had called her at the office and confirmed that indeed his business in Mexico City would take longer than expected and he would not be back for a few weeks. Anaís was glad that prior to his trip they had made every effort to see each other, hungry for their private time together. Yes, she would miss him, but she also felt glad to have the time to explore Varadero and the hotel area where the Russians wanted to build.

Certainly, Isa had to know her way around this second most visited city in Cuba and Anaís definitely needed a crash course on the resort's highlights to handle not only any questions by the Russians but also by any other prospective client. She knew that the brief tour of the beach resort that she had made with the Illinois delegation and her Pinar cousins would not suffice.

Chencha had reminded her that the only way to get there was to take the buses or to hitch a ride with someone. Neither sounded like a pleasant idea. Anaís had seen the buses that went out to the countryside, and they were old, open pick-up trucks that hauled people and animals. She thought about the taxi driver that she had used a few times while she was staying at the hotel with the delegation, but decided that it was too risky to look him up since he might be suspicious of an American still in Cuba after such a long time. Instead, she took the bus to CUBALSE where there were always many taxis catering to the foreign shoppers. She looked for the oldest and most serious-looking *taxista* in the line of taxis waiting for foreigners wanting transportation. Marcelo, a sixty-something looking man was very happy when she said she wanted to hire him for the weekend.

The drive to Varadero was indeed her favorite and she was glad to see that Marcelo insisted that they travel through the Yumurí Valley to see what he called one of the most glorious sites in the world. Yes, Marcelo was recommending a circuitous route to Varadero, but Anaís knew it was well worth the extra time.

The Valley of Delights, as Marcelo said it was affectionately called, was certainly the most beautiful valley she had ever seen, with its lush vegetation and limestone cliffs and the rivers Yumurí and Bacunayagua meandering through the landscape. It was breathtaking.

On their way back to the Vía Blanca main highway, she glimpsed the turquoise sea beyond sisal plantations and lush hills. Marcelo was a veritable fountain of information, something that she had come to expect from just about any Cuban citizen. The Revolution had promised to create a literate and educated workforce, and Anaís would agree that it had kept that promise.

"*Señorita,* do you want take the *Autopista o La Avenida? La Avenida* goes by the ocean, and is much nicer."

"Oh, yes, *La Avenida.* And what I would really like is if you would show me the Varadero that the tourists see as well as the Varadero that only the locals know."

"You have been here before, no?"

"Yes...but I stayed pretty much at the hotel. This time, I really want to get to know Varadero."

Marcelo seemed newly excited. "*Bueno, bueno.* I'll take you to all the special places *turistas* don't know. Should we start now?"

"Sure. Just pretend I'm here for the first time."

Marcelo shifted in his seat, smiling at her through the rear view mirror. "We'll go this way, then." He turned into a meandering road, past the intoxicating scents of hibiscus, oleander and jasmine. "You know, many *Americanos* came to Varadero a long time ago. *La familia DuPont*—the Dupont family, built a private home on the water that's like a small castle. Did you see it on your previous trip?"

"Yes. I saw it. And it is a castle, you're right."

"*Y Al Capone...*"

He pronounced each syllable of the legendary Chicago Mafioso's name: ahl-cah-poh-ne. She remembered that on her visit with the Illinois group to the *Casa de Al* restaurant they had all laughed at the menu which included a Lucky Luciano filet, commenting that not even Castro could get rid of the American mobster's memory.

"And the Russians. Yes, they love our beaches, and Varadero for long time was...how do you say, of they...?"

"It was theirs."

"Yes, theirs..." he repeated the word, trying to commit it to memory. "We *Cubanos* cannot be here, on the best beaches by the good hotels. Only Russians and *turistas*. Then, the Russians. Out." He made a whistling sound with his mouth and hands, as if he himself was throwing out the unwanted lot. "We don't like Russians much here. They think they're the boss of the Cuban people." He drove animatedly. "No more!"

Anaís listened to Marcelo's political analysis while marveling at the beautiful beaches, the white, fine sand like powdered sugar, the ocean every shade of blue imaginable. She understood perfectly why the Canadians and Russians were trying to grab a piece of this area of unmatched natural splendor. Other than the jellyfish which had kept her from swimming in the ocean the last time she had visited Varadero, Anaís could not think of a more spectacular beach anywhere else in the world that she had visited.

He was pulling up the Estrella Caribe Hotel where she had stayed previously. "If you need me, I'll be around the corner."

"No, Marcelo. You take the rest of the day and evening for yourself." She put a one-hundred dollar bill in his pocket. "You have a good time and I'll see you tomorrow."

Marcelo politely did not bother looking at the amount of money knowing Anaís would pay him well.

"Ahhh, and *las Cuevas de Bellamar!* You must to go there soon. It's a cave with...how do you say...*estalactitas?*".

"Stalactites."

"Thank you. Stalactites." Marcelo did his best to imitate her pronunciation. "Yes. Stalactites like *flores*, like flowers, from the roof of the caves."

He kissed his lips in appreciation of the cave's beauty. "And there's a room...It's like being in a church."

"Wherever you think we should go, let's do it. I want to see everything around here."

"*Gracias, señorita.* Enjoy your evening in Varadero."

"You, too, Marcelo."

Sí, she would do her homework and she would be the best salesperson possible for any Varadero business.

CHAPTER 30

March in Chicago

ALRIGHT, THIS WAS THE DAY, ISA THOUGHT, LOOKING OUT HER LIVING room window. Spring was around the corner and she needed to practice her rollerblading. Anaís was registered as part of an office team to raise funds for a women's center. The winter had just been too rough, the layers of clothing too many for her to even think about doing an outdoor sport. Her few attempts with Richard had given her the confidence to rollerblade in a straight line. Now she needed to learn the rest. She grabbed her things and headed out the door. Downstairs in the lobby she exchanged the daily pleasantries with the doorman, promising him more black bean soup the next time she made them.

It was a perfect day outside, dry and sunny and mild for Chicago in March. The 50-degree weather had brought out people taking advantage of the unusual temperature for outdoor activities. Pedestrians strolled leisurely while others on the lakefront enjoyed jogging, biking and rollerblading. The weather still felt very cold to her, but still she could really appreciate the difference in the air as the days were slowly becoming warmer and daylight lingered longer. It was difficult for Isa to understand the weather here. Just a week ago, people were shoveling snow and huge city trucks were spreading de-icing materials on the streets. Today—well today was balmy by comparison.

As she briskly walked along the lake to the spot where she would meet up with Richard, she looked at the bare trees and bushes lining the median, the yellowed grass and the brown flower beds thinking what a miracle that soon everything would be alive and flowering again. At least that was what Richard said she would see in a few weeks. She was excited at the prospect not only of warmer weather but also of seeing for herself how the landscape would be transformed. She had never seen the blossom of a spring, and Isa looked forward to it with anticipation

She was not very far from the agreed meeting spot near the boarded up concession stand. Feeling energized and confident, she decided to surprise Richard on rollerblades.

She sat down on a nearby park bench. The wood felt cold through her warm leggings. She strapped on her roller blades and imagined herself gracefully skating up to Richard and impressing him with her athleticism. In Cuba, she had done a lot of swimming and running, but never skating. And Richard was so very good on skates that she felt envious merely thinking about him gliding, turning and stopping effortlessly.

Steadying herself and readjusting her fanny pack, she took a deep breath and slowly started to skate, staying on the right side like Richard had cautioned her. Bikers and joggers passed her by, and Isa felt childish skating with care and trepidation. She began skating a little faster, balancing herself with outstretched arms. She felt confident, and increased her skating speed a bit more.

The cool breeze tousled her hair into her face and she reached up to brush it out of her eyes. As she did so, she saw Richard about a block away walking toward the concession stand. She skated faster. The wind blew a little harder, tossing her hair even more. She brushed her bangs back and then waved in Richard's direction trying to catch his attention.

Suddenly she realized that the sidewalk ahead was descending into a cross street. She began to panic as she felt her body moving faster and faster toward the intersection. Richard had shown her how to stop by gliding into the grass, but she was moving too fast now to change direction. She heard herself scream as she whizzed past a young couple jogging in the middle of the road, and then heard them gasp behind her as they watched her flailing arms and stiff body jettison towards the street. A loud *¡Ay Dios mío!* escaped her lips right before she felt something slam into her side, throwing her onto the grass.

Dazed and shaking, she didn't know what had hit her. Had she entered the intersection? A car? A biker? She was face down on the grass, a heavy bulk upon her. She lay dazed under the weight, but thankful to be alive.

The weight moved off her, and someone helped her turn over. The bright sunshine of the noon sun made her squint as she looked up at dark sunglasses and a red ski cap.

"Are you alright?"

She looked up at the shadow above her. As she started to turn, a sharp pain shot up her right arm. She must have flinched because the person over her told her not to move, and gently pushed her back on the grass. Isa felt the pain in her arm become sharper as she tried to sit up.

"I'm sorry," she said, pushing the man away and sitting up. "I'm very sorry."

"No, don't move. You shouldn't be moving until we know if you're injured. Where does it hurt? Can you see well?"

So many questions. The man's unsolicited conversation was becoming very annoying. She pushed him a little harder, and he lost his balance and fell back on his heels. They were now both sitting on the grass, facing each other.

"I'm sorry" she said again. "Did I bump into you?"

"No. I pushed you. You were headed for the street...you were going very fast and it didn't look like you knew what you were doing...I mean, it looked like you couldn't stop."

¡Ay, Dios mío! The annoying stranger had thankfully kept her from getting hit by a car.

"Sí...yes. I'm fine." She cradled her arm.

"You're hurt..." He touched her arm. "You should really get that looked at...Let me take you to the hospital...it's right over there..."

"No, thank you..." He helped her get up.

"Isa!" Richard was running up to them. "What happened to you? I saw you waving at me, and then you disappeared." He looked at Isa's face, still covered with dirt and grass stains, and then looked at the man standing next to her.

"Your friend looked like she didn't...like she couldn't stop and she was heading toward the street. I pushed her out of the way. But I think

I've gotten her hurt anyway. She's been grabbing her arm."

"Did you hurt yourself, Isa...I mean, Ani?"

"My arm hurts."

"You really should have that looked at," the stranger repeated. "The hospital is right by here. I can drive you there. I feel responsible for this."

"No, thank you. You stopped me before I got into the street. Thank you. Ouch!"

"Come on. He's right that somebody should take a look at that. Thanks, man."

"No, really, I feel terrible. Let me drive you. I'm right over there."

"What do you think, Ani? I walked over here, so we can take a taxi."

"But why wait for a taxi? Really, I'll take you. Come on."

Isa nodded.

"Let's take your skates off."

Both men hovered over her. Supporting her good arm while the other took off each skate and helped her with the sneakers she had in her backpack. Isa felt her face get redder and redder as people glanced at them.

"I can do that." She tried to bend over to tie her shoes. She winced as pain shot through her arm.

"No, you can't."

The stranger took her skates and Richard held her good arm. They walked in silence for half a block where the stranger opened the door to a large SUV.

"Nice wheels!" Richard said.

"Thanks. It drives pretty well."

They helped Isa into the back seat. She leaned her head on the recliner and closed her eyes, wondering what she had done to her arm. Could it be broken? The two men in the front seat were carrying on a conversation about cars as if they had always known each other. Isa looked at the back of the stranger's head, blonde curls peeping out of the red ski cap. His dark sunglasses lent a mysterious look to his handsome face. He must have felt her gaze because he turned to her. She averted her eyes.

"We're almost there. How are you feeling?"

"Embarrassed."

"Why? Rollerblading is a tough sport. I have my own stories of spills to testify to it."

"No shit! I've got a gash in my knee..." Richard chimed in.

Isa listened as the men shared their sports injuries with bravado. It wasn't long before she saw the sign for the emergency entrance to the hospital and the stranger pulled up to the door. Richard immediately got out and helped her out. The stranger walked in front of them through the automatic glass doors.

"How are you holding up? I hope we don't have to wait too long. Hospitals are terrible." Richard was saying to her. "These emergency rooms sometimes are a zoo."

"Dr. Mitchell? What are you doing here on your day off? Can't get away from us, huh?" A short, heavy nurse smiled at the stranger.

"Hi, Tawana. No, I can't get enough of this place." He tapped her shoulder. "But listen, do me a favor," he said pulling her to a side. "Take this young woman in to get x-rays of her right arm and shoulder. I don't want her waiting here. Her injury is my fault. I'll tell you all about it later."

"You're the boss," nurse Tawana answered.

"I'll see you in there." He winked at them. What beautiful blue eyes, Isa thought, watching the stranger disappear behind a gray door.

"Come on, honey, this way." They followed her into a large, well-illuminated room with several beds, some with drawn curtains around them. Pointing to an empty bed, Nurse Tawana pulled a curtain around them for privacy. "Alright honey. Just make yourself comfortable here. Let me get my paperwork and we'll get you going as fast as I can so Doc can get back to his day off." She disappeared behind the curtain.

"Gorgeous and a doctor, too," said Richard ever feigning that his heart was a flutter around a good looking man. "I think he's straight. Damn! When am I going to get lucky."

Richard moved to help Isa remove her jacket. "How does it feel? How's your arm?" he fussed over her.

"Fine, if I don't move it. How stupid of me, Richard. I should have waited to skate with you."

"Sweetie, shit happens."

"Shit happens? What kind of an expression is that?"

"A pretty appropriate expression for this, if you ask me. Don't you have that in Cuba? I know shit happens there too."

"Yes, it does," she tried to laugh, but her arm was starting to hurt more.

Nurse Tawana pulled the drawn curtain to the side.

"Alright, honey. You can come with me while your husband..."

"Friend."

"Whatever. You fill out these forms, and you come with me. Do you want a wheelchair?"

"Of course not."

"Just asking, honey."

They walked past a series of curtained areas, and then past the nurses' station. Her stranger, Dr. Mitchell, was talking on the phone, dark sunglasses stuck into the collar of his cobalt-colored sweater. Isa thought him the handsomest man she had seen in ages.

"Through here, honey."

Inside the x-ray room, a technician explained how he would need to move her arm and shoulder to get the pictures from various angles. Isa moaned through most of the positions and sighed with relief when the technician said they were done. He escorted her back to the examining area where she found Richard and Dr. Mitchell chatting.

"Well, good news, Ms. Moran," Dr. Mitchell said.

"Doctor Moran" Richard corrected, and Isa looked at him with a reproachful look for emphasizing the title. "She's a not a medical doctor, but still..."

"I understand," the doctor smiled, "Dr. Moran, it looks like what you have is a bruised shoulder. There was nothing unusual in the x-rays. Nothing is broken, and I don't see anything to indicate a dislocation. It will be sore and probably quite painful for a few days until the bruising subsides. So, after a few days of babying your arm, you should be fine. Let me just check your range of motion, before you leave."

He put his papers down and walked toward her. Isa blushed, thinking not about her arm as he manipulated it in different directions, but about how alluring he was. As he moved her arm back, she winced. He apologized. With his strong fingers he applied a light pressure around her arm joint, her shoulder. He was so close and his voice seemed to breathe the questions right into her ear as he probed to check on areas where she felt pain. His voice, his closeness, his looks, made her tremble.

For a moment, she thought he seemed a little flustered, too.

"I don't feel anything unusual. I think we will immobilize your arm for a while. Make sure you get some rest and I'll prescribe some anti-inflammatories, then you should be as good as new in just a few days." The nurse had come in with an arm holster and approached Isa to put it on, but Dr. Mitchell took it from her. "Thanks, Tawana. I'll do it." Tawana's eyebrows arched in surprise. She smiled as she turned and disappeared behind the drawn curtain.

"No rollerblading for a while, though, Dr. Moran. If you were to fall on this arm again before it is completely healed—well, that would not be good." He fitted the holster around her shoulder with care and a gentle touch. "And when you do start to rollerblade again, well, make sure you practice stopping, and no speeding on those things until you feel that you are in total control. Alright?" She looked up into his eyes and thought they were the color of the ocean at Varadero, and seemed almost as deep.

"Yes. I understand." She didn't want him to take his hand off her shoulder.

"I'll be more careful next time." They smiled at each other, neither one moving.

Tawana reappeared around the curtain.

"Ready to go? You need to sign these discharge papers." She started to hand them to Isa, but Dr. Mitchell took them from her and turned to hand them to Richard.

"Let's have your friend sign them for you so you don't have to strain any more than necessary today."

"Alright." Richard handed the signed papers to Nurse Tawana. "Anything else we need to do here?"

Dr. Mitchell helped Isa get down from the hospital bed as if she were a frail and delicate child. "No, she's ready to go," he said as the two of them exchanged a lingering look.

Richard gently pulled Isa's uninjured arm. "Then come on, already. Let's go."

Isa steadied herself against the table. "Thank you for everything," she said, still looking into his eyes.

"Thank you for not suing me."

She smiled. "Sue? You saved my life."

"Nothing so dramatic."

"Yes, you did."

"It doesn't matter." Richard's voice was a little exasperated. "You're both right. Now let's get out of here, Isa. I hate hospitals. No offense, Dr. Mitchell."

"None taken." He looked at Isa again. "You take care of yourself."

"Yes. Thank you." Richard gently guided her out through the automatic doors.

The emergency room waiting area now was even more crowded. As she looked around at crying babies, people coughing, and others holding bloodied towels to some part of their body, Isa realized what quick and special treatment she had just received. Richard must have been thinking the same thing.

"Yes, it was very special, Richard. But I don't think it was personal. He just felt badly because of what happened. Don't you think that's all that it was?"

He looked at her and laughed heartily.

"That room was so hot with the two of you that I almost had to take my clothes off."

She jabbed him in the ribs with her good hand.

"You're terrible."

"Come on, now," he pulled her ear. "You're going to tell me you didn't like the delicious looking doctor?"

"Yes, he was handsome."

"Handsome! I could eat him up." Richard licked his lips. "But, again, all the good ones are straight."

"It doesn't matter what I think, anyway," she said, as they got into the cab that Richard had hailed down. "That was it. As you say here."

"Well, you could sprain the other arm."

She jabbed him again. "You are just terrible." She leaned over and kissed his cheek. "And wonderful. Thank you for being there with me."

"But, of course." He smiled and took her left hand. "And you need to go home and do as the good doctor said. I'll get you settled in and stay with you if you want."

"No, Richard. It's such a beautiful day. Like you said, there aren't going to be many days like this in March here in Chicago. Just drop me off and you go have fun. I'm already feeling, how do you say when your head doesn't feel like your own head..."

"Light-headed?"

"Yes, light-headed. I want to lie down and maybe sleep for a while. I feel very tired all of a sudden."

"Probably the pain killers they gave you. Alright, then, I'll drop you off. But I'll come by later. How about if I bring Chinese and rent a couple of videos?"

She yawned as he helped her out of the cab, taking out the house keys from her fanny pack. "That sounds great. But only if you don't have something better to do than sit with an invalid on a Saturday night."

"Well, you're right. If I get lucky out there you'll be history." They laughed. The doorman asked what had happened and Richard gave him a quick response.

"Are you sure that I can't help you get upstairs into bed, get you some food or something?"

She pushed him toward the door. "Just go. I'll be fine."

"I'll see you later."

"Only if you're unlucky," she said behind her. The two elderly women exiting the elevator looked at her in mild disapproval.

"The expression is if I don't GET lucky," Richard yelled back.

She had fallen into a deep sleep, brought on by the medication and nerves. When she finally opened her eyes with some effort, the room was totally dark. She had slept a long time, and it was almost six in the evening. No wonder her stomach was growling.

Her arm still ached and she was hungry, but she hated leaving the warmth of lying under the down comforter. She lay in the darkness and comfort of her sister's bedroom.

Her phone rang. She flinched as she reached for it with her injured arm.

"You have a visitor, Dr. Moran."

"Thanks, Julius. Yes, send him up." She got up slowly and looked at herself in the mirror. A chill made her nipples harden under the silk long sleeve top that was rather transparent and clingy. Richard could care less.

She heard the knock at the door and yelled out.

"I'm coming, Richard. I am hungry! I hope you have the Chinese—Dr. Mitchell!" She felt the blood rush up to her neck and face as she opened the door.

"I'm sorry. You didn't know it was me? I thought the doorman called you." Dr. Mitchell seemed to be forcing himself to look at Isa's eyes instead of her body.

"Oh. Yes, he called. But he said my friend...not that you are not..."

"I understand," he chuckled. "You thought it was your boyfriend. The one I met today?"

"He's not my boyfriend. Richard is happy. I mean, gay. He's my best friend here."

"Here?"

"He's my best friend...here...everywhere."

"I see."

They both stood awkwardly at the door. Isa looked down at her clothes. "Oh, excuse me. I just got up. I will be right back." She stepped behind the door, disappearing briefly. She reappeared again in a sweat suit. He was still standing outside her front door.

"Yes. So. You're here. Did I forget something at the hospital, Dr. Mitchell?"

"No, not at all. And please call me Sean. And, no, you didn't forget anything. I just thought I'd stop by and see how your arm was doing. It was my fault. I don't usually check in on people who come to the emergency room, of course. But, as I said, this was my fault, and I live close by, and it's my day off..."

Isa looked at the beautiful man at her door. Her heart was beating faster, as it had when he had examined her arm earlier. She only half heard his words. How could anyone have such blonde, almost white hair, and such dark tanned skin? It intensified the blue of his eyes. He was a few inches taller than she was, not tall by American standards. *He is perfect. The most attractive man she had met in a very long time.* What was he saying?

"...so since I see you're fine, well, that's all I wanted to see, really, so..."

"I'm sorry," she interrupted him, opening the door. "I am so rude. Please come in, Dr. Mitchell."

"Sean."

"Yes. Sean. You are so very nice to come to see me." He stepped into her foyer and looked around.

"What a great spot you have here."

"Thanks. Yes, I love it here. Please, let me have your coat. And please... call me Isa. My name is Ana Isabel and most people call me Ani...it is a long story...but I prefer Isa, my parents' nickname for me. Please call me Isa."

They had been talking for almost an hour, and Isa had even completely forgotten that she was hungry.

"One of my best times, a time when I really felt I was helping out, were the two years I spent in the Peace Corps in Guatemala. Have you ever had an experience where you suddenly had to be creative about everything in your life, from which foods to eat when you don't recognize anything on your plate to washing your clothes in a river?"

Isa thought back to her life before Chicago. "Yes, I've had that sort of experience," she whispered.

"Where?"

Isa thought for a second.

"I don't want to talk about it right now, if you don't mind. It is still very difficult for me to think about it."

"I understand," he commented. "It's very, very hard to know that there are people struggling around the world with the basics of life when we have all this." He gestured widely around him.

"But I also learned so much from the people I worked with, Isa. As poor as they were, they were full in their hearts. They owned nothing, yet they had everything." He noticed tears in her eyes.

"I'm sorry. I've made you think of something sad."

Isa got up and stood by the glass wall facing the darkened lake.

"I...I am a Cuban American and have family in Cuba. And life there is very hard. I didn't know how bad things were there until I came here. I mean, until I went there and then came back here." She spoke to Sean's reflection in the glass, not wanting to face him directly.

"It is such a beautiful country, with such beautiful people. Proud and resourceful people. With so little in their lives. And I live here." Her voice trailed off, and she saw Sean get up from the couch and stand next to her. She looked up at him, tears still in her eyes.

It felt perfectly normal for him to take her in his arms, and kiss the top of her head. She hugged him back. He kissed her neck, her ears, her cheeks. Unabashedly, they locked in a deep kiss, and Isa felt her entire body meld into his embrace.

As their lips parted, she pushed softly away from him, feeling ashamed that she had just kissed a total stranger.

"I'm sorry." Sean arms fell awkwardly to his side. "I'm sorry. That was very forward of me. I don't know what I was thinking." He ran his fingers through his hair. Isa looked at him, wondering if his sudden boyish bashfulness was sincere. How could she have allowed herself to kiss him back like that. She felt equally embarrassed.

Sean was still apologizing.

"No. It's alright," she said. "It's my fault, too. But I think..."

"Do you want to go out for some Chinese food? I think I heard you say that you wanted Chinese food when you opened the door." He stopped her from saying no. "Please. You don't have to talk. I'll do all the talking. Or we could go for pizza. Whatever you want. I owe you a dinner, at least...for bumping into you today and all."

Isa fidgeted with the strings on her sweat pants. She saw him smile at her indecision. "Alright. Give me a few minutes to change." She headed for the bedroom.

Sean looked around the elegant living room, admiring all the many unique sculptures and paintings. He wandered over to the wall to wall bookcase and recognized some of his favorite authors. He smiled, thinking what a lucky break it was to have bumped into this unusual woman. He looked at pictures of a teenage Isa on skis, in a running marathon, in world cities that he himself had visited. Some were with an older couple, probably her parents. Many were with friends. He was glad to see that there were no pictures with any one man.

"I'm ready."

She looked beautiful in her black jeans and pink sweater. Isa had one of those curvaceous bodies that he had always admired in Latin women. And the deep, green of her eyes was captivating.

"*Perfecto.* I'm going to practice my little Spanish on you, if you don't mind."

"*Ah, ¿tú hablas español? ¡Qué bueno!*"

"*Sí. Lo estudié en la secundaria, y en la universidad. Pero fue en mi viaje a Guatemala cuando de veras me sentí cómodo en la lengua.*"

Isa couldn't believe her ears. Sean's Spanish was nearly perfect. "You speak very, very well. Your studies and trip to Guatemala really have given you a command of the language."

"Yes, we Americans are a sorry lot when it comes to languages, but some of us can at least get by. Look at you. You learned Spanish from your parents?"

He held the door for her and they headed down the hallway to the elevators.

"My parents." Isa told Sean about Ani's adoptive parents and their insistence on her learning her Cuban culture and language. She waved to the doorman who was talking to a cabbie down the street. They kept up their conversation for a few blocks before Sean pointed out a small pizzeria on the corner.

"We should never forget where we come from, our roots as you say. That is most important."

"Amen." He opened the door to a cavernous looking restaurant. "And here we are. My favorite pizza place. Do you know it? No. Well, you'll never eat pizza anywhere else. *Eh, Mama Luisa, como stai?*" He kissed a round, heavy woman with thick white hair pulled back into a bun.

"*Eh, doctore.* Long time we no see you here. And finally you bring me a *signorina*." She said looking at Isa."*E que bella!*"

"Don't give away all my secrets, Mama," he pretended to whisper in her ear. "*Si, e bella, no?*"

CHAPTER 31

Elián: April 22, 2000

"So, Isa..." Richard handed her a glass of red wine, "how's it going with the doctor?" Richard was using an accent that he said was his Jewish East Coast heritage. They had just finished putting away dishes and had decided to hang out in the apartment to watch a rented video after the news. The low hanging clouds outside her windows made her feel suspended in air.

"He's *perfecto*, Richard. Really, really *perfecto*." She felt her cheeks redden.

"Hmm," he grunted, pretending jealousy. "You certainly have seen a lot of each other these past few weeks. Almost every day?"

She blushed more. "Not every day."

"And so," he used his Jewish accent again, "how's this big Swede in bed? And is he really a BIG Swede?"

Isa laughed out loud. She had never in her life had a male friend who was just a friend. Relationships in Cuba were much more complicated, usually tinged with sexual undertones between men and women, even in the absence of a real sexual relationship. But here in the States it was very different. It seemed men and women could be friends. And with Richard, it was almost like talking to a girlfriend. She thought back to her friends in Cuba again, and wondered how her sister was handling those relationships.

"You are really bad, Ricardito." She sipped her wine. "But this wine... it is really good! What a wonderful taste!" She did not at all miss the homemade brew that passed for wine in Cuba, except Tío Julio's wine which was always special.

"Yes, I am bad. But we know that. And you haven't answered me. Should we toast to his *bigness?*

She laughed again, enjoying the strange openness with which she and Richard could express their thoughts and feelings

"*Bueno*, we have not made love, Richard. Sean is a very patient man."

"Who needs patient? Do you want patient? I don't think so..." he pulled her hair. "I see it in those fiery, green eyes. You're hot for this guy. And why not...he's gorgeous!" Richard batted his eyes.

Isa agreed, but replied that they had only known each other a few weeks and it wasn't proper.

"You're in America now, *muchacha.*" His Spanish accent was always funny to her. "A few weeks! I would have had him in my bed the same night...checking things out, you know what I mean. Don't tell me Cuban women don't do that because talk is Cuban women are *muy caliente.*" He pulled her hair again and they laughed.

The sounds of the television had been droning in the background, when the words Castro and Elián González caught her attention. Richard also stopped his conversation.

A television reporter was saying that the FBI had just raided the Miami home of Elián González's uncle in Little Havana. Pictures of agents running into a bedroom closet and a female agent carrying out a sobbing and scared Elián filled the large screen with nightmarish details. Richard and Isa sat silent, as they heard the details of the dramatic taking of the young boy and that he would be returned to his father and stepmother waiting for him in Washington. Screaming, cursing family members and friends ran after the black FBI van.

Isa was stunned. She felt frozen inside. Richard, on the other hand, had risen from the sofa and was toasting in midair.

"It was about time we had some balls with this. Shit. It's been, what, five months since we've had this little boy hostage here? Would we have stood still even for one day if Castro had kept an American little boy swept up on their shores? Fuck, no!"

Isa turned to Richard, who was excitedly dancing around the room. Yes, the news was wonderful. For Elián, who belonged with his only living parent, and for Ani and herself. If this was all true, and Isa still was trying to believe it, she could now talk to the Senator about their situation.

Richard hugged her.

"Isa. Isn't this great? Now we can get Ani back. And you can stay here. Shit!" He stood arm's length and looked at her. "I'm going to have double trouble with both of you in my life. Can I stand it?" He hugged her again.

Isa smiled and took Richard's face in her hands.

"It is wonderful, isn't it, Richard. Tomorrow, I'll call the Senator. Now there is no reason he can't help us, right?"

"Well, I think it's in the bag." He saw her confused her face. "That means that it's done, a sure thing."

"Should we try to call Ani?"

She dialed the international operator not waiting for Richard's response. She was told that the calls were not going through and that she needed to call later.

"I imagine many people are trying to call there right now."

"Or maybe Castro isn't letting anyone call in, Richard."

"That's possible. I can't ever think the way you do, Isa. It's hard for me to believe one man has so much power over a whole country."

"And I can't think like you, Richard. Even this news, the way they covered this." She pointed to the television news, which now featured anchors analyzing the FBI raid, replaying the scenes of the FBI agents rushing into a small bedroom and pointing guns, then a man and Elián hidden in a closet, and finally a female agent carrying the young boy out to a waiting black van. The images were repeated in their shocking detail. "In Cuba, people disappear. My own parents disappeared. And people continue to disappear. How can I understand that here your media is allowed to film and report such an event. Back home we speak about such things with only our very closest family members, in the quiet and dark of our bedrooms."

Richard looked at her soulful face. The twin sisters were so identical physically that Richard often forgot how different they really were. He knew little about Isa. She was a 38-year-old woman with whom he had only spent the last four months, not the twenty-plus years that he had known Ani. Richard knew that despite the long conversations they had shared about her life in Cuba, he really understood very little about Isa.

"Come here." He opened his arms to her.

For a minute, Isa imagined herself back in Havana, with Chencha saying something very similar in trying to comfort her.

Chencha and Ani. She thought about them so often, wondering how Anaís was coping with the hardships of life in Cuba. In the last months, Isa had begun to understand why America was called the land of the free. She felt free to say what was on her mind without worrying whether her neighbor was going to report her to the Block Committee or the MININT. She felt free to be out at night with her sister's friends without being called a slut.

Americans have no idea of the blessings they have, she thought.

And in many ways, Americans had too much. Her own sister had too much. And now she, too, had too much. Too much food, too much entertainment. Too many bookstores and restaurants. And on TV, too many journalists repeating too many of the same details about Elián's rescue.

The next day, *Arrancapellejo* was waiting for her at her desk.

"So, Anaís, what do you think about the Elián thing? Isn't it great? Well, I think you'll think it's great, right? But, I don't know. Really, what do Cubans think about the Elián thing with the FBI grabbing him up like that in the middle of the night and all?"

Isa sighed as she moved around her colleague and put her briefcase on her desk. She tried hard to think of the expression that Richard used with people like Cynthia.

Something about buying a life, she thought. Definitely, *Arrancapellejo* needed to buy a life.

"I can't speak for all Cubans, Cynthia. Some are on one side of this issue and others think something else...like everything else in this country...many opinions."

"Well, what do you think?"

Isa looked at her for a moment. "I think a child belongs with a parent that loves him and can take care of him," she said.

"See, I do, too. But, the family says that he's going to be brainwashed by Castro, that he'll never have the opportunities he has here..."

"Some of that is probably true." She sat at her desk and took out a couple of files, hoping to give *Arrancapellejo* a signal that she was busy. Cynthia didn't move. Isa started writing on her pad of paper, but *Arrancapellejo* continued standing there. Isa put her pen down. "I don't know, Cynthia. I'm not sure I know any more than you about what is going to happen to him."

She lied. She had a pretty good idea of what would happen to Elián and his family. Elián's father would be considered a hero for bringing the child back. He probably would receive some sort of government job that under other circumstances would have been beyond his reach. Elián would become the poster child for Castro's propaganda against American interventionist tactics. The family would have access to more food vouchers.

"But brainwashing! Don't you think that's just criminal?"

"People think in Cuba, Cynthia. Cubans are a pretty smart, often highly educated, group of people. You saw that for yourself, when we were there, didn't you. Yes, some people allow themselves to get brainwashed. But most of us...most of them think for themselves, even when they can't act on their thoughts."

"Ugh. I couldn't live like that?" *Arrancapellejo* crossed her arms in front of her. "Could you?"

"No," she heard herself whisper, thinking that indeed would be difficult for her to live under the Cuban restrictions she had known all her life.

Isa had tried calling her sister in Cuba throughout the night. She had not been able to sleep, waking up almost every hour, and dialing the international operator. She received the same message every time: We can't get through at this time.

She looked at the clock, wondering if it was too early to call Pablo at the Senator's office. She did not want to sound desperate so she decided to wait until after lunch to make her call.

In her heart, Isa was fighting a battle of emotions. She was elated that the Elián situation had been resolved because that made it possible for the delegation to follow up with the scheduled trip in the fall. And certainly Senator Fernández would now take up her cause and reunite the twin sisters.

But, to tell the truth, she no longer wanted to go back, even for a minute. What had at first been a desire to live out a dream of life in America for just a short period of time was now a passion to remain. And it wasn't the soft life of America as Castro described it that had totally seduced her. It was her new freedoms.

And Sean.

They were going to picnic at the park, and Isa hoped Sean wouldn't be called on his cell phone on any emergency so that they could spend the night together.

They had known each other a few short months, yet she knew it was not only an attraction. She loved him. Isa did not question her feelings like she would have when she was much younger. Her heart recognized love and she was happy feeling totally alive again. Richard had given his blessing, and that was special to her as well.

Now that Sean was in her life...well, life had never been better. Only the thoughts of her sister and the hardships she knew she must be enduring troubled her. She had heard nothing from the Senator's office. However, perhaps now with the Elián issue seemingly on its way to a resolution, everything would finally turn out fine for all of them.

CHAPTER 32

¡Viva Fidel!

"I can't believe you're not wearing a rally t-shirt, Isa."

Anaís looked at Diego, dressed uncharacteristically in old jeans and sporting an even older looking t-shirt with the faded revolutionary *Patria o Muerte*, Country or Death, slogan.

Chencha had not said anything to her about wearing something particular for the *Primero de Mayo*, the May 1st, celebration. Anaís was surprised because Chencha was always careful to instruct her on what Isa would do in a certain situation. Now, Anaís felt tongue-tied, not having a clue about what special t-shirt she should have worn.

"You know, I can't find it. Even Chencha helped me to look, but we couldn't find it."

Diego looked at her in puzzlement.

"I know, our place is so small, I can't understand how it happened. But, that's why I'm not wearing it."

"Well, you can't go to the rally like that." He sped by a procession of old cars, the passengers hanging out the windows, waving large Cuban flags. "We'll go by CUBALSE. Although pretty much everything else in town is closed, they'll be open for the tourists. Our Labor Day today seems to be a favorite day for them to stay away from the city and they'll be shopping or at the beaches. I think they are afraid of being near a demonstration by a million *socialistas* in the heart of Havana."

"Or maybe they just don't want to hear Fidel talk for twelve hours." The comment slipped out of her tongue before she could stop herself. Diego looked at her and laughed.

"Isa! I've never heard you talk like that!" She blushed. "Actually,

I agree with you. Fidel can certainly talk more than anyone I've ever heard. And this year, aside from his comments about where we are after the Special Period, we all know that he will be addressing the whole Elián mess." He maneuvered around more cars honking and waving flags. "Still, you need a proper t-shirt."

Chencha had begged off accompanying them. She was too old to walk amidst the crowd that gathered, thousands bused in from all the provinces outside the city. She also confided to Anaís that she also felt too old to listen to Fidel's speech, which at the May 1st celebrations would go on for hours. And this year with the Elián issue, who knew how long Fidel would talk.

Besides, they had already gone to the *Victoria de Playa Girón* speech in April, and that long afternoon's tirade about the Bay of Pigs Invasion was enough for Chencha for a while, she said. After all, she was an old woman. What could Fidel say that she had not already heard? And what would they really do to an old woman who didn't attend a rally, even if the block snitch reported her to the committee?

Diego had pulled up to CUBALSE.

"Let's go." He opened the door for her and they jogged to the door. Enrique met them at the door.

"You're here?" He seemed to be surprised that they were not at the rally.

"*Buenos días, hombre. Sí,* we're headed to the rally. But this beautiful woman needs a proper t-shirt." Enrique immediately motioned to one of the clerks and smiled as he followed Anaís' swaying gait.

"*La señorita,* she is quite lovely." He smiled at Diego, raising his eyebrows. "She is very special, no?"

Diego smiled back, not responding as he watched Anaís disappear behind a wall of clothes racks.

"Yes, she must be very special to you. She comes here a lot to buy..." Enrique lowered his voice "...and spends many American dollars." He winked at Diego. "Yes, she must be very special."

Diego blinked, startled.

"I think she is one of our best customers these days. Things must be good for you at the *inversiones turísticas* office." He winked.

Diego looked sternly at Enrique as if indicating he had crossed a thin line. The manager understood, and bowing, excused himself.

"Let me know if there is anything I can do for you."

"Thanks." Diego's voice was cold and abrupt.

Isa was still spending money at CUBALSE? Where was she getting the dollars? Was her mysterious cousin one of those American relatives who eased their guilt by sending U.S. dollars through Western Union?

Anaís was back, sporting a t-shirt with Che Guevara's picture. She smiled at him coquettishly.

"Am I alright now?"

"Yes. Now you are. No, let's not stand in line. We're already late. Enrique will put the cost on my bill." They headed for the front door. "And he is very happy...that you are using his store so much."

Anaís noticed a note of sarcasm in his voice. "*Ahh..sí.* With the ID you gave me...and the money my cousin left me...I guess I have been buying a few things for Chencha and the apartment."

He helped her into the car.

"That money she left...it never seems to be depleted."

Anaís did not know what to respond, and instead looked at the gathering clouds. "Do you think it will rain? Goodness, it really looks dark in that direction."

Diego could not get used to her attitude of late. It was so unlike the Isa he had dated a few years ago.

"We'll park here." He pulled into a side street. "This is about as good as anything."

The clouds gathering overhead were not deterring the massive crowd carrying flags and wearing t-shirts with Communist slogans. It was like the street festivals back home, except larger than any Anaís had ever seen. They pushed through the narrow side street and eventually arrived at the broad boulevard at the Plaza of the Revolution.

The well-known bearded figure in his dark green fatigues was at the podium, smiling at the thousands of people jammed in the plaza and down every street as far as the eye could see. Anaís marveled at the sea of flags waving wildly as Fidel stepped up to the microphone. His voice boomed a warm *bienvenidos hermanos* across the square through loud speakers set up around the plaza.

His welcome silenced the wild crowd. However, the moment Fidel began to speak, they exploded into cheers and whistles and chants of *Viva Fidel* at every pause. It was infectious, and she felt the crowd's electricity.

Diego had been very quiet since they had left CUBALSE, and Anaís squeezed his hand tenderly, catching his gaze. She felt his eyes looked at her questioningly. More often than not these days, Anaís felt she saw that look on Diego's face and it concerned her. What was she doing that made him seem so puzzled? When they made love, everything seemed fine. Their hunger and passion for each other had not diminished in all these months, and she actually felt an increased tenderness in his touch and in his eyes when he looked at her in their private moments. She felt he was falling in love with her.

"*¿Qué pasa?*" She kissed his cheek tenderly.

"*Nada.*" His gaze had not changed.

"*¿Es verdad?* Really?" She squeezed his hand again.

"*No, todo está bien.* I just have some things on my mind...with the Russians finally coming next week."

Anaís felt her heart race. They were coming!

"And we'll be meeting with them...you and I...in Varadero..."

"When is that?"

"I'll know more in a few days. But it will be next week some time, after I come back from Pinar."

"You're going to Pinar! Can I come along?" The opportunity of seeing Tío Julio again made her temporarily forget about the Russians.

"Not this time. I'll just be in and out...on business." He saw the disappointment in her face. "But after the Russians leave, let's see if your uncle will let us come by for a few days. I know how you love being with them. And it is a problem for you to get out there without a private car."

Something Castro had said made the crowd rise to its feet, and they also rose and clapped. Fidel was talking about the corrupt American government's kidnapping of Elián, their double standard in how the U.S. applied its own laws. The crowd seemed to be working itself into a frenzy, and with each pounding of Castro's fist, they screamed louder and louder, their cries of Elián and *Viva la Revolución* filling the space around them. The sounds were almost deafening, and Anaís felt even the ground seemed to shake.

Suddenly the darkened skies appeared to respond to the crowd's emotional electricity with its own deafening thunder and an ensuing downpour of warm, tropical rain. Aides rushed to cover Castro with large umbrellas, and the bearded one continued his diatribe, impervious to the water pelting everyone around him. The crowd reacted to the rain with laughter and screams. Diego slicked back his hair and wiped his face, happy to see that Anaís was not wavering. Instead, she stood soaked to the skin, her shirt and slacks sticking sensually against her skin. She threw back her head laughing, trying to drink the pouring rain. Diego felt overtaken with desire to devour her, to lick her dry.

"*Vamos.*" He grabbed her arm.

"*¿Qué?* Don't you want to stay for the rest of the speech?" She heard her mocking tone. Diego ignored her sarcasm.

"In a few minutes there is going to be a mad dash out of the plaza. This torrential rain is only going to get worse and even Fidel will call it a day." He moved them quickly past the rows jammed with people still cheering and chanting. The atmosphere reminded Anaís of a football game back home, where the faithful ignored freezing temperatures and heavy snowfalls to watch their team to victory.

Cold Chicago winters seemed a lifetime away, however. Here, the heavy rain was almost welcome on her hot body. She wished Diego would stop so that she could enjoy its cooling effect.

The rain was quickly becoming a sheet in front of her eyes, and even though Diego was only a few steps in front of her, she could no longer see him. Only his strong grip on her hand kept her assured. Then, as she felt Diego slowing down his pace, the sky seemed to open even yet another floodgate, and Anaís caught her breath as if falling into the deep end of an invisible pool. Behind her, she heard screams and then the sound of people running. Diego gripped her hand even tighter and resumed his run.

"*Ahora sí. Vamos.* We better get out of here."

The thunder of thousands of people running for shelter and the clattering of the rain pellets on the rooftops and pavement were deafening. The sky was almost as dark as night. Now, she could see nothing at all in front of her, around her. She grabbed Diego's arm with her free hand and fell in step with his quick gait. She felt bodies rush past her, laughing, swearing, singing. She wondered if Castro was still at the podium, giving his speech to an ever-thinning crowd under the blackened skies. She doubted it.

Diego stopped abruptly and she bumped into him, pushing him against something she could not see. It was his car. She could hardly believe that he had found it in the blinding storm.

As he searched his water logged pockets for his keys, Anaís looked around her. Briefly, the curtain of rain parted and she was not surprised to see that the people were turning the storm into a party. She had gotten used to the spirit of the Cuban people, usually ready to make the best of any situation. Perhaps, some were even thankful that the storm had cut short their usual long number of hours standing under a hot sun, listening to Fidel. She was sure not many would venture to say so, but she was sure many would be thinking it.

The rain again picked up force and the curtain of water closed before her. The crowd became only a blur behind the rain pellets, their voices wafting through the air. Someone had started to sing lines from the old ballad '*Ahorita va llover',* The rain is coming, and the melody was now heard in waves of voices from different points around the plaza. People crammed the streets, singing and yelling. The party atmosphere had taken hold and her body tingled with excitement from the contagious energy of the crowd.

Diego finally found his keys and opened the door. He helped her in and then moved quickly around the other side and slipped into his seat. They looked at each other, somewhat out of breath from the run, their hair matted to their face, their clothes soaked through and through. He slipped his hands under her water-heavy shirt, feeling her large breasts tenderly. "Let me help you out of these wet clothes, Isa." He pulled the shirt over her head and quickly unsnapped her bra, dropping it to the floor.

"And let me help you." She unbuckled his belt and started to unzip his pants.

"Nobody can see us..." he whispered in her ears as they stripped each other naked.

"No. Nobody can see us."

Their wet, hot bodies slipped on the old, leather seats, and they grabbed each other even tighter, kissing each other hard, fondling, stroking each other hungrily. They made love with the privacy of the torrential rain and fogged up windows around them, the pounding on the roof matching the pounding of their hearts and bodies. And when they both finally screamed in pleasure and fell limply into each other's embrace, Anaís thought she would never again experience a storm without shivering, remembering this magical, uninhibited moment with Diego.

CHAPTER 33

Isa is not Isa

"E*H, QUÉ SORPRESA, ¡D*IEGO! W*HAT ARE YOU DOING IN THESE PARTS?* W*HAT* a surprise!" Tío Julio shook Diego's hand and welcomed him into the house. The old man squinted in the bright sunlight streaming in through the door, his green eyes smiling at the unexpected visit.

"How nice to see you. *Entra, entra.* Come in." He patted Diego's back.

"Good morning, don Julio. Hope I didn't disturb you, but I was here on business yesterday, and thought I'd say hello before heading back to Havana."

"You know you are always welcome here, Diego." They walked past the living room toward the kitchen in the back of the house.

"How about a coffee? I make it nice and strong to get me going in the morning." Diego followed the old man, whose stamina and gait belied his age.

"Please sit, Diego." He pointed to a chair at the long, oblong wooden table. The sweet country smells of wet grass and dewy flowers filled the large room through the open windows. Tío Julio carried two small coffee cups to the table, and brought a little dish with sugar and a small spoon. He sat down at his chair at the head of the table.

"So, on business here?" He added two small spoonfuls of sugar to his coffee, then sipped the hot dark liquid. Diego nodded. "And how is business?"

Diego also added sugar in his cup, weighing his words, knowing that his visit was more than a social call.

"Oh, you know, don Julio. The usual. More headaches, than I want or need. But things are good." He sipped slowly. "There's a lot of European interest in developing partnerships with us, and that is always good for the country. I even have some interest from Japan."

Tío Julio nodded, sipping his coffee.

"Yes, I hear that Varadero gets more and more foreign visitors. We don't see much of that here, of course. And I like it that way." He leaned back in the chair, rubbing his unshaven face. "Yes, I like it that way. And you and Isa should spend more time out here. There's a great peace that comes with being close to nature." The cry of a rooster broke the air. They both laughed.

"Yes, indeed, right on time, *el señor gallo* adds his opinion to our conversation...just as if I had planned it." Diego admired the old man's quick wit and humor.

"And, how is my niece, if I may ask."

Diego shifted in his chair, the old wood creaking under his weight. "*Bien, bien.* Isa is an...incredible woman."

He looked at the old man's kind face, his dark green eyes and classic features reminding Diego of Isa. Shit! What was he saying? Everything reminded him of Isa. She was was on his mind constantly.

"Yes, she is an incredible woman. She has not had it easy, you know." Tío Julio threw back his head drinking the last drops of his coffee. "No, she has not had it easy."

Diego saw an opening for questions, the reason he was really at the farm. "Why do you say that, don Julio?" The old man eyed him intensely for a few seconds, as if carefully choosing his next words.

"Well, you know Isa's parents died when she was still a very little girl. A toddler, actually. My wife and I wanted to bring her here with us to Pinar. But after a while, we realized her best opportunities would be in Havana. Her parents would have wanted that for her. And Chencha, bless her soul, has been like a mother to her. So, we agreed to have her stay in Havana, in the small apartment that she was allowed to keep. I want to think that she grew up with a lot of love and caring. Between us, the family, Chencha...Isa has grown up as happy as we could possibly help her to be. But it's never the same, when you don't have your parents."

The sadness of the conversation suddenly seemed to age Tío Julio as he got up slowly to take the empty coffee cups to the sink. He sighed heavily, rinsing the cups briefly under a small trickle of water from the faucet, then drying each one with a tattered cloth from a hook on the wall.

"That's why we never told her how we think her parents died...although I think somehow she found out." Tío Julio looked at Diego, a member of the same government whom Tío Julio held responsible for the deaths. "...or about her sister."

Diego sat up in the chair, his sixth sense kicking in. "Isa has a sister?"

Tío Julio leaned against the sink, continuing to dry the coffee cups slowly, pondering his words. His green eyes narrowed as he looked at Diego's inquisitive face, saying nothing. Diego watched as the old man continued to dry the small coffee cups, reading Tío Julio's mind. Should he share family secrets?

After a few minutes, Tío Julio put the cups away in a cabinet and sat down across from Diego.

"Had a sister. Now, Diego, you are an old friend of the family, and I know you and Isa have been close in the past...and again are close. And although I know you work for the government..."

Diego interrupted him. "Don Julio, *por favor*. You know me."

Tío Julio put up his hand. "Yes. I believe you are a man of honor. And a friend. It's just that some family secrets...well, in our family, for instance, no one under Isa's age knows about her sister. And Isa is... what...38, 39? So, no one her age or younger knows certain things about the family." He leaned back and closed his eyes as if remembering a long list of sad events that he needed to safeguard. "There are things that are better left unsaid."

He fell silent, and Diego hoped it would not be the end of the conversation. He waited, hoping the old man would continue. But Tío Julio seemed lost in his thoughts.

The moist morning air blew in through the windows, scattering some papers on the counter, and startling Tío Julio from his reverie. Diego got up and quickly. He gathered and placed them in front of the old man. Diego took his seat again. He took a deep breath, knowing he had to pursue his questioning.

"So, what happened to Isa's sister?" he asked in a soft, low voice.

Tío Julio's green eyes grew darker. "She died. She was so young...not even two. We saw her only a few times here on the farm. You know, it was at the beginning of *la Revolución*...everything was...confusing. We heard she died of pneumonia...I was so sorry I wasn't there for her mother at that time, but like I said, everything was so unsettled..." He breathed deeply, sadly.

"Then Isa's parents...disappeared." He brushed his stubbly face. "We...I...decided that we wouldn't burden Isa with all the tragedy, and we agreed not to talk about any of it to any of the younger people." He leaned back in his chair. "What good would it have done? What could have been gained for Isa, on top of not having her parents around, to know that her twin sister had died? It probably would only have made her feel sadder. So, Isa visits an empty grave...with her parents' names on the headstone...horrible memories."

Diego could hardly believe what he was hearing, and suddenly, everything that had been confusing him became very clear. Now he understood why even after his exhaustive search and investigation, he had not found any record of Isa's birth, not in Havana nor in Pinar del Rio. That lack of information is what had brought him to the farm, to see if in some way, without being too obvious, he could figure out how such records could be missing. Now, Tío Julio's openness was answering his questions...and more. Isa had a twin who had died? Hardly!

His mind clicked back to the pictures of the woman who had come to Havana with the Illinois delegation in November...Isa's spitting image. His search for answers about this mysterious relative whom he linked to Isa's changed personality was finally realized. But, could all this be really true?

He needed to get back to Havana. He needed to get back to Arturo's files.

CHAPTER 34

Betrayed

BACK AT THE SECRET POLICE HEADQUARTERS, DIEGO POLITELY GOT PAST the chitchat with the young secretary and quickly retreated to studying the files he had requested. After the conversation with Tío Julio, Diego had used all his influence to gain access to records he hoped would clear up the mystery of the twins and the mysterious woman who was calling herself Isa. He finally located not one but two birth certificates for Buenaventura infants. Seeing the information in black and white still shocked him.

Yes, there were indeed two Isas. Except that he now knew that the older twin by two minutes was Ana Isabel and the younger one was Isabel Ana. Diego found everything difficult to believe. Yet now all his questions about the seductive green-eyed woman with the missing beauty mark were answered. Yes, the Isa he began dating in November was different...because Isa was not Isa. She was Ana Isabel, the twin that somehow had ended up living in the United States and had a different last name.

There was a death certificate for Ana Isabel stating that she had died of pneumonia at the age of 18 months, just as Tío Julio had explained. It was impossible, however, to make out the signature of the recording physician. Not that it mattered. The event occurred at a time when the country was experiencing so much internal and external turmoil that Diego was sure many shortcuts were taken in the less important departments such as birth and death records. Forging a death certificate would not have been difficult.

But Ana Isabel had not died.

Perhaps she had been taken abroad by a relative who then never returned to Cuba. But why all the deception? And did Tío Julio really believe that his twin niece had died, or was he deceiving Diego as well?

Diego leaned back in the chair, closing his eyes tightly. He felt sick inside because his feelings for the woman he was calling Isa but was really Ana Isabel, were battling his loyalty to his investigation.

Yes, he needed to admit to himself that he could not ignore that his feelings were deeper and wilder than anything he had felt for anyone he had previously known, including the real Isa. Yes, the twins were equally beautiful and alluring. But there was something about the woman he had been dating since November of last year, Ana Isabel, a confidence and independence of thought and action that had captivated his soul.

After all these months of being with the dark-haired beauty he wondered why he had not seen that there was too much that was different about her. But the same qualities now both intrigued and confounded him. He had attributed the changes he saw in his former lover to the fact that she was now a little older, had increased responsibilities in her career, and had finally gotten over the loss of her husband. But, in fact, it was none of those things. Now everything was clear.

What was not clear, however, was what he would do with all his newfound information. Diego ran his fingers through his thick black hair. No, he didn't need to report anything quite yet. He needed to know more facts, beginning with what had happened to Isa and Ana Isabel's parents.

Anaís fidgeted in her chair as she stared at the papers in front of her. Relax, she told herself. She had done her homework for this meeting with the Russians and everything would go well.

She had prayed to Chencha's Yoruba gods and the old woman had met with Secundino who reassured them that the meeting would be a success. She had studied key phrases in Russian from the texts and cassettes Isa kept in her desk. The meeting had been moved from Varadero to Havana. There was nothing to be concerned about.

But then she saw them entering the restaurant and she froze, her mind going blank as she watched Diego in his starched white Cuban *guayabera* and two dark suited men heading her way behind the concierge. She took a deep, long breath as she extended her hand to the older man smiling at her.

"*Zdravstvujte! Kak u vas dela?*"

It surprised her to see Diego's eyebrows shoot up as she welcomed them.

"*U menya vsyo khorosho, spasibo. Vy ochen' krasivaya.*" The older man kissed her outstretched hand and Anaís smiled coquettishly.

"*Spasibo,*" she replied.

Diego shook his head in amazement, feigning annoyance.

"*Un momento, mis amigos.* Isa may understand what is going on, but I am a poor Cuban, with no Russian in my studies. We must communicate in Spanish, please." He pulled out a chair and sat down, smiling incredulously at Anaís.

"As you wish, my friend. But what a pleasure to hear our native tongue from such a beautiful and gifted mouth." Vladimir kissed Anaís' hand again then gently let her retrieve it as they all took their chairs.

Anaís was sure everyone could hear her heart thumping and her mind screaming *gracias, Secundino* as it became clear that she would not need to communicate with their clients in anything but Spanish and that she had would do well in this meeting with the few dozen mastered phrases in Russian which she had learned from her sister's tapes. Her prayers had been answered.

"Well, let's talk business before pleasure then," Diego said. "But first, a few *mojitos.*"

"*¡Muchacho!*" The young waiter approached their table with a bow.

"*Pozdravlyayu!* Congratulations on a very good decision," she smiled at her clients. Many *mojitos* and a great snapper dinner had relaxed her. "You have made a very wise decision which will be profitable for both your country and ours. The property you have selected next to the Xanadú Mansion is without equal. Wait until your guests see the beaches there. And the golf! Not to mention the wonderful scandals about the DuPont family, especially about the men and the parties they held there."

The three men laughed loudly, obviously already aware of the Du-Pont history at the three-story estate in Varadero. Vladimir slapped his friend on the back.

"I told you, Alexei. Cuban women are exceptional." He smiled at Anaís. "So...earthy."

Diego waved to the waiter for the bill.

"And Xanadú is so close to..."

"*La casa de Al Capone!*" Anaís filled in. "Another marvelous playground for the guests at the hotel."

"*Da.* Yes. All good!" Vladimir looked at his watch and then at his silent partner. "Alexei...well, unfortunately it is time for us to go." He took the napkin tucked into his shirt. "This has been a much awaited and worthwhile meeting. Isa..." he again took her hand.

"*Do svidaniya.*"

"*Udachi i vsego khoroshego, señores Arsov, Smirnov.*"

Vladimir bowed deeply, then turned to Diego.

"*Muchas gracias, amigo Diego.* And I hope that our Spanish has not been too hard on your ears." He chuckled, looking at Anaís. "Alexei tomorrow will finish the figures and make a call to our office, but I am sure everything will be approved...without a doubt."

"*¡Magnífico!* As always a pleasure to do business with you. And..." Diego winked at both men, "enjoy your next, uh...meeting."

Vladimir waved at Anaís as he allowed Diego to escort him toward the door.

"They are not as wonderful as your Isa, but they will do. *Buenas noches,* comrade."

CHAPTER 35

June 28, 2000

ISA WOKE TO A NEWS REPORT THAT A SUPREME COURT RULING WAS expected against Elián's Miami relatives' request that he be allowed to stay with them in the U.S. If that were the case, the report said, Elián and his father would probably leave Washington for Cuba that very day.

For once, Isa hated to tear herself away from the television set, but she had errands to run. The late June hot weather that Chicago was experiencing reminded Isa of Havana, but here the blue sky peeked around skyscrapers that still amazed her. The trees and bushes that had been bare when she arrived in the city were green once more, and Michigan Avenue had shed its twinkling, white lights for the brilliant colors of potted plants and flowers.

Isa stood in line at the bank, looking at the other customers using the ATM machines that she still could not bring herself to trust using. She glanced at the paycheck she was depositing, thinking as always what a fortune her sister earned for such an easy week's work. What she wouldn't do back in Cuba for Chencha and her family in Pinar with just this one paycheck!

As she walked further down Michigan Avenue, she paused in front of an electronics store displaying their televisions on sale in the window, then quickly stopped when she saw Elián's father onscreen, about to address the media.

"I would like to thank the North American people for the support they have given us. I would like to thank the U.S. Government."

Cradled in his father's arms, Elián smiled at the cameras in the charismatic way the public was now accustomed to seeing. A large jet waited in the background on the tarmac.

Isa listened to Juan Miguel's comments as the translator's voice made it clear in English to the American public that the seven-month long Elián issue had come to an end.

"I think that this has allowed me to meet very beautiful and intelligent people in this country, and I hope that in the future this same friendship and this same impression that I have of the U.S. people, that same thing can become true between both our countries, Cuba and the U.S. I am very grateful for the support I have received. I am extremely happy of being able to go back to my homeland, and I don't have words really to express what I feel." With those parting words and a wave to the people who had come to see them off, Juan Miguel González held tight to his eight-year-old son and followed his wife and infant child unto the jet that would take them back to Cuba.

People who had stopped to listen began commenting on the news, but Isa barely heard them. All she could think of was her sister in Havana, thinking that this type of news would definitely be broadcast by the Cuban government. And how happy Anaís would be to know that Isa now would be able to return to Cuba, so that Anaís could have her life back. But Isa's heart was breaking.

The last time that Isa had called the Senator's office, she had asked Pablo to be candid with her about what the Senator was planning about their situation. Pablo was embarrassed and at first skirted the question. Finally, he confessed that the political drama that surrounded the young Elián boy had put everything on hold and Senator Fernández had said the time was not appropriate for him to initiate any asylum initiative for anyone. Now the plans were for another delegation visit to attempt to pick up negotiations where things were left off before the Elián issue.

Of course, neither Pablo nor the Senator had any idea that the woman in the U.S. who kept calling their office was Isa and that the U.S. raised Anaís was still in Cuba. Only Richard knew these facts and that is how things would remain.

Nothing was turning out as the sisters had hoped. Their plans to be together in Illinois would not easily materialize.

Soon, Isa would return to Cuba with the delegation and the twins would exchange places once more.

———————

"*¡Viva Fidel! ¡Viva Cuba! ¡Viva Elián!*"

Fidel hoisted the young boy on his shoulder like a proud grandfather as the boy's parents smiled sheepishly next to Castro.

The crowds that had gathered in La Plaza de la Revolución seemed as large as those at the May Labor Day celebration, but the atmosphere was more jubilant and excited. Tens of thousands of people had gathered to welcome home one of their own.

Anaís looked around her at the sea of flags everywhere. Fidel smiled as he lowered the young Cuban hero by his side and began to clap along with the crowd.

Fidel stood quietly while the crowd roared its approval, finally rejoicing after many months of waiting for the country's smallest comrade to come home. Standing next to Diego who clapped and whistled along with the crowd, Anaís understood the tears that ran down his face as everyone seemed to be caught up in the jubilation and happiness a family feels when a child who has been lost is finally found.

Fidel raised his hand and the crowd immediately became subdued. His booming voice resonated from every corner of the square.

The crowd once again boomed its accord.

"*Sí*...finally...our youngest comrade, our youngest hero of the Revolution, our symbol of Cuban independence from our northern aggressors...he is finally home." Fidel smiled as the crowd yelled and stomped in agreement.

"The imperialists who allowed the *gusanos*, the worms, in Miami to keep our son from us finally realized that the Cuban people will not be trifled with, that we will defend...to the death...our sovereignty...and that the international community saw their actions for what they are...aggression and imperialism and deceit."

Diego whistled loudly. He smiled at Anaís, his beautiful brown eyes glistening with emotion. Anaís felt moved by the event as well. And she felt that it was not simply because of the coming home of a loved one, but by the spirit of camaraderie and pride that electrified the crowd. Yes, she knew that many of the so-called spontaneous demonstrations that took place around the country and particularly in Havana were in fact contrived demand performances to demonstrate solidarity with Castro, a demand performance that the ordinary citizen needed to comply with or else risk being reported to the block comrade. But today was different. This was the Cuban pride in sovereignty that she had witnessed over the many months of living among the people.

Sovereignty? It was difficult to believe she could associate this word with Cuba after living these many months in a country where the every-day citizen's life spun on the whim of the dictator. Yet, she had learned through listening and watching Cubans day after day struggling to make their lives just a little better than subsistence level that the Cuban people felt the Revolution and Castro had given them back their sovereignty, from Batista and the United States. Anaís was beginning to understand the paradox that was Cuba, suppressed by the Communist leadership, yet fiercely proud to be free from foreign intervention.

They had so little, these Cuban patriots! But today they had Elián, and that was enough.

CHAPTER 36

Fourth of July

TONIGHT SEAN WAS PICKING HER UP AFTER WORK FOR THE FOURTH OF July concert and fireworks in Grant Park. Sean had invited Richard, but Richard instead had told them that he was off with his latest beau for a month to the Greek Islands, and that he was leaving Isa in his hands. Sean was more than glad to oblige.

She started to prepare her *arroz con pollo* for the picnic, a dish that Sean loved and that also reminded her of cooking back in Cuba for special occasions. As she had told him, the dish was not complicated but on the island it was often impossible to find the ingredients so it was kept for only celebratory moments.

Here, she enjoyed cooking, and it was the one luxury she enjoyed spending money on. Richard and Sean swore they had gained weight with her meals, but she insisted she was having the most fun being able to cook what and when she wanted.

Cooking she enjoyed. Baking, on the other hand, was difficult for her and she still had not mastered her sister's chocolate chip cookies recipe which Richard insisted was important for her to learn since it was Anaís' custom to give them as treats to the doormen in her building. Isa was glad that after her last attempt Richard had finally decided that buying the cookies was better than gifting burnt cookies and ruining Anaís' relationship with the building staff.

As Isa sautéed the chicken, she started to daydream about Sean and the happiness she felt with him. She was in love for only the second time in her life and it felt wonderful.

A sudden flash of herself saying goodbye to Sean sent a sharp pain through her heart.

The phone rang, taking her away from her thoughts. It was him.

"So are you ready? Yes, I know it's early, but we will get better places on the lawn in front of the stage. I'll pick you up in one hour? Great!"

Sean. How will I be able to leave him?

The oppressive July heat seemed to envelope the car as Diego sped down the highway, seemingly trying to capture a breeze that could cool their sweaty bodies.

Anaís pulled back her thick black hair on top of her head. It had to be at least a hundred degrees in the shade!

"*Isa. ¿Qué pasa? Es julio.* It's always like this in July." Diego veered around a box in the middle of the road. He glanced at his passenger. Damn, she was beautiful, this Isa impersonator, her green eyes the color of Chinese jade. Yes, the real Isa would never have thought twice about the weather, but this foreigner was feeling the humid Cuban summer heat for the first time and he could only imagine the shock to her northern bred blood.

"Want to stop at Las Terrazas for a dip before we go on to your uncle's farm?" He searched her face for signs of not understanding what he meant by Las Terrazas, but Anaís did not even blink as she nodded. "We haven't been there in years," he continued. "Remember the old shack where we..." Purposefully he did not finish the sentence, waiting to hear what she would say. Anaís seemed to wake up from her heat-induced stupor.

"*Sí.* Of course...let's go there...it was always wonderful."

There was no shack at Las Terrazas! This beautiful area, one of the few remaining forest belts around Havana that had survived Spain's greed for lumber and France's thirst for sugarcane, had been one of Isa and Diego's favorite weekend retreats. He remembered how, along with many other Cubans from the area, they would spend the day swimming and relaxing under the canopy of the lush groves of trees, eating fruit that seemed to be there for their pleasure. But there was no shack associated with these memories.

Diego shook his head, suddenly overtaken by the nagging thought that had been haunting him since he realized that he had been sleeping with an imposter.

He looked at the beautiful brunette next to him, now reclining her head, eyes closed tight, trying to fight heat fatigue. Was she the enemy? His military training kept telling him that she was, that he should arrest her, that he should use her deception to publicly humiliate her and the aggressor to the north. It was precisely what he should do. It was the patriotic thing to do. It might even gain him new notoriety and prestige at the highest levels...

He sighed so deeply that the sleeping beauty next to him stirred perceptibly. He watched her change positions and continue to slumber.

No, he didn't want any notoriety. And...he could hardly believe what he was thinking... he wanted no furthering of his career at any level of government!

For weeks now Diego had been carrying on an internal dialog about the situation with the new Isa. He felt at times that he was two distinct people, carrying on with himself sociopolitical and ethical conversations of the deepest levels he had ever experienced. It was almost as if he would step out of himself and listen to both sides of the issues, nodding in approval to very conflicting opinions. Only now in his innermost private thoughts could he admit that he had been living an unexamined life in many aspects. And the new Isa was making him confront difficult truths about himself, and about the Revolution.

He had found documents that suggested that Isa's parents had been targeted for months before their disappearance for their vocal opposition to certain measures that the new Castrista government was implementing in the early nineteen sixties, especially with the closing of newspaper offices and deportation of foreign journalists. From the sketchy papers that he had managed to gather, orders had been issued to send Isa's parents to one of the jails specifically for dissidents. No other mention was made of them in anything he found. Diego's conclusion was that they had died in jail or worse yet perhaps executed. A harsh sentence, he thought, for speaking your mind.

Yes, he had been G2 for years, but his heart had not been assigned to activities which the government seemed to reserve for its most hardened and older officers. He profiled visitors to the island and often followed their steps, but nothing more sinister than that. Nothing like he heard among other G2 officers, including Arturo.

In Diego's mind, national security was not about torturing or killing Cuban civilians, regardless of how outlandishly different their politics. For that and many other reasons, he had not lasted long in the coveted G2. The *Oficina Para Inversiones Extranjeras* suited him much better.

Indeed, the facts pointed to the fact that Isa and her sister had been dealt a cruel hand not only by fate, but by their own Cuban government. He was not about to hand out more pain to Isa's family until he had thought everything completely through.

"Okay, right here." Sean stopped a couple of hundred yards away from the center stage already crowded with people checking the sound system. He spread the large blanket on the ground, strategically setting the picnic basket and tote bag to hold it in place against the summer breezes battling their efforts.

"Told you we should get here early. Look around." He pointed to the crowds gathered as far as Isa could see. "Every year, they get around half a million people out for this concert if it is a good weather day. And I can't believe you have never come to one of these, Isa, given that you live nearby."

Isa avoided his gaze. She hated the lies she constantly was forced to make up with Sean. The only two things that were true about their relationship were that Isa was indeed her name and that she loved him.

"I guess the crowds bother me. I don't like them."

Sean looked concerned.

"I'm sorry, I didn't know. Do you want to go?"

"No." She immediately corrected her statement. "I don't like them by myself, but with you, everything is different."

He stopped laying out the plates and dishes and hugged her. "Life is different for me, too, my darling." He kissed her tenderly. "I have never been so happy that someone had an accident." She jokingly slapped his cheek. "Well, just think if you hadn't been out of control on those roller-blades. Our paths would probably never have crossed."

That is so very true, Isa thought. She probably would have spent all her time with Richard, waiting for the time to return to Cuba. Now, returning to Cuba was the last thing she wanted to do. Isa now believed in love at first sight. It had happened to her the moment she saw Sean.

"Old Cuban saying: *que será, será*."

"Wait a minute. I think I've heard that before, in a song my mother liked. And it was an American singer, maybe Doris Day."

"Well, but it's a Cuban saying," she chuckled. "Or at least we claim that it is. Are you hungry? I think this is my best *arroz con pollo* yet. I found *azafrán* from the Middle East. I've heard it is the best saffron ever."

"And..." Sean reached into the large tote. "I found the largest, juiciest mangoes ever." He displayed them proudly. "And I know you love them."

"Oh!" Isa took them and smelled their skin. "These are incredible! Where did you buy them? The ones in the supermarket nearby are pretty small."

"Well, for you, I drove all the way to the north side to one of the Latin grocery stores. If you have never been there, we will have to go. I know we like to shop near home, but really, this store is a Latin cook's dream."

They sat and Isa began to peel and slice the mango.

"You have travelled a lot in Latin America, Sean. Did you ever hear the children's story that talks about mango raining down its sweet juice on the people in a poor town? I think it is one of the reasons mangoes are my favorite fruit."

He closed his eyes trying to remember.

"Ah, yes. Where the kids can drink mango juice from the rivers?" She nodded happily. "I never understood that story." He teased her, laughing.

"What? It is such a good story."

"Well, I don't understand it. But then, I don't get the meaning of many songs in Spanish even though I understand the words."

"I see. Well, imagine you are a very young child who doesn't have many different things to eat." Her eyes were lost in the horizon over the lake. "Every day, it is rice and black beans. Or black beans and rice." Sean chuckled.

"Sometimes a small piece of bread. And to drink—water or watered down milk. You almost always wish you could eat more...to drink something really wonderful. And one day, you get to eat a mango, and the sweetness is like nothing you have ever had. You want to eat more, but there is no more. Not for a long time." Her eyes moistened as she remembered their hardships in Cuba and she stopped talking.

Sean was watching her intently, and she feigned a smile and brushed back her hair.

"Well, one day, a friend tells you that on the other side of the moon, whatever you want is there for the taking. That you can drink mango juice from the rivers any time you want. It is a faraway place and a perilous journey, only for the very brave. The story teaches that there is a most perfect place and moment in life for everyone—if you are willing to take risks, and even if it is on the other side of the moon."

The sun was setting behind the tall buildings across from the park. Happy chatter from the concertgoers surrounded them and musicians were beginning to tune their instruments on stage. They looked silently at each other, and for a second Isa wondered if this was the right moment to tell Sean who she really was. She started to speak.

"Well, I guess I understand better now," he interrupted, "even though this idea of the other side of the moon is really too far for me, and certainly out of reach." He grabbed her and lay her down next to him on the blanket. "Besides, for me, wherever you and I are is the most perfect place and moment." He kissed her softly.

"And actually..." he licked her lips, "...you do taste like mangoes."

CHAPTER 37

Cuba by Night

THEY STEPPED OUT INTO THE HOT AUGUST EVENING, DIEGO'S STRONG ARM opening a way for them through the excited crowd. Anaís felt exhilarated by the evening's superb performance. Although her adoptive parents had shown her a love for the arts from a very early age, she could not think of a single ballet performance she had ever attended that had mesmerized her with the artistic and athletic abilities she had seen tonight in the Swan Lake performance by the Ballet Nacional de Cuba.

"This is absolutely excellent, Diego!" she whispered, squeezing his arm as they left the Teatro Nacional de Bellas Artes. The company's performance had been inspired, encouraged by the audience's appreciative screams of delight. At first, Anaís had thought the ebullient chatter and clapping more appropriate to a rock concert. However, quickly she had been caught up in the dancers' dynamic talent and passion.

She felt she had experienced creative greatness and it was difficult to contain her joy. But she could not say this to Diego. Perhaps he and Isa had come here and experienced this incredible dance company often.

"Do you want to walk around a bit, and then down to the Malecón? It is such a beautiful night and you seem...well, I think you need to walk off some of that energy." He kissed her on the lips.

"*Claro que sí.* It's a beautiful night!"

The marble floor of the *Paseo del Prado* looked stark under the dark shadow of the canopy of trees lining the beautiful footpath to the bay. Anaís looked admiringly at the wrought iron light fixtures and the large stately lions spaced tastefully along the way. She could imagine what this path had looked like when her parents walked it decades before, when the marble pavement was maintained, polished and gleaming for the Cuban citizens as well as for the American and European tourists so that they would continue to liken it to the *Champs d'Ellysées*. No broken fixtures or missing light bulbs then, she was sure. And the buildings on either side of the Paseo would all have been brightly painted, black iron porches crowded with people enjoying the robust Cuban coffee and sweets or the traditional warm nuts sold by the *maniceros* immortalized in many island songs about peanut vendors. Instead, the clash of deteriorating buildings next to renovated facades shocked her even now in the softened darkness of the night.

"Havana is so beautiful, *¿verdad?*"

"The most beautiful city in the world for me, Isa."

They walked toward the Malecón in silence. How she would miss this city when she left.

At the Malecón, couples sat straddling the low wall that separated Havana from the sea. Anaís still could not pick out the prostitutes since to her they looked like all other young girls she saw around town. Here in Cuba, however, she knew that women didn't take evening walks by themselves unless they were looking for male companionship.

And especially not around the Malecón, where the young prostitutes hung out hoping to attract the foreign tourists. Times were more and more difficult in the country, and financial need combined with the open sexuality of Castro's new society made the oldest profession flourish.

"How sad that these young women have to sell their bodies."

"They should be arrested." Diego's tone was cold.

"I think if you're hungry you will do anything."

Diego stopped in his tracks and looked at her sternly. "Nobody goes hungry in Cuba, Isa."

Anaís realized she had misspoken. "I don't mean she's hungry. It's just that, you know, how young girls are. They want to have pretty things."

"Ours is not a society about wants." His voice still sounded authoritarian. "*La Revolución* is about equality and brotherhood. So, when times are good, we all have extra things. When they are not, we all share in the crisis."

Anaís kept silent, realizing her sister would never have spoken out as she had.

"Do you feel like there are things that you want that you can't have. Is that the Isa that you have become...since your American cousin was here?"

She didn't like the way he sarcastically said cousin, but she bit her lip, still trying to defuse the conversation.

"Diego, don't get like that. I'm just saying that...well remember when the Russians were here as government consultants?" She remembered conversations with her sister. "Remember how we all hated that they stayed in the best houses or hotels, ate food that had been flown in just for them, used some of us as their nannies, danced in clubs that the rest of us *cubanos* could go to only if we were with one of them or someone like..."

Anaís stopped short of ending her sentence, but Diego seemed to read her mind.

"Someone like me. Someone in a position of power, in the government, like me. Is that what you were going to say?"

"Diego..."

"You know, Isa, it's time that we..." Diego lowered his head and facing her took her hands. "It's time that we..."

His brown eyes were darker than she had ever seen them before. His face seemed sad, a sadness that Anaís could not understand could have been caused by their casual conversation.

"It's time that we, that I take you home. I meet with clients tomorrow morning, and I still have a lot of paperwork to finish."

He hailed one of the many cabs lining the Malecón.

"*A Miramar, mi amigo.*"

They drove holding hands in silence, but the distance between them was immense.

CHAPTER 38

Good News-Bad News

"SHIT, MAN. IT'S BEEN WAY TOO LONG! HOW HAVE YOU BEEN, *MI AMIGO?*" Arturo patted Diego's shoulder heartily.

"Good. Really good. Busy as ever. You know how busy we are these days. All good, though. I like it busy."

They sat down at a small wrought iron table on the veranda facing the ocean. A young man immediately came over to ask for their order. The old Miramar home turned paladar was quiet in the mid-afternoon lull after lunch.

"*Dos cafés*—double sugar in mine." Arturo adjusted his dark sunglasses. "I think I put more and more of that stuff all the time in my coffee." He looked up at Diego and slapped him on the back once more.

"Hell. It's good to see you."

"Same here, Arturo. We just don't seem to run into each other as much anymore. How are things at G2?"

"You know, same. It's the same old shit. But...tell me about you? Whatever happened with the Varadero deal with the Russians that looked so good?"

"It's moving—but slowly. You know, you never know with those bastards. They want everything in their favor. Like they still have a hold on us. After all these years."

"Shitheads! We should have kicked them out long before the wall came down. And now they want favors? Screw that!"

"My feelings exactly. So, we'll see. I think they'll come around to our figures. If not, the Spaniards or Germans are right there, waiting for this deal."

"And who do you think should get it?"

"*Los españoles* are much better to deal with. But I think it's a good idea to spread things out...keep everyone guessing and wanting to work with us. So, probably if the Russians fall through we'll go with the Germans."

"Hmmm. Sounds like good planning...*Gracias*..." He took the coffee cup from the server and lifted it up to his lips, taking a small sip of the black brew. "*Perfecto. Gracias, muchacho.*" The young man nodded and retreated quietly.

"Well, you know, I've been wanting to talk to you about your interest of a few months back with that group from Illinois." Arturo sipped his coffee and looked directly at Diego through his dark glasses. "They're coming back, you know."

Diego felt his stomach contract tightly, but knew that he had to wear his poker face with Arturo. Shit. He wished his friend weren't wearing those impenetrable sunglasses so that he could see Arturo's eyes. He sipped his coffee and answered nonchalantly.

"*¿Verdad?* No, I didn't know. Nobody has told me anything. How is that happening?"

"Well, it came to us about two weeks ago. I figured I'd bring you the news, since you seem to be interested in them." He stopped. Diego didn't respond. Arturo remained silent as well. They looked out to the horizon. Finally, Arturo spoke again.

"Matilde says that you've been over there a few times, spent quite a while going through paperwork. Was there something you were looking into that I should know about?"

Same old Arturo. Diego knew that when it came to the job, no personal relationship ever stood in the way for his old friend. Arturo cut to the chase and was as direct as always.

"Not at all. You know, I was out of town when they came last year. I think I was in Colombia. Maybe it was Mexico. I can't remember. Anyway, I didn't get to meet any of them. I heard that the people assigned to work with them were actually pretty impressed with the group, and that they were not at all the type of *Americanos* that they were expecting to meet."

"How's that?"

"*Bueno*, privately they spoke of being against the embargo...that it is a stupid idea kept alive by the Miami Mafia with a lot of influence in Washington. It seems most people thought they were sincere. And that particular U.S. states could offer some good agricultural possibilities for us." Diego felt more confident as he spoke, feeling he was doing a good job of convincing his old suspicious friend.

"Anyway, they said they seemed really interested in dealing with us, even of finding a way around the embargo. So, I wanted to learn as much as I could about them from the information that G2 gathered before and while they were here. You never know. If we did business with them it would have an impact on the hotel business, indirectly."

"Hmmm. Yes...indirectly, I guess it would."

"Of course, everything went to hell because the U.S. kidnapped Elián."

"*Sí*. But the delegation is coming back." Arturo savored the last drop of his café. "Are you taking the lead this time, although it doesn't seem to have a lot promise with the hotel business?"

"Yes, I think I will. And, no, it doesn't have any promise in the short run. If they change senators all this could be moot. But I think it's worth keeping alive. Sooner or later, they need to realize it's good for their economy to deal with us, on all levels and in all areas, right."

"Hmm," Arturo nodded, adjusting his sunglasses again in the glaring sunlight.

"Well, we'll be keeping an eye on all of them again when they come back. And you let me know if you need anything, or if we should look into anyone you think is suspicious, *¿bien?*"

"You know I will, Arturo. Like you said when you trained me, once a G2 always a G2, right?"

"You're dammed right!"

The two men smiled at each other. Diego felt that he had covered his tracks with his old mentor. But where he was going next with all the information that he had on Ana Isabel and her sister, he still did not know. His heart was telling him one thing, but he had just said, once a G2 always a G2. Was this true?

The ringing of the phone startled her. It's Sean, she thought, teasing her again about his birthday plans for her that evening. She couldn't wait to see him, or to see what he had planned. All he said was that she needed to wear warm clothes. Of course, that could mean anything. And although everyone was saying that they were having a mild fall, to Isa the cold October days were worse than any winter day in Cuba, especially when the temperature dropped in the evenings.

"Good morning, Office of Tourism," she answered the phone softly, expecting to hear her lover's voice on the other end.

"May I speak to Anaís Moran, please?" No, it wasn't Sean.

"This is she."

"Oh, hi Anaís. I didn't recognize your voice. It's Pablo from Senator Fernández' office."

Her heart jumped, as she acknowledged his greeting.

"Well, I have good news and bad news. Which do you want first?" Anaís' heart jumped again.

"It doesn't matter, Pablo. Well, no, you know...tell me the good news first."

"Pack your bags because we're going back to Cuba. Next Friday." He spoke excitedly.

She could hardly believe what she was hearing.

"The bad news," he continued, "is that at this time, with everything just beginning to normalize between Castro and Washington, Senator Fernández doesn't feel like it's a good time to bring up the situation with your sister. But he does want to talk to you about it, at length, he said, while we're down there. To make plans for the moment when he can bring that issue to the table. But nothing will happen on this trip. Optimistically, maybe your sister's process can begin sometime next year."

Isa didn't know what to respond. The thought of seeing her sister and Chencha elated her, but a sharp pain touched her heart. Pablo's news meant that she was going back to Cuba and to her old life, to change places with Anaís as she had promised. Based on what Pablo had just said, there was obviously now no chance of both sisters coming back with the delegation nor any time soon. And that meant not coming back to Sean.

She thanked Pablo and sank into her chair. The phone rang again and she answered it morosely.

"That's a sad hello. What's the matter, Isa?" Sean's concerned voice answered.

"Uh, nothing. I'm just working on something very difficult."

"Well, I hope you finish it all so that tonight your head is totally clear for your...BIRTHDAY." He almost screamed into the phone. "Are you ready for that, birthday girl?"

Isa felt drained and unenthused. Sean. Her wonderful, beloved Sean. How could she leave him, maybe forever? She felt heartbroken and teary eyed. "Uh, Sean, I can't talk right now. I really have to finish this... project."

"Isa, are you sure that everything is alright? You don't sound like yourself. How about if we meet for lunch? I can probably get out of here in about an hour."

"No." She heard the abruptness of her voice. "No," she softened her tone. "I'm probably going to have to work right through lunch to finish. But I'll see you later, tonight like we talked about."

"Remember to wear warm clothes." The enthusiasm of his voice meant to tease her. "You are going to need them. Eight o'clock, okay?"

"Sure. Yes, that's great."

"*Hasta pronto, mi amor.*" She heard his kiss through the wires. "*Ciao.*"

She kissed back, fighting back the desire to cry. As she hung up, she realized that she needed to get out of the office before she would break down. It wasn't quite lunchtime yet, but she grabbed the jacket from the back of her chair and swung her purse over her shoulder. *Arrancapellejo* watched her curiously. Isa waved at her and hurried toward the front door, telling the receptionist at the front desk that she was taking an early lunch to run errands.

Tears filled her eyes even before she exited the door. She decided to walk down the stairs to avoid running into anyone she knew in the elevator. Her emotions overwhelmed her, thoughts of her sister and Sean flashing in her mind.

Outside the office building she hailed a cab and gave the driver her address. The sun shone brightly and the air was charged with the customary dynamic activity of downtown Chicago. She looked up at the buildings that had become familiar to her, the city noises and smells inundating her senses. Soon, she realized, this would be but a memory.

The taxi pulled up to the front of her building and she saw the new doorman rise to open the front door for her. She waved at him that she was not coming in.

She wanted to walk and needed to be alone with her feelings of both joy and sadness. Isa walked the short block to the beach across the street and sat on one of the benches at the edge of the sand. The waves off Lake Michigan shimmered in the distance. The lake always reminded her of the ocean back home, but the water was a different color of blue there, wasn't it? She wasn't sure she remembered.

She couldn't help but smile at the Chicagoans lying on the sand or sitting on benches soaking in the noon rays. Back home, 60-degree weather meant wearing your heaviest sweater.

Home. Soon, she would be back home.

But Sean.

For months now, Isa had been rehearsing how she would explain her situation, how she would confess to him who she really was. She came close a few times, after they had made love and when she felt most vulnerable, but she never managed to confess that she was an imposter.

Tonight? She'd spoil whatever plans he had made for her birthday. No, he didn't deserve that. Not tonight.

Besides, what would she tell him? How would she tell him?

She ran her fingers through her hair, thinking of how much it had grown in the last year. In Cuba, she had never let her hair grow after adolescence, finding it too troublesome to keep her thick hair under control. It was also so much cooler during the hot summers in Havana. She smiled to herself. How wonderful that she could allow herself mundane thoughts about hair! Back in Cuba her worries would be about food rations for the month.

How was she going to tell Sean that she had been living her sister's life and now she had to give it back? She loved him, and although they had never exchanged those words, she felt he loved her too. She felt suddenly guilty that she had not stopped their affair immediately instead of letting herself fall in love.

There was no question in her mind that she had to go back to Cuba and free her sister to return to her real life. These past months with Richard and Sean and the other friends that had become part of her life would always be with her. Isa regretted nothing. Still, her heart felt like it was breaking in two.

She looked at her watch and saw that it was time to go back to work. Certainly it was going to be the most difficult evening of her life knowing her days with Sean were at an end.

Out of nowhere, Chencha's African story about the other side of the moon began to play in her mind like it used to when she was a child and she felt sad. She heard the old black woman's voice describing pools of delicious mango juice fed from gentle rivers, and imagined herself surrounded by purple trunked trees with foliage every color imaginable. Gigantic butterflies could transport you anywhere you desired. The other side of the moon was everything fantastic and exotic that you could envision and more. There, every dream came true, Chencha would always state with conviction.

Isa cried, feeling for the first time no comfort in this story with its empty promise of happiness.

"Happy Birthday, gorgeous." Diego kissed her deeply.

"How did you know?"

"Not easy to forget your birthday when it's the day we celebrate one of our greatest heroes." He looked at her, grinning. "Che's death is not something any good Cuban forgets."

"No, of course not. It's just that...I didn't think you'd remember that my birthday was his..."

"Yes, the anniversary of his death. But, as importantly, your birthday."

"Yes," she smiled. "Yes. Of course. Thank you for remembering."

"And what do you want to do to celebrate?" He touched her body suggestively.

"Yes, we could do that."

Diego laughed. "Well, that's great. But what special thing or place, that you haven't been to in a while that is, do you want to go to?"

She paused wondering what she should say. "Well, there is Tropicana."

"Tropicana, huh? Yes," he embraced her tighter, "that's a good idea. How about if we have dinner at *Los Jardines* and then catch the show?"

Had Isa been there before with Diego? Anaís waited for a minute to see if he would give her any clue. Diego just smiled at her.

"Yes, that will be great."

"Then I'll pick you up at 9:30. And wear something spectacular for our special evening...maybe some of that fake jewelry that your cousin left you." What was Diego's interest in her jewelry? Lately, some of the things he said were perplexing.

The tall, curvaceous mulatto dancers carried their elaborate headgear with the adeptness of any Las Vegas showgirl, their undulating moves belying the heaviness of their headdress. Anaís could see why Tropicana had reigned supreme in the late fifties as the most popular Caribbean hotspot. The club was dated compared to night clubs in the States, but its exotic allure remained.

Dinner was incredibly delicious and incredibly expensive. Seventy-five dollars for each of them. She still had not figured out how Diego could afford a life style which she imagined was beyond most government workers. And she also couldn't figure out why he was always treated with such respect, beyond what one would expect for a tourism department director. Whatever connections he had, they opened doors to see and visit places on a minute's notice, always getting the better seats, the better service, the better everything. Even in Castro's classless society, Anaís' year in Cuba had shown her that despite Fidel's rhetoric, privilege still existed on the island for some, especially if you were with the government.

And Anaís wasn't complaining that somehow Diego managed to get special treatment. It had made her time in Cuba not only a great adventure but also without the hardships that she knew her sister and Chencha usually endured.

The restaurant's specialty of lobster in a Creole sauce was one of the best meals Anaís had enjoyed in Cuba. She could hardly believe the size of the lobster that they placed on her plate. Diego had asked for the beef tenderloins, and after tasting his dish, sent his compliments to the chef. Soft music from a trio serenaded them amidst the tropical plants hanging from every corner. The star-studded sky was the perfect canopy above them.

"You look amazing." Diego took her dimpled chin in his strong fingers. He looked at the emerald earrings and matching necklace.

"And these..." He touched one of the chandelier earrings. "They're fake? Your cousin gave them to you?"

Anaís swallowed hard. She hated the needed the pretense with Diego.

"Yes."

"Unbelievable. Shit. They look so real." He looked at her green eyes, matching the deep color of her jewelry. What a great liar she was! Always unflappable. When was she going to confess to her ruse?

"You know," he continued playing with her earrings. "You have a lot of these...fake pieces, don't you?"

"Yes, some."

"So, you might consider selling me a set, as a sample that I can present to Enrique at CUBALSE at the next meeting on new products for our tourists, to build our economy. What do you think? Your cousin wouldn't mind, since according to her they're so inexpensive." He wanted to break her down, to make her admit her lies about being Isa, admit her lies about caring for him.

"No!" She grabbed at her necklace. "No" she said more softly. "I can't do that, Diego. They're the only thing I have left of my cousin's visit. They're very special to me. I understand what you're saying, but I can't."

His eyes narrowed, watching her panicked face, guessing that the jewelry was not fake.

Isa was waiting for him downstairs by the glass walls. Sean bounded into the lobby, smiling as he hugged her tightly.

"Happy birthday, Isa." He kissed her full on the mouth. Isa didn't want to stop hugging him back.

"Ready to party?"

She had told herself that there was nothing to be gained by thinking about her situation and she wasn't going to say anything. For Sean's sake, she would pretend it was yesterday, when their future still had promise and not the despair that she now knew was their fate. Even though she didn't care about her birthday, it was his night to enjoy surprising her with his plans.

"I am ready. But you're not wearing a lot of warm clothes, Sean." She pointed to a vest over a cable sweater. "Look at me! You told me to dress in warm clothes and I did."

"Well, you have to. You're always cold. I'll be fine. Trust me." They stepped outside and he called a cab.

"So where are we going that I have to dress like a polar bear?" She pulled at his blonde curly hair.

"I can't tell you." He kissed her, and they both continued a deep embrace, ignoring the taxi driver's looks in the rear view mirror.

"I wish we could stay here forever," she said, placing her head on his shoulder.

"I don't know." He kissed her forehead. "It might feel cramped for some things that we like to do."

Laughing, they got in the cab and drove north on Lake Shore Drive. She couldn't imagine where they were going. But she didn't care. Being with Sean made her so happy, so relaxed and happy that she wouldn't care if they simply continued to drive around all night.

"You didn't sound too well this morning when we talked, Isa." He looked into her beautiful eyes, thinking again how amazing she was. "Were you having a bad day at work?"

She sighed unwittingly.

"What a sigh! That bad, huh?"

No, she wasn't going to think about anything except making Sean's plan go perfectly. "It's over. I'm sorry I concerned you earlier." She tried to distract him and changed the conversation. "So where exactly are we going?"

"We're almost there."

"I love you, Sean. And I thought I would never love again." She looked at the beautiful opal ring. "But ..." she swallowed hard. "We can't. This can't be." She turned away from him, her face lit only by the brightness coming from the bonfire that Sean had built for their evening picnic on the beach near the spot where they had met when she lost control rollerblading.

She looked back at him and cringed, seeing the surprise and disappointment in his eyes. After a few moments, he turned away, clutching the ring in his hand.

"You don't love me." The words hung sadly on the gentle wind blowing in from the lake.

"No. That's not it. I do love you. I love you more than anyone."

He looked at her again with the same surprise and disappointed gaze. "Isa. I don't understand. What are you saying? You love me? But you don't want to marry me?" He looked into her eyes as if trying to find answers. "You don't believe in marriage, is that it? If that is it, that's not a problem. I can wait. I'll wait forever for you to feel comfortable with marrying me. Or we'll just live together. Whatever you want, as long as we are together."

"But that's the problem, Sean, I love you. I have never been happier. But we can't be together." She put her fingers to his lips to keep him from talking. "Please listen to me because what I have to tell you, it's a horrible thing I've done letting us get close when in the end we will be apart. What I've done..." She took a deep breath. "I am not who you think I am."

He looked at her in confusion. "I don't care what you have done or who you are. I love you, and we can work through anything."

"No. You don't understand. I am not the Isa that you think. I am working at a job that is not really mine. I live in an apartment that is not really mine." Sean looked increasingly more confused. "Even Richard is not really my friend, at least, not my long-time friend."

He took her hands and tried to speak, but she put her fingers up to his lips.

"Listen to me. Until last October, I was Isa Buenaventura and I lived in Havana, Cuba."

Sean's eyes widened and she nodded.

"I know this is all going to sound crazy, Sean, but it is the truth. I am finally telling you the truth about myself. Until last year, I lived in Cuba and had no idea that I had a twin sister here in Chicago. I changed places with her while she was on a business trip to Cuba. She has been pretending to be me in Havana, and I have been living her life here." There. It was all out.

"I cannot tell you how sorry I am that I have not been truthful with you, mainly out of fear for my sister's safety back in Cuba, and partly because I never expected that we would fall in love. I thought when the day came for me to have to go back, I simply would disappear from everyone's life. But you...you are my love. And I yet look how I am hurting you." She began to sob. "Sean, I go back to Cuba next week."

Her words seemed to pour out of her in a slow and deliberate recounting. Sean listened stoically, blinking in disbelief. His hands squeezed her so tightly that it almost hurt her. Isa didn't care. She wanted to feel his touch.

"And the only person who knows the whole story is Richard. He was on the Cuba trip. He saw right through me because he and my sister Ani have been friends since they were young. And thank goodness for Richard. I don't know what I would have done without him. But look what I've done to you."

Sean had not stopped looking into her eyes, holding her hands in his. He then cupped her face in his hands, brushing away her tears.

"My poor Isa. What a life you've had. How can anyone blame you for what you did?"

"I blame myself, Sean, for thinking that things could be different. And because my sister has spent almost a year living through what I assure you has been a difficult time. Yes, she says she's living an adventure, but Cuba is difficult. And now I am hurting you, the man I love, because I can't stay here, and we can't be together."

"But that's where you're wrong, Isa." He grabbed her hands and squeezed them tightly. "We'll figure this out. There has to be a way, there has to be someone who can help us."

"The someone is Senator Fernández, but he can't help me at this time."

"Then we'll talk to someone else..."

Isa felt an instant terror. "No! You have to promise me, Sean. You cannot say a word of this to anyone. Not anyone. It would put my sister in grave danger. You have to understand. If they found out in Cuba who she was, the international incident this would create would be immense. They could put her in jail." She felt panicked. "Please, please tell me you won't do or say anything. Please!" She sobbed.

"Alright. Alright. I promise." He hugged her to him. "But how can I let you go, Isa? I love you." A strong wind from the bonfire made the wood crackle and sparks floated through the air. The full moon shone on the glass-like surface of the lake, casting a soft light on their faces. Sean took Isa's hand and pulled off the glove. He placed the opal on her finger. Isa started to speak and he kissed her.

"Don't say anything. I want you to take this ring, to wear it. You will come back to me. We will figure this out. I know we will. There is no one else for me, no one else who should wear my great grandmother's ring."

Isa gazed at the smooth stone circled by sparkling diamonds. She had never imagined a man like Sean. His kindness, his openness, his optimism were all characteristics she loved dearly. He was so unassuming, despite his looks and position. In him, Isa felt she had found the best of the best in him.

The mere thought of never looking again into his wonderful eyes or feeling the strength of his body against hers was unbearable. And even more unbearable was the thought of hurting him. She found herself saying words she did not believe.

"Of course, we'll figure it out. And I am honored to wear this beautiful and special ring." She wrapped her arms around him, wishing to never have to let go.

"You'll probably be back in a few months, probably by Christmas." He hugged her so tight that Isa had to catch her breath. "And we'll drive up to Michigan. I can't wait until my family meets you."

CHAPTER 39

Adiós Tío Julio

"Tío Julio, I have something to tell you."

Her uncle pulled the reins on his horse and stared at Anaís' serious expression.

"*¿Qué pasa*, Isa? Are you alright? You don't look well. Is that why you asked Diego to stay back at the house?"

"Yes, Tío. I'm fine, but I have some things to tell you that...well, I probably should have told you before, but when I come to the farm, I am always so relaxed, enjoying every minute of being here. Besides, I still don't know how I can talk about this."

"Well, whatever it is, as long as you are alright, it will be okay." He urged the horses back to a walk. "Trust me, at my age, nothing really is a surprise any more. In fact, I know that whatever it is, it will not surprise me."

"I think this will, Tío."

"Try me."

She leaned over and stroked Lucero's mane. "I don't know where to begin."

"It doesn't matter. Start wherever you want. I'm not that old. I'll keep up with you."

She took a deep breath. "Tío, I'm not Isa. I'm Ana Isabel, the twin niece you thought had died."

Tío Julio reined his horse to a dead stop, staring at her.

"*Mamá* and *Papá* sent me to the U.S. with an American couple known to a priest they knew. The couple...the Morans...took care of me. And when nothing could be done to get Isa out of the country, I guess that's when my parents faked that had I had died of pneumonia. They must have paid someone to falsify the report. Who knows? With the craziness in Cuba at that time, and with all of you far from Havana, I guess it was an easy lie to pull off. The Morans adopted me in Chicago. They gave me a wonderful life. When I was thirteen, they told me the story and gave me my parents last known address, and that's how I found Isa. I didn't know anything about her or any of you until I came here with the Illinois delegation last October. Isa and I exchanged places. That's another long story, Tío."

She looked at her uncle, looking back at her tenderly.

"I'm sorry, Tío. I thought about saying something sooner, but didn't know where to begin. And I am saying something now because the Illinois delegation is returning and I'll be going back to the United States from where I'll do everything in my power to get safe passage to the U.S. for Isa."

"I'm the one who is sorry, Isa. You and your sister have gone through so much. I shouldn't swear, but shit...I thought nothing could surprise, but indeed I have still much to learn, right? And, sí, tell me everything. This is unbelievable."

He clucked, and both horses started walking again. Anaís felt an immense weight lift from her heart to finally be truthful with this uncle that she had come to love so much.

They talked for a long time, Tío Julio listening attentively to the incredible story of two lives torn apart and then exchanged. He said very little until they were back in the barn unsaddling the horses.

"Isa...I mean, Ana Isabel... I can hardly believe any of this! Your aunts love to watch soap operas and this certainly has all the makings of one, doesn't it? If they only knew this real story! Crazier than any soap opera I have ever heard of!"

"Tío, I don't think we should tell anybody."

"No, you are right. This secret has to be between us and Chencha. If even one person carelessly let any of these details be known...It would be disastrous. The fewer people knowing anything the better. I will take this to my grave. But wait...what about Diego?"

She closed the stall door and waited for her uncle to put his horse away. She hugged him strongly. "I don't know. I am afraid. Not so much for myself, but for Isa, who has to stay here. I just don't know what to do. I care for Diego...but can I trust him with this?"

"What I know is that Diego is an honorable man. And he loves you, or at least, my instinct says that he does. Yes, he was G2, the secret police..." Anaís blinked astonished at the new information "But I think he will understand what your parents did, and what Isa and you did. Tell him. It will be alright." He looked at Diego reclining against the banister of the back porch of the farmhouse, waiving at them. "Tell him, child. He has deep feelings for you. I can tell."

"I don't know, Tío. This is big. I've lead a big lie with him. And if he is, or was, with the secret police..."

"I don't think your feelings have been lies. And he will understand your loyalty to your parents and sister." He hugged her and they started walking toward the house. "I'm just sorry that I'm going to lose you just when I was beginning to know the real you, Ana Isabel." He kissed her forehead.

"Me, too. Until I came here, I did not know I had a Cuban family, or this beautiful country and the wonderful heritage which I now know I have."

"One day, my dear, things will be different. You'll see. Things will be different. I hope to live to see that day." He patted her on the back. "Now go to your young man and talk with him from your heart."

―――――――――――

"That was quite a dinner your uncle cooked up for us, wasn't it?" Diego's arm encircled her waist. They walked behind the house under a clear, star-studded sky, the evening sounds surrounding them softly.

"*Sí*. He is an incredible cook. It is always so good to spend time with him."

"You look like him, you know."

She smiled at him. "Do you really think so?" She, too, felt she resembled Tío Julio.

"Did your mother look like him as well?" Diego watched for her reaction, and saw her blink repeatedly at his question.

"Yes, probably." She didn't know what else she should say. Diego never spoke of family. Besides, her mind had been preoccupied all evening during the meal with the dread of her pending confession to Diego, now complicated further with the fact that he had been with the G2.

Yes, she had to tell him the truth. She owed it to him. Not only was Diego a wonderful man, but she had grown to care for him during their months together. It wasn't only the sexual pleasure they shared, but the kindness and quality of the man. She might even love him, although that was something she had not allowed herself to explore in her heart, knowing that she eventually would leave.

If Diego were just another lover, it would be different. She could disappear from his life without a word, and Isa could simply break off the relationship when she came back. But this was her dear Diego, and as her uncle had said, he was an honorable and loving man. He would not use her confession to jail any of them or to make headlines around the world.

"Have you heard anything I've said in the last ten minutes?"

She looked at him surprised to see that they had walked into the barn without her even realizing it.

"What do you mean?"

"You have been deep in thought, as if you were a thousand miles away."

This was her moment of truth. She felt sweat drip down her back despite the breezy evening.

"Yes, I was a thousand miles away, Diego. Actually, I am...from a thousand miles away."

She held her breath, looking intently at his strong features softened in the moonlight that streamed through the barn door. She expected to see a look of surprise or questioning, but all she saw was a smile start to creep on his face.

"It was time you told me, don't you think?"

Anaís felt suddenly dizzy. He knew!

"Yes, I've known for some time now."

Her green eyes gleamed with horror.

"No, don't look at me like that. It's alright. No, I don't mean it's alright that you haven't been honest with me, but I mean I understand. At least, I think I understand what happened. And there is nothing to be gained by making trouble for you, for Isa, or your family. It's alright."

She burst out crying, and he pulled her close, stroking her hair. "Life was not fair to any of you, not to you or Isa. And what may have happened to your parents...well, that was not..."

"I never meant to hurt you, Diego," she interrupted. "This was about my sister, and making sure my parent's wish for us to be together became a reality. I ...I care for you, and that is why it's been so hard to not tell you."

"I know." He hugged her. "And I...I care for you, too." He kissed her face. "And I know you will need to return with the delegation that is coming back from your state, although I don't want to know how the two of you will pull that off." He hugged her tighter to his chest.

"Thank you, Diego." She continued to sob. "Part of me doesn't want to leave you or Tío Julio or Chencha or this beautiful country."

"I wish it were different, too. But right now, two Isas in Havana would be a problem." His simple statement made her chuckle and he chuckled, too.

"I will miss you...but maybe someday... And, if I can, I will help you in any way I can."

CHAPTER 40

Going Home to Cuba

THE WEEK HAD FLOWN BY WITH A SPEED SHE COULD NEVER HAVE imagined. Sean had been overjoyed when Isa asked him to spend her last days in Chicago with her at Anaís' apartment, and they had spent every minute possible together, trying to cram into the short week all the hopes that they had for the future. They cooked together, met each other back at the apartment daily for lunch and every night after revisiting a place that had become special to Isa, they made passionate love with no conversation about the days ahead. They had vowed not to speak about her departure, knowing there would be ample time for sadness in a very short time.

Isa felt that she had never before lived as intensely in the moment. Even when she was exhausted at the end of the day, she hated to fall asleep in his loving embrace, feeling that sleep was wasted time.

She finally got through to Anaís, but her sister's voice was concerned instead of happy. They both knew they couldn't speak freely on the phone, fully aware that no one ever knew which conversations were being monitored. But she could hear the worry in her sister's comments: "Are you sure you want to come back at this time? I'm fine, really. You could leave your trip for later."

Isa knew she couldn't depend on *later*. She had done what she had dreamed of doing, living in the United States and exploring freedom. And she had lived beyond her wildest dreams her sister's incredible life. Unexpectedly, she had even fallen in love, something she thought would never happen to her for a second time in her life. It was time for her to go back to the lot that fate had chosen for her. And for Anaís to regain hers.

Anaís had asked to speak with Richard, and Isa was surprised that they started to talk about sports. She couldn't follow the conversation because she didn't know Chicago teams, but Richard kept saying numbers and changing them until he finally said he understood.

When he got off the phone, he asked Isa to sit down on the couch next to him.

"Okay, Ani is ready to come back if you are, and to keep working to get you here through the Senator's office. Are you ready to go back?"

Isa nodded.

"Are you sure, sure? You're leaving...a lot behind," he hugged her. "And I don't just mean adorable me."

She nodded again, and hugged him back.

"Okay, then. We'll need to sit down and look at the finances, to see where we're going to withdraw some money for you to take back with you."

"What?"

"Ani wants you, as her, to withdraw $10,000 to take back to Cuba for you and Chencha to have while she works on getting you out of there. The problem is not the amount, but she wants it in tens and twenties. That's what will be the issue. But we'll figure out."

"But, I can't do that."

"Sure you can. Your sister wants you to do it and we will." Isa started to protest and Richard put his index finger on her lips. "Uh-uh. There is no discussion about this. It's what we're going to do. We will just have to be creative, space the withdrawals out, I don't really know."

"How did you talk about that? All I heard was sports talk."

"It's our own secret code...goes back to college...we communicated about all sorts of things with sports facts when we didn't want anybody to know." He looked at her baffled face. "We'll teach it to you when you're back here with us permanently."

"Do you really think it will happen, Richard? That one day I will be back?"

"Don't cloud up those beautiful green eyes! Yes, of course, it will happen." He held her hands, trying to sound more reassuring than he really felt.

"Anaís has the support of the Senator here, and you've spoken about that lottery that Cuba has every year which I didn't know about."

"Ricardito, do you know how many people last year applied for those visas to the U.S. which you call the lottery? Half a million! For 20,000 visas! What are the chances?"

He squeezed her hand.

"Well, the Senator, he's a good guy. He won't let you two down. I know it. I know it will happen. Right now, don't even think about these things. Tell me if there is anything I can do to help, or if there is anything you want to do before you leave." His own eyes welled up with tears.

"See, now you've made me cry."

Isa touched his cheek, comforting him.

"You are right, Richard. Something good will happen. Look how lucky I have already been."

"Isa, maybe you should go above the Senator's head, to someone else at the State Department."

"No. I can't bring attention to myself here. It would be dangerous for Ani in Cuba. Swear to me, Richard, that you won't do anything without asking me first."

Isa realized that neither Richard nor Sean understood the terrible fear she felt for her sister's safety if anything were to be known. And if there was any chance for her to one day be in the U.S., it would have to happen through channels, after she and her sister were back in their respective lives.

Elián now was out of sight and out of mind in the U.S. media. Only the Miami newspapers continued to carry daily articles about the González case. In Chicago, in middle America, Elián and his situation were history. Isa hoped that over time, relations would be again such that Anaís could get the Senator to address their situation. There was always hope she thought, trying to be like Sean who was always optimistic about everything.

Richard was upset because he had not been invited on the trip to Cuba because the Senator's office had restricted the number of people in the delegation. The focus of this trip was going to be totally humanitarian, taking medicine and medical supplies for children and the elderly. There would be no talk about trade, and therefore Richard's role was eliminated. He had tried to talk himself into the group, but to no avail. The only reason Isa was going was because the Senator's office thought it was a good idea to return with the only Cuban American from the previous trip.

Richard called Isa daily, trying to sound upbeat but always ending with a teary *hasta luego*. Now it was their last time together.

"Okay, Isa, I have something for you." He said, opening the door of his car.

"Come on, Richard. You know I can't really take much back to Cuba."

"Well, you are taking this. You won't have a problem since you are part of a government delegation." He handed her a pair of new rollerblades plus knee and arm pads.

"Oh, this is wonderful! Thank you!" She kissed his cheek.

"You're pretty good now, but remember to always wear your pads."

"*Sí, papá,*" she teased.

"And you have the money?"

"Right here." She touched the lining of her down jacket.

"Perfect. I never would have thought of hiding $10,000 in small bills in there. You Cubans!" He was trying to make her laugh.

They stood for a moment awkwardly looking at each other. Isa bit her lip, trying not to cry. There was so much she wanted to thank him for.

"Richard, thank you...thank you for everything. *Por todo en absoluto.* I don't know what I would have done without you all these months. You have been more than a friend, almost what I imagine a brother is like..." His eyes filled with tears.

"No, don't cry" she said, "because then I'll cry. And I have to tell you...take care of Ani. I mean, I know you will, but take care of her. And when you see Sean..." her voice broke as she looked at the opal ring on her finger.

"We'll get you back here, Isa," he said in a hoarse voice. "And there is nothing to thank me for. I am now blessed with two sisters. And we will get you back."

She dabbed at her eyes, nodding.

"I know you believe that. Sean says the same thing, too. But I...I come from a different place, where our movies don't usually have happy endings. No, I know you don't want me to say it, but you're my friend, my best friend and I don't want to lie to you. I don't know if I'll come back, and if I do, it may be after many years, maybe when things change in Cuba after Castro dies, but that could be a long, long time away. When I see Ani, I am going to give her Sean's ring to give back to him, because he deserves a happy life now, not in some unknown or faraway moment. But Anaís doesn't know Sean, so I want you to talk to him, to tell him, that I will always love him, and that is why he needs to go on with his life, without me."

They were both crying now, sobbing like children in the empty parking lot across the street from the lake. All the week's pretense of normalcy finally erupted in the terrible sadness that she felt. They held hands and nodded, understanding each other.

"Okay. But you are coming back. I know it. I'm not even going to say good-bye. Only, *¡hasta la vista!*" He made a grand gesture with his hand.

"Ricardito, I've told you only Arnold says that in the movies." She kissed his cheek softly. "*Hasta que Dios quiera.*"

O'Hare airport traffic was not as busy as they had expected, and Sean and Isa arrived well ahead of their anticipated schedule. She had tried to persuade him to say their goodbyes at the apartment, but Sean had insisted on staying with her until the last minute.

Their last day together had been almost impossible to bear. Despite their attempt to pretend it was an ordinary day, neither one of them was able hide the anxiety of Isa's departure. They kissed and touched each other incessantly, making love through the night with their usual passion tinged with feverish undertones of despair. In the morning, they took their customary long walk by the shore despite the harsh winds of the late fall day. Isa chitchatted about the weather and the bare landscape, which only weeks ago was ablaze with red, purple and golden colors. Sean said there would be many other falls that she would see with him when she returned. Her deep green eyes had turned the color of the turbulent waters in the distance.

"You want to get a cup of coffee?" She had just checked in her bags full of clothing and shoes for Chencha. The thought of seeing her old nanny and sister were the only thoughts that gave her joy.

She couldn't wait to wrap herself up in the old woman's powerful embrace. As soon as she got back, they would visit Tío Julio and the family in Pinar. And she would ride Lucero hard across the fields that long ago were rich with *caña*, Cuba's renowned sugar cane.

"Yes, coffee sounds good." She looked at her watch. "I still have about half an hour before I need to meet the group."

"I wish I could go with you. Maybe I can just stay with you until you board?"

"It wouldn't be good, Sean, for them to see us...to meet you. Too many questions might arise that would make it difficult for my sister later on. I've put her through enough."

They sat at a small table facing the concourse, waiting for their coffees.

"I hope you and my sister become good friends, Sean. She's a wonderful person. And she's had an easy life in some ways, money, career... but in others it's been very hard. There's no family here for her. Except for Richard, there's no one really close to her. Back home, we have so many cousins and uncles..."

"If she's anything like you...I can't wait to meet my future sister in law."

Isa couldn't help but smile. If only she had his optimism. That was an American quality she would never understand.

She heard someone call her name, and looking up saw the Senator's aide rushing up to them, two full bags slung over each shoulder.

"Hey!"

"Hi, Pablo. This is my...friend Sean."

"Nice to meet you, Sean. Are you ready, Anaís? The Senator is waiting for us in the lounge. He wants us to go over the agenda for the trip."

"I'll catch up with you. In a minute."

Pablo waved and ran off down the concourse. Sean and Isa looked at each other, squeezing each other's hands. She didn't know what to say. She wanted to memorize his face, every curl on his head, the laugh lines that creased around his eyes when he laughed. She was sure she would not see him again.

"Isa, we will figure this out. You know that, don't you?"

"Yes, I do" she lied. "I know you and Ani will bring me back here. And you'll get to meet Chencha. And you'll love her."

"I love you." He leaned over and kissed her deeply.

"Do you need any change?" the waiter asked as he picked up the cash from the table.

"No, that's fine."

They walked, still embracing. Isa turned to him at the entrance to the concourse.

"It's better if you stay here."

"I know."

"I'll be fine. I don't want you to worry, Sean. I've lived in Cuba my whole life. Everything will be fine."

"And you're coming back. You know that, don't you." He sounded like a man trying to convince himself. He pointed to the opal ring on Isa's finger. "You need to come back so we can make it official."

"Yes, I know."

"You have to come back to me, Isa."

"I know." She put her arms around his neck. "I love you." They kissed with the deep and sweet despair of those saying their last good-byes. "I'll see you soon." Their arms stretched out toward each other until only their fingertips touched. Isa touched her fingers to her lips and blew him a kiss.

"I'll see you soon."

"In my dreams."

She turned slowly, accommodating her purse and duffle bag over her shoulder. She could feel his eyes on her as she walked down the crowded concourse and only turned around when she reached the connecting hall. His arm went up immediately as they caught each other's gaze, and they waved and smiled at each other. She blew him one last kiss, then turned quickly as she felt tears rushing to her eyes, feeling that she was leaving her heart behind.

CHAPTER 41

Cuba! Again!

ISA LOOKED AT THE TURQUOISE WATERS AND THE BEAUTIFUL PALM LINED coastline of Cuba in the distance. Her home, her island lay before her, and despite everything, she realized how she had missed that special color of the sea, the deep lush green of the countryside in the distance. At this altitude, Havana below was a shimmering town of bright colored buildings and winding avenues, not the city in much need of repair that she knew.

Their connecting flight had been delayed in Mexico by bad weather for almost an hour, and Senator Fernández had taken the opportunity to give the group another a pep talk. He stated that despite the tensions between Havana and Washington, he was proud to still have managed to put together the humanitarian mission to Cuba. Their goodwill would hopefully keep the lines of communication open so that once Cuba/U.S. relations stabilized, Illinois products and services would be first in line to the Cuban economy.

The delegation's focus this time, Senator Fernández stressed, was to nurture good relations after the Elián situation and if pressed for opinions on the subject, everyone was expected to stay neutral. They were goodwill ambassadors and nothing more. Their stay was short and focused, and everyone's job was to soothe any ruffled feathers created as a result of the political confrontation.

Isa listened absentmindedly. Her thoughts were with Anaís and wondering how they would see each other in a manner that would not raise suspicion.

The plane's wheels touched the ground. Isa looked at her watch and realized that Anaís would be at work. Perhaps she could take a taxi to Miramar after the reception that evening. She needed to call first, just to make sure that Ani was going to be home. They had so much to talk about.

Arrancapellejo was by her side.

"How does it feel to be back here, Ani? Twice in Cuba in a year. Can you believe it? After all those years of being out of the country, this must be really something for you. But you look so sad. What's the matter?"

Everything was the matter, Isa thought. She felt the warm morning air as the airplane door swung open. Bright October sunshine streamed into the cabin.

"I'm just tired, Cynthia. It's been a long day."

"Yes, but look at this weather! I could come back here any time. Couldn't you?"

I'm here to stay, Isa thought, and her heart felt heavy again as she thought of Sean, Richard and the life she had experienced in Chicago. She smiled wanly and stepped outside. A small group of Cuban officials waited at the foot of the metal staircase. Unlike the elaborate welcome that Anaís had described about her arrival with the Illinois group last year, this time Fidel was not at the head of a long, official line of dignitaries. There were no children with flowers, no band playing the Cuban national anthem. She touched the lining of her down coat nervously.

"*Bienvenida, señorita.*" She shook hands with each of the government officials and felt a warm feeling listening to her fellow Cubans welcoming her home. She loved her people, this island. She hadn't realized how much she had missed them until that very minute when she looked into their eyes, remembering their shared history. Perhaps that's how she needed to reframe everything that had happened in the last year. Chicago had been a dream, a vacation. Now she was back, to her Cuban home and reality.

From a distance, a pair of binoculars followed Isa as she headed for the limousines waiting to take them to their Havana hotel. The dark brooding eyes behind the lenses blinked. Diego lowered his eyes and turned to exit the door behind him, pondering his next steps.

The delegation members separated into different limousines sent to drive them to the hotel. Isa made sure she was not in the car with *Arrancapellejo*, feeling she could not bear her constant babbling gossip and conversation. Instead, she rode with a couple of the journalists. She nodded and smiled as they excitedly discussed the political situation between the U.S. and Cuba, which was quite different since their last visit.

Her mind was elsewhere, on Sean in Chicago, on Anaís a few miles away in the Havana office building. She felt that all her energy in the last ten days had focused on living the moment with Sean and trying to absorb the special places and people of her Chicago life deeply into her soul so that she could savor them some time in the future in Cuba. She realized that she had not allowed herself to think about her return to her old life in Havana.

And now here she was, hours away from resuming her real identity. How would she and her sister pull it off? What would it be like? Could they each pick up where the other had left off? And Anaís? How had she really coped with her life in Cuba during the last year?

The limousine wound its way now through the wide Malecón boulevard to their hotel. Havana at midmorning was a bustle of activity and European tourism. Bicyclists in faded clothes pulling empty carts maneuvered nonchalantly through the traffic of old American cars from the fifties and sixties. Young, voluptuous girls in short dresses swayed down the broad oceanfront sidewalk, smiling or answering catcalls from passing cars. The office buildings seemed small, the streets narrow, the air not clean. Everything was familiar yet different, Isa thought, realizing that it was she who was different.

"*¡Bienvenidos a Cuba!*" The doorman's accent seemed heavy and sugary. He smiled at the tired group. "Welcome to the Melía!"

"Well, let's meet back in the lobby in about one hour," the senator's aide was telling them. "Then we'll have a better idea of the agenda for the next few days."

Isa started to roll her suitcase, but was helped immediately by another porter. She looked at him feeling almost foolish. Soon, she too, would be part of the Cuban workforce not allowed in the hotels frequented by the foreign tourists. How odd it was going to be living her old life again.

In her room she quickly put a call through to Chencha. The phone rang various times, and she could picture the old woman walking slowly from the chair where she usually fell asleep in the midday heat.

"*¿Qué hay?*" Chencha's voice made her almost cry.

"Chencha. It's me."

Screams from the other side told her that her old nanny was still the same, thanking her African gods in a language that Isa had never learned. "*¡Cómo estás, mi niña!* How are you? I have missed you so much."

"Chencha, I've missed you too, very much. And I have so much to tell you. But I don't want to talk too much, you know. Is An...I mean, is Isa at work?"

"No. Today her office was doing some work with a firm in Varadero. She won't be back until later on tonight."

"Well, tell her that I'm here. I don't want to call her at work. But we need to see how we're going to do this."

"I understand. I will tell her. Don't worry. We'll see each other soon enough, child."

"All is well, Chencha. I love you both and I can't wait to see you. I'll call tomorrow. A kiss for you."

She hung up, feeling Chencha's caring reach her through the telephone line. Chencha was truly a second mother. How she had missed her warmth and counsel.

Isa changed into comfortable shoes and slacks and headed for the lobby. The Senator's aide was there passing out an agenda, and she caught him mid-sentence.

"....so, since we're not here for very long, our time has to be spent wisely. Yes," he smiled at the men, "that means you may not have too many opportunities to do the Tropicana, guys. Sorry. But just about every evening we're invited to some shindig or another. Remember all we've gone through in the last year with Cuba/U.S. relations. So, very important that we are all with the Senator at each of these evening events aside from the morning business meetings. Again, sorry. But you'll for sure have the last evening to yourself. I promise that."

"He's an early bird, anyway. We'll have our fun when the Senator goes to bed." One of the journalists whispered to another.

"And tonight," the aid continued, "we are invited to the foreign ministry's affair. So, formal wear, okay."

"What about our Cuban *guayaberas?*"

"Not tonight, fellows. Suits."

"But they wear those here for fancy occasions!"

"The Cubans do. Remember, we need to be extra careful with our protocol. So, suits it will be, okay?"

"Yeah, yeah, yeah."

"Now, this morning we are splitting up into two groups—half of us will be taking school supplies to a few of the schools outside the city. The other half will be talking with the pharmaceutical company here. And here is the schedule."

Isa had been assigned to the school. No negotiations with anyone. Wonderful. It would give her time to think.

"Isa is back home." Chencha hugged Anaís as she entered the apartment.

"Really? That is so wonderful! How is she? When will we see her?"

"She sounded happy. She wanted to see you earlier today, but I told her that you would be in Varadero until tonight."

"Good, Chencha. And did you have a chance tell her that Diego knows?"

"No! This old head of mine. I never even thought of Diego. I hope that I didn't make a problem, child."

"No, Chencha. I just don't want her to be shocked when she sees Diego here. We need to be very careful, for Isa's sake, for all our sakes."

Chencha's eyes turned to the heavens.

"Secundino...he says all will turn out fine. All will be as it was always meant to be."

"Dr. Moran, how was your time at the schools today?" The Senator had greeted her with his usual warmth. Isa was happy to report the excitement of the children and teachers at the grammar schools they visited and how much they appreciated and welcomed the boxes of notebooks, pencils, markers and crayons given to them. Isa knew that each child would use up each and every space on the pages with written work and that they would color with the very last bit of crayon. The school supplies would not be wasted, she told the Senator. He expressed his gratitude for their work, and then left with an aide for a meeting.

She looked around at the lovely setting on the veranda of one of the beautifully renovated colonial style buildings in the Vedado suburb outside Havana. The elegance of the room, the table settings and the decor had the first rate look of a top Chicago event. A combo played softly in the distance. They were being treated royally at this dinner, their first night in Havana, but Isa knew that soon, when she was no longer part of the American delegation, she would be experiencing a different situation, helping Chencha to eke out every bit of cooking oil from the can, to stash away the smallest pieces of soap to add to other soap pieces, to crush the scented petals from the jasmine tree outside their window to make cologne. She was now on the other side once again.

"¿Y cómo has estado, Isa?"

Even before she turned, Isa recognized Diego's deep voice. "Diego!"

"Hola, Isa. My God, you and your sister are spitting images of each other. Except you now have the American woman's look."

Isa couldn't believe her ears, and she stared at him wide-eyed and shocked. Anaís had said nothing about sharing their secret with Diego. How and when had he found out about their deception? Why didn't Chencha tell Ani that Diego had been a G2? Her mind raced, her feet frozen to the floor.

"What's the matter, Isa? Surprised that I know?" Diego's eyebrows narrowed into one long line at the top of his nose."Don't worry. It's alright. I know all about it. Well, at least your sister's version. And I can't wait to hear yours. How you managed to pull this off is…well, frankly, it's unbelievable." His matter-of-fact attitude disturbed her. "Want to dance?"

Diego slipped his strong arm around her waist and led her to the dance floor that had been set up for the evening. They began dancing to the cha-cha-cha that the combo was playing.

"How is my sister? And what are you doing here? And what and how do you know?"

"Your sister is excellent. And, I am here to take you to her, if you want." His eyebrows still were narrowed.

"Of course I do."

"Well, that's what we will do then." He twirled her gently. "But we have time. And I really want to know how all this happened. Your sister told me her story. Now I want to hear it from you."

"When did she tell you, Diego? Why would she tell you something so private? Why, Diego, why?"

The blunt question took him off guard for an instant. He smiled and his tone softened. "I'll go first, then. Isa, I confess I wasn't happy when you broke things off we me years ago." He sounded sincere. "I really liked you and liked spending time with you. Still, I respected your wishes and moved on. But then, last year, out of nowhere when I came back to the office in November after being away on business for a while, you…that is, your sister pretending to be you, started flirting with me. I was at first surprised but glad that you were giving me a second chance."

The song ended and he took her by the arm to a corner of the room.

"We became intimate almost immediately," Diego saw Isa blush, "and from that very first encounter, something seemed very different. This new you was outspoken, with controversial ideas, always challenging me and what I think. I felt that I was with a totally different person, unrecognizable, except for your gorgeous physical appearance. And as we continued to see each other and to be with each other, I forgot about the previous Isa of years ago...I'm sorry, but that's the truth. I felt I was with an entirely different woman, and that is the woman that I have come to...I have come to care for very, very much." His voice was soft and gentle.

And there it was, Isa thought. Diego no longer had any residual feelings for her. He was in love with Anaís, whether they had exchanged those words between them or not.

"What I don't understand, is why you came back," he continued.

"I belong here, Diego. When I met my sister and found out how we had been separated, how our parents had let Father Pat choose whom to take first to the United States and that she was chosen...I wanted to see what it's like...over there." Her voice trailed off into a whisper.

"But do you want to be here?" he pressed. "I think, in many ways, your sister likes it here and is happy here. Perhaps you, too, were happy... there." Diego spoke, wishing he would hear words that he could use to make Anaís stay.

"Anaís has her life back there, Diego. I belong here."

"I see." Diego sighed, knowing that he was hearing the truth. He believed Isa's simple statements.

"Well, then, your sister will go back. It would serve no purpose to create yet another international incident by letting any of this be known. What was done almost 40 years ago, well, we need to let that be. And personally, I thank you. Spending this year with your sister has been..." His voice cracked. "She has become very special to me."

"Diego, I am so sorry..."

He shook his head. "You gave me time with a most wonderful woman. That's what I will remember, when she's gone." He squeezed her hand.

"*Gracias, Diego.*" Her eyes welled up with tears. "I will never forget this."

"*De nada, muchacha.*" He smiled at her. "Life is never easy, *¿verdad?* Now, I'll just mingle until you think you can get away. And we'll go see Isa, or rather, Ana Isabel."

"*Bien.* Let me just tell one of my colleagues that I need to meet with you about something."

"I'll be around the corner waiting."

"*Perfecto.*"

They looked around at the others watching them. Isa shook his hand and joined her table. She grabbed the purse with some of the photographs that she wanted to show Chencha about her life in Chicago. Her heart cringed when she thought that among those pictures were some of Sean, her love, whom she would probably never see again.

"John, I've run into someone that I met last time we were here, from the tourism office, and we're just going to get a drink," she spoke quietly to one of her colleagues at the Senator's table. "I'll take a taxi back to the hotel. Tell the group that I'll see them tomorrow."

On the way to Miramar, Diego's comments about Anaís were evidence to Isa that her short-lived affair with Diego was all but forgotten by him. That was wonderful to hear since theirs had been a casual relationship those many years ago. He loved her sister. That was obvious. And Anaís? What were her feelings for Diego?

They were silent at he turned the corner onto her street. The headlights of Diego's car shone inside the small apartment, and she saw two figures jump to their feet. Chencha and Anaís appeared at the door, not wanting to venture out into the street.

Isa hardly waited for Diego to stop the car and jumped out waving wildly at the two women by the door. Yes, she was home. It was time to get Anaís back to hers.

CHAPTER 42

Going Home to Chicago

ISA FOLDED A BLUE LIGHTWEIGHT JACKET AND STARTED TO PUT IT INTO her sister's duffel bag. Then she took it out again, saying, "I think you should carry this with you, Anaís. It was cold in Chicago when I left."

For a moment, the sisters looked at each other, as if remembering their exchanged lives of the past year.

Anaís stopped putting things in the drawer, crossed the room and hugged her sister. Their arms encircled each other in a tight hug. Tears came to their eyes. After a long, silent moment, Anaís looked at her sister softly, "Isa, I love you. And it is so unfair that you again stay behind. I feel so guilty... "

Isa shook her head.

"I mean it. I feel guilty. Guilty that fate decided it was I who would go to the United States. I'm guilty of leading the life of comfort and privilege that has been mine all my life. While you," she stroked her sister's hair, "you have had to be brave and self-sufficient, and you've made do with so little, during all that time."

The words were like balm to Isa's spirit and she affectionately squeezed her sister's hands.

"This year has been incredible for me, Isa. Despite all the craziness, I would never had done anything differently. Yes, I was drunk when I told you to take my place...but I also think my heart was talking clearly. It was the right thing to do. I have loved every minute... I have learned so much here, experienced so much. My family, the people..."

"And Diego," Isa filled in for her.

"Yes, Diego." They hugged again.

"Can you really leave him, Ani?"

Anaís' eyes welled with tears. "I can't allow myself to think about Diego and me. I have to go back to the States to get this resolved for you, for you and Chencha. And I am going to get you both come to live with me, and for you to go back to Sean." Anaís pointed to the opal ring that she was now wearing instead of Isa. "I know you want to go back, to wear this ring from Sean and to marry him. And it is possible. Even Diego says you can apply to visit me in the States, and once there, you can ask for political asylum."

Isa nodded. They both knew what a long shot it would be to be able to get a visitor's visa, especially with her position in the Tourism Office. But Isa needed to pretend, for her sister's sake as much as for her own.

"Yes," she said. "It will be alright. *Si pasa, pasa.* And if it doesn't happen, that's alright too. You can come to visit me. And we both know that one day, all this in Cuba will change. And we are sisters, soul mates. Now that we have each other, we will never really be alone." Silent tears streamed down their faces.

"And, Ani..." Isa handed her sister the two porcelain dolls. "Take these with you...our mother's things will be safe with you, until we are together one day."

"Don Diego is here," Chencha whispered through the door.

Both Isa and Anaís went out to greet him. A smile on his face made them feel better for an instant.

"He handed Anaís a large box, a look of pride danced on his face. "This is for you. It's from the Russians." They really liked you, and the deal that you put together for them. They asked that I get you something special from CUBALSE."

"My goodness," Anaís exclaimed, opening the box. "They shouldn't have done this. I was doing my job, and you haven't even decided who will get the deal. I can't take this from them."

Diego gave her a scolding look.

"Have you learned nothing about our way of being here? You cannot say no to this gift. It would be a hurt, an insult. They want you to have it. They will be proud when I tell them how stunning you look in their gift."

Anaís realized that he was right. Isa and Chencha too were nodding agreement.

"The perfect dress for your return to your country," he said as Anaís took out a dark green sheath with matching shawl.

"Come," said Chencha. "Let me help you to get ready, child." Chencha's lip quivered.

"Hurry up." Diego warned. "We must be at the airport soon."

Chencha followed Isa and Anaís into the small bedroom. Out of the box, Anaís also took black leather low-heeled shoes.

"Let me help you," Chencha said, holding up the dress as Anaís slipped out of her shorts and blouse. The dress fit perfectly, accentuating her slim and curvaceous figure. The shoes were a little tight, but she was excited to be wearing a new pair.

"Beautiful," Chencha said, stretching to zip up the back. "Bend down, child" she ordered Anaís so she would reach her height. "Now that's beautiful." Isa agreed, a smile on her face. The tears had dried, but it was difficult for her to hide the sadness she felt seeing her sister leave.

"Let's go." they could hear Diego's impatient voice calling from the next room.

"Chencha, please come quickly." Diego put his arm around the old family caretaker leading her to the door. "You need to come with us also. To say good-bye to our girl."

"Yes." Chencha agreed, her voice cracking and tears streaming down her wrinkled face. "Thank you."

They all took seats in Diego's old black Chevy, Anaís in the front seat. They drove in silence. Anaís turned to touch her sister's hand or pat Chencha's face. It was so hard to think of saying good-bye.

They found parking easily in the area reserved for government officials. Diego took out Anaís' single duffle bag and put it over his arm. With the other, he helped Chencha get out of the back seat and handed her the new cane that Isa had brought from the States. Both sisters helped the old woman up on the curb.

"They won't let you past the guards," Diego said, suggesting this was the opportunity to say their good-byes.

"I will find a way of bringing you both to live with me," Anaís said, hugging her sister and Chencha. "I promise."

Isa nodded, while Chencha shook her head.

Not me. I can die now that I have seen both of you together, that I see that you love each other and that the past has been forgiven. I can die now." Her gnarly, wrinkled hands grabbed Isa and Anaís' arms.

"You two—you will be happy."

"I won't be totally happy until both of you are with me, in the States," Anaís said, squeezing the old woman's hand tightly.

"Soon I hope. She smiled that toothless smile that Anaís had grown to love so much. God is very powerful." She reached into the pocket of her wide skirt, taking out a small bottle. "Here is a small remembrance of Cuba for you... When you put it on and smell the jasmine in the air, you will think of us, no?"

Anaís' heart ached as she hugged the old woman, knowing it would be for the last time.

"Thank you, Chencha...for everything."

Diego was now at the glass door, opening it and motioning for Anaís to follow.

"Be hopeful, my sister," Anaís hugged her sister and kissed her cheek.

"Don't worry, Anaís," Isa responded. "We will be fine." Then, with one last hug, she added. "And explain to Sean..."

Anaís nodded. She hugged Chencha in silence, then followed Diego through the doors, waving to her loved ones one last goodbye.

Once inside the building, Diego put his arm around her shoulder and whispered in her ear.

"Everything is going to be okay. Trust me. Don't worry."

Anaís looked at him through teary eyes, then kissed his cheek. Diego had become such a dear person to her in so many ways. Did she love him? Probably, despite their many differences, she did love him. She had not told him how much she was going to miss him too, his kindness and caring. There were so many things she wanted to thank him for, she didn't know where to begin. She wanted to catch his eye, find the moment, but Diego seemed to be in a hurry, scurrying down the hallway, dodging the group of people talking, laughing and crying as they said their good-byes to those leaving the island. Finally, they were at the departure line, and Diego took out his ID card from his pocket and showed it to the thin young uniformed man at the edge of the commotion.

"I'm seeing this *señorita* to the plane. She was here with a U.S. delegation, and I personally want to walk her to her group."

"Your passport please," the officer said, waiting with his hand stretched out for Anaís to take out the documents he had requested from her handbag. The young man looked at the picture in the passport, then at the ticket. Finally he looked and Diego and then read his G2 ID card. Satisfied that everything was in order and knowing that he should not question someone with Diego's authority, he didn't quibble when Diego took the documents before either passport or plane ticket were stamped. Instead, the customs officer nodded and motioned for them to pass through.

Anaís could hear the comments from the people standing in line, and felt embarrassed at the personal attention she was getting.

"Diego, my group is supposed to meet at the bar..."

But Diego had other ideas. He seemed in a hurry to get her to the plane. He tightened his grip on her arm and led her to the exit door where the plane sat on the tarmac. Diego handed the steward Anaís' boarding papers and his own government ID card.

"No. It's better for you to relax on the plane. You probably don't really want them asking you a lot of questions. I'll let them know that you're on the plane." He waved her passport and plane ticket. "And I will give these to your group leader. You don't need them anymore until you land in Miami and go through Customs there." He put the papers in his pocket.

The Mexicana Aerolíneas flight attendant smiled as they approached the door.

"Doctor Moran has been visiting us as part of a delegation for cultural exchange. I would like to personally show her to her seat, if that's possible." Anaís saw Diego's flash his most disarming smile.

"Certainly. No problem, Coronel Mendoza. Please go right ahead," she smiled back at him coquettishly.

"You are very kind, *señorita*" he smiled again, moving Anaís in front of him through the glass door.

The evening breeze caressed Anaís' face and body with its warm tropical sweetness. She was going to miss this type of evening in Chicago, she thought, breathing in the night's charm. She was going to miss everything here. And Diego. She still had not said what she wanted to say to him and they were already ascending the stairs up to the plane.

She hesitated on one of the steps but realized Diego was not stopping his quick race to the top and so she continued to follow him. He hurried Anaís down the narrow aisle to her seat.

"You are all the way at the back," he said, and Anaís turned around to ask why all the hurry when there were no people on the plane yet. Why was he in such a hurry to say goodbye? Perhaps he had already closed the door to his feelings for her, knowing they didn't have a chance together?

Almost at the back of the plane, Diego pointed to her seat by the window.

"Here we are." He said, putting her duffle bag in the compartment above her seat. "You have had an arduous day, Ani. Stay back here and just relax. It would not be good for you to start crying about...well about Isa and everything...when nobody knows what has happened. So just pretend to sleep and your friends will leave you alone I am sure." Anaís knew he was right. She stood next to him, realizing he was about to leave and she still had not told him all that was on her mind and in her heart.

"Take care of yourself...try to call, to get through to us here in a while." He sounded almost matter of fact. "Don't forget us."

Anaís felt her entire body go limp, filled with emotion. Hadn't these months meant anything to him? She couldn't think of what to say first.

"Diego, I don't know how to thank you for..."

He cupped her mouth with his hand. "I know." He kissed her forehead. Then abruptly grabbed her tight and kissed her deeply and lovingly. "I love you. And you don't have to thank me for anything. Maybe this makes up a little for what you lost a long time ago. Just be happy."

He hugged her, and when they again separated tears also filled his eyes.

"I am not going to say *adiós*. Just till next time."

She nodded and watched Diego head down the aisle among the empty seats. Would she ever see him again?

With an overwhelming sadness weighing her heart, Anaís curled into her seat next to the window, looking out as the first passengers started to line up to board the plane. She saw Diego look at the plane once more...he then turned quickly and disappeared into the terminal.

Chapter 43

Final Goodbye

Chencha and Isa were still standing where Diego had left them. He glanced at Isa's drawn face, the long black eyelashes around her beautiful green eyes still wet with tears.

"Let's go, Chencha." Chencha didn't move. "We need to go," Isa repeated. Still, the old woman did not budge. She saw Diego walk quickly past them to the trunk of his car. He opened the trunk and took out a cardboard box, which he handed to Isa.

"Isa, you're going on that plane, too." The words struck her like lightning. Isa blinked, not comprehending what Diego was saying.

"Don't worry about anything." Diego handed her a medium sized cardboard box from the trunk of his car. "Just follow my lead. Take this box and put on the clothes that are in here. Chencha will help you. And hurry, there's no time to waste."

Isa felt numb. She mechanically allowed herself to be guided by both Chencha and Diego through the glass door entrance to the airport. The room was filled with activity despite the late evening hour, and the conversations around her were a jumble of words to her ears. Her mind seemed to have frozen on Diego's words: "Isa, you are going on that plane, too."

What did that mean? What was Diego talking about?

At the door to the ladies restroom, Chencha guided her to one of the small toilet cubicles and started unbuttoning Isa's blouse, her tiny and bent black figure seeming childlike next to Isa. As Chencha was unbuttoning the last button suddenly Isa seemed to react to what was happening. She grabbed her old nanny's hand.

"Chencha, what is going on? Are you both crazy? What is Diego talking about? I have no passport, no ticket..." she whispered, the words pouring out of her head.

Chencha's rough fingers softly touched Isa's lips.

"Child." Isa could barely hear her words. "It's in the hands of God. It's just like Secundino predicted" she said, now starting to help Isa's arm out of the blouse she was wearing. "Diego has a plan, and I know it is going to work. He is going to get you on that plane..."

"What?" Isa interrupted.

"Chencha replied quietly, continuing her task. "I don't know. But Don Diego knows what he is doing. And this is what was meant to be, for you to be with your sister in the United States, like your mother and father wanted for you, for the two of you, from the beginning."

Isa was beginning to understand. Diego was planning to sneak her on the plane with Anaís!

The plan seemed impossible. Still, now grasping Chencha's words, her mind and body changed from a state of quiet shock to incredible exhilaration. Could it really happen? Could her dream of being together with Anaís really be possible? Of going back to Sean? Her heart raced.

Suddenly, she was overtaken by an unbelievable desire to believe that it was possible, that Diego could find a way. If anyone could, Diego was the person who could make this happen.

She began taking off the rest of her clothes in a frenzy. Chencha handed her a dark pant suit and cream colored blouse. The black low heeled shoes looked exactly like the ones Anaís had received from the Russians. Isa felt they were a bit snug, but she wouldn't have cared if they were two sizes too small. All she could think of was how Diego was going to get her on the plane? Her mind kept repeating, no passport, no ticket. But she certainly was now dressed appropriately like a foreign traveler and not a Cuban citizen.

Chencha took the box with the clothes that Isa had just taken off, and with another motion of her finger to her lips for silence, opened the stall door and walked out with Isa. She looked around. The restroom was empty, except for a young Asian tourist sitting in a far corner, nursing a young baby. The young woman and Isa smiled at each other. Isa felt full of excitement and trepidation.

Outside the restroom door, Diego stood calmly by, one hand inside his pant pocket, the other holding a cigarette.

"Your sister made me give them up," he said with a smile, puffing on the cigarette. "She convinced me that I will live longer, maybe long enough to see the things that we've talked about come to be." He took another long puff. "But today," he continued, "I need to smoke."

"Let's go."

"Gracias, don Diego," Chencha was patting his hand. "Thank you for this miracle. It comes from Dios and you." Chencha took his hand and kissed it with an air of reverence.

Diego bent over to kiss her head.

"Chencha, my thanks to you."

Everything was happening so quickly that Isa had not stopped to think that all along, Chencha must have been part of the plan and also that Chencha was not leaving Cuba with her. Diego noticed her panic.

"Don't worry about Chencha. She is coming to live in my house. She will be alright with me."

Isa had no doubt that Chencha would be alright with Diego, but she couldn't leave her, the woman who had been like a mother to her. "Chencha, I can't leave you..."

"Child," Chencha admonished her. "Don't even think of not doing what Don Diego is telling you. This is what was meant to be. Your mother and father entrusted you to me only until your family could get you to the United States to be with your sister. That was what they told me to do," she took Isa's hands, "and today, thanks to Don Diego, I am finally fulfilling that duty." Chencha squeezed Isa's hands in her own. "You have to go."

Isa realized that her old nanny was right, yet, at the same time, how could she leave her?

"We don't have time," Diego was saying.

"But Chencha." Isa replied, her mind trying to think of a way of taking Chencha with her.

"She will be fine. With me. I know you want to take her with you, Isa, but that is not possible now, not today. Today, you need to go. Once you are on the other side, you can find a way. I will help you from here. You know I will."

Isa told herself she needed to believe the words that she was hearing from Diego. She bent over and hugged the only mother she had known.

"Chencha, I..."

"Child, there is no time." Chencha hugged her back with tenderness. Then she looked into Isa's dark green eyes. "This is what was meant to be. And I will wait, right here with don Diego, for you to take me to Chicago, to your new home. And you will show me everything that you have seen...we will catch the snow as it falls from the sky together." They hugged again.

"It's time to go," Diego said quietly. She saw the two women slowly let go of each other, guessing deep inside that it would probably be the last time they saw each other.

"May God bless you, my child," Chencha said, making the sign of the cross in the air in front of Isa's face and at the same time calling on her Yoruba gods. Isa smiled, remembering the many times over the years that Chencha had sent her off with that same blessing, and she felt a sudden embrace of protection.

"Thank you, Chencha. I beg you. No goodbyes, let's just say, *hasta luego,* until we see each other again."

Diego took Isa's arm as the two women slowly separated, letting go of their hands slowly. Chencha stoically stood still as Isa turned away.

"Don't look back," Diego suggested. "It's better. For Chencha. And we don't want to call attention to ourselves." Isa obeyed, and followed him through the growing throng of people heading towards the guards at the far end of the room. She could see the small Illinois group at the head of the line.

Now, what was going to happen? How was Diego going to get her past the Cuban Immigration officers. He was handing her something.

"Here's your sister's passport. I'm so grateful that you are identical twins! And I was able to get you a ticket for a seat at the very front of the plane. Anaís' seat is all the way at the back, with her group. As soon as you get to your seat and strap in, put on this cap." He gave her an old Che Guevara baseball cap. "Pull it over your eyes. Don't move from your seat, don't talk to anyone, don't take off the cap. When the delegation goes by, make sure they cannot see your face. Try to fall asleep or pretend to sleep so that the stewardess doesn't talk to you or sees your face clearly. You can do this. It is a short trip, from here to Cancún and then on to Miami. Once you're off the airplane and inside the U.S. terminal..." he winked, "...remember, *pies secos.*"

Pies secos—dry feet. The old slang for a Cuban getting asylum into the United States if he or she stepped on U.S. soil.

Everything Diego was saying to her felt like it could work. She grabbed his arm.

"Diego..." He silenced her with a kiss on the forehead.

"Isa, like I told your sister, we don't have time for talk. My heart, it goes with Ana Isabel and you."

Isa started to cry. He shook his head and pursed his lips in disapproval.

"No. We don't have time for tears either." He hugged her one more time. "Now just think about that plane, and what awaits you on the other side of that door. I have the passport and a ticket—they are not stamped so you are boarding as Anaís. And remember, once you are on the plane, just keep quiet. Once you arrive in Miami, the moment you step on American soil, you are safe. That is the law there, and you will get asylum."

With one last tender touch of her arm, Isa saw Diego leave her side and walk toward the front of the line. She tried to compose herself, praying silently that this crazy plan of Diego's was possible.

The line moved slowly, as the Cuban immigration officers closely scrutinized all the tourists' credentials.

She could now see the front of the line, and there, next to two armed guards stood Diego, talking calmly and enthusiastically. She wondered why he had left her in line. Was she supposed to pretend not to know him?

Directly in front of her was a German family eagerly chatting about their Cuba trip. Their dark tans contrasted sharply with their pale blonde hair and deep blue eyes. How ironic, she thought, these people from so far away could simply buy a ticket and come and go from Cuba, and she and Ani could not. When would that change?

Her heart jumped as she realized the German family was showing their papers to the short officer standing at the podium near the entrance to the exit hall. She could hear Diego's animated conversation, talking about the latest baseball scores of the Cuban team visiting the Dominican Republic. The officer seemed caught up in the conversation, but still managed to stop his Spanish exchange with Diego to curtly ask the German family how long they had been in Cuba and how long they had stayed. Oh, no. What was he going to ask her, Isa thought. She imagined that Diego's credentials or perhaps his personal acquaintance with the officer was the reason he was able to stand there, nonchalantly talking about sports while the officer proceeded with his job at the last checkpoint. But Diego would not be the one checking her passport, which was her sister's passport, and her ticket. Isa felt panicked.

The German family moved through the door to the glassed-in area, which was the last exit room before going out to the tarmac. She moved forward, handing her documents to the immigration officer, her heart beating so loudly she was certain everyone around her could hear it. She saw Diego, jokingly slap the immigration officer's back and say,

"What about that steal in the fourth inning. I still can't believe how they made that call!"

Obviously this was enough to slightly distract the immigration officer for a second because Isa heard him swear.

"Definitely. That was highway robbery," the officer was saying. "The umpire really had *cojones* to make that stupid call."

Isa and Diego's eyes met for an instant. Isa adjusted her baseball cap. The Cuban officer looked at her passport and then at her. He looked at it and at her one more time, and Isa's heart stopped. Could he be remembering that he had let her sister go through this checkpoint just a while ago? Were she and Diego going to be found out?

"They did the same thing to us last year," Diego was patting the officer's arm. "Remember that game with Javier..."

The officer again got caught up in Diego's sports trivia, and proudly filled in the umpire's last name.

"Yes." He said, stamping Isa's passport and returning it to her with her airline ticket. "Yes, it was Javier Moreno. Now that was really one son of a bitch." He motioned her to move on. "Go ahead, please" he said to Isa. She adjusted her cap and walked through the glass door to the other side of the waiting room.

Isa's head was reeling. She wanted desperately to turn around and look at Diego, to at least send him a smile of thanks. But she knew better. He listened to Diego and the immigration officer continue their baseball conversation.

The German family stood talking to the flight attendant. Isa could hear them commenting on the great vacation they had on the island. She lowered her baseball cap over her eyes, trying to mask as much of her face as possible. This was the last hurdle.

"*Buenas noches,*" the smiling flight attendant said. Isa lowered her head and pretended to yawn as she handed her passport and plane ticket.

"Tired?"

"Yes. Very much," Isa responded.

"Well, it's a short trip...we make a quick stop in Cancún where we don't deplane...then on to Miami. You can probably get in a short nap." She looked at both documents and without hesitation tore off the main part of the ticket and handed Isa the stub. "Thank you for visiting Cuba. Have a good flight."

Isa nodded. She wanted to run to the plane waiting outside on the tarmac, and to her seat, but instead she walked with a measured step, trying to settle the thumping in her temples, the beating of her heart. The German family was ahead of her, climbing the stairway to the plane single file. As she stepped through the exit door, the warm autumn air caressed her skin, slightly cooling the heat she felt in her feverish body. She looked at the plane a few hundred yards from her, watching the people inside sitting by the windows and settling in.

She was leaving Cuba. She might not ever be back. A great sadness suddenly overwhelmed her and almost made her stop her slow and deliberate steps toward the plane. She was leaving not just Diego and Chencha, but also Tío Julio, her family. She was leaving her beaches and her palm trees. She was leaving her homeland.

But another competing feeling captured her mind. She was going back to her new home and to a new life with her sister. And with Sean.

As she looked up the stairway to the plane, she suddenly realized that her parents' dream for them was finally coming true. She was going to finally be free. Yes, there was a lot she was leaving behind, and she knew she would shed tears for all she was losing. But she was going home, to the place where her parents had hoped to take her and her sister so many years ago.

As she reached the top of the stairs behind the German father juggling three carry-on suitcases and a few shopping bags, Isa remembered Diego's instructions and pulled her baseball cap over her eyes.

"Hi," she said to the flight attendant at the door.

"Welcome," was the answer back.

She fought the desire to look to the back of the plane to try find her sister's face. She avoided everyone's eyes. Diego had told her to simply find her seat, 3A, by the window and pretend to sleep. Two older tourists were already seated and when she showed them her ticket, they got up slowly, seeming a little annoyed as they came out into the aisle to let her in to her window seat. She excused herself.

As she sat down, she felt odd with no bags or purse like the other passengers. Pulling the baseball cap over her eyes, she pretended to sleep while in reality her mind was racing.

Every second seemed like an hour as she sat in her seat, listening to the jumbled conversations around her. She listened to the pilot, telling them that they would depart as soon as everyone had taken their seats. After what seemed like a lifetime, the pilot finally announced that they were taking off.

Isa folded her hands in prayer, thanking God in her mind that she and her sister were almost out of danger. For the next few hours as the plane crossed the short distance from Havana to Cancún and then on to the U.S. mainland, she continued repeating her prayer to God and the gods she had grown to know through Chencha, those Yoruba spirits brought from Africa to the islands and still sacred to so many. When the pilot announced that they were over U.S. soil and would land shortly, Isa's stomach churned once more nervously.

The plane touched down easily, and she heard some people clap as the plane continued a slow pace toward the gate and the stewardess welcomed everyone to the Miami International Airport. She, too, wanted to jump and shout with joy, but she remained in her seat, the baseball cap over her eyes. Not until she felt that everyone around her was getting up from their seats did she finally push back the cap and look around. Her eyes actually needed a few minutes to adjust to the light. Everyone was in that special happy mood of coming home.

People were moving down the aisle anxious to leave the plane. She could see that all the passengers were being escorted to a waiting bus. She was almost free! Once she stepped off the Cuban plane and on to the American soil she would be out of danger. Then the only thing left was for Anaís to be safe off as well.

At the back of the plane where the Illinois delegation had taken their seats, Anaís had preferred the silence of looking out at the blackness outside than talking with her companions. Only *Arrancapellejo* had come over twice during the brief flight to talk.

No, she didn't want to talk. Her heart was filled with an immense sadness that she could not control. Her sister, again, had been dealt the wrong hand. Over the year that Anaís had spent in Cuba, she had wondered many times if she would have had the strength and the courage that Isa had shown all those years in Cuba to remain a good person if she had been the twin that fate had left in Cuba so long ago. She was not sure.

Now that almost everyone had deplaned, one bus full of passengers moved slowly toward the main customs building. Her own group at the back of the plane helped each other with the carry-on bags from the baggage compartments and stood in the aisle expressing their happiness at being home.

On most other trips that she had ever taken, Anaís had always felt that it indeed was one of the best feelings ever to come home from a trip. Not this time. Her sadness at leaving Isa, Chencha, Diego, the relatives in Pinar del Río, and the beautiful country that was her birthplace was immense. Would she ever see them again? Anaís fought the tears building up in her eyes.

"Are you alright?" one of her friends asked.

She nodded yes, unable to speak, afraid that if she said anything, all that would come out of her mouth would be a long sorrowful cry.

"Pretty dress," *Arrancapellejo* was saying behind her as they lumbered down the plane's aisle. "Were you wearing that when you left the hotel today?"

Anaís pretended not to hear her. She nonchalantly looked out the plane window at the second waiting bus that would take them to the Immigration area, wondering what and where her sister was at that minute, as she, Anaís, stepped out into the warm Florida night.

Everything around her suddenly seemed magnified. As she boarded the last bus headed for the terminal, the bus struck her in its cleanliness, size and bright lights, so different from the Cuban buses she had grown accustomed to over the last year. There were no armed army officers on the tarmac. It seemed that everyone on the bus was chewing gum.

She felt a sensory overload of strangely familiar things that reminded her that she was back in the United States. Her home. The home she had missed, the home she felt in her heart also should belong to her sister.

Her sister. Where was she right now, what was she doing? Probably Isa and Chencha were drinking a coffee as they waited for a TV soap opera to begin. She hoped they were not as sad as she felt.

The bus came to a stop at the entrance to the terminal area for incoming international passengers. Anaís could see most of the passengers hurrying off trying to be the first in line to go through Customs and on to their families. How wonderful to have a relative waiting for you, your own flesh and blood, waiting anxiously to catch a glimpse of you. Her own flesh and blood lived a very long and divisive couple of hundred miles away.

Then Anaís saw her. Isa's face ahead of her in the crowd of passengers shocked her. Isa was not hurrying like the others to form a line at Customs, but rather stood grinning and waving frantically behind the line forming in front of the Customs Officers.

At first, Anaís could not comprehend what was happening. Her mind raced back to the moment when she first saw her sister for the first time behind the cracked and unpainted door of the apartment in Cuba. She felt the same disorienting and shocked, life changing sensation.

Her sister! Isa was standing in the airport. She was there, just ahead of her! Anaís ran to her.

"What...?" She could not continue and simply hugged her. The members of the delegation started gathering around the two women in dismay.

"Diego," was the only word Isa could mutter, taking off her baseball cap and hugging her sister again.

"He said I'd be alright once I got here, once I stepped on American soil. That I could say that I have a sister here, and get asylum."

"Dry feet," Anais laughed, tears streaming down her face.

"Yes, my dear sister,

Finally what our parents dreamed for us!"

THE END

Acknowledgments

My deepest thanks to my readers who enjoyed *Mango Rain* so much that their constant queries about the future of the novels' characters inspired me to envision both a prequel and sequel to the novel. I am forever grateful. Without their interest, Anaís, Isa, Diego and the others would not have haunted my dreams until I gave them new life in the upcoming works, *Mimi's Path* and *Todos Vuelven*.

My thanks as well to all the important women in my life: my grandmother, whose colorful stories of life in Cuba fed my imagination; my mother whose insistence on keeping alive our Cuban traditions helped me 'experience' the island of my birth even as I grew up in the United States; my two daughters, who are my first and constant cheerleaders; and my granddaughter who helps me stay connected to my inner, creative child.

And to the special men in my life: my father, who left us too early yet has inspired everything I've ever achieved; to my husband, who celebrates 'me' and 'us' as we evolve in our ever changing lives; and to my four grandsons who show me the soft and wonderful hearts that beat under a male's strong exterior.

Gracias to you all.

Discussion Guide

1. Which sister do you identify with more – Anaís or Isa? Do your feelings change for either of them during the course of the book?

2. Imagine the plight of parents having to part with their children and knowing they have to choose between which of their daughters will emigrate to a better life. What do you think about how the parents determined which twin they sent with Father Pat? If you were their parents, what would you have done?

3. In Chicago, Anaís has considerable material wealth and personal freedom. In Havana, what do you believe Isa considers as her wealth? If you were one of the two sisters, what would you find the most difficult to give up?

4. The author draws a sobering portrait of what it means to live in twenty-first century Cuba and how much the people there do without. How does each woman make the most of her situation while living in Cuba?

5. In the U.S., people take pride in the right to express themselves freely. Is this the same for all the characters in the novel? Can you cite examples?

6. (For women) In the book, women in Cuba are portrayed as limited in what they can say or do, while Anaís's confidence sets her apart. How easily could you adapt to those societal limitations? In what area of your life would you have the most difficulty?

(For men) Anaís comments to Isa that in the U.S. men usually restrict their outward/direct comments to a woman regarding her physical attributes. To what do you attribute the difference between male behavior in the U.S. and Cuba?

7. Does each sister adapt equally to her new situation? What challenges does each face, and how are the challenges different?

8. Throughout the book, each of the four main characters – Anaís, Isa, Chencha, and Diego – are faced with a moment when they are given the chance to risk what is most dear to them. Can you identify those moments? What does the book say to us about the rewards of taking that risk?

9. How does the book help you 'experience' Cuba through each character's daily life?

10. Imagine the main characters a year after the story ends. Are the characters' lives still intertwined? How have they moved forward?

An Excerpt from
Mimi's Path

Diego

Cuba, 1961

Her hand tightly clutching her *cemí*, the Taíno amulet of the moon which protected her, Mimi looked out the dirty bus window as the vehicle slowly crept through el Valle de Viñales. She pressed her face against the glass, hoping to see her mother moon, but only darkness and heavy clouds filled the skies.

The previous night, spent with friends who had moved to the outskirts of Havana, she had cried herself to sleep keeping her sobs quiet in order not to awaken her three sleeping daughters curled up on the same bed with her. She had caressed their sleeping heads, wondering how she would tell them that their brother, their hero, had died.

Or had he been killed? There was a hint of that dire possibility in the conversation with the local who brought her the news from Pinar del Río that Diego had been given a proper burial.

How could her baby boy be dead? He was only twenty-three years old. God should have taken her instead. She was already past the half-century mark, an age that many in her town never even reached, including her mother, who had died when Mimi was but fifteen years old. Now, Diego, her firstborn, her pride, was gone and she knew nothing more than that.

Diego had left Baracoa at sixteen. Mimi had always known in her

351

heart that he was meant for bigger things than what their town had to offer. Although important because this was the site of the 15th century Spanish landing and referred to by Columbus as the 'most beautiful place eyes had ever seen', the town surrounded by mountains, where rivers meet with the ocean, and is the greenest part of Cuba, was a small town.

More than six hundred miles southeast from the Cuban capital through the island's largest mountain range, Baracoa was too small for Diego's curiosity and his innate intelligence. His continuous questions about how the natural and physical worlds worked exhausted everyone. Monsieur DuBois, the generous man who was her *patrón*, said Diego had an exceptional memory, remembering everything after the first time he learned it. Diego's first word in the morning as he awakened and the last as he kissed her good night was *¿por qué?* Why? That word was Diego's constant friend.

He had read everything that Monsieur DuBois put in his hands, and quickly abandoned the need to go to the storage shed that served as a school for the local children when they were not working the cacao or coconut fields. Monsieur DuBois, who seemed intent on nurturing Diego's natural intelligence and interest in everything, quietly had assumed the role of private tutor.

The older man almost seemed grandfatherly in his relationship with the young boy, allowing him special privileges that no one else had. This meant that Diego had access to the huge library where he could read and work on projects with Monsieur Dubois, among which was helping to identify, catalog and store the antique gold coins that Monsieur Dubois collected. Diego's trustworthiness had gained him this privilege, one that the collector would not have shared with just anyone, given the value of the coins.

Mimi had not been surprised, therefore, when the kindly old man spoke to her about allowing Diego to leave Baracoa to study at La Universidad de la Habana. Monsieur DuBois had softly explained that he understood it would be a huge sacrifice on her part to let her oldest child leave her side to live in the big city, a city Mimi had never been to herself. Still, he emphasized Diego's special abilities and asked her to consider what he could achieve if given the opportunity. The university studies would give him choices. He could choose a career of his liking, and perhaps even return to the hacienda and become one of the foremen. If she couldn't afford to send Diego there, and they both knew she could not, Monsieur DuBois would pay Diego's expenses if Mimi would agree to learn English with the house British butler's help so she could help with the guests who visited the chocolate factory. Besides, Diego would not leave until he turned sixteen, in three years. During that time, Mimi would adjust to the idea of not having her oldest child and only son at her side.

How could she say no to an offer that seemed so favorable to her son's future? The truth was that she would do anything for her children or, for that matter anyone in her family. Her loyalty to Monsieur DuBois also meant that she would do almost anything he asked. Had she not even agreed to be called Mimi while she worked in his household because he had such difficulty pronouncing her given name Nonúm?

Monsieur DuBois' kindness and attentiveness to his staff was exceptional, and he always had been especially attentive to her and her children, even more so since Mimi's husband and father had died. With the trust she put in Monsieur DuBois' knowledge and kindness, Mimi agreed that Diego's future lay far away from his birthplace.

To say that Diego was elated when Monsieur DuBois proposed he attend La Universidad was an understatement.

"*Bien sûr,* of course, this is a huge sacrifice for your mother," Monsieur Du-Bois had nodded toward Mimi standing quietly by the massive mahogany door to the library as he spoke to Diego about Havana. "She has even agreed to learn English to help here with the Americans when they come on business. So, you as well will learn English with her. That way, you can help each other with that God-forsaken ugly language." His face lit up with a smile as he announced

"Tomorrow you begin...every day...after Mimi finishes her day's work...you will spend some time with Charles."

By the time the day arrived for Diego to leave Baracoa, both Diego and Mimi spoke and wrote English proficiently. Of course, Diego had mastered every lesson, his accent nearly flawless given his age. He had spent every free moment listening to the English lessons on records that Monsieur DuBois had given him. Now Diego easily understood the conversations he heard around the hacienda among the American business men who visited regularly.

Mimi, too, enjoyed her new skill and even started teaching her daughters, Mily, Rosa and Sonia, quoting Monsieur DuBois, "you can never learn too much." She had made a game of trying to speak English with them. Using words about their surroundings, nature, and their favorite activities, the girls seemed to pick up the pronunciation with less difficulty than Mimi herself experienced.

Finally, the day had come in August 1954 when everyone they knew in the town came to say goodbye to Diego. Few townspeople had been to the capital city of Havana. It was clear they felt the young man represented each and every one of them as he went off to the big city. Monsieur DuBois himself accompanied Diego, saying he had business to take care of in Havana anyway. Mimi stoically hugged her son farewell while Diego's young sisters played nearby. She knew that at their young ages they did not fully comprehend the tremendous significance of the event.

"Diego, *toma*, take this." She cupped his fingers around a smooth object. He smiled as he opened his hand and saw the cemí of *pájaro carpintero*, the woodpecker that his grandfather had carved for him so many years before. "It will remind you of your family and our town", she had said. "It will keep you safe from the big city's dangers."

She recalled their conversation and her tender yet clear instructions. "Remember, there, the trees do not talk to you, to help you understand your path. I hear the habaneros, those city people, don't really believe we, descendants of our noble Taíno indians, even exist. To them, Baracoa is a far away and ignorant place. You know better. Be proud of who you are. Do not forget who you are." With that last bit of advice, Diego had left her to follow his own path.

As she stopped reminiscing, Mimi's loud sigh startled the woman sitting next to her on the nearly empty bus. "*Lo siento, señora.* I'm sorry."

The bus stopped at a small wooden structure at the edge of town to let her out. Dawn was beginning to break behind the massive craggy mountains that surrounded the valley, casting tenuous shadows on the darkened streets. Mimi looked around, and seeing no one, sat on a large tree stump nearby.

The air was still damp with early morning dew and a soft breeze rustled the long black skirt of her dress. She had managed to fall asleep for a while during the long, bumpy ride from Havana to Pinar del Río well after the tears that streamed down her face finally lessened and her body tired and listless, had given in to a restless sleep.

Now, sitting in the silence of a town not yet awakened, interrupted only by the sound of the wind whistling around her, memory of her dream made her shudder. She tried to suppress it. The dream turned nightmare was a confusing mix of images of herself as a child swimming in the Toas River with her sister; evenings making love with Diego's father; giving birth to their son under a full moon. Then, a horrific vision of Diego's bloodied body falling into a ravine.

Mimi got up, her entire body quivering from a sudden chill in the air and in her heart. She looked down the path and still saw no one. Perhaps they had forgotten she was coming.

No sense in waiting. She knew where they lived.

Clutching her cemí to her heart she headed down the dirt road to where her grandson was waiting.

"*Lo siento*, doña Nonúm. Please come in."

Mimi smiled. Nonúm, the Taíno word for moon. She had not heard her given name pronounced by anyone in a very long time.

"*No importa*, doña Luz. I think the bus made better time than we all expected. I hope you don't mind that I took the liberty of just coming directly to your house. I'm glad my memory didn't fail me. It was not that far."

"At least fourteen kilometers!" Doña Luz set about lighting a few small lamps in the small living area. "Please sit down. You must be exhausted. Some coffee perhaps?"

"*Sí, por favor*" Mimi replied. She smoothed out her skirt and looked around. A small red rubber ball and stick fashioned like a bat lay nearby. "These are Diego's?"

Doña Luz nodded feebly.

"*Sí*. He fashions himself a baseball player." The edge of doña Luz' black skirt caught on the side of the small, iron stove. As she tugged to free her dress, she spilled some of the water she was about to pour into the coffee pot. Mimi stood up to help her.

"No, doña Nonúm. It's okay. I can clean this up easily. I'm just a bundle of nerves these days..." She stopped short of finishing her sentence, darting a distressed look at her visitor. After all, it was not she, Luz, who had lost a son.

"*Lo siento, doña Nonúm...*"

Mimi understood instantly and shook her head.

"No need to say anything, *mi amiga*. Yes, Diego is...was my son...but he was yours too...He always spoke highly of you as his mother-in-law..."

Doña Luz broke into tears, and setting the coffee pot on the burning stove, walked over to Mimi and embraced her. Both women held on to each other, understanding their shared pain. No need to speak aloud that doña Luz knew first-hand the heartbreak of losing a child. Her only daughter had died in childbirth. No need to express the unfairness each felt that death had claimed their children first instead of them. The shrill whistle from the coffee pot stopped their thoughts, and each wiped away tears.

"Do you take three or four sugars?"

"Four, *por favor.*"

Doña Luz handed Mimi the thimble-sized cup of steaming black coffee and returned to the stove to pour herself another.

"There's no coffee like that of this region," Mimi commented, licking a drop from the corner of her mouth.

"*Gracias*. I agree." Doña Luz smiled gently. "But then, again, I only know this part of Cuba." They both chuckled at the simple facts. Their eyes focused back to the ball and stick.

"What happened, doña Luz?" Mimi leaned close to her friend. "What happened to my Diego?"

Doña Luz fidgeted in her chair. She saw the pain in Mimi's eyes, remembering the dagger she felt that had pierced her own heart as she held her daughter's limp body in her arms seconds after the *comadrona* had cut the umbilical cord at the new-born's birth. Doña Luz' own life seemed irrelevant at the sight of her dead daughter, and she remembered grabbing the knife from the midwife's hand, ready to plunge it into her own lifeless heart. Her husband's and Diego's screams had stopped her hand in midair.

Doña Luz remembered that she had not even felt it when her husband cautiously and gently had taken the knife out of her hands, nor the moment when Diego placed baby Diego in her arms. Miraculously, somewhere in those brief seconds between life and death, her grandson's soul had spoken to her, asking her to stay with him.

How might she comfort the grieving mother sitting across from her, now she asked herself. Her own sadness over Diego's untimely death would need to be attended to later.

"Doña Nonúm, I don't know if I can give you all the answers. I don't know what things are like in Baracoa..." her voice had become softer and quieter, as if someone were listening just outside the front door. "You are lucky in Baracoa, living so far from...everything. Here, in Pinar, we hear more of what is going on in Havana, and right now, it's not all good." She moved her chair closer to her friend.

"Everything seemed to change for Diego last year in Havana when the government closed the newspaper office where he worked." She was now whispering in Mimi's ear. "He would come back here to be with little Diego and raved and ranted about government corruption and was distressed that some of his friends were being dragged off in the middle of the night because of something they wrote which someone in the government found offensive. Even the fact that he spoke English stopped being an asset for him. We were so surprised! At the beginning of *la Revolución*, Diego was so very happy and hopeful for a positive change after the disaster that was Batista, but..."

Doña Luz stopped and looked around.

"He felt he was being watched because of what he was writing."

Mimi blinked, suddenly remembering the last time her son had visited them in Baracoa for baby Diego's fifth birthday. He indeed had seemed preoccupied during the week that he had spent with her, not wanting to meet up with some of his old friends as he had done on past visits. He seemed to prefer simply staying with her, his sisters and his child. Mimi had dismissed his behavior as part of growing up and not wanting to party, to go out *de pachanga* with his friends. Or maybe he now just did not have much in common with small town life or its people. Either way, Mimi had enjoyed having him around, ignoring his often sour demeanor.

"Do you think Diego was involved in something illegal in Havana, doña Luz?"

Her friend shook her head vigorously.

"No, no. Your son was the most ethical man I've ever known...other than my own husband. When we spoke with him, about anything, it was like talking to an old man, and not the twenty-three-year-old that he was. No—nothing illegal. Just that..."

She seemed to choke with emotion.

"One of the last conversations we had with him — just a few weeks ago, he had found out, somehow, that despite all the talk from...well, you understand, despite all the talk about all of us in Cuba now being equal... that no one is privileged...well, that it's not true. With all the speeches from you know who about the virtues and need for rationing everything so that the country can be independent from foreign powers...despite all that rhetoric...Diego said he had sources that were giving him proof that the soldiers —at the top, of course— have no rationing...that they're not making any sacrifices like the rest of us. They're eating lobster and expensive desserts prepared by special chefs, driving fancy cars. They smoke the cohibas that now only are grown and made for...you know who…So, if that is indeed happening with the top level soldiers, then what is going on with…well, you understand. Your son wanted to expose that hypocrisy. I think…I think it got him…killed."

Doña Luz' last word was barely audible, but even before she had finished her story, Mimi knew.

A long pause followed the last statement. Both women stared at each other in stoned and painful silence.

"At the end…what happened? Where is he now?" Mimi asked quietly.

Doña Luz moved herself next to Mimi's chair and placed her arm around her friend's shoulder, hoping to steady the news she was about to give.

"Someone knocked on our door six days ago today. It woke all of us up, including *el niño* so I stayed with him in bed until he fell back to sleep. When I went to the living room…there were three young men. I recognized two as friends that Diego had brought here on occasion. All three of them were in tears, crying like children. On the couch was … Diego's body…dried blood covering his head…"

Doña Luz began to cry and it was Mimi who turned to comfort her friend as she finished her story.

"They said they were in a bar, one of those that only locals frequent, off the beaten path in Havana, talking politics…when half a dozen soldiers came in asking for Diego. His friends immediately said there was no one there by that name, but Diego stood up and identified himself. They fought to keep the soldiers from dragging him out to the street… heard a gunshot…then a car speeding away…and the last soldiers that were holding them inside the bar told them to watch who they made friends with from that moment on. Outside…they found Diego's body… in a ravine next to the road."

Mimi could barely move. She thought of the dream and nightmare she had had on the bus. Maybe she was still dreaming. It was not possible that her son could have been shot by soldiers of an Army and a government that he had celebrated with so much joy only a few short years ago.

It was not possible that Diego's body was lying in a grave in a cemetery within walking distance—maybe she had passed it earlier on her walk from the bus stop. How could she have gone by her son's last resting place without knowing it, without feeling his soul calling to her from the darkness of his tomb?

The sun lay low over the mountains now, casting slivers of magenta and purple hues peeking through the tree tops that sheltered the cemetery.

Since her conversation earlier with doña Luz, Mimi had been sitting at Diego's freshly laid tomb. Her stomach growled. She knew that the thimble size cup of coffee shared with her friend earlier would not sustain her much longer, but she couldn't bring herself to leave her son's side.

All day long, sitting at the gravesite surrounded by clumps of dirt left strewn about from the newly dug excavation, between tears and sobs, Mimi had spent time reminiscing every moment she could remember of Diego's life. She thought of the joy he had always brought to her and to those around him. Such goodness in her little boy, how could he be gone? She could not imagine a greater pain in the world than for a parent to lose a child. Her heart felt as if at any moment it would disintegrate in grief.

Mimi glanced at the cemí of the woodpecker that doña Luz had given her earlier, saying she had found it in Diego's pocket. Mimi reassured her that she had done the right thing not to bury it in the simple wooden casket with her son's body. The cemí was so special, a symbol of Diego himself. Mimi could not thank her enough for her thoughtfulness in keeping it for her.

Years before, while walking in the forests around Baracoa with Baba, her father, who was the local *behíque,* gathering plants, herbs and animals for his medicinal preparations and spiritual cleansings as the shaman to the community, Mimi and her father were surprised to discover young Diego hiding behind bushes and trees to stay out of their sight. At three, he was not allowed to go on these searches with them since, if they were lucky, they collected venomous snakes and spiders for the curative effects their venoms provided. These searches were dangerous unless you knew exactly how to handle the forest creatures.

Her father had been amused instead of angry, seeing Diego crouching behind a magnificent cypress, and decided they all should sit under it to listen for the tree's message.

Mimi recalled Diego's face, full of childish joy at being welcomed instead of scolded. He followed his grandfather's tacit instructions to lay fallen branches on the ground under the tree forming a circle inside which the three sat as his grandfather then spoke a few Taíno words of praise for the tree, and all fell silent around them.

For hours, the three sat in the stillness and beauty of the magnificent cypress, when then suddenly they were startled by the sound of a small branch that fell next to Diego. Mimi recalled Diego's wide-eyed amazement as he watched his grandfather listen to the branch and then remarked that the tree had stated its desire.

Days later, Diego was given his own Taíno amulet, the cemí of the woodpecker that inhabited the tree. His grandfather said Diego was like the *carpintero real* of the region: colorful, playful, intelligent and unique. Among all the woodpeckers in the region, the *carpintero real* was the rarest of all.

Mimi would give the cemí to little Diego and share the story of his father and great grandfather.

Then she hoped doña Luz would understand why she was going to take little Diego with her when she headed back to Havana.

About the Author

Berta Isabel Arias

Berta Isabel Arias, Ed.D., is an accomplished Cuban-American woman of many talents and the winner of numerous awards garnered during an illustrious career as a professor in world languages and international education. Throughout her career, Dr. Arias channeled her creativity by writing poetry and short stories. Now, in her next stage of life, she has moved to Amelia Island, Florida where, when she is not writing, she champions the cause of nurturing education and protecting the environment. She is the collaborator and translator of the Amazon best-seller, *Cápsulas Informativas Constitucionales,* the first ever book explaining the U.S. founding documents in Spanish (Constitutional Sound Bites by David Shestokas). Visit the author at www.bertaariasauthor.com.

CPSIA information can be obtained
at www.ICGtesting.com
Printed in the USA
LVHW091319180520
655784LV00001BA/26